EXTRAORDINARY ACCLAIM FOR LAURA BAKER'S BOOKS

Legend

"Laura Baker's LEGEND is a page-turner from beginning to end. A skillfully crafted mystery, laced with Native American mysticism and romance is a sure-to-please read."
—Dinah McCall

"Laura Baker is a truly dazzling new find. Her second novel, LEGEND, is a marvelous example of romantic suspense deftly blended with Native American beliefs."
—*Romantic Times*

Stargazer

"A fast-paced, well-plotted story. A larger-than-life hero and a heroine who is his match. Here's one you'll enjoy!"
—Kat Martin

"STARGAZER is absolutely magical. Laura Baker has created a wonderful hero, and a tale to savor. Don't miss it!"
—Megan Chance

"Promising new author Laura Baker makes a winning debut with this uniquely spellbinding tale.
—*Romantic Times*

"STARGAZER is a wonderful Indian romance filled with mysticism, time travel and adventure. . . . If you like time travel and Indian mysticism, STARGAZER is the book for you!"
—Kristin Hannah

"A lovingly crafted tale . . . M . . . . . yhem, and sweet roma . . . . . ime-

—Nan Ryan

"STARGAZER is . . . . . pense, desire, and fascinat . . . . Laura Baker's powerful story hold . . . . . than a few unexpected twists and is guaranteed to keep you up until the wee hours."
—Christina Skye, author of *Three Wishes*

BROKEN IN TWO

LAURA BAKER

St. Martin's Paperbacks

BROKEN IN TWO

Copyright © 1999 by Laura Baker.

All rights reserved. No part of this book may be used or reproduced in any manner whatsoever without written permission except in the case of brief quotations embodied in critical articles or reviews. For information address St. Martin's Press, 175 Fifth Avenue, New York, N.Y. 10010.

ISBN: 0-312-97175-3

Printed in the United States of America

St. Martin's Paperbacks edition/October 1999

St. Martin's Paperbacks are published by St. Martin's Press, 175 Fifth Avenue, New York, N.Y. 10010.

10 9 8 7 6 5 4 3 2 1

My hero is . . .

    the boy who asked me what I dreamed of;
    the first love who made my heart catch at the brush of his hand;
    the friend whose knowing gaze sees to my heart;
    the man who trusts me with his anger, not just his laughter.
    He is my first wonderful memory, my last words in the day . . .

                                    To Tom
                              my husband

WITH WARMEST THANKS

to the Storybook Cabins in Ruidoso. I swear they
exist . . . though they are too good to be true.

to three wizards of plotting: Robin Perini, Laura
DeVries, and Alice Orr. A blur of days and nights
stretching to a mythic weekend. Somehow we never
let the fire go out.

to Robin Perini and Sandy Elliott. You both humble me
with your talent, your patience, your unflagging dedication . . . who knew magic could happen at Carrows?

to my family, who endure haphazard meals and a
house where every day is a scavenger hunt.

GLOSSARY OF TERMS

Aha-ay-hay! Ki-ah'vakovee! Kak nam yet ka toe' (Hopi) Listen to me! Someone is coming! Soon everyone will be crying and mourning.

'Ahéhee' Navajo: Thank You

Alch'i'i Navajo: The place they come together

Bahana Hopi: White person

Balolokong Hopi: The Great Water Serpent

Bika anilyeed Navajo: I need help

Bilagaana Navajo: White Person

Doo yá'áshóo da Navajo: It is bad

Do Tah Navajo: Emphatic Response

Éiyá ndagá Navajo: Oh no!

Háadi Jenny Navajo: Where is Jenny at

Hash yiniłyé Navajo: What is your name

Kiis'áanii Navajo: Hopi Indians

Kikmungwi Hopi: Village chief

Nakee ts'iil Navajo: Broken in Two

S'aa'akó tee Navajo: You are all right

Sáni Navajo: The old one. Also a term of endearment.

Shash'la yádii, T'áá'akó téé Navajo: It is all right

Shimásání Navajo: Grandmother

Shi yázhi Navajo: Term of endearment

Sitsóí Navajo: My grandchild

T'áá shoodi Navajo: Please

Tségháhodzáni Navajo: Window Rock

Ya'at'eeh Navajo: It is good; Good morning

CHAPTER ONE

A CANYON IN NORTHERN ARIZONA

Tikui awoke, a scream lodged in her throat. Her pulse beat furiously through her veins with a certain threat, one she feared more than death. She clutched the ragged Pendleton blanket close round her old shoulders.

Tikui looked to her guardian. The long-legged bird gazed down at her with one eye, his usual stance perched mid-air on the rock wall just above the etched deer. He had not deserted her. But did he still protect her?

Tikui glanced sideways, furtively, almost afraid to see whether her offering had been refused, but there lay the paho sticks with fetish stones . . . and the feather of the water bird was gone.

Good. Good. Her offering was accepted.

But her silent assurances didn't calm her. She peered through the darkness in her cave to the night beyond, yet the familiar stars could not comfort her—anymore than they had for the past seven nights . . . anymore than they had so long ago, in a distant place.

Then, she had been young, living among her people, until they could no longer bear her screams in the night, or allow one more of her terrible premonitions to cast the village into chaos.

She pressed her eyes closed against the dark memories, but she could never forget the day she had left Hopi—a castaway from the pueblo. She had walked away an outcast, a Tikui, the name she had carried ever since.

That had been long ago, before she climbed high in the cliffs, away from those who would ridicule her, call her crazy.

It had taken thousands of nights, thousands of days, for her to find the strength to let go, to sever the cords from her heart to the people in that village. Eventually, the voices in her head abated, first becoming whispers, then dying, quieted in the utter lonely stillness of this canyon.

If she heard rumblings of dissension, carried to her on the winds, she let the sadness pass through her, breathing deeply on it for only a moment—a wisp of the lives she no longer shared—then breathed out in release. They neither wanted her nor her concern.

Finally, she had found inner peace to match that of the solemn cliffs . . . until one week ago.

Tikui pushed herself up from the ground. The movement rustled her grass mat and released a breath of dried sage and fresh-cut sweet grass. The usually comforting scents now seemed cloying, annoying her with their faint promise of serenity.

There was no more peace tonight.

Tikui hugged the blanket closer against a sudden chill and walked to the front of the cave. The dead of night still held the canyon in total darkness. Tikui's steps, as always these days, were labored, but her feet were sure on the familiar, comforting ground. Every step she took released stories from the earth, stories from those who had walked that path before, stories the earth gathered and held until Tikui's bare feet pressed the secrets loose.

What men forgot, the earth remembered . . . and she would exact her lessons. Tikui's throat clutched at the dark powers her people would face.

But she would not leave. Here, the legends of her ancestors' determined migration sang through her. These murmurs from the past were her only companions and they brought her no recriminations, only joy.

No, she could not leave.

She looked beyond the mouth of her cave to the opposite plateau. As if from nowhere, black, somber clouds had amassed low over the mesa and moved toward the cliffs.

A light at the bottom of the canyon caught her attention. It tripped along, flickering and dancing like a twinkling star bobbing at the end of a string. Tikui glanced away, then back, testing her own failing vision. The strange light persisted and drew ever closer. Now she recognized the path: the erratic light followed the arroyo, vanishing then reappearing from behind the walls of clay. Someone was walking into her canyon—an event Tikui had not experienced for many years. There were no roads within twenty miles of this desolate wilderness, no important ruins to investigate, no deep streams to fish, and no easy way through it—all the reasons Tikui had selected this insignificant box canyon.

The sound of men's voices drifted up the cliff walls. Tikui crouched at the edge of her cave, thirty feet above the canyon floor. She could make out two men: a smaller one walking ahead and the one with the flashlight following, its light on the back of the first man as if the beam were a rod pushing him forward. A sense of foreboding wound through Tikui, a tightening coil of apprehension.

The arroyo took the men straight to the base of her cliff. They stopped directly below her and the night's crisp air carried every word clearly to Tikui.

"You don't need those things." It was the smaller one talking. He had the voice of a Navajo—his words clipped and guttural.

"Don't tell me what I need, Eddie. I paid you for the job and now you're holding out." It was the taller man, the one with the flashlight. Tikui heard the Anglo world in his voice.

"I'm not holding out. I told you what I kept." The one called Eddie turned into the direct glare of the flashlight. "I am doing you a favor—you can't sell the ceremonial pieces anyway."

The white man chuckled, an ugly, derisive sound that

skittered down Tikui's spine. "Is that so?"

The next instant, he raised the flashlight and hit Eddie square on the head, sending him to his knees.

Tikui sucked in a breath. Fingers of lightning struck the ground directly across the canyon.

"What I do is none of your business." He yanked Eddie's head back by a handful of hair. "And I don't like having my plans messed with."

"You don't . . . understand. The stuff is illegal. That Denver dealer . . . he can't tell anybody."

"Well, well. Seems like you gave this a lot of thought." The white man paced around Eddie, who was crouched in a ball on the ground. "So what did you think you'd do with the pieces?"

"Give them back . . . to the tribes." Eddie looked up and, even with his eyes squinted against the light, his expression was defiant. "They . . . are special."

The white man chuckled. Tikui gritted her teeth against the harsh sound.

"That would make you some kind of hero, wouldn't it, Eddie?"

"I'm not trying to be a hero, just do the right thing."

"So now I'm the one who's wrong?" He kicked Eddie in the back and sent him sprawling to the ground. "Listen to me, you miserable little thief, you picked the wrong man to mess with. I don't give a *damn* about your pathetic noble causes." He grabbed a fistful of hair and yanked back. "Now, where's the rest of the stuff?"

"You're doing this . . . just for the money?" Eddie's words came out choked, perhaps from the pain. But Tikui heard despair, as if he had just realized a lie.

"Not the right answer." He hit Eddie upside the head again, producing a low groan.

The earth rumbled, a sound so deep it was almost inaudible, only felt.

Tikui's heart beat violently. *How could they ignore the warnings?*

"But the truth . . . isn't it?" The beaten man pushed himself up in agonizing slow motion.

Tikui looked at his adversary. Now he held a gun. Frantically, she glanced around her dark cave searching in vain for something she could use as a weapon.

"Tell me where the Hopi tablet is, Eddie."

At the mention of the tablet, Tikui forgot her search. She held her breath, tried to quiet the thunder of her racing heart. Leaning dangerously close to the edge of the ledge, Tikui strained to hear every word.

Swaying the slightest bit, Eddie faced the white man. Then he smiled. "Over my dead body."

The shot rang through the canyon, the sound ricocheting off the cliffs and reverberating through Tikui. She clapped her hands over her mouth, holding in her scream, her outrage, until she felt choked by the black emotions lodged in her throat.

A dull, resonant roar resounded through the subterranean streams, up through the mantle of the earth, into the soles of her feet, her legs, to the place in her belly.

Suddenly, the ground gave a great heave—a roil just beneath the surface.

Balolokong! The great serpent of the underworld!
What had awakened him?

The earth undulated. Thunder boomed and lightning cracked the sky.

Tikui grabbed the rock wall, pulled herself against it. She peered over the side. The man had fallen. He scrambled to his feet, kicked Eddie's lifeless body and cussed, as if Eddie's death were just one more frustration. He paced a few steps and swept the ground and cliffs with his flashlight.

Tikui scrambled from the edge and pressed her back against the cave wall. The beam penetrated her sanctuary and skimmed over the rocky craggs within inches of her. Even when the light disappeared, Tikui sat there frozen, her thoughts snared on one thing: the Hopi tablet.

Was the legendary stone within reach of her people? Tikui's mind raced with hope.

Is this white man the one?

But no, he couldn't be. He had killed another man, a Navajo. He could not be the man of honor promised by Spider Grandmother. Tikui's thoughts tumbled in confusion.

A flash of light, catching her cave then jerking erratically skyward, brought Tikui back to the immediate danger. The white man had not left and was now searching a way up the sheer cliff.

How long before he discovered the trail carved by the cunning ancient ones to their cave?

Tikui forced herself to move. She gathered the most important of her few belongings, rolled them within her grass mat, tied the ends, and slung the bundle over her shoulder.

She stepped onto the narrow ledge. A glance over her shoulder confirmed that the murderer was scaling the canyon wall. It would take him time in the dark to find his way to the caves. By then, she would be on the mesa top.

Tikui inched her way in the opposite direction, working her feet along the barest support of rock. Her fingers skimmed over the sandstone and found the ancient toe- and handholds. They had been carved into the rock centuries ago, during that dark time in her tribe's history when the ancient ones feared the most terrible of enemies—their own people.

Now, there would be no safe place—for her or for any of her people—unless she could discover where this Eddie had hidden the promised half of the tablet. The old woman took a last look at her sanctuary, the rock walls of her beloved cave, her home for fifty years, the one place where she had been safe from suspicious eyes and ridiculing words.

They no longer wanted her in Hopi. They might not even listen to her. But Tikui could no longer ignore the calling.

Tikui bid goodbye to her waterbird guardian and turned her gaze to the mesa and the path home.

WINDOW ROCK, ARIZONA, NAVAJO TRIBAL POLICE HEADQUARTERS

The personal effects of the deceased amounted to no more than car keys, a silver-case lighter—but no cigarettes—and a used-up black wallet, worn to white at the corners, with forty-seven dollars inside. No wedding ring, Frank noticed, but there was a frayed picture with curled edges that was bent to the timeworn contour of the wallet.

Using the tip of his pen, Frank slid the photo from the pile. It was of a little girl. He stared at the small, somber face in the picture. She was maybe three years old and already looked so serious. Was this Eddie Honanie's daughter? Did she understand his death, that she would never see him alive again? Did she know that before long she wouldn't be able to remember his voice? Only in her dreams would his face, his eyes, the way he talked, be crystal clear.

Life is so goddamn precarious. What is the point?

The old anger bit at Frank's gut. For a second he had the nearly overwhelming urge to hurl the table and all of Eddie's belongings straight through the nearest window.

Instead, he pressed his fists to the table and took a deep breath.

When the hell would he be able to let go? That's all he wanted to know. When would he get some peace? It had been three years and he could still instantly conjure the images, still smell the gunpowder rising from the bloody holes in her blouse, still taste the salt of his own tears. If Mary had lived, the baby inside her would now be a child nearly the same age as the one in this photograph.

Stepping back from the table, he wiped a shaky hand across his mouth and considered leaving now, passing this case on to someone else. He could catch a plane—would there be another one today from Window Rock to Denver?—and be back at the bureau by this afternoon.

Frank's heart slowed, the rush of blood that had pounded at his temples lessened—just at the thought of backing away, giving up, crawling back into his cubicle.

He investigated stolen art, not murders. Not for three years had he been involved with murders.

"Special Agent Reardon, I'm Officer Coriz."

Frank started at the unexpected voice, then covered his lapse by gesturing at the sparse pile of Honanie's belongings. "Is this everything from the crime scene?" His words caught on the knot of emotions in his throat and he gave a small cough.

"That's it," Coriz answered, a bit sharply.

Frank glanced at the man beside him. The Navajo officer stared back, unsmiling. "No gun?" Frank asked.

"No gun found on him or with the rest of his possessions."

"And the rest of his possessions are *where*?"

"In a suitcase in the basement."

"All of his possessions are in a suitcase?"

"Seems so." Coriz's voice carried the tone of a shrug, though he didn't move, and Frank could swear he hadn't even blinked, only stared at Frank with dark, unapproving eyes.

Another Indian with an attitude about the FBI.

That was no more than Frank expected.

"How did you come to find all his possessions in a suitcase, Officer Coriz?"

"Guess he was living in his truck."

Frank looked back at the table. The little girl with a round face stared up at him from the old black-and-white picture. "No residence?"

"His car registration and driver's license gave the address of his sister." Coriz read from his notes. "According to her, Eddie didn't live there, either."

"And who's the little girl?"

Coriz leaned closer for a look. "Might be Jennifer Honanie, the DOA's daughter. She's a teenager now."

"And? Where is she?"

"She lives with her aunt."

"What do they know about the murder?"

"The daughter was vague on his whereabouts, his friends. She had nothing to tell us."

"And the aunt? She have the same attitude?"

"Not quite, but she wasn't any more help."

Frank shoved Honanie's meager belongings back into the envelope and reached for the manila file folder from the medical examiner. Clipped to the top were photos of Eddie Honanie's body.

He stopped at the third picture, a close-up of Honanie's upper arm showing a tattoo of a long-legged skinny bird near his shoulder. Some kind of water bird, Frank figured, which, of course, made no sense in the middle of the desert.

Frank shuffled through the pictures of various angles of the body. He saw a young man, dressed in jeans, a plaid shirt, and tennis shoes. Normal-looking, if you looked past the blood and the obvious massive trauma to the head where Eddie had been hit with something before he was shot. Whatever the murderer had wanted from Eddie, Eddie had not been easy about giving. And it finally got him a bullet right behind the ear.

Frank's jaws clenched at the cowardly, execution-style murder. God, how he hated being back on *any* Indian reservation.

"You about ready to go see the witness?"

Coriz's harsh impatience got Frank's attention. "Have you got a problem with me, Officer Coriz?"

The Navajo raised calm brown eyes. "No problem, Agent Reardon. You're just what we need: another agent on the rez."

Frank met the sarcasm. "I couldn't agree more."

He replaced the pictures and closed the file. "Just how do you pronounce—" Frank took another look at the name. "Tikui?"

"Te-koo-ee." Coriz sounded it out as he started for the door.

"So, in what context did she mention the Denver art theft?"

Coriz walked ahead. "It just kind of came out."

"Kind of came out," Frank muttered and drew a breath for patience. "How about you let me see your notes?"

"They won't do you any good. I'll take you to her and you can ask your own questions."

"Just point me to the room. I'll handle it."

"Oh, she's not here, Agent Reardon. We have to go to her. Assuming she's where I last left her."

At Frank's sharp, quizzical look, the officer explained. "I had her with the nurses at St. Michael's, but she walked out. A patrol car found her on the highway. Guess she was going to walk all the way back to her canyon. That's one hundred twenty miles across land that birds don't even fly over." He shook his head in apparent disbelief.

"Why did you take her to a hospital?"

Coriz stopped just outside the front doors and faced Frank. "She needed some attention, cleaning up. I wanted them to look her over."

They stood in the gravel parking lot, the bright sun flashing off the aluminum roofs of the outlying buildings. Despite the clear blue sky, Frank could see a dark cloud looming—Coriz hadn't told him everything.

"What's the problem, Officer Coriz? What aren't you telling me?"

"Actually, she's in good shape considering . . ."

"Considering what?" Frank gritted his teeth waiting for the cloud to rain.

"Considering she has lived her whole life in a cave," Coriz said, then added, "and considering she's crazy."

They found Tikui on the top floor of the hospital in what the nurses called the solarium, a description at best misleading. Frank stepped into the long, dark room and was immediately hit by the stale smell of cigarette smoke. Though large square windows lined the length of one wall, the huge cottonwood trees beyond captured all the sunlight.

From the gloomy shadows came the sounds of low whispers and occasional coughs. Frank could make out gray figures of patients and a few visitors. Coriz led him to the far end, past worn-out couches and threadbare chairs, to an old woman, pressed against a window, staring out.

"Tikui? It's Officer Coriz. How are you doing today?"

Frank didn't know what he expected in appearance from someone who lived in a cave, but this wasn't it. Glistening white hair hung long down her back. She stood straight as a rod, one hand resting on the windowsill. She didn't move or say a word, but stood stock-still as if she were a marble sculpture. Frank looked past her shoulder, at the view beyond, but all he could see were some red-rock bluffs in the distance.

Coriz touched her on her shoulder. "Tikui, I've brought someone who wants to talk to you. Agent Reardon is from the FBI. He has some questions."

Frank spoke. "Tikui, I'm here because of Eddie Honanie's murder. What were the exact words you heard before Eddie was killed?"

" 'Over my dead body.' "

The startling words came clear and strong. Frank looked at Coriz, who shrugged. "She must have been medicated," he said to Frank.

Coriz angled in front of her, tried to get her attention. "Tikui, can you remember any of the conversation between Eddie and his murderer?"

" 'Listen to me, you miserable little thief, you picked the wrong man to mess with.' "

Frank stepped back and nodded to Coriz. The officer joined him. "We aren't going to get anything from her," he whispered.

" 'I don't give a damn about your pathetic noble causes.' "

Frank stared at Tikui. She stood motionless, this frail, elderly, little woman staring out the window.

Coriz walked over to Tikui and placed both his hands

on her shoulders. He leaned close to her face. "What else did the murderer say, Tikui?"

The old woman took her gaze from the window for a moment and looked at Coriz. " 'I paid you for the job and now you're holding out.' "

Frank stopped. "Did he mention what job, Tikui?"

She turned to him. His first full view of her face and all Frank could look at were her eyes, the lightest gray and so clear—as if they alone had never aged since she was a child. "You must find the Hopi tablet," she told him.

She said it with such earnestness that, for a moment, Frank wondered if this were a direct instruction. "Did the murderer want the tablet, Tikui? Is that what he killed Eddie for?"

Her eyes hardened. "He is not the one." She spat the words out.

Frank ran a hand through his hair, unsure of whether to press any further. When he looked back at Tikui, her gray eyes were staring straight through him, giving Frank the uneasy sense she sought something within him.

He shook his head, breaking the contact, and stepped back. "Thanks for your help, Tikui."

A firm grasp on his arm stopped him. Frank glanced down with surprise at the spindly fingers holding him. When he raised his head, the fast hold on his arm was matched by the determined gaze he saw in Tikui's eyes.

"The earth quaked. *Balolokong* is angry." Her tone beseeched him to believe. "You must find the Hopi tablet and return it or the sorcerers cannot be stopped."

Her gaze held his and Frank didn't know what to say. How do you comfort a crazy person?

He tried a reassuring smile. "I'll do my best, Tikui."

Frank raised a brow to Coriz and turned to leave, but Tikui's hand still held him.

"Are you the one, Agent Frank Reardon?" she murmured.

*   *   *

Frank walked ahead of Coriz, wanting only to get out of the building, leave behind Tikui's searching eyes, her soft voice, the impression of her desperate grasp on his arm.

There, for a moment, in the depth of her gaze, Frank could have sworn he saw understanding and, even worse, hope in him.

The thought tore at him like a rusty knife dragging across his chest tearing jagged lines in his thick skin. Well, no amount of probing would find any hope left in him. He had buried that along with any faith in humanity when he buried Mary. If people expected any more of him they were wasting their time.

Frank stepped from the chilly building and slanted a look at the overcast sky. A thin gray haze stretched to the horizon. To the right were the bluffs he had seen over Tikui's shoulder. From her little window on the landscape, they had looked red. Now, in full view, they were drab brown ordinary. Nothing worth noticing.

He donned his shades and walked to Coriz's Jeep. Tikui's ramblings had only confirmed that Eddie had held out on someone and got a bullet in the head for his trouble. One luckless son of a bitch. And all Frank had was a dead suspect and a crazy woman for a witness. "Was she that bad off when you first talked to her?"

"Worse." Coriz looked up at the solarium window. "It was almost all babbling. About earthquakes, a man of honor, a Hopi tablet." He shook his head, then looked at Frank.

Frank was surprised by the compassion in the officer's eyes.

"Story has it *she* is some sort of Hopi sorceress." Coriz stared at Frank too long.

Frank opened the door to the Jeep. "Well, maybe that's how she first escaped from the hospital."

"Maybe," Coriz said, barely above a whisper.

A moment later, he looked at Frank, his eyes all business. "I need to get back to the station, but I'll get someone to take you to the sister's place." Coriz tapped the top of the Jeep with his keys.

"She was the uncooperative one?"

"I didn't say she was uncooperative. She just didn't have any information for us. Problem is, she's up by Shonto."

Frank folded himself into the front seat. "Fine. Just point me in the right direction."

Coriz seemed to consider Frank. "I thought you knew."

"Knew what?"

"We've had problems up there. Reports of Indians with guns. Couple of tourists were stopped, scared pretty bad. FBI has been all over it."

A cold hollowness yawned in Frank's chest. *Indians with guns. FBI.* Did it ever stop? Was there ever enough?

"Agent Reardon, we don't need any more trouble," Coriz said.

Frank's attention jerked to Coriz, his instincts honed on the Navajo. Did Coriz know about Red Earth?

The Navajo stared back, his hard, unwavering gaze revealing nothing.

"I'll be fine," Frank forced out. "Just tell me where the hell I find this sister."

"Her name's Ella Honanie. She gave me the impression she didn't have a lot of use for her brother. She seems to have her hands full just running her store. Pretty rare thing, an Indian owning a trading post."

Frank jerked his attention to Coriz. "Eddie Honanie's sister owns a trading post?"

"Red Rock Trading. I'll draw you a map."

Frank couldn't believe his ears, or his luck. He could see the light at the end of this investigation tunnel and it led straight to a trading post selling stolen art.

CHAPTER
TWO

Today she would kill that bird.

She didn't care what Ben said about bad luck or omens. She wouldn't let one more of his singsong stories capture her imagination—or her sympathy. That old Hopi was more than likely making it all up, anyway. She simply couldn't allow that magpie to mess on one more thing in the store.

Decision made, Ella's hand closed steadfastly on the pellet rifle, and she started down the hallway. She paused at Jenny's open door and glanced into the empty room. Jenny had torn through the trading post after Eddie's funeral, straight out the back door to the horses, blurting out through choked tears that she had to be alone.

Ella understood being alone, gathering her thoughts, taking the time to temper any emotions. Jenny especially needed the latter. If she would only let the anger go, time would heal. Time healed anything, Ella reminded herself firmly.

She carried the gun to the main room of the store—only to come to a quick stop at the door. An older man and his rather sweet-looking wife loitered at the jewelry case. Ella hid the rifle in the folds of her skirt.

Tire-kickers, Ella surmised, and a waste of Ben's time. She wished he would cut them loose. She needed him to cut them loose. She had her sights set on that bird—something she could do something about.

But Ella could tell he was intent on reeling them in.

Already, she noted with a salesman's respect, Ben's "obliging Indian" routine had softened up the husband enough that his arms weren't locked across his chest.

"You don't want to spend so much money, but you want the real thing, yes?"

"It's so hard to tell," the wife said. "We've seen so much."

"You look no more. This piece has been waiting for you." Ben bent below the case. Ella could hear him rummaging through the shoe box of overstock jewelry. When he stood, he held an old tourist bracelet that he presented to the woman with great ceremony. "This belonged to an Indian maiden. It was a gift to her from her lover. A young buck. So sad." He lowered his gaze and shook his head solemnly. Even Ella was taken with the performance and she knew it was all theatrics.

"What happened?" the woman asked quietly, staring at the bracelet in her hand.

"It is such a sorry story. He loved her. Intended to marry her. But it could not be. He was Navajo. She was Hopi. Like me." He smiled proudly, then fixed his face in seriousness. "Bad blood."

The words found their instant mark in Ella, a defenseless place in her she never visited and one she would not indulge now.

". . . forbidden by the fathers." Ben's drama continued. "The young buck made this bracelet with symbols of his love. Crossed arrows here and here. And this design? This is the sign of two hands clasped." He put his own hands together, fingers curled, to demonstrate. "An ancient sign carved on the rocks. One unbroken line for everlasting love. He gave his woman this bracelet, so he would always be with her."

Ben's voice lowered, became confiding. "And these small drops of silver around the one perfect turquoise? These are his tears."

The woman drew the bracelet close and ran a gentle

fingertip over the stone. She looked close to buying, but then she raised a questioning brow. Ben didn't miss a beat. "You wonder how I have it to sell, no?"

"Well, yes."

"That is even sadder. The two lovers were made to marry other people. That Indian maiden became an old woman. Still she kept the bracelet until the day she died. But her children, bah!" Ben swept the air, as if batting away something awful. "They did not care. Children do not understand love. They sold it to me." He smiled knowingly at the woman and to her husband, who looked ready to buy the bracelet just to get going. But Ben was not quite done.

"I keep the bracelet. I don't know why." He shrugged his shoulders. "I guess I believe in love."

"Yes." The woman's voice cracked.

"I could see. When you walked in together, hand in hand. I could see that." Ben smiled again at the husband, then he stood there silent. Not another word. Nothing about the price, or how well it looked on the woman, or how she would treasure it, none of the hackneyed closing lines of an amateur. Ella barely dared to breathe.

"What do you think, honey?" the woman asked her husband. Ella knew the sale was made.

Ben took the man's money, quickly wrapped the bracelet in tissue, and the couple left smiling.

"Quite a story," Ella said. "Too bad it was a lie."

"I don't know if it was a lie. She believed it, so that made it real. As real as this one hundred fifty dollars." He waved the money in the air. "You want to argue with the proof?"

"I know better than to argue with a con man." She added, reluctantly, "Especially when I need the money."

Ella unveiled the rifle and walked to the back of the gallery. She could hear Ben hurrying after her.

"You're not going to shoot that bird."

"Yes, Ben, I'm going to shoot that bird."

The bird's sharp call echoed from the high ceiling in the gallery. Ella craned her neck to see into the shadows of the beams.

"You can't do that, Ella. He's a magpie. We never see magpies anymore."

"Ben, he's ruining the merchandise. Already I've had to clean four rugs."

Ben reached her side. "You'll bring bad luck. Ella, he has chosen this place as home."

"Then he is a stupid fellow," she answered, "because if he *could* bring good luck, now would be the time. Now is when I need it," she muttered to herself.

The errant thought instantly added to her annoyance. Since when had she begun wishing for luck? Luck didn't get her through the day, any more than being hopeful or sentimental.

Ben laid a hand on her arm. "How can you challenge the stories passed down for centuries about magpies? Don't you have any respect for your heritage?"

Ella threw him a withering glance. "And you do? You just completely fabricated a story about Indians in order to sell a bracelet."

Ben's eyes twinkled. "I made a woman happy. All in a day's work." Then he sobered. "I did not murder a magpie."

"And you won't have to now, either. I'll do it." She trained the pellet rifle on the fluorescent fixture hanging inches below one beam. She was sure the magpie hid in there.

"Ella! Wait! You have to stop. This bird, I think, is important."

"Not to me."

"That just about sums up everything, doesn't it, Aunt Ella?"

Jenny stood just inside the back door, the entrance to their living areas. Though she was only across the room, her niece seemed to be a million miles away, unreachable. Her stance, as always, was slouchy with an edge—as if daring anyone to say a word, and if they did, she wouldn't care.

Yet, through Ella's eyes, Jenny glistened—a beautiful child with so much potential. If only Ella could find the right words to say.

Then Ella saw the overstuffed backpack slung on Jenny's shoulder. "Where do you think you're going?"

"To Great-grandma's." She slanted a challenging look at Ella.

"Of course," Ella said, forcing a casual tone.

Jenny's gaze turned suspicious. "You can't make me stay."

Ella swallowed her retort. The point wasn't whether she could make Jenny stay. What mattered was that Jenny didn't want to stay. She would rather sleep on the dirt floor in a mud hogan with a grandmother who was about to become homeless than live here, with Ella. All the possible things Ella could say, all the reasons why Jenny was wrong to leave, crumbled like dry sage in the face of Jenny's cold stare.

Finally, Ella said the only positive, nonthreatening words she could think of. "Grandmother will be glad to see you."

"She would be glad to see you too if you cared. If you would finally help her."

"I've tried, Jen, but she doesn't want my help. She wants a miracle."

"All she wants is to stay where she's always lived! Where she was born. She just wants to be left alone. Is that so much?"

"Yes, it is. She fought and she lost, Jen. The courts back the Hopi. It's as simple as that and no one who encourages her otherwise is helping her."

"You mean like Daddy tried to?"

There it was. The source of Jenny's rage glowed with a fire in her eyes—an eternal flame she carried in her like a torch for some hero. A hero who never wrote, who had only rarely visited his only child.

Ella's hands drew into fists at her sides. She hated Eddie for the lies he had told Jenny, the lies of a hero's life always fighting the noble cause.

He had been nothing but a foolish man who got himself killed. And his murder made him all the more a hero in his daughter's eyes.

Jenny deserved the truth, but Ella saw that she needed the lie, the one that gave her own life meaning—because if Eddie wasn't a hero needed everywhere else, then why hadn't he been here?

"I know you don't believe me, Jen, but things work out the way they're supposed to. They will for Grandmother, they will for you."

"Like they did for Daddy? Why don't you say it, Aunt Ella?" Tears welled in Jenny's eyes.

Ella reached a hand to her, but Jenny swatted it away. "Don't," she spat out.

"Hush! Both of you! I'm trying to hear this."

Ella had forgotten Ben was even there. She now saw he was absorbed in some television newscast. He showed no more interest in the words exchanged between Ella and Jenny than if they were an insignificant conversation. Ella felt the steely hold she'd had on her composure slip.

"Look at this!" Ben's nose was only inches from the picture, his hands pressed to each side of the small screen as if holding on for dear life.

Jenny stepped past Ella to look over Ben's shoulder. "It's an earthquake, Ben."

"Yes."

A map of Arizona appeared on the screen with concentric circles spreading out from the Grand Canyon, evidently the epicenter of the quake.

"Two hundred miles from here," Jenny said, with obvious disinterest.

"The second one in two days." His low tone drew Ella close, too. "The first one happened the night of Eddie's death."

For the next few minutes, the only sound in the large room was the voice of the reporter on the television.

"Park Rangers are still checking all the campsites," she said. "So far, there are no reports of any injuries, but they have not yet been able to contact the overnight groups at the bottom of the canyon."

"Guess the tourists are getting their money's worth," Jenny muttered.

Ben glanced back at Jenny. "I don't care about the tourists."

Jenny smirked. "Interesting admission coming from you."

The old man swiveled the chair to them, his face lit up like a child's with a secret he couldn't keep. "This is a momentous occasion!" He jumped from the chair. Startled, both Ella and Jenny stepped back.

"Ben, what are you talking about?"

"Why, the prophecy, Ella. The Hopi prophecy." He was pacing now. "I thought of it when the first of the white buffalo calves were born. And again when the comet came two years ago. Then I wondered if it might be possible when the second white calf was born. And now." He gestured wildly, his steps quick, almost as if this squat, round man were about to break into a dance.

Suddenly, he turned, facing them, his arms spread wide, a huge grin on his face. Both Jenny and Ella must have looked completely bewildered because Ben sobered and offered a smile. "I'm a bit excited."

"I think he's had too much soda," Jenny said, hiking up her backpack and heading for the door.

"You're leaving. Yes. You tell your great-grandmother that her miracle is about to come."

Jenny paused at the door. "It's not her miracle, Ben. You said it yourself. It's a Hopi miracle and Great-grandmother is Navajo. Nobody in this family even talks about being part Hopi." She gave Ella a sharp look.

Ben's eyes smiled. "You tell your great-grandmother,

child. It's a miracle for everyone." He started pacing again. "Now, we have to find the tablet." He was muttering and pacing, back and forth.

"Well, that should keep you honest for a while, Ben. Let me know what you find." Jenny had her hand on the door.

"No! You don't understand! The ones with fire will come unless the man of honor returns the tablet."

"And that would be you?" Jenny's sarcasm sliced clean through Ben's excitement. "I don't have time for this."

"This is the fifth sign," Ben said quietly. He looked from Jenny over to Ella, his face worried, his eyes beseeching them to listen. "The one we've been waiting for." He nodded and turned back to the television.

Stunned, Ella stared at the back of her friend's head. Had he suddenly lost his mind? She looked to her niece and found Jenny staring back at her, concern pinching her forehead, her eyes asking the same question of Ella.

Ella put a hand on his shoulder. "Ben, you're not making any sense."

Ben's dark eyes took her in with their familiar warmth, the eyes of a friend. "Ella, you've been looking for something to believe in, this is it."

"I have not!" Her denial rang off the abrupt silence. She recovered her equilibrium and lowered her voice. "I'm not some tourist you can scam, Ben. This is Ella you're talking to—and Jenny." She let the threat hang in the last words. *Do not involve Jennifer in any ludicrous scheme.*

"I'm outta here. I'll tell Great-grandmother about the miracle, Ben. She needs some hope."

"Jenny, wait. How will you get there?"

"I have a ride. I'll call." She was out the door.

Ella saw no car, no truck, nothing but the wide-open vista that seemed to reach all the way to Black Mountain. Ella's thoughts tumbled in a confused rush. "What ride? Jenny, you can't go. Not now, I mean—"

"Then when, Aunt Ella? If I wait as long as you to have

a life . . ." She shook her head then turned and walked away.

The insult sliced through Ella's heart. She couldn't move. She couldn't make herself run after Jenny. She wanted to. She wanted to haul Jenny into her arms and make everything all right. But something stopped her, a barrier she couldn't get past. Words she couldn't say about herself or even about Eddie. She was afraid to speak for the rage building inside her against Eddie, or for the pain leaking from her own heart.

When Ella finally found her voice, Jenny was nearly at the turn of the road. "Jenny! Eddie loved you. He loved you enough to leave you here with me."

Jenny stopped and faced her. Ella drew hope from the quiet look on the child's face, but then Jenny spoke, her words clear and defining. "Daddy didn't mean for me to die here on the vine with you."

Ella watched the slowly diminishing form and her heart broke with every step.

"Let her go, Ella." Ben's short, strong fingers grasped her arm. "She'll be fine at the grandmother's. She will only have her thoughts and they will come back to you."

"No, her thoughts will be of Eddie. And of grand adventures. And miracles." She looked at Ben. "Did you have to talk about miracles?" Ella walked past him into the store before he had a chance to respond. She didn't need to hear another word.

She picked up the gun and walked to the far end of the gallery. She heard Ben's hurried steps behind her.

"Ella! Wait! You have to stop!"

Ella glanced at Ben over the barrel of the gun. He looked truly agitated—a state she had never witnessed on the passive Hopi. His eyes pleaded with her to listen.

"The signs. Didn't you listen? Who knows what this magpie means?"

"He means nothing, Ben, but more work."

"You're angry. I understand. Why must you do this now?"

"I'm not angry, Ben. I'm frustrated. This is something I *can* do." Ella's throat tightened around the words.

She pulled the trigger.

The magpie let out a scream and flew to the other set of lights.

She kept the bird in sight and pulled the trigger again.

Frank slid the Jeep to a grateful stop at the front of the trading post. The old vehicle moaned over the troublesome roads with a last tiresome creak before settling into a dusty silence. Frank surveyed the hodgepodge building that spread before him. It began with stone, moved on to rooms of logs, and finally finished with adobe bricks of clay and sticks. It meandered over the tough ground like some feral low-to-the-ground creature, at one time domesticated but now gone wild, looking for shade, just trying to survive.

He had no doubt Miss Ella Honanie had conjured her own plan for survival—a plan he was about to happily destroy.

He had about reached the door when he heard a shot. Frank slammed his back against the wall of the building, pulled the gun from his holster, and eased toward the window. He peeked in and couldn't believe what he saw: a slender Indian woman was aiming what looked like a child's shotgun at the ceiling.

"There it is!" she yelled, and let off another shot.

Another Indian, a short, very round man, was waving his arms, as if to distract her.

What the hell was going on?

Frank pushed open the door to the trading post. At the sound of the chime, the woman turned, her face surprised.

She immediately lowered the gun to her side. "I'm sorry. It's a bird, you see—"

"Don't bother, Ella. He's a cop." The man had keen, intelligent eyes that stayed focused right on Frank.

"FBI, actually," Frank corrected.

"So what do you want?" he asked.

"And you are?" Frank countered.

"A Hopi." Ben crossed his arms over his chest.

"Your name."

"Yours first."

"Ben, I'll handle this."

Frank heard the irritation in her voice. He also noted, however, that she didn't offer any apology for Ben. She walked to the counter and put down the gun. "Are you here with information about Eddie?"

"I'm Special Agent Reardon, FBI. And you are?"

"Ella Honanie, Eddie's sister. Have you found out who killed him?"

"And Ben's last name?"

"Talaqueptewa," Ben answered, sounding out each syllable as if talking to a child. "You need me to spell it?"

"Ben, when was the last time you saw Eddie?"

"This afternoon."

Frank saw the spark of mischief in Ben's eyes. "Alive," Frank added.

"The day before he was killed."

"Where?"

"Here."

Frank faced Ella Honanie. "Why was he here, Miss Honanie?"

"To visit," she answered. "Why are you here, Agent Reardon?"

"And Eddie's daughter." Frank checked his notes. "Jennifer? Is she here?"

"No."

Frank looked up and met the unflinching gaze of Ella. "But she lives here, right?"

She didn't respond, but Frank saw her gaze flit to the side before returning to her constant stare at him. "What is it you want, Agent Reardon?"

"Well, now, Miss Honanie, your brother is dead. You don't seem too eager to help with the investigation."

"Just what are you investigating?" It was Ben. "If you're looking for any answers here, you're wasting your time. No big surprise for the FBI, I admit."

Frank walked the room a few paces and stopped in front of the jewelry case. A closer look delivered some surprises. There were actually some fine pieces set among the usual assortment of souvenir fare. In fact, half of one shelf offered a selection of old pieces. "Some nice stuff. Where do you come by your inventory, Miss Honanie?" Frank made mental notes of the pieces to check against his lists of stolen art.

"Different places. Mostly Indians, some traders, and some pawnshops in Gallup."

Frank sauntered around the room. The walls were a crazy quilt of sandpaintings, Navajo rugs, and watercolors. Shelves ran the circumference of the room and held dozens of kachina dolls. Even from a distance, Frank could tell that many were not authentic Hopi kachinas but instead replicas carved by Navajo.

"And Eddie, did he supply some?"

"No."

He stopped at one of the shelves and fingered the tag hanging off a kachina. "Now, you see, Miss Honanie, I find that hard to believe. Eddie didn't have a job, no visible means of support. And here you are with a thriving store. You didn't help him out with income?"

"A thriving business, Agent Reardon?" She gave a small laugh. "And if I helped Eddie, what difference would that make? He was my brother. Just what are you getting at?" Her smile was gone and her gaze now held Frank's—straightforward, earnest, as though she truly didn't have a clue where this was going.

For a second Frank questioned his own assumption about her culpability—but for only a second.

"What am I getting at, Miss Honanie?" He leaned across the counter. "I'm getting at the reason why Eddie was murdered." He was close enough to see the pulse at her throat.

"Why?" The so-quiet question was almost a plea. Her lips stayed parted.

Frank leaned closer. "For the stolen art, of course. Why don't you tell me about it?"

"Eddie was killed for stolen art?"

Frank watched Ella's face closely. Her brow creased. In confusion? Concern? Suddenly, her gaze locked with his.

"Indian art, Agent Reardon?"

Her question surprised Frank. He nodded.

"That can't be. He wouldn't," she declared.

"But Eddie could steal *other* art? Is that what you're saying, Miss Honanie?"

She didn't rise to the bait, but returned his unflinching stare. "If you're investigating stolen Indian art, Agent Reardon, I can tell you that Eddie had nothing to do with it."

"The witness to the murder says otherwise."

"Tikui? That old crazy woman? She lives in a canyon."

Frank narrowed his eyes on Ben. "You seem to know more than you should about the investigation. You want to tell me how?"

The Hopi stared back, unblinking. "I will tell you this, no one listens to Tikui. She is an outcast from the pueblo."

"You have no right to call her that." Ella's voice quivered slightly with what seemed barely controlled outrage.

She was glaring at Ben and the Hopi looked more than bewildered.

"Ella, that's what Tikui means: 'outcast.' I'm not making a judgment."

"I know what Tikui means, Ben. Don't use it."

The Indian's mouth fell open as if Ella had grown two heads.

Frank immediately wondered why this meant so much to Ella.

The next instant, she turned her attention to Frank and asked, "So this woman witnessed the murder? What else did she tell you?"

"She heard Eddie mention a Denver art dealer. What would you know about this, Miss Honanie?"

"I know either she misunderstood or you have made a mistake. Eddie would not steal art."

"Are you sure? We can't always account for everything our family does."

"I don't *have* to account for anything Eddie did." Her eyes held a hard, impassable sheen.

"Oh, but you do. That is, if you want to catch Eddie's murderer." Frank pushed off from the counter and paced a few steps around the main gallery room, purposefully directing his gaze to the full cases and the crowded walls. He faced Ella, hoping to catch a sign of guilt, or even anxiety.

Instead, he saw understanding descend across her face. "You're investigating me," she murmured and Frank didn't miss the flicker of pain that pinched her brow.

A chuckle pulled Frank's attention to Ben. "You FBI guys sure don't disappoint. How long does it take to train you to be narrow-minded, shortsighted, prejudiced sons of bitches?"

Frank's lips curved slightly. "Just long enough to teach us to recognize a con when we see it."

"That long, eh?" The smile stayed as Ben shook his head. When he again considered Frank, however, his smile had died. "Then again, it's easy to just assume every Indian is on a con."

Frank knew that attitude—that arrogant platitude so convenient, so useful, so *insidious,* because it counted on your humanity, the humanity that rebelled against injustice. It preyed on the guilt every white person should feel for the crimes against Indians. And finally, it relied on your very innocence to be tortured by guilt . . . the more innocent, the better.

Frank's gut churned with frustration . . . and hatred, which seared straight up to a point behind his eyes. He leveled his gaze on Ben. "I believe what I see."

A flutter from above drew Frank's attention. The next instant, a flash of black and white descended on a swoop and a call.

A bird landed on his shoulder.

"What the—"

"The bird—" Ella started.

"A magpie, Agent Reardon." The Hopi took a few steps toward Frank. His wide eyes were on the bird.

CHAPTER
THREE

This can't be," Ben said. The Hopi sounded truly disappointed.

Frank caught Ella's glance to where she had placed the gun.

"You don't want to do that, Miss Honanie."

"What?"

"Try to shoot a bird off my shoulder."

"No . . . of course not."

Though she didn't look at all convinced. Her deep brown eyes, first on him then the magpie, were laced with annoyance.

"I just don't understand," Ben said. "Why land on him?"

Frank had a moment of irrational pique at the Hopi's obvious disenchantment with this bird.

"Because he's the tallest in the room, Ben. Or maybe because this bird is stupid, and not so important."

Frank could not understand the argument over this bird on his shoulder. At that exact moment, the bird decided to tweak Frank's earlobe. The sensation tickled him down to his toes and he couldn't help a chuckle.

"Please, Agent Reardon, don't humor Ben."

Humoring Ben Talaqueptewa was the last thing on Frank's mind and his annoyance grew over this whole situation. "Miss Honanie, if you will simply open the door,

I'll step outside.'' Frank took a step toward the door.

"No." Ben hissed his demand barely above a whisper.

"Ben, I want the bird out of here."

She breezed past Frank and a scent of sweet grass wafted over him, such a totally pleasant smell he hesitated a moment too long before realizing Ella held the door open. Frank took brisk steps out the door and beyond. The magpie bobbed along on his shoulder, chortling happily at his ear.

"Shoo!" Frank swung his hand toward his shoulder.

The magpie fluttered, but didn't fly away.

"It's a miracle," Ben murmured.

"Ben!"

Ella's glare had no effect on the old Hopi, who continued to stare at Frank's shoulder in amazement.

Frank jerked his shoulder, waved his arms, even jumped from one foot to the other. The bird flapped, chortled, and dug his feet into Frank's jacket.

"Ella, no!"

Frank looked up just in time to see Ella emerge from the trading post with the pellet rifle, her skirt billowing, her face set with determination.

"Put the gun down, Miss Honanie."

She aimed it skyward and pulled the trigger.

The magpie screeched and fled to the top of the trading post.

"There." She turned, walked back into the post, and slammed the door.

Frank shook his head and started for the store with a last glance to Ben, who stood there staring at the bird on the roof. The store was empty and Frank's patience with both Miss Honanie and Ben came to an end. Did she seriously think she could dismiss him and be done with the trouble?

He walked to the middle of the gallery. "Miss Honanie!"

"You don't have to yell."

Frank turned toward her voice and caught sight of her beyond a door behind the counters, sitting at a desk. "We're not through here."

"I've told you all I know about Eddie, Agent Reardon." She didn't deign to even glance up from her paperwork. "I have work to do."

"I see. More important than my investigation into your brother's murder?"

"You can think what you want, Agent Reardon. Most people do. Open minds take a lot more work," Ella said, her quiet, practical tone confusing his anger.

"Most people care about the murder of a loved one."

She looked up then and stared at him, so intensely, the distance between them seemed to shorten. He could see the glisten in her eyes, as if his words had pricked at someplace vulnerable. Suddenly, she asked, "You say you believe what you see?"

"That's right."

She swept past him, stirring the air. That same faint scent of sweet grass lingered in her wake as she walked out of the room. When she returned, she held a picture frame, which she presented him. He could see it was a picture of this post taken before the addition of some rooms. A family stood in front, but their small faces were blurred. The old black-and-white photo had been shot from enough distance to include the whole rambling building, yet it captured none of the details of the humans. "And?" He held the frame out to Ella.

Her eyes glistened with pride. "That's my family. My father, my mother, Eddie and me. And the post. It was taken the day Father took over the store."

She paused, an expectant look on her face, but the significance of the photo still eluded Frank. Ella sighed and set the picture on the counter. "A lot has changed," she said, staring at the photo. "All that remains from this picture, twenty years later, is me and the post."

She turned to Frank. "If you believe what you see, Agent Reardon, then look hard at this picture. What you're looking at is my life. A hardworking, honest life.''

Frank couldn't tear his gaze from her. Determination flashed in her eyes, tinted her high cheekbones with pink. Even her black hair shone brighter, as if she could bring every part of her to bear.

He recognized that look of commitment; he had seen it enough on Mary's face, usually followed by some tirade against bureaucrats and paper-pushers—except Ella Honanie did not seem prone to tirades, or displays of any kind.

He studied Ella, the thought forming—again—that maybe she was sincere. She probably was. Just as sincere as Mary had been . . . and just as sincere as the Indians who had caused her death.

If you believe what you see. Ella's words settled on Frank like rain damping down dust, clearing his head of any distraction.   .

''I believe you, Miss Honanie.''

Her quick smile only made Frank take a breath before continuing. ''I believe you care about this store. I can see this place means the world to you. I even believe what you said earlier about times being hard.''

''I manage—''

''Question is,'' Frank continued, ''how far would you go to keep the business?''

For a second, Frank thought she might implode. Her mouth dropped open and the pink in her cheeks turned bright red.

But it was the immense sadness in her eyes that took him aback.

''I think it's time you left, Agent Reardon.''

''This problem won't just go away, Miss Honanie.''

''It will when you walk out that door, Agent Reardon.''

She raised her chin the slightest bit in an obvious struggle for control and once again left him at a loss. She hadn't gotten angry, defensive, belligerent—any of the emotions he would expect from someone he had practically just accused of being a criminal.

He looked away from her and his gaze took in the gallery, the hodgepodge of merchandise, the old wooden cases. Maybe she was all that she said—a lone woman just trying to make a living.

Then his gaze settled on the fake Hopi kachinas. A trademark of any successful con was a good front and he knew, sure as those kachinas were fake, so was she. Frank felt the familiar satisfaction of his instincts clicking in.

"I'll need to see your books: income, disbursements. Also a list of vendors and of the inventory."

"You have no right—"

"Oh, but I do."

"I own this trading post, Agent Reardon, not the Navajo Tribe, not the BIA, and not the federal government. Me."

Frank ventured a look at Ella, hardening his thoughts in the face of her fierce look. "You don't own the land, Miss Honanie. I'm sure I don't have to remind you that the federal government holds this land in trust for the Navajo. And I'm the federal government."

"I've already told you I don't know why Eddie was killed. You're wasting both my time and yours."

"You'll have plenty of time to get the information together for me, Miss Honanie. As of today, this post is closed." Frank started for the door.

"You can't—"

Her quiet plea drove straight through Frank. He paused for a second at the door, then kept on walking.

A few paces toward the Jeep, Frank heard the creak of the post door, followed by the soft crunch of boot heels on the hard-pebbled earth. He knew it was Ella by the *lack* of harsh sounds: no slam of the door, no sharp invectives hurled. But he could feel her gaze on his back, impaling him to the spot.

He slanted a look over his shoulder at her, his fingers already on the door handle of the Jeep. She approached him with all the sure, deliberate aim of a bullet. The swirling skirt at her ankles, billowing sleeves of her blouse, the gentle rise of her hair in the breeze—these were all dressing, a veil of softness covering a steely purpose.

"Agent Reardon, I have a deal for you."

"So soon? That usually comes after the arrest."

Her lips flattened and she considered him. Then, "I meant *compromise*. Are you always so quick to judge?"

She couldn't have known those were the exact words to reopen old wounds, Frank told himself even as bitterness bubbled up from deep scars. "Sometimes not quick enough," he muttered, before he could stop himself. He opened the door.

"Stop and listen to me, Agent Reardon." Her hand gripped the window frame, slender fingers risking his anger. "I must keep the post open."

"That sounds more like a demand than a compromise, Miss Honanie."

"People depend on the store. For groceries, staples, cloth for dances."

"A real hardship to go without cloth for dances."

"You really don't understand, do you? Look around you, Agent Reardon. This isn't one of a hundred corner stores. Where else will the families go? You assume I've committed a crime, even without evidence. Are you so sure that you're willing to also punish the families who depend on me?"

He had to admit a grudging respect for her determination. "Just what is your compromise?"

She pulled folded papers from her pocket and handed them to him. The white-lined sheets looked as if they had been ripped from a child's spiral notebook. Double columns of neatly written script on the front and back of the two papers listed close to two hundred names; most were Indian, others Frank thought might be names of Anglo traders.

"It's not complete, but—" she said.

"I need it complete." Frank started to hand it back.

She stopped him with her palm out. "It includes the people I trade with often. I've been toying with the idea of an Indian arts market. Like a fair. Maybe in September. There are the rodeos and . . ." Her voice had become wistful.

Frank glanced to her, but she looked away with a shrug as if she decided what she held important was of no interest to him. Then she leveled her gaze on him. "Let me keep the store open. Please."

Frank slid into the seat and started the Jeep. When he tried to close the door, he noticed that her grip on the frame had turned her knuckles white.

"Is Ben's name here?"

Her eyes narrowed. "Why, yes, but—"

"All right, Miss Honanie. You have your compromise. But I want the rest of the paperwork in two days."

She stood for a moment still gripping the door, looking as if she might want to change her mind.

"Don't make me regret it, Miss Honanie."

"You won't. Thank you." She released the door and took a step back. She didn't look so much relieved as she did *resigned* to one more burden.

Frank refused to feel the slightest bit of responsibility. He pulled the Jeep around and headed down the dirt road, but he couldn't resist a last look in the rearview mirror. Ella had already turned back to the store with sure strides, a small figure becoming ever more indistinct in the vast distance.

Are you always so quick to judge?

They were words Mary might have uttered to him, just before she stormed out the door on another crusade. And his answer was always the same. *Yes.*

Even when the time had come to judge him.

The hollowness in his chest turned cold.

If he spent a lifetime, he could never redeem himself for that one moment at Red Earth.

He drove east, down miles of dirt road, then highway, with only his headlights breaking the enveloping darkness. Occasionally, he would see the flicker of a light as if a lone star had landed on earth, and he thought of what Ella had said about the far-flung families depending on her.

If he gave a damn about anyone, he might hope she was innocent.

Of course, he *didn't* give a damn about anyone. Not anymore.

For the two-hour drive to Window Rock and the Navajo Police Headquarters, Frank's thoughts centered on that lone trading post and its inhabitants, especially Ella Honanie. Beneath that quiet façade was a woman who did not let much stand in her way. He just might be the first brick wall she had met.

At the Navajo Police Headquarters, Frank accessed the data base and typed in Eddie Honanie's name. An instant later, he had the personal information including tribal number, but no criminal activity. That was no surprise. Any arrests would have been part of Eddie's file. It also didn't mean Frank wouldn't find something at the FBI office in Phoenix.

Frank pulled Ella's list from his pocket and started down the names. Four hours later, and almost to the end, Frank had nearly two dozen names of suspect individuals, with crimes ranging from disorderly to driving while intoxicated to burglary. He made notes on each, though only the ones charged with burglary held any promise.

At the next name, Frank's lips curved up. He typed in Ben Talaqueptewa's name. A moment later, personal information ran down the left side of the screen. But what Frank was looking for glowed in satisfying amber on the right side: Ben's criminal record.

Though a short list, the nature of Ben's record showed a pattern. There were two complaints filed for misrepresentation of Indian arts, yet he had never been charged or tried. The victims of misrepresentation had seemingly dropped from sight. Tourists, Frank figured, who probably refused to delay their vacation. Another complaint had been filed, just six months ago—this one for trafficking in illegal Indian art. Frank's gaze stopped at the name of the complainant, a dealer in Gallup . . . and one of the sources on Ella's list: Joe Miller.

Frank stared at the screen, but his mind was on Ella. Did she know of the complaints? If so, she also had to know how bad it looked for her—openly employing Ben in her store: a person accused of fraud. Or did Ben keep secrets from her, even lie to her? Frank thought of how Ella had hurried to provide the list. And he remembered the expression on her face: not stricken, as if she knew the list contained incriminating information; instead, she had looked weary.

Frank squeezed the bridge of his nose to exact focus. Whatever Ella knew or didn't know would be revealed in time. One fact at a time until he built a case, that was his job.

Frank noted the names and dates from Ben's record, then continued through the entries on Ella's list. He came to the last one, Chandler—just that, no first name. Instincts told him it was an alias. He typed in the name and wasn't surprised when he drew a blank screen.

He exited the file and leaned back in the chair, notepad in hand. He shook his head at the list. Miss Honanie had to hold the record for the most dissimilar collection of associates—and most of them disreputable. She was acquainted with a veritable potluck of deviants—society's discards of the deranged, depraved, and degenerate. With this gold mine of shady characters, it would be a wonder if she *weren't* doing something illegal.

Gallup, New Mexico, boasted of being the entrance to Indian country. From Frank's vantage as he descended on Highway 666, Gallup looked less of a gateway than a clog in the arteries. Two-lane roads radiated in from the south, north, and northeast—desolate highways bringing in Zuni, Navajo, and even Hopi from the far reaches of the reservations. Brick buildings lined Main Street, none venturing more than three stories—as if content with the limited view further restricted by the surrounding bald, sandstone dunes. Chinese restaurants, souvenir shops, bars, pawnshops, Indian stores—many with the names of Arab proprietors—were all crammed into an area less than a mile long. Huge red letters on windows screamed wholesale prices to the public. Gallup might consider itself a gateway, but Frank bet the passed-out cowboy collapsed against the wooden Indian would call it a dead end.

Frank parked the Jeep right in front of Miller's store. The low chiming of a bell announced his entrance and a burly man, with enough girth to double as a bouncer at the bar next door, ambled in from a back room.

"Mornin' to you. Anythin' I can help you with, you just let me know." He smiled, one thumb curled around a suspender.

"Agent Reardon, FBI, I'm looking for Joe Miller, the owner."

The man's smile died. "That's me."

"Well, Joe, you can tell me how you know Ben Talaqueptewa."

"Why?" Joe's tone was a challenge.

That was not the response Frank expected from the man who had filed a complaint on Ben. He shifted gears and faced the man dead-on. "When was the last time you saw Ben?"

"It's been a while."

"How long a while?"

"He keeps himself up the way in Shonto."

Joe crossed beefy arms across his chest as if that was all he had to say on the subject.

"You want to tell me why you won't talk about Talaqueptewa? I came across your complaint—"

"Who's complaining? Dammit, I told that man in Austin that I just needed some time. I have his name, you call him." He went for his wallet. "Between the feds and the state you guys are killing me."

"*Your* complaint, Miller. The one you filed on Talaqueptewa."

"What?" The big man leaned on the case. Miller's face was already red with anger. Now he looked ready to bust Frank in the nose.

Frank returned the glare. "Do you have a reason you don't want to remember this complaint, Miller?"

"Yeah. My reason is I didn't file one."

Miller didn't blink or flinch and Frank wondered whether the man might be telling the truth.

"You're wasting your time here, Mr. FBI," Miller continued. "My books are straight. I've got nothing to hide."

Frank doubted that. "Just how do you know Talaqueptewa?"

"I'm in Indian arts. It's a small world."

"And in this small world, how did you come across Talaqueptewa?"

The big man shrugged, testing his suspenders. "Everyone knows Ben. I don't remember how I met him."

"You buy things from Ben?" Frank ventured.

"He brings me things from time to time."

"Like what?"

"Stuff. I told you it's been a while."

"Stuff," Frank repeated and took a tour of the store. He decided on another tactic. "How about Ella Honanie? You know her?"

He glanced at the big man and caught a flicker of something on Miller's face, almost like a smile at his lips. "Yeah, I know Ella. What about her? If you believe a complaint on her you really are stupider than you look."

"What would your association with her be?" Frank said as he studied another case of jewelry.

"We're both in the business."

"And what about her brother?"

"So this is all about Eddie?"

Frank glanced over at Miller and found him shaking his head, as if in disbelief.

"I get it now," Miller said. "You're investigating Eddie's murder." He pushed back from the case, still shaking his head. "You think someone in the business was involved? You really are dense, aren't you?"

"Why don't you enlighten me, Miller? What do you know about Eddie Honanie?"

"I didn't know Eddie well. But I can tell you one thing, he wasn't involved in the Indian arts business. Whatever Eddie was up to, Ella wasn't a part of."

"What *would* Eddie have been up to?"

"I haven't got a clue." Miller's lips drew into a tight, straight line.

"Oh, I think you do have a clue, Miller. And I have to wonder what kind of game you're playing. You file a complaint, but don't file charges, and now you deny any knowledge of the complaint."

"Are you hard of hearing? I did *not* file a complaint. You suits have got the wrong information."

"Now, I have to wonder what would make you *forget* about that complaint," Frank continued as he wandered to a case full of old kachinas. "Maybe you decided you need what Ben provides. Money has a way of assuaging guilty consciences."

"You get the hell out of my store." Joe rounded the corner of his cases and, more quickly than his size indicated, was across the room and facing Frank.

Frank had to lift his chin to meet the big man's gaze. "Whatever game you're playing, I'm going to find out. You can count on that."

Miller's eyes shone with anger and a barely constrained rage. "You're fishing for something, but you won't find it here, FBI. Now get out."

Frank took a last look at the kachinas, committing them to memory, then walked to the door. He paused, hand on the knob, and turned to Miller. "By the way, you know someone called Chandler?"

Miller barked out a laugh. "Why don't you go check that computer of yours, Mr. FBI?" Then he disappeared into the back room.

For the thirty miles back to Window Rock, his mind was on Joe Miller, Ben, Eddie, and Ella. Whatever reason Miller had to *forget*, the complaint was strong enough for him to stand up to the FBI. Large sums of money was a great persuader . . . large sums of money or large crates of art.

At Navajo Headquarters, Frank walked straight to an empty desk with a computer and tapped in the keys for the complaint index. He highlighted Ben Talaqueptewa and punched enter. The Miller complaint jumped up on the screen. Frank scanned down to the bottom of the complaint and stared at the empty space for the officer's name who took the complaint.

"Agent Reardon, what are you doing in here?"

Frank glanced up at Officer Coriz, then back to the computer. "Can you tell me why this information is incomplete?" He jabbed his finger at the blank space on the monitor.

"Did anyone say you could access those files?"

Frank turned his head to face Coriz. "You know I don't have to ask."

"Most agents do, Agent Reardon—out of courtesy. You, in particular, are supposed to keep me informed of your investigation."

Coriz stared back with no effort to veil the dislike in his eyes. Either this Navajo knew about Frank's involvement in Red Earth or he simply had no use for any federal agents. Whichever reason, Frank didn't care. The distrust was mutual.

"That cooperation goes both ways, Officer Coriz. Are you going to answer my question?"

Coriz stared at Frank for a beat longer than necessary, then looked at the screen. "I can't tell you why it's blank." He straightened and returned his gaze to Frank. "Who is the complaint on?"

"Ben Talaqueptewa."

"A complaint on Ben?"

"You sound as if you know him."

"Everyone knows Ben. What's this about?"

Coriz's casual, almost friendly tone when speaking of Ben, and the fact he used nearly the same words as Miller, instantly ratcheted up Frank's annoyance.

"What about Joe Miller? Do you know him, too?"

Coriz's eyes went blank. "No. What about him?"

"He's an Indian trader in Gallup. He's the one who filed this complaint."

"No, don't know a Joe Miller." His tone implied that ended his interest.

Frank ran a frustrated hand through his hair. "Where would I find the paperwork on this?"

"What is this about, Agent Reardon?"

"Illegal trafficking in Indian arts," Frank said, watching Coriz.

"Oh, no, you've got it wrong. That was *misrepresentation,* not illegal trafficking, and the charges were dropped. That happens out here. People misunderstanding." He gave Frank a pointed look.

Frank returned the stare. "Different complainant, different complaint on something that is not *supposed* to happen out here, Officer Coriz. Now where is that paperwork?"

Coriz leaned toward the screen again, reached his hand to the keyboard and scrolled up to the top of the complaint, where the cursor blinked beneath Ben's name. "I didn't know anything about this one," he said. His voice was thoughtful. "Just a minute."

He left the file room. Minutes later he returned, manila folder in hand bearing Ben's name. "I tried to check the day and time against who was working, but there isn't any paperwork here on that complaint."

Coriz stared at the monitor. "It's like this complaint just appeared in the computer."

"It can't just appear, Coriz."

Coriz didn't say anything.

Frank's thoughts were on Miller and his denials of making the complaint. Instincts told him Ben had something going with the trader, but did it have to do with Eddie and

Ella? Frank couldn't say, but those same instincts fired every time he thought of that remote trading post.

He pushed back from the computer and started for the door. Coriz stopped him with a hand to his arm. Frank turned, ready to tell this Navajo to back off, but then he registered the concern in Coriz's eyes.

"What brought you to this complaint to begin with, Agent Reardon?" Coriz asked.

Frank hesitated to answer. Memories of past betrayals—Indian to white, officer to officer—made him clench his jaw. But he had to cooperate with Coriz. "I'm looking at the people involved with Ella Honanie and her trading post. Somebody has to know about that stolen art."

"You've tied Eddie to the stolen art, then?"

"Tikui tied him to the art, remember?"

Coriz's eyes flickered with amusement. "That's it? Because she mentioned Denver? She also mentioned earthquakes, sorcerers, and a Hopi tablet."

That Coriz had just about summed up the extent of Frank's case didn't amuse Frank. "I'm waiting on Denver to confirm Eddie's prints on the storage locker. They'll match, Coriz, take my word for it." He gave a glance to Coriz's hand on his arm, but the Navajo didn't budge.

"You're here as a courtesy, Agent Reardon. So far, nothing ties Honanie's murder to that art. The last thing we need are unfounded speculations about an Indian trading post."

"What has you so worried, Coriz? I would think you would want to root out any illegal businesses, *Indian* or not."

Coriz's black eyes turned to flint. "Those troubles I told you about up there? It's between the Hopi and Navajo. Now, you're investigating a trading post on Navajo land, run by a woman part Hopi, part Navajo. Do us all a favor, Agent Reardon, and keep me abreast of what the hell is going on."

CHAPTER
FOUR

Three twisted wire bracelets, two cuff bracelets, four Yazzie etched bracelets . . .''

Ella recited each piece as she wrote it down—her latest strategy to keep herself awake. She had stopped drinking coffee an hour ago. The strong brew had kept her going for the past twelve hours, but her stomach rebelled at the thought of one more cup.

Ella set down her pen and flexed her fingers. Tingling sleepiness raced up her arm. Her gaze went to the boxes of jewelry stacked on the cases. Her handwritten list already filled two yellow pads. The words blurred and drifted into an endless scrawl.

She wouldn't get this done today. There was no way she could meet Reardon's deadline. She had been a fool to even promise him.

And without the list, Reardon would never believe she had nothing to do with the stolen art.

I believe what I see, he had said.

If he just looked around, he would see she was barely making ends meet. Did he really think she was doing this for the money? The absurd notion bubbled up into a coarse laugh. It was all Ella could do to squirrel away money for Jenny's college. Ella didn't keep this place to get rich. She kept it to provide stability for Jenny.

She had made a home with no drunkenness, no angry arguments . . . no abandonment.

Except Jenny wasn't here. She had left.

Futility stole over Ella.

Her exhaustion muddled her thoughts and feelings into a swirl of words and emotions, until only the simplest phrase floated coherent: *It doesn't matter what I do.*

The thought pinched Ella's heart, letting the old sadness leak past barriers. Bone-weary fatigue cracked her defenses, flooding her with an unreasonable grief that rose swiftly, unmercifully, pricking behind her eyes. She had no strength to muster against the overwhelming emotion.

In that irrational state she felt deserted: by Ben, who had left in pursuit of that silly tablet, some stupid belief he placed above her own real crisis; and by Jenny, who obviously believed the home Ella had provided offered her nothing. Instead, Jenny chose Grandmother—a woman as passionate in her beliefs as Eddie and as far removed from Ella as you could get. Jenny and Grandmother understood each other . . . to the exclusion of Ella.

Taking a deep breath, Ella pushed up from the chair she had planted herself in hours, maybe days, before. Numb legs buckled beneath her and Ella barely caught herself with an outstretched hand to the counter.

In that instant, the memory of another time collided with the present. Ella saw her father struggling to stand, bracing a hand on the counter, staggering upright; her mother stood at the door, a pitying, resigned look on her face right before she walked out the front door and out of their lives.

And Ella saw herself, a disconnected image of a child, alone, with no one to turn to because Eddie had already stormed out. The stricken expression on her own young face was burned into Ella's soul. *She* had somehow caused her mother to leave, she knew it in a place deep, deep within. Now, Jenny had left. If only Ella had been better, not created that trouble before, the bad things would not keep happening.

An uncontrollable shudder swept through Ella. With extreme effort, she expelled the image from her mind and replaced it with the adult Ella. She relegated those extreme emotions to where they belonged: out of her thoughts and heart.

Extreme emotions, just like adamant beliefs, were dangerous.

Ella's gaze took in the boxes of jewelry waiting to be inventoried for Reardon, all because of what *he* believed: that she was capable of dealing in stolen art. That he was even demanding all this impossible paperwork was mean-spirited and narrow-minded.

She pushed away from the counter. This didn't deserve her attention and Reardon would believe whatever he wanted. Ella had more important things to do than to pander to the whims of this FBI agent.

Ella awoke to pounding at the front door. She lifted her head and squinted at the bedside clock: five in the morning. Now she could hear muffled yells along with the incessant knocking. Ella dragged herself from bed, grabbed her robe, and walked to the front of the store. She flicked on the outside light and peeked out the window. Mitchell Lopez jerked his head to her, his eyes wide, his face desperate.

"Miss Ella! *T'áá shoodi! Bika anilyeed!*"

"Is it Shirley? Is the baby coming?"

"Yes, yes. Please, you help her!"

Ella nodded and gestured to Mitchell to give her a minute. She ran back to her room, threw off her robe and nightgown, dressed, grabbed her bag of emergency first-aid supplies, and ran out the back door.

She drove around to the front where Mitchell waited in his truck, engine running. Ella pulled behind and followed him over one dirt road and down another for the thirty-minute drive to the Lopez house. The whole while, Ella's heart thumped in her chest. She had delivered babies, but the fearful look on Mitchell's face worried Ella.

Inside Mitchell's cinder-block home, an elderly woman sat on the couch, three small children hugging close.

"Ya'at'eeh," Ella greeted the woman, who she assumed was Shirley's mother. The old Navajo stared back, her lips in a thin line.

Why did she sit here instead of helping her daughter?

A terrible foreboding spread through Ella.

She glanced to Mitchell, who waited impatiently at the opening to a small hallway, gripping his baseball cap so tightly his knuckles were white.

"Bika anilyeed?" he pleaded.

"Yes, Mitchell, I will help her," Ella answered with more confidence than she felt.

She took a deep breath and followed him into a tiny bedroom. A bare bulb from the bedside lamp cut hard shadows across the walls and cast Shirley's face in harsh yellow. She had the blanket pulled to her chin, her gaze on the ceiling. Her lips moved, but she didn't make a sound. Every line in her face was drawn in terrible strain.

Ella set her bag on a wooden chair and leaned close to Shirley, pressing a hand to her forehead. "It's Ella Honanie, Shirley. Let's see how you're doing, okay?"

Shirley didn't respond, only continued muttering, staring at the ceiling, her eyes fixed there.

Ella heard a small cry, the sound of a baby. She pulled back the cover and lost a breath. A tiny boy, still bloody from birth, lay beside Shirley.

"Doo yá'áshóo da."

"Mitchell, what is bad?"

She turned to the husband and stopped. His face was hard and so fearful; his gaze was set on Shirley's belly. Ella went to the end of the bed and pushed the cover over Shirley's knees, where she saw the crown of another baby's head. More blood soaked the sheet beneath Shirley.

Ella poured antiseptic over her hands, then placed her fingers at the baby's head. "Shirley, push."

The woman didn't move.

"Mitchell, Shirley is exhausted. She just needs help."

Mitchell didn't move. He muttered *"Doo yá'áshóo da"* over and over again.

"Mitchell, go to Shirley!"

Ella shot a glance to him. He stood frozen to the spot, his face stricken with fear.

"No, two," he whispered.

Suddenly, Ella understood. It wasn't the birth he feared. They were frightened because of the twins. In the presence of anything strange or unusual, Navajo were immediately cautious. In the case of twins, their caution turned to superstition—an omen of bad luck for the mother, the father, the whole family.

Mitchell would stand there and Shirley would suffer excruciating pain, or worse, until she passed out—all to deny life to this baby . . . because their tradition told them to be afraid.

"Damn traditions," Ella hissed. She shot her best glare at Mitchell. "If you don't help, Mitchell, Shirley will die. Do you want that?"

His gaze went to Shirley, his face so full of pain, Ella's heart caught.

"Go hold her hand, Mitchell. You tell Shirley everything is fine," she whispered. "You tell her you love her. Now!"

Her command jolted him to action. Ella heard Mitchell murmuring to his wife, felt the bed creak with her movement. Shirley groaned, then hissed through a contraction. Ella talked to her, urging her, all the time gently working the baby's head. The crown widened. Soon, forehead, then nose, then chin, appeared. Ella felt for the cord and breathed easier when she found it wasn't tangled.

Finally, the whole baby emerged. Ella stopped the flow of blood in the cord, snipped it, and stood with the baby. Shirley's face glistened with sweat. Mitchell's features were still creased with concern. Neither one smiled or reached for the baby.

She walked to where Mitchell leaned on the bed. "You have another boy, Mitchell."

She sat down beside him and smiled. "Two boys now, born for your clan."

Mitchell stared at the bundle, his face a conflict of love and fear. The fear clearly kept his hands locked in his lap.

Ella's heart clenched at the hard, unforgiving wall of beliefs this new, fragile life faced. She struggled to find the words to break through the barrier, to wrestle free the love she knew must be inside Mitchell and Shirley from the stranglehold of their beliefs.

Her only hope, Ella realized, was to find something *within* their beliefs she could use. She racked her brain, trying to remember Navajo legends, none of which she ever knew or had paid attention to.

She suddenly remembered something about warrior twins from the Creation Myth. Were they boys? What was the story?

She stared in mute frustration at the helpless baby. If she said the wrong thing, he might be turned away, orphaned, and she might have her ignorance to blame.

Too, he could face the same fate if she said nothing.

Ella drew a tentative breath. "Every day, you live the Navajo Way, Mitchell. Changing Woman knows this. These twin boys are gifts to you from Changing Woman because of your good lives. Would she give you something bad?" Ella leaned to catch Mitchell's gaze. "Would she, Mitchell?"

He shook his head, though reluctantly.

"No, she wouldn't. She honors you. She brings you twins." Ella paused, so unsure, yet she had to say it. "Twin boys, Mitchell. Just like the warrior twins."

Mitchell's gaze locked on Ella. She saw the unmistakable flicker of hope in his eyes. She wanted to jump for joy that she'd made the right guess. Instead, she kept her eyes and tone serious.

"It's true, Mitchell. You know it. You are blessed tonight."

Tears welled within his eyes. He reached out for the baby and Ella laid the tiny boy in his hands. Quietly, but as quickly as possible, she left to get hot water and blankets.

She returned to find Mitchell curled around Shirley, the babies resting between them. Ella worked swiftly and gently, cleaning the babies and wrapping them warmly. She gathered her supplies back into the black bag and went to the door.

"*Ahehee,*" Mitchell said, barely above a whisper.

Ella turned and smiled. "You're welcome."

Ella stepped out the front door and came to a halting stop. The grandmother stood rigid on the front porch, her gaze set on the east.

"*Shash'la yádii, T'áá'akó téé,*" Ella offered.

The old woman glanced at her, then averted her stony gaze to the horizon.

Ella took a few steps toward her, keeping a respectful distance away. "It is all right," she repeated. "This is a good family. Changing Woman would not punish you."

"*Do tah!*" The grandmother's sudden command sent a bird flying from a nearby tree.

She faced Ella, small black eyes staring so hard, Ella thought she could feel their sharp focus within her.

"*Hash yinibyé?*" she demanded.

"My name is Ella Honanie."

The old woman's eyes narrowed. "You are Hopi. What do you know of Changing Woman?"

"Half Hopi," Ella said. "I am half Navajo."

The answer did nothing to appease the woman. She made a dismissive sound and waved Ella away.

Ella wanted to reach out to the woman, tell her to please give these babies love, to let go of her terrible beliefs. They are only superstitions, Ella wanted to yell. Instead, she backed away, and climbed in her truck.

She drove the road home. Dawn hugged the horizon; arms of gray pushed the dark night away from the earth. No doubt, it would be a beautiful day, but the thought wouldn't register past the frustration and pain clenching Ella's heart.

She had tried everything tonight, even whispering a legend in order to convince Mitchell—a legend she didn't really know, and wouldn't believe. She had even resorted to admitting her heritage, in the hope that her half-Navajo blood might sway the grandmother.

Still, that child might be banished.

Damn traditions! Damn her heritage!

Ella slammed her palm against the steering wheel. The truck swerved, caught a rut, and veered off the road. Ella pressed on the brake.

Anger trembled through her veins, sending shudders through her that she hadn't known since childhood. She folded her arms tight, hugging herself against the tremors.

How had this night become one of so much anger, so much sadness?

She steered the truck back onto the road, lowered the window fully, and stuck out her head. She breathed deep of the crisp morning air. Her eyes stung, but Ella told herself it was the wind.

In the early morning, Frank pulled up to the front of Ella's post. He wasn't the first there. Three Navajo men stood casually on one side, one leaning against an old Chevy pickup, the other two propped against the hitching post where a horse stood tied. Whatever conversation they had been sharing died as Frank stepped from the Jeep.

He saw their sideways glances follow him to the front door. Not until he tried the knob did he notice the red and white Closed sign in the front window. Undeterred, he walked around the side of the rambling building, ignoring the stares of the Navajo. He approached the back of the trading post, kicking aside another tumbleweed, his mood darkening with every step.

He had driven two hours—the last half hour on hard-packed, corrugated ground that would break a cow's ankle—only to find no Ella Honanie.

Everywhere he turned in this investigation led to a dead-end . . . or back to Ella. The damn woman might live out in the middle of nowhere, but she managed to be at the center of *something*.

He circled the back, saw no sign of a vehicle, and continued around the building to the front. The Navajos watched him approach. Frank stopped at the hitching post on the near side of the door. As soon as he leaned his hip against the railing, the Navajo restarted their conversation—as if they could finally resume now that he had settled.

Twenty minutes later, another Navajo drove up in a truck, a woman beside him in the cab and four kids in the back. The driver climbed out, gave Frank a furtive glance, then joined the other men. Soon, another truck and two more horse riders joined the ones already waiting. The late morning sun beat down on the roofs of trucks and gleamed off silver buckles, and no one showed the least amount of impatience with the interminable wait for Ella Honanie.

Frank pushed off the railing and paced to the end of the building and back to the hitching post. He looked at his watch and cursed.

Where the hell was she?

All that nonsense about being hardworking, how people depended on her . . . she really was something.

A plume of dust followed still another truck as it bounced over the road to the post. It was a veritable gathering of Navajo out here in front of a closed store in the middle of the desert, with everyone seemingly content to wait forever, if need be.

Frank's instincts fired on the sudden realization: Ella Honanie could easily have packed up and left.

His blood ran cold and he strode to the window. As much as he could see, the gallery was just as he had left it yesterday—rugs hanging, jewelry in cases, kachinas on the shelves. Would she simply drive off and leave everything?

He thought back on when she had shoved the picture frame in his hand and told him this post was her life. He remembered the desperation on her face when he threatened to close the store, the sincerity in her eyes when she promised to provide all the information he requested.

He had believed her.

He also remembered thinking she might be capable of

doing whatever it took to get whatever she wanted.

Frank cursed and walked to his Jeep. He opened the door, then noticed the Navajos moving to the front of the store. The truck turned off the road, skidding over the dry earth. The window lowered and a slender arm waved.

"*Ya'at'eeh!*" she called out to the Navajo.

Frank stared as Ella disappeared past the building. Surprise and relief at her appearance only lapped against the wave of anger already flooding him.

Who the hell did she think she was?

He tore after her, walking through flying dust to the back. He rounded the side just as she was backing the truck into a lattice-weave shelter of branches. She had her head turned, long dark hair sweeping across her chest. She eased the truck to a stop and turned it off, but instead of climbing out, she rested her head on hands curled over the steering wheel. Her small shoulders rolled forward. She looked like a woman in dire need of something—rest, or comfort . . . or consoling.

Frank stepped in front of the truck, his boot heels crunching on dry earth.

Ella's head jerked up. Weariness limned her eyes, making them even darker, deeper, than Frank remembered. Frank clenched his jaw against a wave of concern. "Where have you been?"

She closed her eyes and drew a heavy breath. "I've been out, Agent Reardon."

"That much I can tell."

Frank walked to the driver's side. "You do have the information I asked for?"

She sighed. "I did what I could, Agent Reardon. That will have to be enough."

Her defiance surprised Frank. "And Ben? Where is he?"

"Now you want me to account for Ben, too?" Her voice was tired.

"What I want are answers to my questions, Miss Honanie. When will Ben return?"

"I don't know."

"Doesn't he work here?"

"He comes and goes. He doesn't answer to me."

She reached for a black bag on the seat and, with effort, hauled it onto her lap. "Now, if you'll just step back so I can open this door, I have a business to run. I think you noticed I have people waiting."

Frank didn't budge. "Did you know that there are complaints filed against Ben?"

Frank noticed the slight crease at her brow. For a second, she didn't say anything. When she did, it still wasn't an answer. "This may come as a surprise to you, Agent Reardon, but I don't keep track of Ben."

"Oh, that's no surprise, Miss Honanie. So far, I haven't found one person you *have* kept track of." Frank heard the sharp edge in his voice, but couldn't stop himself. He had no reason to be so angry with her. She hadn't disappeared. She hadn't refused his requests. Yet, she seemed so damn *complacent* about the investigation. "You've denied all knowledge of Eddie's actions. You've said you have no idea what Eddie could have been up to. You don't know where Ben is, when he's coming back or even *if* he's coming back."

Frustrated, Frank shoved a hand through his hair. "You made it thoroughly clear yesterday there are legions of people who depend on you. But you know nothing about the people closest to you? What *do* you have the answers for, Miss Honanie?"

Her brow pinched as if she were in sudden pain. She glanced away, swallowed, then leveled her gaze on Frank. Her deep-set eyes were a dark, dark, glistening brown. "It just so happens, Agent Reardon, I am fresh out of answers."

CHAPTER
FIVE

Frank cursed himself inwardly. Since when had he become such a bully? Why did her quiet, controlled demeanor pull such rage to his surface? He took a step back. "I'm sorry," he muttered.

She looked surprised, then shook her head. Her black hair gleamed in the sunlight. "No . . . you're right. I don't know what's going on with the people closest to me. I guess I thought—" She stopped. Her gaze went to the window, her eyes set on the distance. "I guess I thought that's how it was with the ones you love. You try to let them go their own way. You try not to interfere. You assume they're doing their best, because you're doing the best you can—" Her voice broke. She raised her chin, obviously struggling for control.

It was the same reaction as when Frank had accused her of doing anything for her business. Emotions had nearly overcome her then, too—as if the worst she could endure were to have her motivations questioned.

The thought pricked at a wound on his heart Frank was sure he had long ago hardened with scar tissue. Best intentions weren't good enough and they were no excuse for wrong decisions. He had learned that the very hardest way, and he had accepted the harsh consequences. The world had no mercy, no matter how much you needed it . . . and a part of him resented anyone who would think otherwise.

Yet, here he stood, unable to tear his gaze from Ella, somehow drawn to the very naïveté he knew to be a weakness.

Frank shook his head to cast off the daze. He walked from the truck. "I'll be in touch, Miss Honanie," he said over his shoulder.

"Ella."

"What?"

"Call me Ella."

"I don't think—"

"Are you afraid of getting to know me, understand me, maybe even like me?"

"It's not my job to like you. It's my job to find out who killed your brother and why."

After a few moments, she broke the silence. "Wait."

Frank heard the creak of the truck door and stopped. He took only a half-step back.

Ella noticed he didn't completely turn, but stood at an angle. The indirectness did not suit Frank. He looked unwilling to face her, as if he would have preferred, instead, to walk away. That she needed him *not* to walk away, Ella didn't understand. That she would care what Frank thought of her, Ella couldn't explain. Most amazing of all, how could this nearly total stranger make Ella reconsider her own motives? But he had.

"I've thought of someone you can talk to about Eddie," she offered.

He cocked his head as if considering her. "Who is that?"

"My grandmother. I think she had seen more of Eddie lately."

"Your grandmother." He sounded disappointed. "What would she know?"

"He was trying to help her. There's a dispute with the Hopi. I just thought she might be able to tell you something."

"I see." He looked to the horizon for a moment, then

back to Ella. "I suppose she's worth talking to."

Ella slammed the door to the truck. "If you'll come inside, I'll draw you a map to her place."

She took a few steps, but Frank hadn't moved, just stood there staring at her, his face drawn in horror. His eyes filled with a deep pain and before Ella could utter a word, he was at her side, his hand on her arm.

"What happened? Who did this to you?"

"What do you mean—?"

Then Ella followed his gaze to her waist. Rusty brown stains smeared the bottom of her shirt and the top of her jeans. "Oh, it's blood. From the baby." She extended the hem of her shirt with her fingers. "I delivered a baby this morning."

She looked up with a half-smile and met Frank's worried eyes.

"From a baby," he repeated. "Not from you?"

"No. Really, I'm okay. There was quite a bit of blood on the bed," she added, concerned now about his reaction. Anyone could see she was fine, but he still held her arm. An urgency carved the lines of his face and he stood too close, as if sure she had come to harm . . . as if he were about to do something.

An odd sensation curled through Ella's belly, tripped by his intense, almost protective stance. The sensation pulled deep inside, to a need she had long forgotten, a need she could not admit.

Ella took a step away. "They were twins, actually," she explained quickly. "It was early this morning." She stepped around Frank and headed for the back of the store. As she turned the corner, she chanced a look over her shoulder at him.

He wasn't looking at her, but off at some far distant point.

"Do you want the directions to Grandmother's?" she asked.

He jerked his gaze to her and nodded. "Yes."

His voice was hard, as if pushed past an obstacle, and

Ella wondered, as she walked into her home, at the vulnerability in Frank she had just witnessed, at the pain she'd seen in his eyes.

In the kitchen, she pulled out a notepad and pencil and drew the map as well as she could. At one point, she couldn't remember whether it was the fourth dirt road, or the third; and she had to guess at the distances, having really no idea of the mileage.

She finished and found Frank standing outside the back door, in contrast to his usual directness. Ella paused, notepad in hand. As if sensing her presence, he turned, facing her, then averted his gaze. The intensity on his face had been replaced with sadness—and Ella suddenly wondered what other layers lay hidden in Frank.

"Do you have the map?" he asked.

Ella realized she had been staring. She pushed open the back door and handed him the paper. "I hope it's right."

He quirked a brow.

"I'm just not sure about the number of dirt roads you pass before her turn. What you want is to climb Black Mountain Mesa," she explained. "That will get you to Grandmother's."

He considered the map, looking not at all sure.

Ella winced at all the squiggly lines. "She lives on the disputed land, off Highway 160," she added, as if that would help. Ella realized he would never be able to find her. She drew a breath and offered, "If you want to wait . . . that is, until I close—"

"No, I'll go now," he interrupted. "Thanks."

Then he left, without so much as looking her in the face.

Frank was lost within half an hour of turning off the highway. He couldn't follow Ella's map. Hell, he couldn't even concentrate on the map. His thoughts were stuck on Ella.

Images of her were juxtaposed one on top of the other: the sight of her slumped in exhaustion over the steering wheel mutated to the one of her brandishing the pellet rifle, determined to shoot the magpie. He saw her imploring eyes

when she begged him to keep the post open, and then her
deep-brown gaze glistening with tears. She was stubborn,
yet complacent; seemingly sincere, yet uncooperative—until now. She had to be independent to live that far out, yet
the first reason she gave for keeping the store open was
that people depended on her.

Try as he might, Frank couldn't get a fix on her.

More disturbing was that he couldn't get a fix on his
own reaction to her. The sight of Ella, her blouse and jeans
smeared with blood, plumbed straight to a spot in Frank
for which he had no defense. He wasn't such an idiot as
not to recognize the cause. He knew it was because of
Mary.

Even though, as many times as he went back over the
image of Ella stepping from the truck, and seeing the blood
on her shirt, it was not Mary he had seen standing there.
God help him; he had seen only Ella.

That truth tore at his heart, made his chest tighten against
a pain greater than missing Mary . . . the pain of forgetting
her.

He closed his eyes and imagined his fingers running
through Mary's hair, the silkiness tickling the sensitive
flesh at his palm, the pad of his thumb tracing her jaw,
finding her lips.

Pain arced through him in brutal, punishing strokes,
making him breathe more quickly—short gasps of cruel
life, his penance. All the while, his mind strained to hold
the vision of Mary's face, to see her eyes gazing at him,
crushing his heart with her tenderness.

Her face turned to wisps of ghostly air, slipping out of
his reach. His whole body tightened in a desperate rush,
struggling to reclaim what he already knew to be lost, until
all that remained was a black void.

Frank's eyes flew open, his hand pressed against his furiously beating heart. He stared across the road and the
desert beyond. The vista stretched forever without interrup-
tion of mesa or mountain, just clumps of sagebrush, cholla,
prickly pear, and the occasional cedar bush. A damned in-

hospitable environment for most, but Frank found the stark vastness satisfying. What you saw was what you got, with no pretense of anything but the bare minimum for survival. A land windblown to the bone. He could relate.

He sat there gazing on the desert, the utter desolation somehow consoling. No matter that he was hopelessly lost.

Ella walked out the back door and past the corral. The sun's hand pulled the blood of the earth to the surface in the last moments of the day. The earth and surrounding sandstone cliffs pulsed with bright red, saturating the landscape, bleeding into a magenta sky.

She saw Apache, his compact, furry body limned in the sun glow. He stood erect on the small mound of dirt at the center of his prairie dog domain as if he too appreciated the sky's drama; this creature from the underground paying homage to the day. Slowly, the sun relented and released the earth, letting the bloodred color drain to pink.

Apache looked over his shoulder and squeaked "hello." He dropped down to all fours and scuttled over the ground to Ella, stopping just a foot away.

"Hello, my little sentinel."

The prairie dog lifted his nose in the air, then drew his whole body upright until he stood perfectly balanced at her feet.

"Sorry, Apache, I don't have anything for you tonight."

His nose twitched, seeking a scent, and his jaw worked back and forth, as if already chewing on the anticipated treat of nuts.

Ella smiled down at him. "You will just have to forage on your own, Apache." The last remnants of pink fled from the sky.

Frank rounded the corner of the post. A faint giggle drew his attention. There in the fading pink of the sunset stood Ella looking down at a small animal perched on its haunches. A prairie dog, he realized. She was talking to a prairie dog. A sharp sound of disbelief pressed through his teeth.

Suddenly, the creature darted a look in his direction then scuttled away, disappearing into a hole. Ella's head snapped up, her eyes wide. Her hand went to the side of her skirt, slipping between the folds.

"It's me, Ella, Agent Reardon."

She pulled her hand from her pocket, though Frank noticed she still looked tense.

"You talked to Grandmother?"

"Actually, no. I didn't find her."

"She wasn't there?" She took a few steps to him.

"No . . . I mean, I never made it to *there*."

"Oh."

Frank had hoped she would remember her earlier offer to take him there. If she did, she didn't look ready to make it easy on him. He walked closer.

Ella heard him approach, though she kept her gaze on the setting sun. She knew he wanted her to take him to Grandmother's. She just didn't know if she could. Every bit of her resisted another argument with *Sáni* . . . and every bit of her pulled just as hard to see how Jenny was doing.

All of a sudden, Agent Reardon was standing in front of her, giving her no choice but to look at him.

"So my map wasn't much help," she said.

"Look, I know it's late—"

"Yes."

He looked surprised at her answer, but Ella didn't care. She already felt the tremblings of the certain argument she faced with Grandmother—and probably Jenny, too—because she would not only be appearing with a federal agent, but one with questions about Eddie.

"But you'll take me," he said.

Ella glanced up. He was so sure, so completely confident of nothing standing in his way. For just a second, she saw Eddie standing there—fearless, intrepid Eddie, always ready for a challenge. But there was a layer beneath that most people didn't know—the Eddie searching for himself and his place in the world.

She considered Agent Reardon. No, she thought, shaking her head, he probably didn't have that problem.

"So you won't take me?" he suddenly asked.

"What?"

"You were shaking your head just then."

"Oh, no, I was just thinking of something else." Ella took a few steps away. She would have loved to put some distance between her and this whole conversation.

"Look, can I use your phone? All I'm getting on mine is static."

"Yes, of course. There's one inside the kitchen door."

He nodded and walked away.

Apache poked his head up and Ella smiled at the sneaky fellow. "Just waiting for him to go, were you?" She chuckled and crouched next to the prairie dog. "Yes, well, I don't think he will simply go away, any more than I can avoid going to Grandmother's. At least I will see our Jenny, eh?"

She gave a scratch to Apache's neck and stood, just as Frank appeared from the kitchen.

"I need that ride, Ella."

"Yes, I know."

Her sudden agreement surprised Frank. Just as swiftly, she turned on her heel and walked to the lattice-weave shelter of branches.

Frank folded himself into the front seat. The first twenty minutes passed in silence, save for the rumble of the truck and the creak of everything metal as Ella negotiated the dirt road. In the gathering darkness, only a weak green light from the dashboard illuminated the cab, reaching to Ella's fingers on the steering wheel. She kept the gear in second, her clenched knuckles on the wheel.

Frank wondered about her obvious reluctance to go to her grandmother's, and what could have changed her mind. He doubted it was his request. From what little he knew about Ella Honanie, she seemed to have a mind of her own.

The silence stretched for miles. By the time Ella pulled onto the blacktop, Frank's usual reluctance to converse now felt constraining in this tiny cab.

"What was that between you and the prairie dog?" His

low voice was barely audible above the grind of the truck.

"Oh, Apache, I give him nuts."

"You named the prairie dog?"

"Yes," she said. That was it. Frank had never met a woman who could stop with one word.

"And you talk to this prairie dog?"

"Yes."

"About what?"

"Things. The day, the sunset." She ended with a shrug.

"Uh-huh." He couldn't help the sarcasm in his tone any more than he could help feeling frustrated with the conversation. He looked out the window to utter blackness. The only light came from the truck and managed to penetrate a mere hundred yards down the highway before admitting defeat to the dense nothingness. "Damn lonely place," he muttered.

"Yes."

Her quick agreement surprised Frank. He looked at Ella. She stared straight ahead at the highway, her arms locked on the steering wheel. The dashboard light cut a crisp silhouette of her against the night beyond her window—a small woman surrounded by the darkness, traveling alone . . . regardless of the fact that Frank sat right beside her.

He could imagine her driving this highway many times, always alone, and he had the sense she would look the same way—her thoughts closed, her emotions guarded—even when by herself.

Suddenly, Frank felt as if he had no more presence in this cab than a sack of groceries.

"You know you're wasting your time."

Her sudden break in the silence had the impact of a statue talking. The image struck Frank funny and he chuckled.

"You think I'm amusing?" She sounded alarmed by the thought, and Frank found that even funnier. His chuckle turned to laughter.

"What's amusing, Miss Honanie," he finally responded,

"is the irony. I'm not the one wasting time. You are, if you believe I will simply go away."

"One could hope."

Her honesty kept the smile on Frank's face.

She turned the truck off the highway and, with a wild bump, they were again on a dirt road. Ella steered the truck down gullies, up rocky ridges, through dense clutches of sage and tumbleweed in a serpentine path that more resembled an ambling horse trail than a road. When she finally pulled the truck to a blessed stop, Frank's ears rang in the sudden deafening silence.

He stepped from the cab into a dome of stars. Billions of twinkling lights pinpricked the enveloping night; their light was so bright it reflected off the earth. Cool air breathed through his shirt. Frank figured they must have climbed a thousand feet from the desert to the top of a mesa. This truly *was* the middle of nowhere.

Ella's door slammed and Frank heard her walking over the ground away from the truck, her strides quick. He turned to see Ella stopped before a huge mound of earth.

"Ya'at'eeh, shimásání," she called out, a little too loud, a little too concerned.

She waited a moment, then opened the door, and Frank followed her into a mud-and-stick hogan. The last embers of a fire glowed in the middle of a round room. In the shadows beyond, Frank could see an old woman sitting up in bed.

"Sitsóí? It is you?"

"Yes, Grandmother."

But Ella didn't approach her grandmother. Frank watched her scan the small room as if seeking something, drawing his own gaze into the shadows where there was nothing more to see than this woman's sparse belongings.

"Shi yázhi, you brought a friend?"

Ella snapped her attention back to her grandmother. "Grandmother, this is Frank Reardon. He's—" She stopped and gave Frank a speculative look before finishing. "He said he would like to meet you."

Frank wondered at Ella's omission of his occupation, and even more about her furtive behavior.

The old woman tilted back her head and met Frank's gaze. "You bring this man to meet me?" Her eyes twinkled with delight. "Come in, come in. Stop standing there like a tree! I am Annie Ben, but you just call me Annie."

She gestured to rugs layered around the fire hole. Frank sat cross-legged on the ground and watched the little woman bustle about adding more sticks to the fire. She then set a tripod contraption over the fire from which she hung a pot of water. Soon, the room filled with more of the aroma of burning cedar. And Frank felt for all the world as if he had stepped back in time one hundred years.

Ella, however, paced as much as the small space allowed, a few steps to the wall, then back again to the fire.

"Shimásání, háadi Jenny?"

Frank had no idea what Ella had said, but it made the old woman frown. "You speak Navajo in front of your friend?" She nodded to Frank.

Ella didn't even look at Frank, her eyes busy flitting around the room and back to the grandmother. "Just tell me if Jenny's been here."

"No, child, she hasn't. Sit down. You're stirring the air."

Ella crouched next to her grandmother, her feet planted on the ground as if ready to spring up. "Please think, Grandmother. Did she come to see you two days ago?"

"I am not feeble, *shi yázhi*. Jenny has not been here since lambing."

Ella did spring to a stand. "I see. I thought . . ." Her words disappeared in a vacant glance around the room.

"You make me worry, *shi yázhi*. Sit. Tell me what happened."

"No, it's okay," Ella said, sounding distracted, and her gaze settled on some point on the wall.

"I wish she were here. I miss seeing Jenny. And you," the grandmother finished quietly.

"If you came home with me, Grandmother, you could

see Jenny all the time." Ella turned to her grandmother and the young fire flames caught a look of hope on her face.

"Not if she is gone."

"She'll come home."

"Yes, I expect that child will go home. And this is my home."

Silence expanded in the small room. Frank watched the two women. There seemed to be a lot more left unsaid, but neither one was willing to start.

He soon ran out of patience with the silence and decided to ask his own questions. "Annie, I have to ask you something about Eddie." Frank paused, noticing Annie's sudden attention to him. "Did he ever come by here with friends?"

"Why do you want to know, Mr. Reardon?"

"Because I'm investigating his murder."

Her eyes narrowed on him with keen focus and Frank felt the old woman's full force of concentration. It was obvious where Ella got her own stubborn determination. "And you look to his friends?"

"I look everywhere I have to." Frank could feel Ella's hard stare, but he kept his gaze on the grandmother.

"The boys he brought here would not hurt Eddie."

"How do you know that?"

"Because they came to help me."

"Help how?"

"Against the *kiis'áanii*." She spit the word out, as if it were distasteful.

"The Hopi," Ella said.

"Don't say that word here!"

"I'm half Hopi, *Sani*," Ella said.

For a moment, no one said another word. Frank finally broke the silence. "Annie, I need the names of those boys."

"They have nothing to do with Eddie's murder."

"But they might know something."

The frown deepened on her brow. Then, "Tillen Chavez was one. The other boy Eddie just called Flint. If you stay here, they will be back. They are going to help."

Ella sighed and approached the old woman. "Grandmother, they can't do anything," she said, putting a hand on the grandmother's shoulder. "You know you have to leave."

"No!"

Ella's hand jerked up as if the grandmother were electrified. "I know you don't want to," Ella began haltingly, "but—"

"You would take the side of the *kiis'áanii*? My own granddaughter?"

"I'm only telling you what has to happen now. If you won't leave, then sign the lease agreement with them. They'll let you stay."

"On their terms. On their land. With their council telling me what I can do, where I can go, where I dig for clay or salt. No." She shook her head violently. "They think they can steal my home," she muttered. "They have no right. And you would let them."

The grandmother glared at Ella with such startling ferocity Frank's own breath caught, but Ella didn't waver.

"The court decided and the . . ." Ella paused. "The *kiis'áanii* won. The battle is over, Grandmother."

"This is your home, too, *shi yázhi*. You were born here. Your cord is buried here."

"Grandmother, hush." Ella threw a quick glance at Frank.

"That embarrasses you? To talk of your cord of life?" She made a sound of disgust. "That is your problem, child. You don't know what is important anymore."

"*You* are what's important to me, Grandmother, not some things buried here."

"Aiee! Talking to you is like . . . " She looked at the fire, then back to Ella. "Like climbing smoke. I make no progress."

Ella smiled a little, her face softening, though worry lines still creased her forehead. "You know that's exactly how I feel, too, talking to you—that I can't make any progress." Ella placed her hands on each side of her grandmother's face and made her look at her. "Come with me tonight, *shimásání*. I have a good home with a room for you. If you want, we can come back and dig up the cords. We can bury them again at Shonto.''

Ella's eyes glistened in the fireglow and Frank thought no one could resist such a compelling stare. But the grandmother did.

She shook off Ella's hands and stood, pulling her five-foot body into an erect, almost regal stance. She stared at Ella, her mouth opening then closing, as if she couldn't speak her thoughts. Then she turned and went back to her bed. ''If Jenny comes I will tell her you look for her,'' she said, and pulled the quilt over her.

''Grandmother! This problem isn't going away! Don't you understand? In two weeks, the Hopi council will evict you, pile everything onto a truck, and drive you off. You don't have a choice!''

The old woman turned her head on her pillow to look at Ella. ''We always have a choice. I choose to stand and fight. You should learn to do the same.''

Ella backed off, retreated, in the face of such a flint-black stare.

''Eddie would understand,'' the grandmother whispered, as if sharing a secret with her pillow.

''Why would Eddie understand?'' Frank asked.

''Don't,'' Ella said, maybe to him, though she still stared at her grandmother, her face drawn into a tight mask.

''He never abandoned a fight,'' the grandmother answered quietly.

''Eddie didn't know when to *stop* fighting, Grandmother.'' Ella's voice held an edge of anger and also regret—as if uttering the words caused her pain.

''And when will you learn to *start* fighting, *shi yázhi*?''

''Never, *shimásání*.'' Ella's eyes glistened, too bright, and Frank thought he saw tears. She bent, kissed Annie's forehead, and whispered. ''Some of us just tend the wounds, Grandmother.''

CHAPTER
SIX

Ella slid behind the wheel with barely a sound. A moment later they were off, winding down the mesa, though this time they drove slower than the ascent, almost at a crawl, as if the truck were in neutral and Ella was allowing gravity to pull the great weight of steel and humans to the bottom of the mesa.

She barely attempted to steer, one hand merely rested on the wheel, as if she would just surrender to the inevitable. Her elbow was bent on the side panel, her fingers splayed across her lips. Her eyes stared into the black night to somewhere else—as if she could see disaster coming right at her, but was helpless to avoid it.

The conversation with her grandmother seemed to have taken the life right out of Ella, which bothered Frank more than he could understand. "I gather that you and your grandmother see things differently."

"She is very traditional," Ella said, but her voice sounded detached from whatever thoughts her mind explored.

"And you don't share her strong beliefs?"

"No."

She said it too fast, too firmly. Frank wondered what nerve he had hit.

"But Eddie shared her beliefs?"

Ella shot him a quick glance and Frank saw a flicker of pain in her eyes, then, just as swiftly it disappeared as if yanked back in place by an inner hand. Frank knew that determination firsthand and a part of him flinched in response to Ella's inward control. He had never met a woman with such a tight grip on her emotions.

Frank had to wonder why the thought of Eddie and their grandmother being close should bother Ella.

"Yes, Eddie shared her beliefs," she said, once more staring ahead into the night. "He gave her hope."

"Hope for what?"

"For a miracle." She gave a short laugh. "Do you believe in miracles, Agent Reardon?"

"No."

"Neither do I." Her voice trailed off into a murmur. "But sometimes I wonder if it wouldn't be easier if I did."

Frank thought of how Annie had delineated the difference between Eddie and Ella: Eddie would stand and fight, Ella didn't. But Frank didn't see it that way. She had defended her business to him, refused to give up until *Frank* relented and let her keep it open. And Frank had watched Ella try to reason with Annie.

Even in the face of the old woman's ranting about Navajo gods and umbilical cords, Ella had continued with calm patience, only to finally be insulted and dismissed. Someone so forthright and practical didn't have a prayer competing with superstitions and miracles.

"If what you say is true, that the Hopi will take Annie's place, she'll see you were right," Frank offered.

Ella glanced at him, a sad smile tugging at her lips. "All she will see, Agent Reardon, is that her chances died with Eddie and she'll blame me for not believing."

Frank still didn't understand her need to make Annie leave now. "If the Hopi will eventually make Annie leave, why not let her stay until that moment?"

"No!"

Frank started at her adamancy. "Why not?"

She stared straight ahead. Frank saw the clench of her jaw and the cab's light reflected off her glistening eyes. Then finally, "She needs to leave before they come for her," she said, so quietly, Frank barely heard her above the grumble of the truck.

She shook her head. Straight black hair, gleaming with its own life, swept over her shoulder. "Ironic, don't you think? Eddie's dead, probably for some fool noble cause, and that only makes my grandmother believe him all the more. And the one with only common sense to offer, no grand solutions, no righteous indignation—well, that one must be the fool, the traitor."

Her words were a repetition of the heart of the chasm that had torn Frank and Mary apart. He stared at Ella, knowing at his core her frustration. He felt a sudden inexplicable empathy for this woman he barely knew.

But that didn't change what he now knew about Eddie Honanie.

"Eddie didn't die for any noble cause, Ella. I just confirmed his prints on the storage locker in Denver. He stole the art and someone killed him for it."

"No, that can't be." Ella looked at him, her brow creased.

"Facts are facts. Something I would think you would understand."

"Then Eddie must have been framed. You should know that you can't believe everything you see."

"All right, let's assume he was framed. Either way, I have him tied to that stolen art." Frank shifted in his seat to face her. "Have you considered that Eddie may have had some *reason* to steal the art? Maybe it fit into some plan he had?"

"Eddie didn't have plans, Agent Reardon. He just had a lot of . . . emotion." A quiet laugh filled the cab and Frank saw Ella's face soften. "He felt strongly . . . about everything. Right and wrong. This side and that. He had it all divided in his head."

Ella glanced at Frank, a knowing look on her face. "Probably not unlike you, Agent Reardon. I bet you also see things as black and white, right and wrong, don't you? That's probably something *you* can understand."

With an aggravating bump, the dirt road changed to blacktop. In the sudden lurch, Frank bounced, hitting his head on the cab roof.

"Son of a—" He cut his curse at Ella's sharp look.

"Too close for comfort?"

Ella's words and her sarcastic tone dogged Frank for the length of his lonely drive to Phoenix and the Field Office. She had compared him to Eddie, a criminal, for crissakes!

Hell, yes, he saw things as having two sides, as being right or wrong. Distinct. Immutable.

Criminals didn't. They saw a gray area between. They blurred the edges, finessed the sides, whatever it took to get whatever they wanted.

Frank's thoughts went to Ella. How could she confuse him with the likes of Eddie?

How could anyone?

Pain seeped from a raw wound, one that wouldn't heal. He had buried the wound beneath veneers of indifference and denial. Layer upon layer, he had built up the scar tissue, believing that, with enough time, enough determination, he could convince himself to be healed.

And he had pretty much succeeded, until this case.

Or was it a woman in a broomstick skirt?

Frank parked and walked into the low brick building, headed down the linoleum hallway, immediately in familiar territory. No matter the city, or how big the force, or how new the building, every FBI office had a particular quality of sameness: a bare cleanness, not sterile like a hospital, but lean like a sleek black limo, where the men inside looked out, and civilians couldn't see in. It was the quality Frank liked . . . and the very aspect of the FBI that Mary had hated.

She would have stripped the tinted windows and turned off the air-conditioning, opening the FBI to the smothering heat of the real world. But then it was exactly her openness that had gotten her killed.

He pushed the pain down deep, into the very recesses

of his own impenetrable façade that Mary had hated. If she were here, he couldn't imagine she would understand, but then Frank had decided long ago that understanding was overrated.

As far as he was concerned understanding was merely the flaky paper skin on an onion—a thin, fragile veneer that fell apart when handled.

After only a few steps down the hallway, Frank could hear more than the usual activity for any bureau—considering the predawn hour. He followed the sound of muffled voices to a glass-enclosed conference room where three suits huddled over a fax machine, their expressions expectant, as if the machine were about to deliver.

Frank pressed a hand against a heavy glass door, but had barely opened it when all three men faced him, guns drawn, in one swift, manual-perfect motion.

"Special Agent Frank Reardon, Denver office," he said, palms out, obviously empty.

"Where's your ID, Agent?" It was the shorter of the three who spoke, slightly balding, with piercing blue eyes.

Frank turned sideways so they could watch him slip his hand into the back pocket of his jeans. He held out his identification. The same man took it, gave a nod, and the guns disappeared. Then he spoke aside to the other two men and they turned back to the fax machine.

"Let's go to my office, Agent Reardon." He ushered Frank past the conference table and through another glass door to an adjoining room, also walled in by glass. Frank realized he must be talking to the Special Agent in Charge.

"Have a seat, Reardon."

The door shooshed closed behind Frank and he had the instant sense of walking into an airtight container. He could see the men talking in the next room, but not even a muffled sound penetrated the thick glass walls.

The agent rounded his desk but remained standing. "I'm Harris, Special Agent in Charge. You're down from Denver investigating the stolen art and Honanie's murder, am I right?"

"That's right," Frank said, only mildly surprised that the agent should make the connection. "I need computer access to check some leads."

"Sure." But Harris didn't make a move from behind his desk, just continued studying Frank with a curious expression as if matching Frank's face with some mental image—giving Frank the uneasy sense he was about to be caught at a disadvantage.

"Weren't you at Red Earth?"

That Frank's instincts were right gave him no satisfaction. "Yes. I was at Red Earth."

"Damn mess."

Harris's pronouncement could just as easily have been the official FBI opinion. It didn't offer Frank any hints to the agent's own stance.

"You lost your wife there."

Frank felt the instant reaction of his body and set his jaw. He pinned the agent with his own stare. "Yes," he said, the word just a fact forced out between clenched teeth.

"Damn shame."

Frank kept his silence and hoped the topic was now closed.

"Several agents killed, too."

"Yes."

"I imagine you've got pretty strong feelings about that whole situation."

Frank's gut knotted with the effort to control just those feelings. Tightness spread through his chest, up his neck, to the top of his head, until every fiber of Frank was pulled as taut as the spring in a trigger.

"You left the field after that, didn't you?"

"Yes." His own voice sounded alien, abnormal, as if stretched so thin it might tear.

Harris broke his gaze and shook his head. Only a slight shake, but enough that Frank got the full measure of the agent's disdain. "The computers are down the hall to your right, Agent." Then, without so much as a nod, he returned to the conference room.

Frank watched him join the other men. Beyond the thick glass he could see their lips move—a silent conversation within the club.

Frank walked out and down the hallway. He found the room with several computers and shut the door, leaning all his weight against it, wishing he could just as easily shut out the memories. But they were right there, always right there.

Hell, yes, I left, Frank wanted to yell. *Otherwise I would've killed every last son-of-a-bitch murdering Indian terrorist.*

He closed his eyes and let the anger and frustration trip through him, quickening his heart, jerking his pulse down to his stomach and up to his throat, short-circuiting his body temperature with rushes of heat and fire.

At the brink of nausea, cold sweat popping at his brow, he felt the abyss open before him, a black yawning hellhole at his feet, beckoning him with a final weightless, nameless release—a promise of relief.

He had the sense of choice: take that step over the edge and find terror . . . or final retribution.

His heart ached for the possibility, that he could finally receive a measure of forgiveness.

But his mind rebelled in a guilty anger. He had himself to blame for Mary's death, no one else. No one could change that fact.

Slowly, Frank opened his eyes and willed himself to focus, to walk to a desk and sit. A few minutes later, he regained normal breathing and the dizzying blackness subsided. Only a dull ache survived in his chest, the lingering reminder of the hollow place inside.

Whatever insanity awaited him in that black pit was a more detached, cocooned existence than he had earned.

What he deserved was cold reality, including whatever disdain and judgment others would heap on him.

Frank's hands were clenched so tight it hurt to flex them. He stretched them out and a flood of blood tingled to his fingertips and made them heavy as he poised them over the keyboard.

Frank stared at the black computer screen before him. All he had left to himself was a job to do.

First he queried Ben Talaqueptewa and, to his surprise, found nothing in the federal database about the Hopi. He typed in Joe Miller and, again, found nothing. Frank had been sure he would find something on either the con man or the store owner.

He entered the names of Eddie's friends that Annie had provided. Neither one had any arrest record. But at the bottom of the screen, the cursor blinked beneath the words Frank had hoped he would never see again: suspected member in the American Indian Rights Organization.

His pulse beat behind his eyes, pounding blood, narrowing his vision on the people who had changed his life, taken from him the only good thing in the world . . . and damned him to purgatory—neither good enough nor bad enough for even the bureau to give a damn, let alone himself.

Eddie had been involved with these bastards. Frank knew it. His fingers typed furiously, demanding Eddie's record from the computer. But the cursor blinked on a black screen. Frank slapped a hand against the monitor as if he could force the computer to cough up the information Frank knew was there.

He stared at the cursed screen, his thoughts nailed on Eddie and AIRO. What was the connection?

The leaders of AIRO moved through an underground world like nightcrawlers, worming their way into communities already weakened by crisis. AIRO burrowed in, protected by a network of radical supporters, a loose affiliation of criminals and liberals ready to supply an isolated cabin for a meeting, a place to sleep, get food, even weapons. They were lawless extremists, the Indian version of the Black Panthers of the sixties or the current-day militias. And just as secret, just as careful, and just as deadly.

Frank thought of Ella's description of Eddie. In her own

words, he was emotional, driven by the cause—just the type of fanatic AIRO liked.

No, it was no leap to connect Eddie to AIRO. And no more of a leap to suspect AIRO of murder.

The stabbing pulse behind his eyes spread to his temples in murderous pain. No, he didn't have to suspect . . . he *knew* they were capable of murder.

But could he connect AIRO to Eddie's murder? Or even connect AIRO to the stolen art?

He pressed his fingers to his temples and rubbed, knowing he couldn't assuage the pain—it came from a source too deep for him to touch.

Frank pushed back from the desk and stood, ignoring the laser strike of agony to the back of his head. He had too many questions, but the man in the other room just might have some of the answers.

He found Harris just as he had left him—still in the conference room, standing over the fax machine. The other two agents were yards away, one standing at the window, the other pacing at the far end. Whatever they were waiting for hadn't come and no one looked happy about it.

Frank pushed open the door. The agents stiffened, but Harris didn't even turn from the machine, his gaze fixed on the inanimate object as if his power alone could will it to obey.

"I need whatever you have about AIRO here in Arizona," Frank asked the agent's back. "What members' names do you have? What information—"

"This isn't your business," said the agent who had been standing at the window as he now approached Frank.

"What do you mean, *this* isn't—" Frank looked back at Harris and the silent fax. "You're working on something about AIRO now, aren't you?"

"And you don't work with AIRO anymore," the agent countered, stopping only a few feet from Frank. "Not since Red Earth."

"Why do you ask about AIRO, Reardon?" Harris faced

Frank. The weariness in the man's voice was echoed in deep, haggard lines on his face. But his eyes were still a clear, steely blue.

"AIRO has come up in my investigation of Eddie Honanie. If something is going on with AIRO here, maybe they're related."

"I doubt it. Eddie Honanie was a small player."

"You knew Honanie was involved with AIRO?"

"We know the members."

"And you didn't consider that information important to share with the investigating agent or, at the least, the Navajo police?"

A sharp, derisive laugh from one of the men sliced the air. "Tell the enemy what you know? Is that how you botched Red Earth, Reardon?"

The accusation knifed nearly clean through Frank, leaving only a thread of his control.

Suddenly, the fax machine rang. Harris nodded to one of the agents, who was suddenly at Frank's side, grabbing his arm.

"Harris, what the hell is going on?"

"Get him out of here," Harris murmured, his attention on the paper slowly drawing within the machine.

The agent pulled Frank to the outer door. Electronic noise indicated the end of transmission and, just as suddenly, the room was silent.

"At least we know he's okay," the other agent said.

Suddenly, Frank understood. "You have undercover in AIRO," Frank yelled over his shoulder.

The agent shoved him to the door. Frank took advantage of the forward momentum, swung around, caught the agent's leg with his own and sent him sprawling to the ground. The next instant, the agent had his gun out, aimed at Frank. Frank leveled his gaze on Harris. "Are you going to deny you have undercover in AIRO?"

Harris held his palm out to the armed agent, who lowered his gun. "Yes, Agent Reardon, we have a man in

AIRO. And I don't need any more complications. If your investigation leads to AIRO, you *will* tell me. Understand?''

Harris didn't take a step toward Frank. He didn't have to; his gaze delivered the threat.

Frank returned the stare. "I'm telling you now. You want to tell *me* what the hell is going on? Why are you so worried?''

"You'd like that, wouldn't you?'' He advanced on Frank until he was only a foot away, then pushed past Frank toward his office. "Do your own investigation, Reardon. And don't screw up mine.''

He was late and there would be hell to pay.

He idled the car down the dirt road, headlights on so the gunmen wouldn't mistake him for an intruder. That thought brought a chuckle, which he quickly suppressed. Even in the privacy of his car, he didn't break the role.

He parked and got out, giving a nod in the direction of one of the lookouts he knew was posted in the deep shadows.

From the outside, the rundown dwelling had as much significance as any other dilapidated mud house at the end of a long dirt road. But not everything was as it seemed.

He knocked and, on request, gave the password. Sanchez opened the door. "Where the hell have you been?''

"Where's Leonard?''

Sanchez nodded toward the closed door at the side of the room.

The little adobe had only a front room, a kitchen, and three small bedrooms. There was barely enough room for the dozen men, let alone the countless others who came, bringing food, newspapers, sometimes even money collected from supporters. Automatics, rifles, and handguns sat on end tables, the kitchen table, and leaned against mud walls as casually as a man's keys or hat.

Anonymity on the outside. War strategy on the inside. In a way, the house matched the men. And just like the mud falling off the walls, the façade on this pathetic operation was about to crumble before everyone's eyes. Only they didn't know it.

He smiled inwardly at his own analogy, careful to keep his outward expression passive. This close to his goal it wouldn't do to let on now there was an intelligent mind in their midst. As hard as it was to endure their stupid arrogance, he could play the part of the mindless fanatic. Soon, he would be the one giving the orders.

He crossed the living room and knocked again, then walked into the bedroom—what Leonard called the War Room; all the furniture had been removed, except for a scattering of chairs and a long banquet table covered with maps.

The table also had the only lamp and in its yellow globe of light he saw Leonard. He was bent over a map with the two advisors who were constantly at his side.

The lean one, a wiry Sioux, quick with his temper and a knife, straightened from the table. "He's here, Leonard."

The big man didn't raise his gaze from the maps. "And where have you been?"

"Getting the information."

"You get lost?"

He set his teeth against the snide tone as he lowered his head slightly and assumed the expected apologetic stance. "It took longer than I thought."

Leonard rose to his full height. His shadow climbed the wall and bent up the ceiling. "You were supposed to be back yesterday."

"I wasn't getting groceries, Leonard." He slanted a look at the leader. "What I found out was worth the time."

The lamplight cast an amber glow up Leonard's face, reaching just the bottom of his eyes, as if a fire smoldered there just beneath his jet-black gaze. He had the look of a leader all right . . . it would be particularly satisfying to see that look turn pathetic.

"And just what did you find out?"

"First there's this." He threw the oblong package on

the table and it slid to Leonard, who tore back the brown wrapping and revealed the stack of cash. "That's from the front men in Gallup, Window Rock, and Phoenix."

"This will help." Leonard fingered the money. "And what did you learn in Window Rock?"

"Your man at Tribal Headquarters says about half the force will back you."

"And the other half will walk away," Leonard said with confidence.

"You're right," said the Sioux. "They won't fight us. They can't fight ten thousand people."

Leonard handed the money to his other advisor and bent back to the map, obviously through with the conversation.

"There's one more thing, Leonard." He lifted his head to stare straight at the big man. The reaction to *this* he wanted to see. "One of your loyal supporters is not so loyal." He made his gaze serious, his brow furrowed in concern. "There's an informant."

Leonard leaned across the table. The yellow light made his red skin an ugly orange. "Who is it?"

"I don't know yet. I got the word from a trader in Gallup who has connections to the FBI."

"The FBI." The hate in Leonard's voice was echoed in the flint-black of his eyes. His gaze shifted to the window, as if he could see through the drawn curtains and into the night. "They can inform all they want to," he murmured. "This time, they won't know what hit them."

"As soon as I know something more, I'll tell you."

"You do that." It was the skinny Sioux. He rounded the table and opened the door, ending the conversation.

"That *bilagaana* makes my skin crawl," said the Sioux after he closed the door.

Leonard poked a finger between the curtains and drew it back just an inch. There was nothing but blackness for as far as he could see. He knew his guards were out there—silent, deadly, loyal. They could crouch in one position for hours if necessary. They would die for him. Just as he would die for the cause, if that's what it took.

He thought of the ones who had already died and the others in jail, but the feds, with all the resources of the whole corrupt white government behind them, had still not managed to bring AIRO to its knees. And now, if everything went as planned, Indian brothers and sisters would rise up across this land and show their power. In just five days, the rules would change. This time, AIRO would capture the attention of the whole world.

Leonard turned from the window. "I don't trust him, either," he said. "Keep an eye on him."

CHAPTER
SEVEN

The last television station signed off and Jenny stared in frustration at the static. She clicked off the television, stood, tossed the remote onto the bed, and walked to the motel window one more time for the same view she had had for the past day: a stretch of parking lot to the highway.

How could he just dump me here and leave?

She had half a mind to walk out. She glanced at her backpack on the nearby chair. She could grab it and go. There was no one to stop her.

But there was also no place to go. The only people she knew in Gallup were traders and friends of her aunt's. They would call Ella, Jenny just knew it. And then she would be back where she started two days ago: stranded at the end of a dirt road in the middle of nowhere, dying a slow death of lifelessness . . . just like Ella.

She was *not* going to die on the vine like Ella. This was her chance to make a difference, just like her father had.

Except she had never pictured her father whiling away hours, even days, in a stupid motel room. Whenever he had visited the store, he had always seemed in a hurry to leave again. Another important meeting, he had quickly explained. Jenny had never minded; no, never. She had known he was needed in so many places, instead of with her.

The familiar lump constricted her throat.

Jenny turned away from her backpack and flopped down

across the width of the bed. Her gaze lit on the same sparkles in the ceiling she had stared at innumerable times, even to the point of counting the tiny glittering specks. But now she swore that a group of the sparkles were lined up in a silhouette of her father's face: his high forehead and arched brows, even the thin line of his nose. In her mind, she connected the specks, filled in the details, added the dark gleam of his eyes. Soon she had her father looking down at her, gazing directly at her. She could almost feel the fierce intensity from his eyes, boring straight at her, only for her. As if she were the only one who could understand him, who would follow him.

The tightness in her throat spread to her chest, made her heart beat fast and hard. "But I don't know what to do, Papa. I don't know what *you* would do."

The plea rang in her ears like a childish whine. Jenny set her jaw against the prickling sensation at the back of her eyes. She wasn't a child. Her father *could* count on her. He should have counted on her long ago. "You should have told me things, Papa." An edge of anger broke through the tightness—that stranglehold of fear on her throat. "But I'll figure things out. I won't let you down."

Sudden bright lights swept the room. Jenny's heart jumped. She leapt from the bed and ran to the window. The headlights straightened directly on her room and a car pulled into the space. *Chandler's car, finally.*

Jenny fumbled with the chain lock and the dead bolt, at last getting the door open. Too late, she remembered her promise to Chandler to never, ever open the door to anybody, not even him, not without the code phrase.

Chandler stepped from the car and into a span of light cast from the lamp in Jenny's room. One look at his face and her heart bumped.

"Get back inside," he hissed.

Jenny backed up over the threshold. "I'm so glad to see you," she murmured.

He grabbed a duffel from the front seat and slammed the car door. He came around the front of the car and Jenny slanted her gaze, careful not to watch him limp. He hated anyone seeing him limp.

"Move," he said when he got to the door, but then pushed past her without giving her any time. The sharp stitched corner of one of the nylon straps dragged across her bare thigh. Jenny bit her lip instead of emitting a sound and laid a careful hand across the stinging scrape.

Chandler dropped the bag on the floor and headed for the sink. "So you already forgot the code."

"No, I—" But her words died in the full force of water running from the faucets.

Jenny closed the door, then stood there, watching him run water over his face and under his long hair to his neck. Droplets clung to strands at his temples. She wished she had the nerve to walk closer, greet him in the way you would a boyfriend, but she had no idea. Instead, her social experience with men had been confined to the four walls of that damn store. If only Aunt Ella had not been so strict, Jenny might know how to behave now.

Jenny's thoughts fled to the only experience she had, observing Aunt Ella with the Indians and customers. She pictured her aunt greeting someone, and pasted a welcoming, bright smile on her face.

Chandler raised his gaze to the mirror and caught Jenny's eyes on him. "What the hell are you grinning about?"

"I'm . . . glad you're back."

He braced his hands on each side of the sink and his stare lengthened, intensified, with narrowed eyes focused on her so fiercely Jenny could barely breathe. His look made her think of her father and she nearly raised her gaze to the ceiling, but something told her Chandler expected her full attention.

With simultaneous twists of his wrists he shut off the water. "You better not get me killed, chickadee."

His long fingers curled around a hand towel. He whipped it from the rod and covered his face, wiping it dry as he turned to her. Jenny's heart beat in such a jerky pattern she thought she might faint and all she could think was, *Don't make me leave.*

He lowered the towel and stared at her, his gaze taking her in from head to toe. The fierce look in his eyes changed to something different that yanked her pulse down to her stomach. He tossed the towel on the floor. "You won't make that mistake again, will you?" His low voice circled around her.

Jenny managed to shake her head, though her eyes were fixed on him. When he smiled, the pulse down in her stomach yanked back up clear to her throat. She swallowed.

"You were gone so long, was all. I thought—" Jenny stopped herself from complaining. Maybe she had misunderstood about him being gone only a day. It didn't matter now. He was back.

"So you missed me, eh?" he asked, still smiling, as he walked to her. He ran his index finger down her cheek, dragging the ragged edge of his fingernail over her skin. Jenny didn't let herself wince. She wouldn't ruin this. She had to make everything all right . . . so he wouldn't send her away, back to Ella.

She raised her eyes to his to let him see her sincerity. "I was worried."

His eyes flashed sudden anger. "You were worried. The little Indian girl was worried about me."

His hand slid beneath her hair, encircling part of her throat. "That's rich." He angled in front of her and, as he pressed close, he whispered in her ear, "I don't need you to worry. I need you to do as I say." He gave a sharp, startling squeeze, then just as quickly let go and strode to the window.

Jenny's blood rushed to her head as if the floor had disappeared beneath her feet. She couldn't speak, she couldn't even move. She felt strangled and trapped as if she were surrounded by a net of unseen wires, any one of which would trip her up again.

"Maybe you wish you hadn't come," he murmured, staring out the window. "Maybe—" He turned suddenly and faced her. "Maybe you thought this would be easy. Is that it, chickadee? Well, it's not easy. And it's dangerous. But you're the one who begged to come along, remember? You told me you wanted to help Eddie."

At the sudden mention of her father, Jenny's eyes stung with a need she couldn't even name. But that need drove through her like a rod of steel giving her strength and purpose. "I'm not afraid." Her trembling voice belied the words, but Jenny continued. "I want to help, Chandler. You can count on me."

He smiled. "Good. Because you're the only one who can do the next task."

Relief surged through her, producing a smile. "Anything."

"Tonight you go back home—"

"No!"

"And you find what Eddie left there and bring it to me."

"What he left there? But—" Jenny shook her head in confusion. "I don't know what you mean. He never lived there."

"But he visited you, didn't he?"

"Yes—"

"Then he could have left something."

"Like what?"

"Like a backpack or a duffel." He paced the room, both hands pushing through his hair. "I don't know what it's going to look like! But you have to find it. Does your aunt have a safe? A secret place? I mean, with all that money."

He looked at her expectantly. An uneasiness spread through Jenny. "She doesn't have a lot of money," she said quietly.

"Every trading post has money. And a safe. For crissakes, Jenny, where does she put expensive things at night?"

"The whole back office is a vault," Jenny said. "But it has an iron door. I don't have a key."

"That's it." He stopped in front of her and put his hands

on her shoulders. "And she has to leave it open during the day, right?"

"But there's no backpack or duffel there, Chandler. My dad wouldn't leave anything there."

"It has to be there, chickadee. And you have to find it."

He squeezed her shoulders so hard Jenny felt his nails biting through her denim shirt. "I'm counting on you, chickadee." He paused, then added, "Eddie is counting on you."

Back to the store. It was the last thing she wanted to do. And once there, how would she ever get away again? Ella would never let her go, not after the disappearing act she had pulled this time. "And you'll wait for me outside?"

"For crissakes, no! Your aunt can't know that you're with me. Don't you get it? I'll be down the road. You just bring what you find with you."

Jenny looked up to him. He would be there. He hadn't lied to her. And he was the only one she could count on.

"I'll do it."

His face spread into a smile and Jenny's insides melted.

Ella set the steaming cup of strong coffee on the desk and clicked on the lamp. Outside, a stripe of faint yellow outlined the horizon and Ella watched the color brighten and widen, a part of her appreciating, as she did every day, that the builders of the post had followed Navajo custom and faced the front of the building to the east.

Through the window, she could hear mourning doves and sparrows, their quiet coos and chatters her only company in the gray dawn.

All night she had lain in bed, her thoughts like boulders in the sand that she kept tripping over. She stumbled from one to the next in an awkward, haphazard path of no coherent direction that had left her feeling so disconnected and frustrated she had finally given up on sleep.

She knew the source of her restlessness: Jenny. The night was incomplete with the bedroom down the hall empty. Ella had even tried imagining her niece there, snuggled safely under the covers. She had hoped to fool her own heart, picturing Jenny contented and happy. But that image never held.

Because that Jenny—satisfied, calm—didn't exist. Even as a child, Jenny had never been simply content. She had attacked each moment with tenacity. Like some half-wild pup, she would sink her teeth into the neck of any situation and not let loose until she had squeezed out every last ounce of drama.

Why couldn't Jenny learn to just let things be? Why must there always be a conflict? As if there weren't already enough stress just in living, just in meeting each day.

With her hand, Ella swept grit off her desk. Each morning, it was the same: every surface had to be cleared of the endless silt drifting from the roof through the wood beams. If there were winds, the whole inside of the trading post took on a dull brown cast, but the desert had been as still as one of the paintings on her walls. She pulled the stack of bills from her box, blowing off more of the light covering of dirt.

She stacked the bills according to priority and drew out her yellow pad where she kept the list of everything she owed. It seemed that for every one she marked off paid, she had to add two more. It was a constant juggle and had been for the last three years. She had hoped this year would be one for which sales from the store would be up and credit for the Indians would be down. When would she ever reach the day when she could open a bill and pay it, instead of writing it down and praying that the money would come in before the demanding phone calls began?

Ella reached for the first bill when a flicker of motion at the window caught her eye. She looked out and saw the flutter of the silvery leaves on a nearby olive tree, caught in a slight breeze. Yet the other trees in the cluster didn't move, as if the wind selected only that one to circle around.

She heard a low whistle. Ella's gaze went to the ceiling.

It was that damn bird again. She rose, intent on taking care of the magpie, once and for all.

Movement at the side window drew her attention. But no tree or bush was planted out there. Ella took a few steps toward the window. The desert beyond was still gray, spotted with the darker clumps of sagebrush and juniper. She could only figure that the movement had been a bird flying low across the building.

As she turned, a flash of *something* rose above the sill. For a second, she thought she saw a man's face.

Ella screamed, stumbled back, and ran to her office. She fumbled with the bottom drawer of the desk, pulled out her gun, and crept to the front counter. The knob turned on the front door, followed by the sound of a key fitting the lock.

Jenny opened the door. "Aunt Ella, why are you up so early—" She stopped, staring at the gun. "What are you doing?"

Ella's joy at seeing Jenny bubbled through her fear in a confused mix. She lowered the gun, but her eyes went to the window and back to Jenny.

"Aunt Ella?"

"I—" Ella took a few steps to peek around Jenny out the door. "I just didn't expect you, sweetie."

"But why the gun?" Jenny had not moved past her first step into the store.

Ella reached around Jenny to close the door; as she did, she took a closer look outside, then pulled the door shut. "You came alone?"

"Why do you ask? Why the gun, Aunt Ella?"

Jenny had shuffled only the slightest bit out of the way of the door and Ella now saw the stricken look on her niece's face. Ella slid the gun into her skirt pocket. "I heard something, is all. Never mind. I'm so glad to see you." She pulled Jenny into a hug, but the child was stiff and only after a pause did she raise an arm around Ella's back. Ella hugged her niece tight, ignoring the weak press of Jenny's arm. It didn't matter. Jenny was home.

She stepped back and held Jenny at arm's length. "I worried about you. You weren't at Great-grandmother's."

"You went to *Sáni*'s?" Jenny's stricken look narrowed to something bordering on alarm, then she looked away. "You followed me around?"

"I didn't follow you around. You told me you were going to Great-grandmother's. Where were you?"

"I'm old enough to go where I want, Aunt Ella." Jenny shrugged loose.

The magpie let out a long whistle.

"Hey! The magpie is still here?" A smile spread on Jenny's face as she looked up into the ceiling beams.

Ella felt a pang of irrational jealousy that the damn bird got Jenny's smile. She took a deep breath to quell a sudden ache in her chest. "You're also old enough to call and tell me where you are, Jenny."

"I knew it would be like this." Jenny's audible sigh filled the gallery. "Look, I'm just here to pick up some things." Jenny started down the hall to the courtyard and bedrooms.

Ella's heart jumped and all the conflicting emotions jammed within her chest. "You're not staying?" The words came out choked.

"Just until I get what I need." Jenny's voice faded down the hall.

Ella stared long after she heard the slam of the courtyard door, long after Jenny's steps on the cobblestone died away. Her heart pounded hard under the effort of stilling all the questions pressing at her throat. She finally walked back to her desk, but as she stared at the stack of bills all she saw was the look on Jenny's face when she had first opened the door; that surprised expression, as if Jenny had not expected to see Ella.

Of course, that was absurd, but Ella couldn't rid herself of the feeling that Jenny had meant to sneak in, gather her things, and leave again without even a word. It hurt Ella that Jenny would go to such lengths to avoid her.

Ella's hands rearranged the legal pad and stack of bills,

straightening, aligning, as if urging herself back to the task. She picked up her pen then set it back down again, unable to muster the slightest interest. *What difference did it make?*

Unbidden, the image of her mother filled her mind. She saw her sitting at this very desk, the pen poised in her hand, but her gaze out the window and beyond—a look of desperate longing on her face.

Is this how her mother had felt? Overwhelmed? Inadequate? Had she finally just given in to some secret longing when she left?

It seemed to be a fatal flaw in this family: Her mother had left; Eddie had chased some greater need all over the reservation—and now Jenny.

Ella stared out her office door across the vast main room of the post. The early morning sun shone through the windows, capturing the silent, peaceful dance of dust motes in the rays. This was all Ella had ever known. All she had ever wanted was to provide a home for Jenny, to create a family with her. She didn't remember any dreams before that, any longings, any goals, even any expectations other than that she would always be here.

No, leaving was not a choice. Chasing after some vague needs and longings was dangerous, irresponsible . . . and hurtful, to the ones left behind.

Ella took a deep breath and let her gaze settle on the impossible stack of bills. She reached for the first one, opened it, and methodically entered it on the list, then went on to the next. It was more than a routine, more than a chore done by rote with no thinking. It was her responsibility.

Ella finished the bills about an hour later. By noon, she had fielded six calls from vendors and worked with maybe twenty customers—not a busy morning. Certainly not busy enough to keep her mind distracted from Jenny. She itched to peek in on her, but Ella didn't want another argument and that seemed to be the result no matter what she said to Jenny.

Jenny wouldn't join her for lunch and the afternoon

dragged on the same way as the morning, except that as each hour passed, Ella found herself wondering if Jenny would be there at the end of the day. She resented every customer who lingered, poking through everything, as if they had all the time in the world. By six-thirty, she could barely restrain herself from flicking the lights on and off in order to budge an old couple from their leisurely study of a map. She did, however, practically walk them to the door and then shut it firmly closed. She didn't bother to count the drawer, settle the batch of receipts, or even lock the office.

Crossing the courtyard into the kitchen, Ella could hear Jenny's voice coming from the small yard outside. Then she heard Jenny laugh, the sound so unexpected and wonderful Ella broke into a smile. Ella walked closer and, through the screen door, she could see Jenny crouched in the red dirt, the furry figure of Apache beside her. The prairie dog nuzzled Jenny's palm, no doubt finding it full of nuts.

Ella leaned against the tile counter, and watched, drinking in the scene. Her mind flooded with memories of just such moments with Jenny. Before Ella's eyes, the teenager became once more the child of seven, giggling and coaxing Apache from his hole. When Apache appeared, Jenny had been so delighted she ran laughing into Ella's arms. Sunlight stretched ahead of them promising endless days of love and laughter . . .

. . . a promise Ella never should have believed.

Ella's throat clenched. She would do anything to have those days back again, when life with Jenny had seemed carefree and the child had gazed up at Ella with adoring eyes.

Nothing like Jenny's gaze now, with so much anger and even contempt. The tightness spread to her chest, pressing emotions into such a knot she could barely breathe.

Ella couldn't understand. All she had ever wanted was to provide a home with love for Jenny—a home unlike the one she and Eddie had had with their parents. A home

Eddie himself had found impossible to provide for his own daughter.

Ella had been more willing. She had been determined. She had struggled against a mountain of debt and overwhelming exhaustion from the endless hours, all to try to provide a life for herself and Jenny.

None of this had concerned Eddie. He had bigger problems, more important than spending time with Jenny. More important than letting her know he loved her.

Now he was dead and Ella was left with picking up the pieces, but she feared that nothing she did or said could ease Jenny's rage—the confusion of a teenage girl who saw her father as a hero.

Damn Eddie and his oh-so-important beliefs.

Shame for her anger wrapped around Ella's cold thoughts like a wet blanket—a heavy, comfortless burden.

Apache pushed his nose back into Jenny's palm and she smiled. Envy at Apache's ease curled round the knot in Ella, tightening it, but she couldn't tear her gaze away.

When had the distance between her and Jenny become so great?

Jenny wiped her hand down her skirt, then raised her gaze to the painted sand dunes. They were pale now in the late afternoon light, but you could see the faint layers of lilac, dusty rose, and the slightest orange. Jenny sat that way, hands resting in her lap, her sight ahead, so purposeful, so focused, she seemed to look past the dunes to somewhere in the distance.

Ella's heart caught.

She couldn't bear it if Jenny left again.

She pushed away from the counter and went to the back door. At the sound of the squeaking hinges, Jenny looked over her shoulder, then frowned when she saw Ella. She quickly turned back to the sand dunes.

"I saw you from the window," Ella began. "It reminded me of all the times we sat together out here."

Jenny sat still as a shadow.

Ella gathered her skirt and settled next to Jenny. "Apache is good company, isn't he? Remember the time

Apache didn't know that a horse was standing over him when he peeked from his hole?''

Jenny smiled. "He just knew the sky was black."

"And Apache dove back underground." She chuckled. "The little fellow was so confused, he didn't come up for the whole next day."

Jenny chuckled, the sound so carefree Ella's heart hurt for her.

"We've been lucky," Ella continued, "that he never moved away."

Jenny gave Ella a quick look. "Could he do that? I mean, would he?"

"Sure, if he wanted to. But he must like it here. He has a pretty good life."

"I've missed Apache," Jenny murmured. But then her smile waned. "How long do prairie dogs live?" she asked.

"I don't know," Ella said. "Apache has already been living here nine years. Maybe one day he'll just go underground and never come out," she offered.

"No, Apache is a warrior," Jenny said firmly. "He would die defending his family."

When Jenny looked up, her eyes were darker, shinier; and Ella knew the child had been thinking of her father and his sudden violent death. The sheen deepened on Jenny's eyes.

Jenny lifted her chin, and in that small defiant gesture, Ella witnessed the profound bravery in this child—and Ella's heart lurched with new fear.

Ella took a breath. "Jenny, if you want to talk . . . about your father . . ." She put a hand on Jenny's shoulder. "I know it's hard."

Ella felt a shudder pass through Jenny. "Honey, please talk to me."

Jenny looked at Ella, her eyes full of sadness. "Now he won't ever be back," she said. A tear slid down her cheek.

Ella wrapped herself around Jenny. "Shh, now. I know, I know." She rocked Jenny in her arms. "I'm here, Jenny. I'm not going anywhere. We'll be okay."

Suddenly, Jenny pushed back. She wiped her eyes with a hasty hand. For just a second, she stared at Ella, as if she didn't know her. Then she stood and walked to the kitchen.

The knot of emotions in Ella squeezed her heart until she thought she would cry out in pain. Instead, she took a ragged breath and called out, "Where are you going?"

"Inside. I want to be alone."

The wake of Jenny's furious energy washed over Ella and all she could think was that Jenny was just like her father; and Eddie had been just like his own mother: three people who dealt with everything the same way, by storming out.

CHAPTER
EIGHT

An hour later, Ella walked down the hallway to Jenny's room. She really had no clue how to approach Jenny, how to again get close to her. It seemed that no matter what Ella said, how carefully she couched it, she angered Jenny. But she had to try. She had to let Jenny know that she cared, that she was here for her.

She knocked lightly on the door. "Jenny? May I come in?"

No response.

Ella turned the knob and opened the door.

Jenny wasn't there. Neither was her backpack.

There wasn't a sign Jenny had spent even a minute here, not a trace of her, not even the slightest indentation on the pillow. Worse, there was no indication she meant to come back, as if she would simply disappear for good.

Panic sped through Ella. She ran across the courtyard, threw open the door, and raced into the main gallery. The store was empty, but the front door was still locked from the inside. Jenny had to be here somewhere.

Then Ella noticed that the iron door to the office stood open.

"Jenny?"

Ella thought she heard a sudden gasp. But it could also have been a breath of wind through the eaves. A glance out the window framed the same still, listless scene as it had been all day.

Ella started for the office then heard the unmistakable wheeze of the heavy safe door. Her heart jumped. "Jenny?" she called again.

The crunch of tires outside and sudden headlights through the window nearly peeled Ella out of her skin. From the corner of her eye, Ella saw a flash of neon-blue, the distinct color of Jenny's backpack. "Jenny!"

Jenny emerged from the shadows, the strap of her backpack clutched in one hand, her gaze downcast.

"What were you doing in there?"

"Nothing." Jenny's eyes cut sideways to the sound of footsteps approaching the door. "I have to go."

Ella caught Jenny's arm as she rounded the counter. "Jenny, stop. Tell me what's going on. What were you looking for?"

"Just some traveling money. That's all, okay?" She broke loose and swung her pack onto her shoulder.

"But where are you going?"

Jenny's hands were already on the door and the dead bolt. "I'll call you." But her tone held no promise.

"Don't do this, Jenny. Don't cut me off. I love you."

"No! You don't love me!" Jenny reeled from the door, her eyes so dark and hard they reflected no light at all. "You don't know *how* to love. Love means taking a risk, fighting for something. You have never fought for anything!" She glared at Ella. "You are scared to death of taking a risk. Well, it doesn't scare me."

"How can you say I don't love you or that I don't fight for anything?" Ella heard her voice grow loud, but she couldn't stop herself, any more than she could quiet her heart thundering against her chest. "Every day, I fight to keep this place, to keep this business. All to make a home for you, for both of us."

"I didn't ask you to."

"No, but your father did, Jenny. He knew I would take care of you. He knew you belonged here, would be loved here."

Jenny's eyes flared with pain, then hardened. "Like

you've told me before, Daddy made a lot of mistakes. This was one of them."

Ella's heart cracked. "What is it you want, Jenny?"

"I want my own life. I want to make my own decisions!"

Ella drew a sharp breath. "Then make one now, Jenny. Make your *own* decision. Be your own person. Don't be what you *think* you're supposed to be."

The door opened and Jenny stumbled forward, her eyes wide with a panic that reached right into Ella and clutched her heart.

Ella grabbed the first thing she could lay her hands on: the marble bear. Her fingers closed on the cold stone and she raised it over her head. A man's leg stepped beyond the door. Ella took a deep breath, readying herself to throw the sculpture.

"Aunt Ella, don't!"

Frank found himself facing Ella and a marble bear. Her arms wavered and Frank saw the strain on her face.

"Here, let me help you with that." He slid his hands near hers to get a grip. "I've got it," he said, though the words came out as a grunt. He set the bear on a nearby iron pedestal. "God, lady, you could have crushed my head." He was amazed that Ella had been able to lift it over *her* head.

"Who are you?" A girl stood apart from Ella, her young face skewed in worry and surprise.

"It's all right, Jenny. It's Agent Reardon," Ella said.

Frank realized it was Jenny he'd heard yell not to throw the bear. He had also heard her yell much more at Ella, painful accusations that still hung in the electrified air. "Guess I owe you one, Jenny. Thanks for stopping your aunt from hurling the bear." Frank smiled at the girl, but Jenny's expression had changed from surprise to alarm.

"FBI?" she murmured. Her eyes widened and Frank noticed her quick glance at the backpack on the floor by his feet.

"I'm sorry if I scared you," he said to Jenny.

"You shouldn't sneak up on people, Agent Reardon," Ella said.

Frank faced her. "That's what I do."

Ella's face was still pale, her nervousness right at the surface, yet she stepped between him and the niece, in an obvious protective maneuver. "Well, you have arrived at a very inconvenient time, Agent Reardon." She put her hand on the doorknob and raised her gaze to his. "My niece and I were talking."

"No, we weren't. I was leaving." Jenny slipped around Ella and grabbed her backpack without missing a step toward the door.

Frank saw the flash of panic on Ella's face, a gut-wrenching look that grabbed him and made him want to help her.

The irrational thought surprised him.

He pulled his gaze from Ella to Jenny. "That's too bad, Jenny, because I came to talk to your aunt about your father. And you might be of some help."

Ella intercepted. "She doesn't know anything. She's just a child."

Frank's gut twisted at the battle he saw on her face between sparing Jenny from his questions and her own near palpable need to make Jenny stay.

"I'm not a child, Aunt Ella." The unmistakable message in Jenny's hard, defiant tone even made Frank wince. She faced him, though she didn't move from her easy escape out the open door. "What about my father?"

"What do you know about Tillen Chavez and Flint?"

Jenny's eyes narrowed on Frank. "Why?"

"Jenny, I'm investigating your father's murder. Don't you want to help?"

Jenny stared back and Frank had to admire her obstinacy even in the face of his authority. He wondered if Jenny had any idea how much she resembled her aunt.

"I met them at *Sáni*'s," she said finally. "My great-grandmother," she added at Frank's questioning look.

"And what did they talk about?"

"I don't know. Things."

"Helping *Sáni* in her fight with the Hopi, maybe?"

"How did you know—"

"Your great-grandmother already told me that much, Jenny."

"You went to see *Sáni*? Who—" Jenny's eyes flashed to Ella. "You took him?"

"I was looking for you, Jenny."

"You just can't trust me, can you?" Jenny shook her head.

"Maybe she was worried about you." Frank caught Ella's quick look from the corner of his eye.

"You have no right—" Jenny started.

"And maybe she is smart to worry, Jenny. Do you know anything about Tillen and Flint?"

"They were friends of my father's."

"Did you know they are members of the American Indian Rights Organization?"

"No, but so what?"

"Was your father a member of AIRO, Jenny?"

"I don't know."

Frank saw the flash of pride in her eyes and knew he had his answer. He looked at Ella, but she was staring at Jenny with alarm bordering on horror.

"What do you know about AIRO?" Ella's question was a demand.

"Nothing." Jenny broke Ella's stare and confronted Frank. "Anyway, why are you asking *me*? Doesn't the FBI have fat files on AIRO?"

"Jenny, if you know something about Eddie's involvement with AIRO, tell Agent Reardon. Tell him what you know."

Ella's plea to her niece caught Frank totally off guard. He had expected Ella to play the cool one when he brought up AIRO—she had certainly maintained that posture every time he was with her. But her anxiety nearly electrified the air.

"I don't know anything."

"Jenny, AIRO is trouble," Ella said.

"AIRO is trouble?" Jenny gave a sharp laugh. "That's right, Aunt Ella, you just go on and blame the only ones who are trying to help."

"Help how? By causing trouble? By making everything an issue of Indians against whites?"

"They stand up for things! And they stand up for people who are too afraid to do it themselves!"

Jenny's yell echoed through the gallery.

Ella gasped.

For a moment, Frank was speechless. Jenny's words knifed clean through to Frank's gut like a poker jabbing smoldering coals. She was a child for crissakes, proclaiming her devotion to that murderous group.

Jenny's face was bright with pride and fearless righteousness and Frank had the nearly overwhelming urge to haul her inside, slam shut the door, and lock her in her room—anything to keep her from the certain danger she just couldn't comprehend.

He looked at Ella, saw the blatant pain on her face—a pain that matched what he felt inside himself. In that instant he knew what he had resisted acknowledging from the beginning: Ella had very little to do with her brother. Whatever Eddie had been involved in, Ella abhorred . . . and, right now, feared.

"You think those men in AIRO are brave, don't you, Jenny?"

She tore her gaze from her aunt and faced Frank, her eyes glittering with defiance.

"They gather at night, talk about rights for the Indians, all very secretive and daring, isn't it?"

Jenny just stared.

"It's them against the world, right? Letting nothing stand in their way. They must seem like heroes to you." Frank took a few steps toward her.

"They are heroes." Her words forced past clenched teeth and jaw.

"You see them willing to risk anything." He walked

closer, until she had to look up at him. "And what do you think they do when they don't get their way?"

Though Frank towered over her, she didn't back down or back away, but stared up at him, her eyes full of courage . . . and worse: blind loyalty. She was so young, so idealistic. Just the kind of innocent they preyed on. It took all Frank's will not to grab her, shake some sense into her.

"Do you know they have kidnapped people, Jenny? Dragged them off in the dead of night because some poor soul didn't do as they asked, or they didn't trust him *or her.*"

"You can't prove any of this. If you could, you would arrest people."

"And then there's the stealing. From hardworking people. AIRO doesn't care, though. They have to live, they have to buy guns, right?"

She blinked, but didn't retreat.

Frank advanced. "What about murder, Jenny? Is murder okay?"

"They're not murderers." Angry red splotched her cheeks.

"How do you know, Jenny? Do you really think they wouldn't kill someone who stands in their way? Isn't that exactly what you like about AIRO, that they fight for what they want?"

"They're not bullies, like you, trying to scare a kid." Her eyes gleamed . . . with rage? Or was it fear? Better if it was fear. Better still if it was fear *of him.*

He closed the small gap between them. "Damn right I'm trying to scare you, Jenny. And you better listen. You better take me seriously. Because you do *not* want to get caught in the middle, do you hear me?"

"I hear you, Mr. FBI." She shot a glare at Ella, lumping Ella right then and there with the hateful FBI.

"Jenny—"

Before Ella could finish, Jenny was out the door. Ella bolted past Frank, screaming for Jenny to stop. Frank caught up to Ella standing at the edge of her dirt lot, staring into the night. There was no sign of Jenny. It was as if she had been consumed in the darkness.

"Would she just walk out across the desert? Is she crazy?"

"Desperate," Ella said and looked at Frank. "She's that desperate." Her black eyes shone in the moonlight. "But I think she had a ride waiting. She mentioned one the last time she left."

"Do you know who that would be?"

"No, I don't," she said.

Her tone spoke volumes about all she didn't know about Jenny. Her gaze was back on the road, the road that must have delivered Jenny's ride and then taken her away—and Frank almost felt as if he could read Ella's thoughts: Where did that road lead for Jenny?

Ella looked as if she might stand there all night staring. Frank touched her shoulder. "Is there anyone you can call?"

Ella shook her head.

"How about friends of Jenny's?"

"She doesn't have—" Ella's words came out choked. She paused and cleared her throat. "She has always stayed to herself."

"How about a friend of yours?"

She only shook her head again, then turned back to the store.

"Maybe she heard at least some of what I said," Frank offered. "Maybe it scared her off AIRO . . ." Frank turned to Ella and the rest of his sentence died. Jenny may not have heard, but Ella had. In the light of the trading post he saw that every bit of the terror he had tried to invoke in Jenny was carved in Ella's face.

"She heard," Ella said. "That's why she left." Ella walked into the store and started shutting off lights.

Did she blame him for Jenny leaving? Was she making him responsible?

Then he remembered the argument he had overheard when he first approached the post this evening. "Jenny was already on her way out the door when I got here. What were you arguing about?''

Ella glanced at him from across the main gallery. ''Family arguments are not meant to be overheard, Agent Reardon.'' With a flick, she cut the overhead lights, throwing herself in darkness. Frank could only hear the rustle of her skirt and the soft pad of her steps across the room.

She couldn't blame him for Jenny leaving. That wasn't what happened—that was the *last* thing he would do.

Ella emerged into the dim light cast by a lone bulb overhead. She walked by him and Frank's hand shot out and held her arm. ''You aren't worried that Jenny may be getting in over her head?''

Her eyes were full brown and luminous, as if barely holding within a wealth of concern. ''I worry about that every day.''

For a second, gazing at her there in that singular light, with only deep black behind her, Frank saw a hint of the immense responsibility she carried, as a lone woman running a store and trying to raise a teenager—a situation so immense, so demanding, he didn't have the first clue how she coped.

Frank's hand dropped to his side and he saw a flicker of sadness in Ella's face. Then she lifted her chin only slightly and the shimmer in her eyes receded, as if draining to some limitless well.

She brushed past and Frank followed her into the office, but there she didn't turn off lights. She stood in the middle of the room, staring at the open safe.

''But there wasn't any money here,'' she murmured.

''What?''

Ella jerked her head in Frank's direction, a look of surprise on her face, as if she had forgotten he was even there. ''Nothing,'' she said, then swung closed the safe door and twirled the lock.

''Ella, are you all right?''

She stopped and stared at Frank. He didn't blame her

for her bewilderment; his concern was just as unexpected for him.

She considered him for a moment, then said, "I'll be fine. Thank you for asking."

He recognized that denial: It was the same one he employed on a regular basis because explaining the problem came too close to baring emotions. Suddenly, Frank saw through Ella's calm demeanor as if she were transparent . . . and what he saw looked familiar.

Frank ran his hand casually down the counter. "I bet you have to be a good listener running this store, dealing with all sorts of people."

"Yes," she answered cautiously.

"So tell me this," he asked, coming to a stop right next to her. "Who do *you* talk to? Who listens to your problems?"

Her mouth fell open slightly. "I—" She paused and Frank watched her regain her equilibrium. "Why do you ask, Agent Reardon?"

"Well, in my line of work, I have to be a good listener, too. Thought I might offer." Frank immediately regretted the invitation. What in the world had he been thinking? He had no business getting involved in this woman's concerns. She would turn him down, he knew it . . . she had to.

"Have you had your dinner, Agent Reardon?"

"What?"

"It's only green chile stew. Do you want to join me?" she asked quietly, casually.

She looked ready to accept his polite refusal, even anticipating it; and if he did, Frank knew instinctively she would react with the slightest tilt of her chin and that veil of control would again descend over her eyes.

For a reason he could not explain Frank couldn't let that happen. He wanted to know more about Ella Honanie. "Green chile stew sounds great," he answered.

He followed Ella down the hallway and out a door to an open courtyard. He glanced up to a night sky filled with stars. They looked so close, like a sparkling roof suspended just beyond reach.

Ella crossed diagonally to another door and Frank stepped into the kitchen, a long narrow room that mirrored the front gallery with the same brick floor and beamed ceiling. But where the gallery walls were covered with paintings, pottery masks, and Navajo rugs, the walls of the kitchen were mostly bare.

His gaze went to Ella, who stood at the stove patiently stirring the stew. For the first time he noticed that she didn't wear any rings or bracelets, none of the silver and turquoise that she so proudly displayed in the store cases.

The contrast between the stark utilitarian here and the rich color and texture of the gallery made Frank even more curious about the proprietor, Miss Ella Honanie.

Did she have no use for the art she sold? Was it simply a way to make a living?

On the nearest wall, Frank noticed the only personal touch to the room: some old photographs in cheap frames hanging in a haphazard array. He walked closer to study them. Most featured the store, with either a group of people outside or an Indian at the counter with a smiling old man whom Frank took to be Ella's father. An exception was a picture of a young girl crouched down, her hand extended to a prairie dog—caught just at the moment the animal must have taken something from her hands: her face was beaming with a huge childish grin.

"Looks like your history with rodents goes way back," Frank said.

Ella looked over and he nodded to the photograph.

"That's Jenny," she said.

"Can't be." He looked again. "She looks exactly like you."

"Yes, well, people used to say that." She gazed for a moment at the picture over his shoulder, a slight smile on her lips. The smile died and she returned to stirring.

"How did Jenny come to live here?"

"Eddie brought her when she was six. His wife was

gone. He was trying to find work. He asked if I would watch her.''

Simple as that, her tone implied, as if there had been no question of how *long* Eddie meant for Ella to watch Jenny—and further, that Ella would never even have asked. Frank shook his head at Eddie's audacity, at the incredible presumptuousness needed for Eddie to dump his child at Ella's doorstep.

''And so you raised her,'' Frank said, unable to keep his low opinion of Eddie to himself.

''Yes, I did.'' Her tone was defensive. She turned from the stove and faced him. ''I see you're still making quick judgments of people.''

''And you didn't judge Eddie? You didn't think it was callous and selfish that he would hand off his daughter so he could get on with his life?''

''Why would I condemn Eddie for the very thing that has brought me so much joy?''

Frank stared at her, for a moment speechless that she could be so evenhanded. ''I can't believe you weren't ever angry at him.''

''That's a waste of time. It's like being angry at . . .'' She paused, shaking her head as if looking for the right word. ''At the weather. It just is, whether you like it or not.'' Her eyes sparked with conviction, but Frank couldn't buy it. She could just as easily be trying to convince herself. He had seen plenty of people eventually eaten up inside by an anger they wouldn't let out.

''All the same,'' he said with a smile, ''you look awfully angry for someone who says she isn't angry.''

''There's a difference between anger and frustration, Agent Reardon. And right now, I'm incredibly frustrated.''

She ladled stew into two bowls, set them on the table, and took a seat. Frank pulled out the chair across from her, but Ella didn't look up—her full attention was given to stirring her spoon around and around in the bowl, making endless swirls in the stew. And Frank had a good idea of exactly where her thoughts were: on Jenny. And that was exactly where Frank intended to apply the pressure.

He touched his hand to hers, stopping the motion. "Ella, you have a right to be mad, even at Jenny for walking out."

She glanced up and Frank couldn't tell if her eyes glistened because of the rising steam from the soup. "It doesn't help being angry. That doesn't tell me what to do or how to get her back."

She looked past him into space, her brow furrowed as if she were trying to decipher the incomprehensible . . . the exact expression she'd had on her face as when Frank had found her staring at the open safe. "What did you mean when you were in the office and said 'But there wasn't any money'?"

Her gaze slid to his. "Jenny had been in the office. She said she was looking for money."

"And you don't believe that."

"I don't know what to think . . ." Her voice trailed off. She set the spoon down and looked at Frank. "Ever since Eddie died . . ." She stopped, then started again. "She lost her father. She lost a part of herself when Eddie died and a part of this rebellion comes from that. She wants a life of her own. I understand. But it's more than that. She just doesn't seem the same. You should have seen the look on her face when I found her in the office. Jenny would never steal from me, but . . ." She shook her head as if trying to understand.

Frank thought of the young girl and her fierce defense of AIRO. "Does she want a life of her own or her father's life?"

Ella's heart jumped—an instant response to a sudden threat. "Eddie didn't have a life," Ella said.

"That certainly sounded like a judgment, Ella."

"It wasn't a judgment," she countered. "It's a fact. He went from one interest to another. He could never settle down."

But she heard her condemning tone, pushed from her heart without a moment to stop it.

"Ella, I think one of his interests was AIRO."

"That doesn't surprise me," Ella said.

"And I believe Eddie stole the art to somehow help out AIRO."

"But that doesn't make any sense." Her frustration level ratcheted clear up to the top of her head, where it pounded right behind her eyes. "Agent Reardon, AIRO would have no more to do with stolen Indian art than Eddie would."

"Maybe he planned to sell the art and give AIRO the money. Those bastards think nothing of using someone for their own purposes."

His eyes flared with hatred. Ella's breath caught. "You hate AIRO," she murmured. "Why? What has AIRO ever done to you?"

A swift stroke of pain lanced through the smoldering hatred in his eyes. Just as quickly, the pain disappeared as if Frank had thrown some internal switch. "Those bastards are cold-blooded murderers, Ella, and Eddie was just the kind of fresh blood they live on. I think Eddie was a loose end for AIRO. A loose end they tied up by getting rid of him."

His words came through clenched teeth, like the snarl of a barely controlled animal threatening destruction. Ella's heart pounded at the fierce energy and her whole body reacted to the emotional assault with waves of tremors. She fought to regain equilibrium, her usual calmness.

"Exactly what are you saying?" she managed.

"I'm saying exactly what you think I am." His black gaze held hers.

"You're accusing AIRO of killing Eddie?" Ella's heart absolutely leapt to her throat on a wave of fear. "That's crazy. They wouldn't kill an Indian."

"They would kill anyone who got in their way."

Frank's eyes were dead serious and he wouldn't look away from her—as if he needed her, almost desperately, to agree.

"Why is it so important to you that I believe you?"

His gaze flickered, for a fraction of a second, then refocused on her. Yet Ella had the uneasy feeling he wasn't truly seeing *her*. "Because they're dangerous. If Eddie was involved with AIRO and Jenny is now following in his footsteps—"

"Jenny is *not* involved with AIRO." Ella's heart threatened to beat right through her chest, as if pounding to escape a certain terror.

"You don't believe that." His voice was quiet, compelling. "You saw her face, you heard her. She called her father a hero."

"Don't," she said, unable to get the words above a whisper. "Don't push your anger on me. You talk about them like they're animals," she murmured.

He raked a hand through his hair and pushed back from the table. "And what if I'm right, Ella? What if that's what Jenny is doing, trying to help AIRO like she thinks her father was? What if she *wasn't* looking for money, like she said, but for something of Eddie's? Something AIRO wants?"

Ella didn't doubt Eddie's involvement in AIRO and she didn't doubt that Jenny, in some way, was trying to discover her father. What if Frank were right and Jenny was in danger? That possibility was worse than the nightmares that kept Ella awake at night, worse than her fears that Jenny would just run away.

Just run away. That's all she had worried about—that Jenny would disappear for good and not return. But not this. Not this.

The rush of blood through Ella's body finally reached her head in a dizzying rush.

She heard a scrape of chair and then felt a hand beneath her arm.

"Ella!"

She felt his breath on her cheek and turned to see black eyes, worried, staring at her. "What is it you want, Agent Reardon?"

His gaze turned hard. "I want to stop AIRO. I want to stop those murderers."

"And what about Eddie's murderer?"

"They're one and the same, Ella. And they're connected by the art. I know it. I have to find that art."

"Whatever Eddie was involved in was his own world, and he didn't bring it here. He knew I wouldn't allow it any more than I will allow anything to happen to Jenny."

"Ella, I won't let anything happen to Jenny. I swear it."

The fierceness had returned to his eyes. A harsh edge that truly scared Ella.

She couldn't ignore the *conviction* in his eyes. She also couldn't ignore the fist of fear in her stomach. Reardon was a dangerous man on a lethal course with AIRO. He couldn't guarantee Jenny's safety. She could *not* let herself—and more importantly, Jenny—get caught in the middle.

"Agent Reardon, you're just a man. Don't make promises you can't keep."

CHAPTER
NINE

Ella's body still trembled from the force of Frank's anger, his hatred of AIRO. Even as he drove away and she watched the taillights of his Jeep fade in the night, his cold loathing of AIRO lingered, chilling Ella to her bones.

Ella briskly rubbed her arms and hugged them tight to her, but she could not stop the shaking within. What reason could any man have for that much hate for others? Whatever the reason, he had no right to impose those extreme emotions on her.

She left the window and paced the gallery, hardly aware of what she was doing, driven by an anxious need to put distance between her and Frank's vehemence. Her gaze scanned the familiar surroundings of her life: creations of silver, marble, acrylic, clay. She ran her fingers along the jewelry cases, over the cool stone of the bear sculpture, seeking calmness, detachment, from among the inanimate objects. No matter the thought and care each artist bestowed on their creations or their skill of execution; no matter the beauty or uniqueness of each piece; they were simply things to sell, to help make a living, to provide a means to Ella's goal.

They engendered no emotion in her. They *demanded* no emotion from her. It was an existence Ella found immensely safe.

You are scared to death of taking a risk!

Jenny's words sliced through the comforting cocoon of

Ella's thoughts. She saw Jenny, her dark eyes accusing and unforgiving. Ella's heartbeat tripped on the injustice, the unfairness. How could the very stability she offered be twisted and contorted into something wrong?

She couldn't understand it, didn't want to understand it— didn't want to come close to feeling the kind of emotions that would turn a person inside out, shatter control, and expose raw, vulnerable need.

Yet she seemed to be the only one terrified of that path. Everyone else around her sought the precarious, dangerous route of extremes: Grandmother, Eddie, Ben with his belief in miracles, and now Jenny.

But Jenny had no idea what she was getting herself into. No fifteen-year-old did. She was so wrapped up in the fantasy of her father, she didn't see that Eddie's choices were wrong. All Jenny saw was the promise of adventure, all she heard was the power of conviction . . . regardless of the fact that Eddie's convictions had finally led to a dead end.

Ella shuddered uncontrollably. She gripped her sides in a vain attempt to quell the tremors, but the wave of anxiety rushed through her blood, down her arms, until Ella thought she might faint.

She would *not* allow Jenny to take that path.

Ella walked to the window, her legs steady, her mind set. This was Jenny's home, whether Jenny wanted it so or not. She belonged here.

She had only one place to look for Jenny: Grandmother's. Another shudder traversed Ella's back, her body's immediate, instinctive plea for avoidance. Ella stifled the reaction and willed herself to endure whatever combative, uncompromising attitude Grandmother harbored.

She gazed out at the pitch-black night and thought she had never felt so alone.

Frank awoke with a start to hear the rumble of Ella's truck pull out from the post. He straightened from the extremely uncomfortable slouch in which he had fallen asleep. His neck screamed with tense muscles, and he kneaded them with his hand, as he watched the inimitable Ella Honanie head off down the road.

That he had been right was of minimal consolation—it only proved his instincts were dead on: Ella Honanie was keeping a secret. The fact she didn't trust him bothered him more than was reasonable.

It shouldn't matter to him. He had the sense she let very few people into her thoughts. He bet he was only one of many whom Ella kept at a distance as she went about her life.

No, it shouldn't matter at all that his promise to protect Jenny had fallen on deaf ears, that Ella had more faith in her own abilities than she did in his . . . despite the fear he had seen in her eyes—a fear he had deliberately *provoked.*

He had reasoned that Ella would confide in him, trust him, even if relying on him was the last thing she wanted. He had made sure she would see no other choice. And he had done his job well: He had drawn on every bit of hatred in his soul to convince her, only to realize he had succeeded in making her fear *him.* He had seen it happen right before his eyes and had been helpless to stop, pull back, give her room to breathe and be safe with him.

When she had asked him to leave, Frank had had the nearly overwhelming urge to offer her comfort. But he didn't.

He had watched her most of the night through the window, circling his Jeep back across the desert and parking just up the road, close enough to still be able to watch the front of the store.

He had seen her pace, stand at the window, distress etching her face. He watched her clutch herself as if struck with acute pain . . . and it had taken all Frank's will not to stride back inside. But he didn't.

He watched. He waited. And he told himself that none of what Ella was suffering should bother him. But it did: He had not forced a criminal out into the open; he had provoked Ella out into the night.

He stayed half a mile back and followed her over the

dirt road to the highway. She turned onto the blacktop and headed west, in the same direction as Annie's.

Behind Frank, the night lightened to bands of gray, then light yellow, as day reclaimed the sky. Concerned Ella might recognize his Jeep, Frank kept his distance on the highway, though he worried over every rise that she might disappear down a side road.

When Ella turned onto the dirt road that led straight to her grandmother's, Frank slowed even more, certain now of her destination.

He muscled the Jeep over rocks and ruts, as the path wound up an incline. A loud scream raised the hair on his arms. It didn't sound human, more like the descending screech of a hawk.

Frank drove closer, rolled down the window. The scream had died down, but then rose again, as if on a new breath. Frank shifted down and applied gas to gain ground up over a rise. There ahead was Annie Ben's solitary hogan. Ella's truck sat out front with the door hanging open, as if Ella had jumped out.

Frank killed the engine and threw open his door. Another scream drifted over the rounded earth home. Frank ran to the back of the hogan, but there was no sign of Ella.

Just beyond the hogan the ground dropped off. In the distance, probably fifty miles away, stretched a chain of mountains. Frank stood on the edge of a plateau with nothing but sky surrounding him.

Shrieks rose from the shallow valley below. One shriek on top of another, a breathless chain of wails that filled the valley and seemed to echo from the distant mountains and back.

Frank spent precious seconds searching for a way down, finally gave up and half slid down the rocky slope, grabbing at juniper branches to brake a free fall down the mesa. There was no trail, not even a vague path leading to the valley, and twice Frank stopped, legs tensed for balance, and listened for screams to lead him. He negotiated around a boulder the size of a house. The ground leveled.

The screams were hoarse now, heartbreaking travesties of sound as if wrenched from a person's soul. The intensity froze his steps. Frank had never heard such grief—the razor's edge of sanity, the black color of despair.

He saw a flutter of denim. *Ella*. Frank pushed through tangled clumps of sage; the ragged cries were more piercing than the sharp, jagged branches.

He emerged at a small clearing. Ella crouched on the ground, her arm across Annie's back. Frank couldn't tell if Ella was all right. "Ella?" His voice pushed past a painful tightness in his chest.

Ella glanced over her grandmother's shoulder and Frank's breath caught at the sight of her face, stained with tears. He took a step toward her. Ella's eyes widened, as if just now focusing on him.

"What are you doing here?"

Before Frank could answer, Annie straightened, raised her face to the sky, and another wail sliced the morning sky, though with measurably less energy.

His boots crunching dry earth, Frank stepped to the front of the women and stopped, appalled at what he saw.

From among scattered mounds of freshly dug sand protruded little bones and skeletons—the fragile remains of children. More pieces littered the area, flung far and wide in the violent desecration. For a moment he thought coyotes might have done this, but then Frank saw shoe prints. They had trampled the ground, as if in some final act of violent desecration, the offenders deliberately stomping over the exposed, defenseless bones, crushing them.

His heart caught at the horrific scene. He crouched next to one print and confirmed it had come from the rubber tread of a tennis shoe. It looked no larger than a size nine. A small man or, more likely, given the shallow depth of most prints, a teenager.

Annie had gathered fragments together onto her wide skirt. Shaky, arthritic fingers reached for a bone and pulled a tiny skull from the dirt. The old woman cried out—a ragged moan squeezed from some infinite well of sadness.

She rocked from side to side, as if teetering on a precipice. Ella caressed the little woman's back and whispered in Navajo. Annie continued rocking, lost to anything but her obvious grief.

Ella began to hum, rocking with her grandmother, ever so slowly easing the old woman, quieting her. Ella laid a hand on her grandmother's fist. Annie clenched a dirty rag encrusted with dark, reddish-brown stains.

Frank walked carefully to Ella's side and crouched.

"Do you know who could have done this?" he whispered.

Ella's thick raven hair reflected white sunshine.

"Kiis'áanii." Annie spit the word.

Ella lifted her gaze to Frank and his heart tripped over as he met her fierce black eyes. He hadn't thought she had this depth of anger in her. "Hopi," she said, her voice tight.

She glanced over her shoulder, her face so taut with pain that Frank could see the slender blue veins in Ella's forehead.

He looked at the devastation lying before them. "What is this place?"

"We don't speak of it," Ella said.

For a moment, Frank thought she might leave it at that.

"We call it *alch'i'i.* 'The place they come together.' " Ella's voice caught on each syllable. "It's our place for the living and the dead."

Frank did not understand. Ella must have seen the bewilderment in his face, because she added, "Here is where we bury the umbilical cords from the living and the babies who did not live. This is the place Grandmother could not leave behind, the reason why she would not move—" Ella's words were choked off on a stricken breath.

Frank's gaze went to the rag Annie clutched and he now recognized the stains as blood—from a baby Annie had buried? Or blood from the birth of a child Annie raised? He stared across the trampled ground, at the tiny crushed bones, and his gut twisted at the thought of whatever depraved excuse for a human would do this.

Ella wrapped both arms around her grandmother and rocked with her. *"Shimásání, shash'la yádii, s'aa'akó tee. Shash'la yadii,"* Ella said over and over in a comforting tone anyone would recognize.

Frank leaned close to Ella. "Ella, let me help you and Annie to the Jeep."

She nodded. Frank stood and moved to Annie's side. He slipped a hand under her arm and one around her back.

"Come now, *shimásání.* Come with me," Ella said.

"Nakee ts'iil," Annie said suddenly, though her hoarse voice barely carried.

"I know, *shimásání.* I know. Let me help you up."

"Nakee ts'iil." The words became a cry, rippling through the old woman.

Frank felt Annie shudder and squeezed both hands tenderly to the old woman. "Come with us, Annie. You can't stay here."

She tried to stand, then slumped to the ground, as if drained of all her strength. She rocked from side to side, murmuring, *"Nakee ts'iil. Nakee ts'iil."*

Frank glanced to Ella. "What is she saying?"

"She says, 'It's broken in two.'" Ella's voice caught and she looked back to Annie.

Frank crouched beside Annie and leaned close. "Annie, you can't stay here," he repeated. "Come with us and I promise to find who did this."

Ella looked at the man kneeling beside her grandmother, his features drawn tight, with the look of deep sorrow for this old woman. She watched, speechless, as he bent, reached beneath her grandmother, and lifted the old woman tenderly into his arms. He stood and stumbled back one step, then caught his balance and started up the rocky slope with barely a look behind to her.

Ella followed, knowing she had discovered a depth to Frank Reardon she would never have believed existed.

Ella led the way up the trail, glancing back now and again to check Frank's progress. Grandmother filled his arms, her small round body a substantial burden, but he didn't show any strain. He held her high and close, Grandmother's head nestled against his shoulder. She had been quiet since they started to climb, and Ella wondered whether Grandmother might have even fallen asleep, held in Frank's arms.

Her heart expanded to the man whose strong arms and broad chest provided comfort right now. She didn't know how Frank had gotten here, or why he had come, but she was grateful.

She reached the top of the rise and heard her name called barely louder than a whisper. She turned to see Frank standing still twenty feet behind her. With a nod, he gestured her closer.

"Go ahead and get her things," he said quietly. "We'll wait here." He bent his head to Grandmother. His lips curved slightly, as if he were gazing on a sleeping child.

Ella nodded, though Frank didn't notice, and she walked away pondering the odd image of the reserved FBI agent cradling her grandmother.

Ella started through the door of the hogan and gasped at the pile of her grandmother's things tossed about like so much rubbish: cooking pots, her blankets, clothes spilling from her trunk, even Grandmother's cot—both mattress and frame—littered the ground. She could barely comprehend the amount of damage. Everything Grandmother owned had been swept off shelves, off the walls, from the cabinets.

Toeing aside canned goods, boxes of candles, old Indian pots, she was barely able to avoid stepping on something. Her gaze settled on a can resting on its side. From its mouth pure white sugar drifted onto the red earth.

Ella realized it would take her considerable time even to find clean clothes to pack for her Grandmother.

She left the hogan and went to find Frank. He stood where she had left him, still holding Grandmother in his arms, except now he faced the mountains. He had his back to Ella, his long jean-clad legs in a casual stance, with one bent slightly and his foot resting on a small rise of ground.

He seemed planted there, unmoving, not even shifting weight.

Ella paused, taking in the scene. He looked as if he could stand there forever, oblivious to his burden, and stare indefinitely across the wide valley, his tall frame against the utter wilderness beyond.

He *fit* that spot.

Ella felt a twinge of envy and swiftly shook off her absurd reaction. Yet she couldn't take her eyes from Frank, and a question rose unbidden in her mind: How he could look so much a part of this place, as if he belonged?

She approached Frank and placed a hand on his arm, careful not to surprise him and Grandmother. Through the fabric of his shirt, Ella felt taut muscles. He turned to her and she saw his large hands—one spread across Grandmother's back, the other curled over her legs. When she glanced up to him, she expected to see evidence of his effort reflected on his face.

Instead, she saw sadness, as if some well of pain within had overflowed into his eyes. She had never seen a man cry.

Abruptly, he looked away. "Ready?"

That's all he said, but Ella couldn't miss the choke of emotion in his voice. She wanted to ask why. Her hands moved to touch his arm, but she stopped within inches and let her arm drop to her side.

"I just came—" she started, but had to clear her own throat before continuing. "I was going to ask you to go ahead and take Grandmother to the Jeep. It will take me a while to pack some things for her."

He nodded but didn't move to leave, only turned his head to the mountains. "She has a beautiful spot here."

Ella almost said that it wasn't Grandmother's spot anymore, but she couldn't. She realized she would always connect this place with her grandmother.

Her gaze settled on the trail they had just climbed, the path leading to *alch'i'i*. Ella suddenly wondered whether

she would ever stand here again looking out over the valley
to the purple mountains.

"Yes, it is beautiful," Ella said. Suddenly, it was even
more beautiful than she had ever realized.

Ella turned away. "I'll get a few of Grandmother's
things," she said over her shoulder, and walked to the hogan.

She started putting everything right within the hogan,
but her energy was gone, her thoughts heavy with memories, one on top of the other, as layered and tangled as the
pile she tried to sort. So many things she recognized: a
basket she had used during walks with Grandmother gathering berries and flowers for wool dyes; a hairbrush that
brought back the memory of Grandmother's tender hands
on Ella's head. Each item she touched sparked another
memory—an old memory, one she had forgotten until this
very moment.

The thought struck her cold. She couldn't think of the
last time she had crouched at Grandmother's knee and felt
the soothing sensation of brush bristles through her hair; or
sat by the fire and listened to Grandmother tell stories, her
words swirling on the plumes of smoke floating through
the top of the hogan.

All the more recent memories were of arguments.

Ella felt a pang of guilt for every one of the confron-
tations. She wished she and Grandmother could go back to
the days when Grandmother smiled easily, and no one ever
imagined that she could have her home taken away.

The old wound opened in Ella and before she could stop
the memories, they rushed through her.

*Hundreds of bonfires that circled the village in a wall
of fire.*

*Large hands gripping her tight, so tight. She could
barely breathe.*

*A blanket wrapped around her so she couldn't move,
only hear all the angry voices.*

Screaming. The Navajo must go!

Her mother crying.
And the small child knew it was her fault.
She had just wanted to see the snakes.

Pain flooded Ella. A sob rose swiftly to her throat. She had only wanted to be with her brother. That was all. That was all.

Emotions wracked her body, clenching her heart, suffocating her. She couldn't bear them!

Ella stood. A pile of Grandmother's clothes fell from her lap. She stared at the rumpled heap, her focus blurry, disconnected. For a moment, she couldn't remember what she had been doing.

Her gaze went to the sorted stacks of Grandmother's belongings. Her hands lifted some clothes, brushing off dirt, her mind concentrated on a task . . . and her heart shoved the memories and the pain deep.

She grabbed the mattress to set it on the cot. White dust drifted from the mattress onto the ground. Ella stopped, frozen at the sight.

She knelt and reached a finger to the dust, holding her breath, praying she was mistaken. When she raised her hand, the pale ivory dust of bone clung to her skin.

Ella crumpled to the ground, overwhelmed by the sheer, calculated meanness: The sacred bones had been carried from *alch'i'i* and deliberately tossed onto Grandmother's bed. She stared, unable to comprehend the evil heart of the person responsible.

Ella pulled herself from the ground and staggered away from the mattress, unable to bring herself to brush off the other remnants, unable to even think. She only knew she had to leave.

Her gaze lit on the trunk. She righted it and dug through the contents for some clothes. Inside, she spotted a knapsack, and stuffed it with some of Grandmother's clothes, shoes, and toiletries, including the hairbrush.

Without a look back, Ella walked to Frank's Jeep. She could see Grandmother sitting up in the backseat. Ella stopped. She willed the tears in her eyes to subside, the pain to unclench her heart. She had to be strong for Grandmother.

She walked straight to the back door and opened it, offering her grandmother the knapsack. "I packed a few things for you, *shimásání*."

Her grandmother's eyes filled with tears. Ella's resolve wavered. This old woman did not deserve so much pain, not in one day.

Grandmother laid a warm hand on Ella's. "Thank you, child."

Ella stared for a moment, not understanding. After all the times she had tried to persuade Grandmother to leave, all the arguments Ella had employed to convince Grandmother to prepare for this day, Ella had never expected her grandmother to willingly drive away from her home. Even now, evidence of Grandmother's grief and the hard tears still etched the old woman's face.

"It is all right, *sitsóí*," Grandmother said. "I have what I need here. Thanks to Mr. Reardon." Grandmother tilted her head to a towel bundled on her lap.

One hand held tight the bunched ends of a towel, the other caressed the lumpy mound as a mother might a swollen belly.

Suddenly, Ella understood what Frank had done for Grandmother.

Ella was at a loss for the right words to thank him. She glanced up at Frank and met his gaze in the rearview mirror. Compassion lit his eyes, and Ella's resolve to remain strong wavered. Her eyes stung with an immediate need she would not acknowledge.

Ella averted her gaze and swallowed hard. With purpose, she shut the door for Grandmother and walked around the Jeep to Frank's side.

"I hoped you wouldn't mind," Frank said. "It seemed to . . . comfort her."

In the dark, solemn depths of his eyes, Ella saw a sad reverence. He didn't look away. But she had to.

"We should go," she said, and walked quickly away.

CHAPTER
TEN

Frank stared after Ella, his thoughts caught on the deep pain in her eyes. He knew that particular haunted look from inside himself, a gaze drawn inward to someplace dark, a place where fears brewed and threatened your sanity.

Maybe it was only her sorrow for what had happened to Annie. He was simply imagining something more, Frank told himself.

He heard a hum coming from the backseat and glanced to the mirror. Annie cradled the bundle of remains and hummed a monotone chant in minor. Though Frank didn't understand a single word, his heart couldn't miss the message of comfort—it was a song of welcome for the beloved remains. The image gave him a feeling of inner peace.

He backed the Jeep off the path and waited for Ella. The next moment, she drove by, going too fast for the rutty ground, her hands clenching the wheel as the truck bounced and bottomed out, metal creaking.

Frank pulled in behind her, but she was already far ahead, flying pell-mell down the mesa, as if in a desperate mad rush to get away.

He gave the Jeep gas, clenching his jaw against the awful risk he was taking on the winding road, a sheer drop on one side. A tire caught the edge of a rut, throwing the Jeep off course. Frank muscled it back, his heart pounding. Then he saw Ella's truck swerve to the edge of the road, obviously out of control. A geyser of sand and rocks spewed from the truck's tires. Adrenaline rushed into Frank's chest, down his arms. His breath stuck in his lungs until he saw Ella bring the truck back onto the road.

Frank gave a quick glance to the rearview mirror and Annie. She had her head down, as if in reverence for what she held in her lap. Her voice rose until she filled the Jeep with her song, seemingly oblivious to the wild ride down the mountain.

Ella continued driving the same way for the entire serpentine road, and picked up even more speed when she reached the bottom flat road. With barely a pause, she careened onto the blacktop, and tore down the highway, where she pulled so far ahead, recklessly passing other cars, Frank soon was left behind.

An hour later, Frank turned into the lot at the trading post and drove around back, passing a group of Navajos gathered at the front. A few glanced up and their eyes widened as if surprised to see a white man driving a little Navajo woman to the post.

Ella's truck rested within the lattice shelter. Frank would not have been the least surprised if it had let out a long hiss and groan after that nonstop race home.

He walked through the back door, the kitchen, across the courtyard, and down the hallway, finally locating Ella within one of the bedrooms.

"What the hell was that all about?"

"What?" Ella asked, barely glancing up from tucking in the bedcovers.

"The way you drove. You scared the hell out of—" Frank paused, uncertain of what he meant to say. "You scared Annie," he finished.

"Annie was in your car, not mine," she said simply, and rounded the bed. She had yet to look up at him.

Frank took a hard breath, calming the fury of emotions storming through him. This was crazy. She was fine. Anyway, Ella Honanie was not his responsibility.

"Do you want to bring her in?"

"What?"

"Grandmother. Does she need help?"

Frank pushed a frustrated hand through his hair, took a step back to the door, glanced at Ella again, and finally walked out of the room, more confused than when he had entered.

He lifted Annie from the Jeep and carried her into the building, through the kitchen, courtyard, and hallway, back to the bedroom. Ella stood at the window, looking out across the desert, her back to the door. Not until Frank crossed the room and settled Annie on the bed did Ella turn around, only to walk directly to her grandmother.

She removed Annie's soft leather boots and tucked her legs within the covers. She laid a hand on Annie's forehead, gently brushing back hair, then leaned close.

"You rest now, *shimásání*. I'll bring you some tea in a while."

Ella straightened and walked to the door, brushing past Frank, still averting her gaze from him, though he couldn't miss the pinched look at the sides of her eyes. He followed her back to the kitchen, but she had continued on through the back door and outside. There she stood, gazing off in the direction of the sand dunes, though she looked to be focusing far beyond.

Frank stepped in front of her, blocking her view, forcing her to look at him. When she did, though, he wished he had not been successful. The haunted look in her eyes had deepened, filling them. She appeared almost as disconnected from the moment as a person in shock.

Frank put a hand to her shoulder. "Ella, what's wrong?"

"I can't—" She stopped and drew a breath. "I'm grateful for what you did, Agent Reardon."

Her voice held a tone of dismissal. Frank bent his head to capture her gaze. "Ella, if you're worried about Annie, she'll be fine. It might take time, but—"

"Yes, of course." She turned back to the building.

"Ella!"

She paused, her hand on the door, and turned halfway to him. "I'm glad you were there."

"I'm glad I was there, too, Ella."

"Well, thank you again, Agent Reardon."

"The name is Frank."

She looked up at that, directly at him, and Frank saw in her eyes a flicker of sincere gratitude within the sadness.

Just as quickly, she returned to the door and walked inside.

Frank pulled into the Navajo Police Headquarters and parked. After the rumble of the Jeep died, he could hear the sound of humming. A lone man's chant rose and fell, drifting over the parking lot from the desert beyond, in what seemed like one continuous, breath-defying monotone.

Frank sat in the Jeep, the sound surrounding him, and his mind traveled to Annie and her love song for the bundle. Each note had reached out to him, embraced him, delivering an incomprehensible serenity he hadn't felt in years . . . a serenity Ella had obviously not shared.

For the entire drive to Gallup, Frank had been dwelling on the haunted look in Ella's eyes, and he had found himself wishing to know what tormented her.

He didn't know what had driven her to race away from Annie's as if chased by demons. Instincts told him, however, that those demons resided within her, behind those dark, troubled eyes.

He knew about demons; you could bury them deep, cage them within the dark recesses of your soul, only to have your steely control defeated by the merest wisp of a memory, a song, a scent, allowing the demons to crawl free from the dark, enclose you, make *you* the prisoner.

A shudder fled through Frank—the rumble of dark thoughts threatening to escape.

Frank slammed the door to the Jeep, strode to the building, and pulled closed the outer door, shutting out the man's song.

In the duty officers' room, Frank commandeered a desk, settled in the chair, and forced himself to focus on the job at hand: writing a report on the vandalism at Annie's. He struggled to keep himself to the facts, trying as best he could to detach himself from the horrible sight, the pain he'd witnessed in Annie. Remnants of Annie's song drifted through his head, distracting him, tangling his emotions, and he had to stop and take a breath before continuing.

When he was finished, Frank shook his head at the meager information he had been able to provide. At the very least, this might give Coriz another reason to increase patrols in that area, considering the trouble Coriz had already mentioned happening in the western res.

Frank entered the names of Tillen and Flint, hoping to discover something more about Eddie's two friends. Without Flint's last name, Frank came up empty, but Tillen had an arrest record with the Navajo Nation ranging from stupid to pathetic: drunk and disorderlies, brawling, and shoplifting. His file also carried an attachment from New Mexico with arrest information for assault.

Apparently, Tillen had not agreed with the repossession clause on the contract he signed with a quick-cash company. The man who bailed him out and guaranteed his court appearance was Henry Fuller—none other than the same New Mexico art dealer who had had his merchandise stolen in Denver.

Frank's hands froze over the keyboard. What the hell was Fuller doing vouching for a loser like Tillen?

His thoughts reviewed everything he knew: Eddie's prints were on the storage room in Denver; Eddie and Tillen were friends and Tillen was involved with AIRO; and, Frank confirmed with another disbelieving glance at the computer screen, Tillen knew Henry Fuller.

Frank picked up the phone and punched in the numbers for Fuller's store.

"Fuller's Indian Arts," Henry Fuller answered.

"Mr. Fuller, FBI Agent Frank Reardon. I'm investigating the stolen art, sir—"

"Have you found it?" Fuller interrupted.

"Sir, I'm calling to clarify a few things."

"So you haven't found my art yet."

Frank ignored the question and asked his own. "Sir, can you tell me how you know Tillen Chavez?"

Dead silence filled the phone. Then, "I don't know Mr. Chavez well. I've only met him a couple of times."

"But you know him well enough to bail him from jail and vouch for him?"

Fuller coughed. "Well, now, you see, Mr. Chavez came recommended to me by a man named Chandler."

Frank recognized the name from somewhere. He jotted it down. "Recommended for what, Mr. Fuller?"

"As a driver. I occasionally need things brought up to me in Taos, or brought down from Denver."

"Things?"

"Artwork, paintings, things that I don't want to ship."

"This is what you hired Tillen Chavez to do?"

Again, the long pause. "Just once," he said finally. "Haven't seen him since," he added.

This man was hiding something. Frank could hear it over the phone and practically taste it at the back of his mouth. He added Eddie's name and Tillen's name to his pad. "Your acquaintance with Tillen Chavez would have been helpful information to know when the art was stolen, Mr. Fuller."

"Yes, yes, of course. Maybe Chavez knows something about the robbery, do you think?"

Yes, Frank thought. Chavez knew something. And so did Fuller, he just wasn't saying. Frank drew circles around the names on his pad: Eddie, Tillen, Chandler. Where did he know Chandler from?

"Is that all, Agent Reardon?"

"Just a couple more questions, if you don't mind. How do you know Chandler?"

"He's a trader. Stops by here every once in a while. I buy old jewelry from him on occasion."

That was it. Frank now recalled seeing Chandler's name on Ella's list of vendors.

"I really have to go, Agent Reardon. I have a business, you know—"

"Just one more thing, Mr. Fuller. I was looking at the list of stolen items you provided and don't see mention of a tablet." Frank drew a breath and waited to see what he would hook.

"Tablet? Why do you ask about a tablet?"

Frank noticed that Fuller didn't answer the question, but instead tried to distract him with another question. "I'm asking you, Mr. Fuller. Should there have been a tablet listed in the items stolen?"

"No, of course not. Why would there be? Now I have to go. Thanks for keeping in touch, Agent Reardon," he added, just before hanging up.

Reardon stared at the phone, every one of his instincts firing. Fuller knew about a tablet, yet didn't want to talk about it. The only reason Frank could think of was that Fuller meant to keep the tablet a secret—but from whom? And why?

He glanced back at the notepad and drew lines between Eddie, Tillen, and Chandler.

"Well, Agent Reardon, good of you to check in."

Frank didn't need to look up; he knew the voice, and the shadow crossing the desk, belonged to Officer Coriz.

"I don't have to clear my agenda with you, Officer."

"But you *are* supposed to keep me informed."

Frank glanced up and casually covered the notepad with his hand. "If you have a problem with me, Coriz, take it up with Harris in Phoenix."

"And he'll get behind you? I don't think so, Reardon. He's not a big fan."

Frank barely concealed his surprise at Coriz's on-target assessment. "So you talked to my boss. Is that supposed to engender some sort of trust from me?"

"He called *me,* Reardon."

Frank's eyes narrowed.

"Asked me how the Honanie case was going."

"The hell—"

"That's right, Reardon."

Why the hell would the field agent call the Navajo cop?

Why would he even be interested in the Honanie murder? And why didn't he just call Frank?

"Now, I have to ask myself why the FBI went behind their own man?"

Frank slanted a look at the cop. "What is it you want from me, Coriz?"

"I want to know what the FBI is up to."

Frank snorted. "Good luck, Coriz. You'll have to work your informant angle on someone else."

"Like your boss tried to work on me? Why *was* he checking on you?"

"I have no idea."

Coriz's eyes narrowed to two creases in solid rock. He had the keen, intelligent stare of an officer on the scent of a lie. "Are you really that stupid? Or is it that you think I'm that stupid?"

"Back off, Coriz."

He didn't back off. "The FBI is a clean machine, Reardon. They like things very tidy. You're messing something up. What is it?"

Coriz had the tenacity of a bulldog. And instincts, good instincts. He was right about the FBI—the bureau did not like loose ends.

Frank's thoughts went to that night in the FBI office, when Harris had warned Frank to stay out of his way. Suddenly, Frank realized that Harris didn't trust him to do just that. Worse, Harris was making sure Coriz knew the FBI had doubts about Frank.

Frank pushed up from the desk, pocketing the notepad in one swift movement. "Instead of worrying about me, Coriz, here's something you can look into." Frank handed the officer the report he had written about the destruction at Annie's.

"What's this?"

"An old woman had her property destroyed."

Coriz looked at the paper and back at Frank. "You filed a report on vandalism?"

"Just keeping you informed," Frank said, and walked away.

As soon as Frank pushed open the outer doors, the song from the lone singer enveloped him. He stared in the direction of the sound, the desert beyond the gravel lot. Even here, the capital of Navajoland, the wildness of the country encroached in a tangle of sagebrush and grotesque cholla.

Frank followed the sound, drawn more by curiosity than by concern, only to come up against a chain-link fence. One hundred yards beyond rose Window Rock, the colossal arch framing a bright turquoise sky. And at its base sat the huddled figure of a man.

Frank walked beside the fence for several sections, but didn't find a gate or any break in the steel barrier. He could see that the fence curved around to the back of the arch, seemingly encompassing the whole area. Probably a half-hour walk all the way around.

Why in the world was it fenced off? he wondered. And why was this man here, singing such a mournful, sorrowful song?

Frank stood at the fence, his fingers hanging on the steel, and listened, but what he saw was Ella and her haunted eyes. And right now, alone in Navajoland, with both the FBI and Coriz not trusting him, Frank felt his strongest connection to a woman with dark, troubled eyes.

She should be happy. She should at least be satisfied. She had Grandmother here, under the same roof. After everything Grandmother had endured, she was now safe, in a new home. But Ella couldn't find the room in her heart to be happy. She couldn't get past the grief; and she couldn't get past the memory of that night so many years ago when her whole family had been banished.

She had thought she had buried the pain too deep to ever be felt again, but from the moment the past invaded her mind in Grandmother's hogan, Ella's heart could *only* feel the pain, the grief . . . and the guilt.

To be thrown from your home, the only one you've known . . .

Ella's eyes stung with unshed tears, just as they had all day.

She longed for someone to convince her everything would be all right, that whatever mistake she had made so long ago had been forgiven.

Ella walked out the back door just as the day's last light caught the bands of color in the sand dunes. Her gaze rose to beyond the dunes, to a place beyond her vision: a far-off canyon with a one-room shack—the family's home after they left the Hopi.

She had never returned there since the day her father made the trading post home—but Eddie had. He would take a horse out for a whole day, and when he returned, he would sit so quietly. It was one of the few times he wouldn't carry on about causes or adventure, but just sit, his mind drawn inward. And Ella knew he thought of his childhood, in that stark, lonely cabin.

She had never confided to Eddie what had happened to their family, why they lived in that shack instead of with other Indians. In the beginning, he had been too young. Then later, Ella thought she had been protecting him.

Now she thought her silence had been another mistake. If Eddie had known they were outcasts, he might not have become so driven, so passionate about anything Indian, so willing to *fight* for anything Indian . . . and he might still be alive.

A sob filled Ella's throat. How many mistakes had she made, all because she wanted to believe everything would work out?

She had tried so hard to make things right. She had told herself that banishment was her punishment and from that night forward she would be neither Hopi *nor* Navajo.

She had told herself she had only to build a life where no one could find fault.

In truth, the episode at Grandmother's had tapped into

a deep need, one Ella had never acknowledged: a need for peace, for stability.

Everywhere she turned, she found conflict. It seemed everyone in her life was on one side or another.

She knew it was irrational, probably the sign of some deep-set imbalance within her, but she had the nearly overwhelming urge to yell at the whole world: *Why can't we all just get along?*

Was she so flawed as to believe in happy endings?

She walked to the corral and Chuska ambled over, presenting his nose for a rub. She leaned across the railing and wrapped her arms around his neck, snuggling her cheek into his. His coarse hair prickled her skin, tickling her, drawing a soft chuckle.

For the first time in her life, Ella wished she had someone to talk to, to confide in, but she didn't know how—and she didn't know who she could turn to.

Frank's face filled her mind. She remembered his deep, concerned voice saying "I'm a good listener." A part of her believed that—the part that had seen him cradle Grandmother; the part of her that still warmed at the thought of him gathering up some of the *alch'i'i.* She had witnessed unexpected gentleness in Frank.

She had also witnessed stark, barely controlled anger and hatred, rising so swiftly within him from a source just beneath the surface. For all his gentleness, he drew harsh lines in the sand and placed himself squarely on one side . . . and he placed Eddie squarely on the other.

Ella thought of her brother, his own anger and passion, and she remembered Frank's words: "Eddie didn't die for any noble cause, he died for a hoard of stolen art."

Was it possible? Had Eddie been so consumed he would do *anything,* even steal?

Ella glanced over her shoulder, beyond the sand dunes. If it were true, she thought, she knew of only one place where Eddie might have hidden something.

*   *   *

Frank heard the screen door of the post bang quickly open and shut, then saw Ella, in jean jacket and riding hat, stride to the corral.

"You're going for a ride at this time of evening?"

She turned to him, one hand on the corral gate. He noticed she didn't look the least surprised to see him, which, inexplicably, made him smile.

"Do you always drop in on people unannounced?"

He considered for only a fraction of a second. "Yes, I do," he answered. "I like to catch them off guard."

"Well, I'm never on guard," she answered simply and turned her attention back to the horse.

Frank was tempted to say, "That's not true." She had certainly been on guard this morning at Annie's and here at the post. But he let it go. For a reason he couldn't name, he didn't want to argue with Ella.

He walked to the corral and raised a foot on the bottom railing. "How is Annie?"

This time, Ella looked up with surprise, and she considered him for a moment before answering. "She slept most of the day."

"That's good." Frank had told himself he came to the post to ask Annie more about Tillen, but he had known that was a lie. His reason for being here was now saddling a horse and getting ready to ride off.

Frank looked across the corral to nothing in particular. He considered mentioning it was awfully dark for a ride. Then he thought he might point out she hadn't yet provided him with the inventory list. Maybe he could remind her of the trouble in the area, and she might not be safe.

Damn it, he couldn't think of what he should say.

While he considered and dismissed half a dozen responses, Ella had already readied the horse, but instead of mounting him, she tied the reins to the post and walked into the stable, emerging with another horse.

"I've thought of someplace Eddie might have hidden the stolen art. Do you want to come?"

Now it was Frank's turn to be surprised. "You just now thought of this place?"

She shook her head. "Do you ever just believe the next person?"

"Not very often," he admitted. He cut her a sideways glance and half a smile as he walked into the stable for riding gear.

Ella walked her horse out of the corral and waited for Frank, then led him north of the post, past the sand dunes.

She kept a steady, sure pace, angling her horse along narrow washes. The landscape gradually changed from scrub desert to squatty bushes of juniper and cedar, then small trees. The air was a little cooler, though so dry that the dust raised by Ella's horse still lingered in the air when Frank passed through. She didn't keep her horse to any one wash, but climbed up and over dunes and crossed parallel washes, finally choosing another to follow for a while. At one dune, Frank looked back on their path and was surprised by the tangled maze of dry washes coursing down in the direction of the trading post—now only a memory beyond the bulging dunes. He hoped to hell Ella knew where she was going.

CHAPTER
ELEVEN

The wash deepened to an arroyo, then widened twofold, and fourfold, until Frank realized he was riding into a canyon. Cliff walls sliced the sky and cut out the moonlight. The night steepened to deep black and Frank was glad he had caught a few hours of sleep back in Window Rock.

He nearly missed Ella's departure from the path. Just beyond stood a small, dilapidated adobe building. Frank slid from his horse and followed Ella to the door.

Anywhere else in the country, this little rundown place would be called a shack: It would have been made of wood and then long ago fallen to the weather and the countless passing years. But here, in the desert, the weather was like a dry-freeze, the lack of moisture in the air forever preserving even the most unremarkable, undeserving dwellings . . . like this one.

He followed Ella inside. She was immediately swallowed in total blackness. He couldn't see six inches in front of his face and hesitated before taking another step. Then he heard the strike of a match. Ella stood maybe twenty feet away, her hand lowering the flame to a candle resting on a niche in the adobe wall.

The soft glow of light did nothing to enhance the pitiful dwelling.

He heard the creak of the door. "Ella—" he started.

"It was a waste of time," she said, her hand on the door. "There's nothing here. I thought maybe . . ." She shook her head. "But I was wrong." The look on her face said she could barely wait to leave.

"Why did you think Eddie would bring the art here? What is this place?" he asked.

Ella glanced to him. "We lived here once," she answered simply, her face expressionless in the candlelight.

Frank looked around the small room. "Here? You and Eddie and your parents?"

"Yes." Ella's gaze took in the room. "And it seemed small even then. And dirty."

She looked at the ground, at one spot near the fireplace. Frank followed her gaze and saw a nondescript stone broken in half. On the adobe wall just above where the stone lay, there were flecks of rock chips imbedded in the earth as if the stone had struck there, cracked, and fallen to rest on the wooden mantel.

Frank picked up the stone that held Ella's interest, and fit the two pieces together. In the dim candlelight, he thought the whole piece faintly resembled a heart. Had it been hurled in anger? By whom? How many years had passed since?

He looked at the tiny, shabby room—a place where Ella had lived. The room where Eddie had grown up. And he saw clearly how driven they both must have been to get out.

Harsh shadows cut across the walls and a dark, earthen floor. "How did—" He didn't finish asking how anyone could live in such a hovel. He saw the answer on Ella's face, etched deep with dark memories.

"We didn't have a choice," she said. "Outcasts don't have a choice." Anger sliced through her words.

He barely recognized her voice past the anger. "What do you mean, outcasts?"

She glanced to him. The candle's light reflected against the hard black of her eyes. "I mean packed up in the middle of the night and told to leave. *Outcast*."

"Like Annie? You lost your home like Annie did?"

"Yes, just like Grandmother. Ironic, don't you think?"

Her brow creased deep, as if reacting to some inner pain.

He understood now her wild flight from Annie's. She had been reliving her own terror. He saw again the destruction of the sacred place, the horror on Annie's face, heard the anguish in her song.

His gaze went to Ella. He thought of the heart-wrenching pain of experiencing it *again*. "All of that happened to you?"

"No. It was different."

He held his breath, hoping she would confide in him. But she turned back to the door, as if to dismiss everything—this room, the past, him.

He couldn't let her. He needed her to talk to him. *Did she never let anyone help?*

He strode to her, touched her arm. "Ella, talk to me. How was it different?"

"Because it was my fault. Because I—" She stopped. She looked straight at him, her eyes haunted.

Frank's heart caught at the sight of her torment. His hands flexed, aching to grab the demons within her. "What was your fault?"

"I don't know." Her voice was small, like that of a scared child, not understanding. Her gaze went to the ground, to one spot near the fireplace. "They never explained," she continued.

He heard the confusion, her pain . . . and more than that—guilt for something she couldn't comprehend, had never comprehended . . . and yet, she had been blamed.

Gooseflesh raised in a shudder over Frank's arms. His thoughts fled to another place, his own private source of terror.

"If only I could go back, change things—" she said, barely above a whisper. "But I wouldn't know how."

Helpless panic clenched Frank's chest.

"I would make it right," she continued. "I would fix it so the mistakes don't keep happening." Her voice was now firm, determined. "That's why I came here. I hoped the art was here."

She looked at him, her gaze so frightened. "Now, where will you look? What will you do?"

Frank struggled past the emotions strangling him. "I'll try to find Tillen," he managed. "It's a good bet he was involved."

"But you don't know where he is."

"Not yet."

Her gaze ran over the room as if searching for something. "So you're back where you started."

The alarm in Ella's voice drew Frank straight. "Not quite," he offered. "Anyway, it's not for you to worry about."

"Not for me to worry about? You have no idea what my concerns are—" She abruptly stopped her outburst.

Sadness filled her eyes. She opened her mouth as if to say something, then closed it in a flat line and turned to the door.

Frank reached a hand to her, but she took another step away. God, she was shutting him out!

Frank's heart slammed hard in his chest, demanding he do something, but he didn't know what. His only experience was with Mary, but she had never lacked the drive to tell him everything on her mind. Yet Ella closed everything off inside and then erected barriers.

"Ella, it will be all right."

She whirled from the door, a look of utter disbelief on her face. "It will be all right? You're the one who ranted on about AIRO. You're the one who planted all the horror in my head and gave Jenny even more of a reason to seek them out!"

She advanced on him, fire in her eyes. Frank was so taken with the sight, he could only stare.

"Did it ever occur to you to keep your anger out of sight and keep your judgments to yourself?"

She stood inches away, her head tilted up to his, her brown cheeks pinched red, and her eyes—Frank couldn't take his gaze away from her eyes.

A shudder ran through her, reminding Frank of the af-

tershock tremors from an earthquake. She wrapped her
arms around herself, her face turning crimson. "I'm sorry,"
she said. She shook her head. "It all seems so hopeless."
Her dark eyes filled and she lifted her chin in that oh-so-
familiar brave stance, willing the tears to subside.

Frank reached a hand to her, but she pulled out of reach
and walked through the door.

She had her horse on the trail almost before Frank could
mount his. Frank pulled alongside Ella, half expecting her
to nudge her horse ahead, but she stayed even, though never
once looking over at him.

They rode in silence out of the foothills, across dunes
and down washes, single file with Ella at the lead. The
bright moonlight cast strange shadows from the junipers
and yuccas—an unreal endless landscape of gnarled
branches and pointy fronds, with no end in sight, no light
ahead beckoning them. The desert stretched seemingly forever, with no sign of human habitation, not even small
flickering lights in the distance.

And so utterly still . . . no hint of a breeze, no scurrying
of any night animals. Frank felt surrounded by stillness that
stretched in every direction and simultaneously closed in
on him.

He and Ella were absolutely alone.

An unworldly feeling swept over Frank—as if this jour-
ney might never end and he were somehow caught in an
interminable, deliberate trip to nowhere. Suddenly, Frank
wanted nothing more than to be beside Ella—he wanted a
connection in the midst of this lonely land.

The urge took hold of him—a need he hadn't experienced in years and was defenseless to control. He tried to
maneuver his horse parallel with Ella's, but the wash was
just too narrow and Ella moved languidly forward, seemingly oblivious to him.

They climbed a small hill and, Frank saw, finally, their
destination. As they neared, the air cooled, as if the earth
had tilted and they were climbing rather than descending.
He was about to deliver a swift kick to his horse when he

noticed something peculiar. Heavy, dark clouds hung over the sprawling, awkward building . . . *only* over the building.

The sight was awesome and unreal, as if that solitary post were the *target* of the storm.

Tendrils of wind curled around Frank, then grew ever more powerful, like the muscled body of a huge snake pushing against his body, pulling at the horse. Even from this distance in the dark, Frank could see that small trees surrounding the post were bent nearly to the ground.

His horse's ears pivoted, then lay back, nearly flat. Both horses resisted going any closer, sidestepping and tossing their heads. With home in sight, they planted their feet in the ground, refusing to go any closer.

Frank slid from his horse.

"Give me your reins!" he yelled to Ella above a thunderous roar.

A blast of wind knocked Frank off balance. His hand shot out to his horse and found a fistful of mane, steadying himself. He looked to Ella's horse and found an empty saddle. Then Frank saw her at the front, bent nearly in half leaning into the wind, tugging her horse forward.

Frank joined her and had to put all his weight into dragging his horse one step at a time. The wind was an angry banshee, screaming, hurling fistfuls of sand, and tossing huge clumps of tumbleweed. On a glance back, Frank saw the horses' eyes were wide with an uncontrollable fear.

"Let them go!" he yelled over to Ella. "We'll find them later!"

She turned her head only slightly, her eyes squinted against the constant assault of sand. "No! We're almost there!"

If he'd had the breath, Frank would have cursed her stubbornness, instead he grabbed the reins higher up to the bridle, forcing his horse's head down. Then he wrapped his hand around Ella's, adding his weight to her own.

Together, they made it to the stable. While shelter provided some relief from the wind, the racket of debris and loose boards banging against the wood walls was deafening.

"Go on inside! I'll settle them!" she yelled.

Did she seriously think he would leave her here? Frank shot her a quick glance of disbelief, but she was already busy tying off a halter rope to a metal eye in the wall of the stall. He did the same on his horse, then walked to the adjoining stall. He tugged at the saddle on Ella's horse just as she reached for it. Frank grabbed her hand and made her face him.

"Ella! I'll finish! Go!" He hoped a glare in his eyes matched his harsh tone. "Now!"

She gave a quick look to his horse, apparently affirming Frank had tied him down, then turned on her heels. Frank watched until he could see her reach the back door of the post.

He pulled off the saddle and checked the knots on the tie-downs, careful to stay away from the horses' stomping feet. Both horses still had a wild look. Frank spotted feed bags in the walkway and tore two long strips that he tied over their eyes. After one last check of the knots, he headed for the trading post.

His hand barely on the doorknob, Frank heard a crash and a muffled scream. He unsnapped his gun.

Shoulder to the wood, Frank slammed open the door to the kitchen, ran across the courtyard and into the hallway, only slowing down when he was close to the gallery. Adrenaline pricked his chest. He stopped a few feet short of the big room and held his breath to listen for the slightest sound, both hands on his raised gun.

"What do you want?"

Ella's cry triggered a spark at every one of Frank's nerve endings. He drew in a deep breath and stepped into the gallery, taking a few careful, soundless steps, his elbow bent, the gun barrel pointed to the ceiling.

The room was pitch-black, but he could hear shuddering breathing.

Frank swept his hand over the wall, his fingers in a silent, frantic search for a light switch. All the while he scanned the room, staring hard into the blackness for any shift of light or shadow.

Then he saw him. A flicker of white and black in the corner.

"You there! Stop!"

Ella gasped.

An ear-splitting yell rent the air. Frank spun, faced the corner, gun gripped in both hands.

The man's scream fell to a monotone note. Then he called out, "*Aha-ay-hay! Ki-ah'vakovee! Kak nam yet ka toe'!*"

The wind crashed violently against the walls. The roof beams creaked, as if supporting some great weight.

Without warning, fire erupted—a flash so bright it blinded Frank. He blinked, refocused, and saw a hideous painted face beyond the ball of fire.

Frank aimed and shot once, twice.

The face contorted in a macabre leer. Then the figure leapt through the window.

All of a sudden, it was deathly quiet. All the noise of the wind ceased. There was no more screeching, no more pounding of objects against the walls.

The abrupt, eerie silence raised the hair on Frank's arms.

"Frank, are you all right?"

He heard a crack in her voice.

"Over here, Ella. Can you turn on a light?"

He heard her footsteps. Then, suddenly, there was light . . . and everywhere he looked, destruction.

Ella stood at the front door, her hand frozen on the switch, her gaze fixed on the room. In four strides he was at Ella's side, his hand at her back. She leaned into his arm, but still stared at the gallery. Her pale expression scared Frank.

"He's gone," he said. "It's all right. *You're* all right."

"*Éiyá ndagá!*" Her eyes widened and she shook loose.

"Ella, what?"

"Grandmother!" she yelled over her shoulder as she ran from the gallery down the hallway.

Frank ran after, slowing as he approached the door and heard Ella talking with Annie. He peeked inside and saw Annie sitting up in the bed, Ella alongside, talking softly. Then she rose and joined Frank at the doorway.

"She had been asleep," she whispered, as they both walked into the hallway and she shut the door. "The shot woke her up. I told her everything was all right."

She glanced at Frank and he saw her face was still pale. He put an arm around her shoulder and walked back with her into the store, but at the archway, she came to a full stop.

She shook her head. "How? The window—"

Anxiety for her raced through Frank. She was obviously in shock.

"Ella, you're safe."

She shook loose. "No, look! The window!"

Frank whirled from her, gun poised. There was no one there. His gaze went to the window, where it froze: The window was closed.

"This doesn't make any sense," he said.

Ella already knew that.

She watched Frank walk over to inspect the window, his boot heels crunching on debris, but Ella didn't have to go any closer to know what she would find. She already knew the window was locked, just as it had been for at least twenty years.

He fiddled with the locks, pushed on the frame, ran his fingers down the seams. Ella turned away from Frank and his preoccupation with the window—her mind struggled for reality—only to have her gaze filled with the heartless devastation of the gallery.

Paintings, weavings, pottery masks, now lay in crushed, crumpled, shattered heaps on the floor. She lifted one of the rugs. The broken remains of a clay canteen hit the floor.

Ella's heart beat so close to her throat, she could barely breathe. She let the rug drop from her hands.

Why?

It was as if the violent wind outside had cycloned through the gallery like a whirling dervish, sweeping everything from the walls. Then she noticed that other items had been left untouched: solitary sculptures still stood on their pedestals, and the jewelry cases seemed intact.

But her office wasn't.

Ella's breath caught at the sight of the wreckage. Everything was upturned, overturned, or torn from the walls. The file drawers—full of receipts, correspondence, research, all the evidence of twenty years in the business—had been pulled out and thrown across the room, some crashing into far walls with a shower of adobe and paper. Even her desk stood on end, the massive, solid oak desk that had never been moved . . . until now. Ella swallowed at the thought of the brute force and power expended in this small room.

She heard Frank's heavy steps cross the gallery and stop at the office door. "Are you all right?"

The concern in his voice very nearly undid her. "I'm not hurt," she answered, glancing at him briefly, then moved away, busying herself picking up paper.

"Leave it, Ella. The police need to see this."

"I can't live like this," she said over her shoulder. But the job suddenly seemed overwhelming.

Frank's hand settled on her shoulder. "Leave it, Ella."

The warmth of his hand seeped through her, straight to some vulnerable part. He pulled her up and into his arms and her defenses cracked clean through to her heart, releasing a flood of aching emotions.

"Why?" she said aloud, but the word came out choked.

"I don't know, Ella. But I'll find out."

Frank's arms tightened around her and for the first time in so long, Ella leaned on someone. Tears stung her eyes. She blinked furiously to keep the tears from falling. Yet she felt the wetness on her cheeks. She pressed her hand to Frank's chest and saw the darkened spots on his shirt from her tears.

They were like stains: the proof of her uncontrolled

emotions. In horror, she pushed out of his embrace.

She didn't dare look into his face for fear of seeing his pity. "I'm sorry," she said quickly. "I'm really okay." She bent to the floor, tried to focus her blurry eyes on the tiny pieces of broken pottery.

Frank stood there a moment, his arms open . . . and empty. He had seen her fight her emotions. The barely controlled shudders running through her still echoed within him; for a moment, the strong, independent Ella had leaned into him.

In that moment, Frank had felt able to protect. He had wanted to hold her, press her even closer. For the first time in years, he had *wanted* the closeness, not distance.

Then suddenly, she had pulled away.

He stared at her crouched on the floor, so intent on the smallest pieces of broken pottery—methodical, all business—as if her momentary emotional lapse had occurred only in his imagination. In seconds, she had regained composure.

Without even knowing it, or thinking about it, Frank reached out to her, took hold of her arm, pulled her from the floor. He meant only to walk her out of the room, but then he saw her eyes: shimmering in dark brown, full of emotion.

Instinctively, he wrapped his arms around her. "You don't always have to be the brave one," he whispered into her hair.

A wave of tremors rippled through her beneath his hands. He squeezed harder.

"Don't." She pressed a hand to his chest.

This time, Frank didn't loosen his hold, but held her closer.

CHAPTER TWELVE

Frank ran his hand up and down Ella's back. Ragged shudders tumbled through her, the fits and starts of someone struggling for control.

"It's all right," he said. "Let it out."

"I don't know what I did wrong—" Her voice broke.

Her plea to understand the incomprehensible tapped a wellspring in Frank. Long-forgotten emotions swirled through him: protectiveness, longing, passion. They rushed on his blood to every nerve ending, a dizzying wave that tightened his arms around Ella, bent his frame to hers, spread his fingers across her back. He pulled her closer, closer, to experience more.

His need possessed him down to his bones—as if Ella, finally in his arms, sated some precious ache in his body, some craving to hold her, protect her.

God, don't let her push me away.

His lips grazed her forehead, her temple. Ella's scent of sweet grass filled his senses. His fingers followed the gentle dip of her spine, so straight, so delicate. Like her, Frank thought. When he reached the slender curve of her waist, Frank longed to encircle her, wrap his arms around her middle, lift her, press his lips to hers . . .

The headlong intensity of his desire startled Frank. His hands stilled. He realized he could barely hear for the thunder of his heart in his ears.

What the hell I am doing?

He took a staggered step back; with a finger, he raised Ella's chin to meet his gaze—completely ready to apologize, humble himself. His breath caught on the softness in her gaze.

"Are you all right?" she asked quietly.

That she would be asking him that question, when he had meant to comfort her . . . A chuckle rumbled up Frank's chest and escaped his lips.

Ella still had her hand on his chest and felt the timbre of his laugh beneath her palm. The vibration trilled through her fingers, through her pores. She flattened her hand to absorb the sensation. Frank took another step back, and Ella suddenly realized he meant to pull away.

All at once confused and embarrassed, Ella let her hand fall to her side, and sought her own composure. She had felt such comfort in his arms, surrounded by his strength— an altogether foreign phenomenon.

She averted her gaze from Frank. "I need to . . ." Her voice died as she took in the wreckage of the gallery.

"What you need is to get out of here, Ella. Get some things together."

"No." She heard the anger edging her voice and was immediately sorry, but couldn't say so. She was too confused by all the emotions running rampant through her.

He shot her a quick glance. "You're upset," he muttered as he kicked aside trash. He uncovered the phone and then yanked it by the cord from the floor.

His face was drawn tight in anger, or frustration, or maybe both.

Ella watched him punch in the numbers on the phone, then listened to him as he spoke rapidly, relating the incident and giving directions to the post, all with logical, unemotional precision. When he hung up, he let his hand rest on the receiver a few beats before looking up at her.

"All right, Ella, let's see if you can think of anyone who would do this." His face matched the composure of his voice on the phone and Ella felt a sudden sadness well within her.

"I don't know," Ella heard herself answer, though what she was really considering was Frank's transformation from consoling friend to interrogator.

"What about the words he spoke, Ella? What language was that?"

"Hopi," she said. "Something about how everyone will be crying and mourning."

"Who do you know that's Hopi?"

Ella immediately thought of Ben. Oh, he would love this. He would talk of miracles and magic. She could picture his face wide with wonder as he listened to the tale of a painted man flying through walls and locked windows.

"I know many Hopi. This is a store, remember?"

"Including Ben Talaqueptewa, right?"

Of course he knew about Ben. And she didn't miss the tone of disdain in Frank's voice.

"Including Ben."

Frank stared at her for a few beats, then paced the room. "I just don't get it. This man wrecks the place then talks about people mourning? It doesn't make any sense."

And then he leapt through a locked window.

She looked at Frank and knew he was thinking the same thing, but neither one of them said it. Somehow, just that silence comforted her: Frank had no more use for the magical than she did.

That left the two of them standing there in awkward silence, unwilling to talk about what had happened.

"Can you tell if anything is missing?"

Ella looked back at the gallery, and tried to replace, in her mind, all the art back on the walls. "I don't think anything has been taken. It's such a mess." She felt the wound reopen and quickly continued. "What was worth stealing is either still in its cases or smashed on the floor."

"But he must have been after something."

All Ella could think was that none of it made sense. No one had ever attacked the post. The store was, and had always been, the one constant in the lives of the surrounding families.

"Maybe it wasn't *supposed* to make sense," she said.

Frank circled the small office, moving papers aside with the toe of his boot. He stopped right in front of her. "Whoever did this was looking for something." He paused. "Not long after Jenny was looking for something," he added.

Ella's heart lurched. "That's just a coincidence."

Frank shook his head. "I don't buy coincidences, Ella."

"Jenny wouldn't be a part of this." Ella heard the edge in her voice.

"I didn't say she did anything, Ella." He walked toward her. "But she *was* in here and you know, in your heart, that she lied to you about looking for money."

"Jenny would *not* do this," Ella repeated.

Suddenly, the room felt too small and Ella felt too cornered. This couldn't involve Jenny. Her heart just couldn't accept it.

Ella backed away from Frank. "You're jumping to conclusions because you have nothing else to go on. And this"—she swept her arm around the room—"you have no way of explaining this. Or the window," she added pointedly.

"It was dark, Ella. We don't *know* what we saw."

"Well, I saw a man in a painted mask, he spoke Hopi, and—" Ella glanced to the window. She still couldn't believe what she'd seen. She faced Frank. "And none of that has anything to do with Jenny."

"*Sitsóí?* What about Jenny?" It was Grandmother.

Ella jerked her head to the hallway and back at the mess in the gallery. *Sáni* shouldn't see this. The old woman would only worry.

"Coming," Ella called out and hurried across the gallery.

Sáni already stood in the doorway, staring at the destruction, the wrinkles in her face deep with concern.

"*Sitsóí,* are you all right?"

"It's okay, Grandmother." Ella put a hand to *Sáni*'s elbow and tried to guide the old woman back to bed. But *Sáni* wouldn't budge.

"Who did this, child?" she murmured.

"A burglar," Ella said and threw a glance to Frank, one she hoped would implore him to be quiet.

She realized she needn't have bothered: He was gazing at Grandmother with sincere concern in his eyes.

"A burglar would do this?" *Sáni*'s tone was incredulous. She took a few steps into the gallery. "Why? Why to you?"

Ella's throat tightened around the injustice. She shook her head, swallowed, fought to find something rational to say to assure *Sáni*.

"Burglars don't much care what they destroy, Annie," Frank said.

Ella looked at Frank. He gave a small shrug of his shoulders.

"Frank's right, Grandmother."

"Burglars *steal* things, child. Not destroy. Agent Reardon would know that, too, I would think."

Ella and Frank exchanged glances over Grandmother's head.

"Maybe this one didn't know the rules," Frank said dryly.

"Sometimes things just don't make sense, Grandmother."

Sáni took a few steps into the room, then turned and faced them both. "I thought you were an investigator," she said to Frank.

Frank smiled. "I am, Annie. I'll find out who did this, I assure you."

"Grandmother, it's really not as bad as it looks. I'll clean the gallery and everything will be fine."

"Some things cannot just be cleaned up." *Sáni* glanced to Ella, then away.

Ella saw the flash of pain and knew Grandmother thought of the destroyed *alch'i'i*. Ella's own heart tore at the wound Grandmother now bore.

"Come on, Grandmother, I'll help you back to bed."

Sáni stopped in front of Frank and held his arm with her small, old fingers. "When you investigate, Agent Reardon, you remember that there is always a reason.''

Ella thought of the painted man standing just over there, offering words of warning . . . *everyone will be crying and mourning.*

She thought of Grandmother's heart-wrenching wails at the *alch'i'i.*

Was the man right? Was there even more sorrow to come?

Her mind went to Jenny. Ella's heart leapt.

A soft touch at her arm sent a jolt through Ella.

''What is it, Ella? What are you thinking?''

Ella looked up at Frank and his strong, reassuring face. He had promised to keep Jenny safe. But could he? Did he even know where to begin?

She could feel Grandmother's gaze on her and Ella forced herself to look confident. ''I'm just thinking I should put Grandmother to bed.'' She took *Sáni*'s arm. ''You need to rest.''

Grandmother shuffled down the hallway, her shoulders bent, her head down. But Ella could hear her mumble, ''. . . destruction.''

At the door to her room *Sáni* stopped and grabbed Ella's arm.

''I like Agent Reardon, child, but he is wrong about this. This was not a burglar.'' *Sáni's* old eyes clouded. ''I'm afraid I caused this. I think whoever was mad at me is now mad at you.'' Her voice cracked.

Grandmother blamed herself?

Ella wrapped her arms around *Sáni*, hugged her, held on to her. ''No, *Sáni*, this is not because of you.'' Ella's throat tightened around a knot of emotions. ''You didn't do anything wrong.'' She could barely get the words out.

She guided Grandmother into the room and settled her on the bed. The bedsprings creaked beneath her weight. Ella pulled the covers over *Sáni*. She gazed down at her grandmother—the old woman's face was deeply lined with worry. ''You didn't do anything wrong,'' she said again. And she would have repeated the words a hundred times, a thousand times, all night, to be sure Grandmother heard and believed . . . and never felt guilty.

Ella stood up from the bed, turned off the bedside lamp, and walked to the door.

"A burglar did not do this," Grandmother whispered into the darkness.

No, Ella thought. A burglar did not do this.

But someone did. Someone who spoke Hopi.

Unbidden, her thoughts went to Ben. Would he know what this was about? He was, in fact, of everyone she knew, the most mysterious—showing up unexpectedly with a smile on his face, then just as abruptly disappearing again into any one of a dozen guises he inhabited: as a tourist guide, a trader, a con man. He might even go back to Hopiland—to the village of Hoteville, where it was rumored he held some important position. Of anyone Ella might consider, Ben was the most likely to know something.

She could go to him. Tonight even. Right now. She could tell Frank . . .

Ella's hand stilled on the doorknob. She couldn't forget that Frank considered Ben a criminal. Frank wouldn't let her go to Ben alone, and if she took Frank along, Frank could very well arrest Ben before he could tell Ella anything. For all Ella knew, Ben might even lie, if forced to talk in front of Frank.

No, she would go to Ben herself, without Frank, without even telling Frank. In fact, she would have to just walk out the back door and leave, or she would have to face Frank's questions, his keen eyes, his strong face . . .

An odd flutter twirled through her stomach.

She didn't want to deceive Frank. She also didn't see that she had a choice.

Ella made a decision.

She looked over at *Sáni,* whose breathing had already slowed. Ella tiptoed back to the bedside table and flicked on the light. She rummaged through the top drawer, but couldn't find anything to write on. She pulled several tissues from the box, smoothed them out on the table, and dug for a pencil from her pocket, glancing over her shoulder every few seconds at the door. Now that she had made up her mind, her pulse quickened at every noise she heard from the hallway.

Quickly, she wrote a note for Grandmother, then wasted several precious moments deciding where to put it. She finally decided on tucking them into *Sáni*'s skirt pocket.

That done, she walked quickly to the door, opened it, and peeked down the hallway to the gallery.

The front door chime sounded, startling her so that her pulse took off. Ella strained to hear who was there. Frank greeted somebody, another man. She was able to catch a few words and soon realized it must be the police Frank had called.

That was good. Frank would be busy, at least for a while, giving the report.

Ella took a deep breath, stepped out into the hallway, quietly closing Grandmother's door. Then she fled to the courtyard and out the back door. She idled the truck out of the shelter, around the back of the store to an arroyo on the side, the whole time navigating without the headlights.

Half a mile away, she pulled onto the dirt road.

She checked the rearview mirror and saw only the night behind her. She had done it.

On the heels of that thought, she felt a wave of remorse for not confiding in Frank. What would he think of her now?

Tikui hummed the ancient song as she walked down the road—just as she had for the past day and the night before that. For hours and hours she had walked, the song rising and falling on her breath, her weary footsteps shuffling the beat. Now the song owned her, pulling her forward to Hopiland—to the ancient village of Hoteville—giving her legs strength, her lungs air. If she stopped walking, the song would die and so would all hope for winning the battle.

In the song was the power to reach Hopi and walk into the village. No one could stop the one who dared sing the hymn of *Balolokong*.

The night rippled with light along the horizon—waves of demonic brightening behind a curtain of threatening clouds. It was as if thunder were now visual, its echoes undulating light like a silent, deadly snake uncurling in the darkness.

From the corner of her eye, Tikui saw coils of light whip along the distant ground. The hair rose on Tikui's arms. The earth rumbled beneath her feet. Tikui stumbled. Her voice faltered. In that instant of silence, the ground heaved with the violence of an earthquake.

She stared ahead, sang louder, her exhausted voice cracking, every ounce of her strength given to keeping the song alive.

Ella had no idea where to find Ben and only one place to look: Hopiland, a place she had not been since she was a child. If she didn't find him there, or find someone who could tell her where he was, she would be at a dead end.

She ignored the tightening in her chest, telling herself it was only concern over her need to find Ben, that she was overly tired and overwrought from everything that had happened.

It had nothing to do with her destination.

But she knew that was a lie.

She stared into the pitch-black night ahead of her. Fear built in her with the threat of a nightmare. Her knuckles gripping the steering wheel were white. Her gaze flitted to every passing mile marker—now only ninety-five miles, now only ninety-four miles, now only ninety-three, taking her closer to the brink of something terrible, a place where something horrible had happened.

A place where people had to escape in the dead of night to save their lives . . . with only bonfires lighting the way.

A diesel horn blasted through Ella's thoughts. A pair of headlights bore down the highway straight for her. Wildly, she swerved back to her lane, overshot, and sped onto the shoulder. Her heart pounded. Tires slid from asphalt to sand, spewing rocks.

Ella brought the truck to a grinding halt. She pressed a hand to her chest, fingers splayed across her beating heart, and closed her eyes against the memory.

Gradually, the images dissolved, receding into the past, but she couldn't rid herself of the terrible fear. It clung to her, gripping her heart, tearing through her veins.

This was a mistake, going back to Hopi. They didn't want her there. She didn't belong there. She had no right to go there and ask for help.

A shimmer of light streaked across the horizon. Heat lightning, Ella told herself, except it was unlike any she had seen: It hugged the earth in a tight, bright glow, as if that were the edge between day and night.

Ella blinked. The light vanished, then reappeared, closer, and closer, broader, advancing toward her.

Her hands went to the steering wheel, turned it hard to curve back onto the road and return home.

"Where are you going?"

Ella jerked at the sound of a voice. An old Indian woman stood at the passenger side, her hand on the window frame. She swayed slightly to and fro as if rocking a child . . . and she was humming.

"Where—" The rest of the sentence died in Ella's thoughts. She could only stare at what had to be an apparition.

"You are going to Hopiland, yes?" asked the woman in mid-hum, then started again with the monotone.

"I was," Ella answered.

The woman smiled. Hundreds of wrinkles spread across her face. "Good, good. You can give me a ride."

Before Ella could object, the woman opened the door and climbed onto the seat. The scents of the desert filled the cab: Dry sand, fresh wind, and sweet grass swirled around Ella.

The Indian sat on the edge of the bench, still humming

quietly as you would a lullaby, her small feet planted on the floor. A long, dirty brown dress hung loose over her gaunt frame. Stark white hair peeked from beneath a woolen shawl draped across her head and thrown over her shoulders. She might be Hopi—though Ella couldn't be sure—and she looked to be at least ninety years old.

What in the world was this old woman doing in the middle of nowhere?

"Where did you come from?" Ella asked.

"*Tségháhodzáni,*" she answered in Navajo.

"Window Rock?"

The little woman smiled at Ella.

"You're Navajo," Ella said, somewhat surprised.

"No, but you do not speak Hopi, do you?"

Ella blinked. "So you're Hopi?"

Sadness passed over the woman's face. "People of peace," she murmured. "I hope this is true."

Ella shook her head in confusion. "Please, what is your name?"

"Tikui."

Ella's heart leapt to her throat. *Outcast.* The name the Hopi had given Ella's mother because she was Navajo.

The childhood memories surged. She saw her mother at a doorway facing a crowd of people. She looked so tall, so brave. But then someone pointed past her, to Ella. Then her mother whirled and grabbed her up in a whoosh of air, so fast, scaring Ella. She could feel the bite of her mother's short nails through cotton. But it was the fear in her mother's eyes that seared the memory on Ella's heart.

And it was all Ella's fault. Because of what she had done. Because she had not been a good girl. Now everyone was angry.

Their anger surrounded her, suffocated her. She buried her face in her mother's chest. And was afraid, so afraid.

A hand caressed Ella's arm, spreading warmth, sending the chill fleeing, and in its wake, a feeling of safety flooded Ella.

She looked at Tikui. "Why would you want to go back there?" The words fell from Ella's lips.

"It's home," she said simply.

She was so old, so alone, and walking the roads at night to return to Hoteville, where they had obviously not wanted her. Suddenly, Ella felt the need to comfort Tikui. "You don't have to go there. Home is where *you* want it."

Tikui smiled. "We have only one home. Hopi is mine. I need to be there."

Ella had already made her decision to go back to the store. She would find another way to reach Ben. She did *not* want to go to Hoteville.

But she couldn't leave this woman out on the road at night.

"I'll drive you to Hoteville," she heard herself say.

The smile on Tikui's face broadened. The sky gave a last bright flash.

"Look at that," Tikui said.

Ella saw only pitch-black night. "The heat lightning is gone."

Tikui stared at the dead calm. The great serpent had been silenced, not by her, not by her song. She gazed in awe at the woman beside her.

"What is your name?"

"Ella Honanie."

"You're Hopi!"

"No."

"Then you are Navajo?"

"No, I'm neither."

Tikui wondered at the hard, fast answer.

"I own a store near Shonto," Ella said.

She stared straight ahead as she pulled the truck onto the highway.

Tikui wondered about this young woman who would admit to being neither Hopi nor Navajo. Yet, she had seen the pain on Ella's face when Tikui had said her own name—a stark, unprotected pain provoked by a word . . . "outcast."

Tikui gazed out the window. The clouds were gone and stars reached to the earth. It was the picture of serenity.

And Tikui knew this woman had more to do with peace than herself. For the first time in many nights, she truly felt strong enough to face *Balolokong*.

"It's time," she murmured.

CHAPTER THIRTEEN

Can you describe the intruder for me, Agent Reardon?"

"It was dark."

"You said that. You also said he was standing by that window over there." Officer Coriz glanced up from his notes. "There was a full moon tonight. But you can't give height, weight, hair color, anything."

Frank knew Coriz expected a response. He might even hope for an embarrassed explanation from this FBI agent who had absolutely no description of the perpetrator. But Frank was not about to mention the grotesquely painted face, the balls of fire, or how the man had leapt through the window . . . a closed window.

At the worst, this Navajo officer would go with his preconceived notions: The FBI were clueless on the res. Frank could live with that. Hell, it was the assumed position.

He stared back and didn't say a word.

Coriz broke the stare first and went back to his notes. "You said he spoke Hopi."

"Something about everyone will be crying and mourning."

"I don't suppose you'd know why he said that, would you?"

"No, Officer Coriz, I wouldn't."

"I see." Coriz strolled over to the bear sculpture, standing pristine amid the debris. "So what we have here, according to you, is someone who destroyed certain things, muttered in Hopi, and left.''

Frank knew the officer didn't buy the story. Hell, *he* didn't buy the story.

''How about Miss Honanie? Would she know?''

''She didn't seem to.''

''Do you think I could ask her myself?''

''She was pretty upset, Coriz.'' Frank slid a glance to the hallway and Annie's bedroom. He hoped she was all right. ''If it's necessary, she can come talk to you later today.''

''Has she mentioned other break-ins?''

''No.''

''Any unhappy customers? Tourists or Indian?''

''She didn't say.''

''Would she tell you, Agent Reardon?'' Coriz slanted a studied glance up to Frank.

Frank thought of all Ella had told him—secrets that caused her so much pain Frank was sure she had not risked mentioning them often yet she had shared them with him.

''I think so,'' he finally answered. He looked to Coriz and found the officer staring at him.

''Interesting,'' Coriz said. He raised his brow. ''By the way, how is the grandmother?''

''Better. Ella's with her now.''

''Terrible thing that happened.''

Coriz still stared at Frank, his black eyes so intensely focused as if to measure even the slightest reaction.

''Yes,'' Frank agreed. ''It was terrible.''

''Heartless and cruel,'' Coriz added, his gaze unwavering.

Frank had no idea of what exactly Coriz was after.

''Weren't those the words you used? Heartless and cruel?'' Coriz pulled a paper from his pocket, unfolded it, read silently for a moment, then, ''Yes, here it is. Under 'Detail of Destruction' you wrote, 'burial ground trampled; family bones, childrens' bones, kicked around, crushed to powder; heartless and cruel destruction of a private place.' '' He looked up at Frank.

Frank didn't remember writing those words, though he recalled only too clearly the heart-wrenching pain in Annie's wails, the sadness he'd felt . . . the song of love Annie sang for the remains.

"You *did* write this, Agent Reardon?"

Frank glanced to Coriz. "Yes, Officer, I wrote the report. And have you investigated?"

"You know, I find this choice of words very interesting," Coriz said, still looking at the report. "Not your normal unemotional, detached account. Is this the new, kinder FBI?"

Frank only stared back.

Coriz looked up and smiled. "No, I don't think it's a new FBI," he said, ignoring Frank and answering his own question. "Is it?" His eyes narrowed on Frank.

"You know, you're wasting a lot of time on two words, Coriz."

Coriz ran a hand through thick black hair. "What do you know about the Hopi–Navajo land dispute, Reardon?"

"Nothing."

Coriz stared, unblinking.

Frank sighed. "Just what I saw at Annie's."

"You saw that it's more than just land, that it involves a family's whole tradition."

"Is this leading somewhere, Coriz?"

Coriz drew a deep breath. "The point is, Reardon, emotions are high. And when emotions are high, people are vulnerable to powerful words, words proclaiming rights, religious freedom, liberty."

Reardon knew those words. He stared across the room, but he didn't see the gallery. What he saw were Indians, a crowd of them standing on a windblown hill, their fists raised to the sky, their features etched in defiance . . . and twisted with hatred.

They had spoken about noble causes, but it was all about

hate; hate born of poverty, unemployment, alcoholism—
every bit of it blamed on the white man's government.

He could hear Mary's voice, her dedication to their
cause, her understanding and sympathy.

But God help the white person who crossed the line and
tried to talk peace. The peacemaker didn't have a prayer
against all that hate.

"You were at Red Earth, right?"

Frank jerked his gaze to Coriz, expecting to see a glint
of disdain, even hatred, in the Navajo's eyes. Instead, a
worried man looked back, his brows creased in concern.

"What makes you ask that, Coriz?"

"There's talk."

Frank's gut knotted in frustrated anger . . . and guilt.
"There's always talk," he muttered. He would never escape the talk.

Frank walked behind the counter and grabbed the
broom.

"More than usual," Coriz added.

"Really? Well, I don't give a damn, Coriz." Frank took
a violent sweep with the broom.

"I see. I thought—" Coriz walked to the door, obviously ready to leave.

"You thought what, Coriz? That because of two words
on a report I was a sorry son of a bitch and ready to apologize? You can go to hell."

Coriz looked surprised, then laughed out loud. "You
really are a sorry son of a bitch. This isn't about you, Reardon."

"But I thought—"

"You thought I meant you when I said there's talk? Oh,
there's plenty of talk about you. The agent who screwed
things up at Red Earth. Agents dead. Wife dead. AIRO
leaders who got away."

Frank's blood ran hot. He gripped the broom so tight,
his fingers tingled. "Get to your point, Coriz." Frank's
tone held a warning.

"That *is* the point. Those AIRO leaders you didn't get in South Dakota are now here in Arizona."

"I'm not surprised." But he was surprised this Navajo cop was talking to him about AIRO.

The silence stretched.

"Is that it, Coriz?" he asked, his tone careful.

Coriz looked up, his gaze unfocused. "No, that's not all of it," he said, his tone heavy with concern. He gazed off to the side, his brow furrowed.

Frank wondered what weighed so heavily on this Navajo's mind. *Something* had Coriz stuck in one place—unable to leave, unable to say what he was thinking.

"It's rumors I'm hearing," Coriz said finally.

"About what?"

"A show of sovereignty."

Frank's instincts sparked, seeking a connection. "And just who is talking?" Frank nailed Coriz with the same look he would use in interrogation—the stare that demanded truth.

Coriz returned the look, his gaze now intense, as if seeking an answer in Frank.

For a moment, neither one spoke—two cops sizing each other up.

"At the station," Coriz said. He didn't blink or look away, his gaze still pinned on Frank.

Frank took in the admission: Navajo cops talking sovereignty, maybe even insurrection? He set the broom against the counter. "What are they saying, Coriz?"

"Nothing specific, but I have heard AIRO mentioned."

"In what way?"

Coriz hesitated. Frank held his breath, sure for an instant the cop was about to turn and head out the door before he said another word. "Recruiting," Coriz said. "I've even been approached."

"Recruiting? AIRO is recruiting members from Navajo Law Enforcement?"

"It seems so."

"It seems so? You're pretty damn calm about it!"

"I don't jump to conclusions."

"Meanwhile, AIRO is infiltrating your force." Frank's blood pumped hot. Coriz was studying him and Frank tried to ease the intensity he knew was in his eyes, but he couldn't. They filled with the bloody vision of the Red Earth disaster. He squeezed his eyes shut against the images, but his thoughts rang with the rumors of collaboration. Some had said South Dakota tribal cops had warned AIRO; others accused an FBI undercover agent of turning. In the end, they had lost two agents, five civilians, and his Mary lay dead.

Taking a deep breath, Frank refocused on Coriz. "If you didn't jump to conclusions, Coriz, then why are you telling me all this?"

Coriz's gaze didn't waver. "Because I need to ask you what part the FBI is playing in this."

"The FBI doesn't recruit for AIRO."

"But they do stand by and watch, don't they? In fact, they even do some sideline encouraging, just to see where it leads, right?" Coriz's eyes flickered with something close to barely concealed hatred—a hatred of cowardly instigators. It was a hatred Frank understood.

"Why would you think for a second that if I knew anything I would tell you?"

Coriz's black eyes narrowed. "Because the FBI doesn't trust you. Because I think you have something to prove. And because I think you *do* know something."

Every one of Frank's muscles tensed against the dead-on assault.

"I have a question for you, Reardon. Why would the FBI plant that complaint on Ben Talaqueptewa?"

"What—"

"You heard me." The boulder of a man crossed the room to Frank. The floorboards creaked beneath his steps. "The complaint by Joe Miller? The one about illegal trafficking of Indian arts?"

Frank's breath came tight. "What do you mean, planted?"

"Just what I said. Never did find any paperwork. Then something you said, made me think."

Coriz waited, expectantly.

Frank bit. "I don't remember accusing the FBI, Coriz."

"You said the complaint couldn't just appear on the computer. Got me to thinking. I put one of our computer whiz kids on it and bingo. He discovered it was sent from another system using FBI codes."

Frank couldn't believe what he was hearing. Why would the FBI plant a record on Talaqueptewa?

"Did you plant the information, Reardon?"

Frank's hand flexed on the broom handle. He saw Coriz's glance and Frank, with deliberation, set the broom against the wall, then faced Coriz. "What do you think?"

The sharp black of Coriz's eyes sparked, like a knife struck on stone. "Are you the enemy, Reardon?"

Frank drew a harsh breath. "That's the problem, Coriz. You think the enemy must be white."

"And you don't get it, do you? AIRO isn't the enemy. We *know* what they're up to. What I don't know is what the FBI is doing."

"You know what AIRO is up to, Coriz? Are you one of the conspirators?"

"If I were, would I even be talking to you?"

Frank ran a frustrated hand through his hair and paced to the end of the gallery.

At the same time, Coriz let out a breath. "I'm talking to you because I think you're in the middle of something, I just don't know what."

Frank whirled on Coriz. "What the hell are you saying?"

"For one, Eddie Honanie's murder investigation. Then there's the false complaint on Ben Talaqueptewa. The destruction at Annie Ben's. Now this." He gestured to the wreckage surrounding them.

"The one common denominator? You. Hell, yes, I think you're in the middle of something. You want to start talking?"

Frank wasn't listening. His thoughts were racing over what he knew of Eddie's murder—bits and pieces that wouldn't fit together any more than the broken pottery at his feet. Eddie stole the art; Eddie and Tillen were connected to AIRO; and the FBI had undercover working AIRO. That much Frank knew for sure.

He also knew AIRO had killed Eddie. He just couldn't prove it.

Frank brushed past Coriz toward the door.

"Where are you going?"

"To Phoenix," Frank said, without even knowing exactly what he would do. But there had to be information he had missed. A way to find Talaqueptewa, Tillen, or Flint . . . or maybe face down Harris. The prospect made him smile.

"You're going to the FBI."

"To their computers, Coriz."

Coriz grabbed Frank's arm. "So you can spill your guts to your bosses? I didn't confide in you, Reardon, just to see it all blow up on the tribe."

"What did you think I was going to do, Coriz? Drive back to Tribal Headquarters with you? And tell them what? That half of them could be involved with AIRO? Or maybe you thought I would spy on the FBI and pass along information to you. Sorry to disappoint you, Coriz, but you had me figured wrong. Now let go."

But Coriz's grip tightened. "I had you figured for a smart man, and guess what? I was wrong. You want to win at whatever game you're playing? You're on the wrong team. Trusting the wrong people."

"I'll bear that in mind." Frank bit the words out and with a sharp twist freed his arm.

"Bear this in mind, too: This isn't about a warehouse of stolen art anymore, Reardon."

Frank turned and looked at Coriz. The Navajo cop stared

back, his reddish-brown features expressionless as if he had truly expected no more of this FBI agent than to be un-cooperative, distrustful, and, ultimately, a disappointment. And still, Coriz had confided in him. Why?

Frank decided Coriz deserved one more bit of infor-mation. "By the way, the intruder had a painted face and body."

The news seemed to startle Coriz; his brows rose over widened eyes. "Painted how?"

"Black, white, and red. Wide, grotesque lines, like some sort of a monster."

Coriz's mouth dropped open slightly. He shook his head. "That can't be. Did you see his hands?"

"No."

Coriz kept shaking his head.

"What is it, Coriz? You know this guy?"

"No. It's just that I heard rumors. But they have to be wrong. It's a bad time for a snake dance."

Frank did not want to hear about any dance that included snakes, but he had to ask. "Why?"

Coriz paced the room. "It's held in late summer to thank the snakes for rain and send them back to the underground with messages for the ancestors. Not now, in the spring, when the ceremony can bring floods." He stared at Frank, a stricken look on his face.

"A cop scared of a little rain?"

"No, Reardon. A Navajo scared of a Hopi ceremony." Fear etched Coriz's face. Then he turned and continued pacing. "They can't do the snake dance," he murmured. "The snakes are full of poison now."

An eerie sense of foreboding slid through Frank.

"It's some sort of show of power," Coriz continued, talking as he paced.

"It was just one man, Coriz. Aren't you jumping to conclusions?"

But Coriz didn't stop pacing. "They won in the courts. Why now?"

"Coriz—"

Coriz was shaking his head and pacing. "They're marshaling their forces for a confrontation."

The foreboding spread through Frank in a skittering of icy pinpricks. "What confrontation, Coriz? What haven't you told me?"

"It doesn't make any sense." Coriz wouldn't stop pacing. "The only confrontation I've heard about is the show of sovereignty by AIRO. Something to do with the highways."

"What about the highways?"

Coriz let out a breath. "There's talk of closing all the roads at the boundaries of the res. Including the highways."

Frank advanced on the Navajo. "Does the tribe know about this?"

"I'm afraid so."

"Do you people even care you're playing right into the hands of AIRO?"

Coriz's eyes flared. "Some would say it's the white man who has pushed us in that direction." Coriz waved a hand in the air as if dismissing something insignificant. "That's not the point, Reardon. Why would the Hopi be doing a dance for power now?"

"Better question, Coriz, is why would a Hopi man appear here, at Ella's?"

Suddenly, Coriz stopped pacing. "What was it the man said?"

"That everyone would be crying and mourning."

Coriz faced Frank. His black eyes were like sharp flints of jet, piercing Frank with their intensity. "What else aren't you telling me? Don't hold back, Reardon." He crossed the room to Frank. "Was he carrying anything? Anything unusual?"

Frank thought of the ball of fire and immediately dismissed it. That had to have been his imagination. He refocused on Coriz and found the cop studying him, as if Frank's thoughts were written on his face. He shrugged. "It was dark."

Coriz stared. "Listen to me, you son of a bitch. I don't

know if you're deliberately difficult or just ignorant." He advanced on Frank. "Or maybe it's the Indian *beliefs* you think are stupid."

"What I think is stupid," Frank said quietly, "is a cop who threatens an FBI agent."

Coriz took a deep breath and stepped back, his boot heel crunching on broken pottery. "Look around you, Reardon. You don't think this was done by a burglar." He turned slowly in place. "They tear things off the walls but leave the jewelry untouched?"

He walked toward the office. "And you can't possibly think that one man did *this*." He gestured to the total upheaval. "He would need superhuman powers."

Frank's gaze slid over the file cabinet and upturned desk. He had already considered everything Coriz was saying. He knew that neither of the explanations were possible. But that left him with no rational answer.

"Do you remember what Tikui said?" Coriz's voice came from right behind Frank, as if breathed down his neck.

Frank turned. "That crazy woman?"

"A *Hopi* crazy woman," Coriz corrected. "She said, '*Balolokong* is angry.' Do you know who *Balolokong* is?" he continued. "He's the underground serpent. He rules the snakes and the water and the underworld."

"You sound like you believe all this, Coriz."

Coriz seemed not to even hear him. " 'He is calling the ones with fire,' " Coriz intoned, repeating Tikui's words.

Frank's heart jumped at the mention of fire. He drew a silent breath. "For crissakes, Coriz, she lives in a cave. If you talked to her now, she'd be rambling on about flying saucers and aliens."

Coriz gave Frank a sharp look. "I *can't* talk to her now. She's gone. Walked out of the hospital yesterday." He walked straight to Frank. "The last thing Tikui said to you was that you must return the Hopi tablet or the sorcerers cannot be stopped." He paused, then, "The man who came here and did all this?" He gestured to the destruction around him. "That man wasn't talking to Ella, Reardon. He was talking to you."

Frank saw the painted man, the ball of fire dancing in his hands. His mind leapt to Tikui, her old hand gripping his arm, her black eyes staring into his. *Are you the one?*

He shook his head to dispel the images.

She was crazy. Coriz was crazy to even be talking about sorcerers and underground serpents.

Frank found himself in the corner, standing by the window . . . a closed, locked window. He traced the unbroken seal with his fingers. Frank could feel Coriz's gaze on him from across the room. He dropped his hand to his side and faced the Navajo. "Whoever did this is not some sorcerer."

Frank crossed the room, opened the door, and stood there, his gaze on Coriz. "We're through here, Coriz," he said finally. "Let me know what you find out about the break-in."

Coriz accepted the rebuff with a solemn shake of his head. Then he stopped midway out the door and looked back. "Take my advice, white man, and stay away from Hopiland."

"No problem," Frank answered and swung the door closed behind Coriz.

CHAPTER
FOURTEEN

Frank watched as Coriz swung his Jeep back and away from the gallery, the headlights slicing through the windows, one after another. The strobe of light echoed Frank's thoughts—one on top of the next, rapid-fire, yet disconnected. His mind would light on one only to be distracted by another. How in hell had a murder and stolen art dragged Frank right back into the middle of chaos, dealing with AIRO conspiracies and militants?

He shook his head in frustration . . . and anger. He hadn't wanted to come here in the first place, dammit. For years, he had kept himself as far off Indian land as possible—away from their problems, their disputes. As far as he was concerned, that's what borders were for, and he had made a concerted effort to stay on his side of the line. How had his investigation of Eddie's murder entangled Frank in Indian disputes over land and legends of Hopi sorcerers?

His gaze took in the destruction around him—the destruction of Ella's store, her livelihood. Was Coriz right? Had the painted man's message been for Frank, not Ella? Had Frank, somehow, visited all this destruction on her?

A wave of irrational panic washed over him, a riptide of memories sucking him under, forcing him to relive the same hell—right down to the detail of involving someone important to him.

Frank's thoughts closed on Ella. When had she become important? When had he begun thinking of her that way?

What kind of fool was he, anyway, to have his thoughts distracted by a woman on the res? She was the last one he should be interested in. And he was exactly the wrong one to be thinking about her.

Frank kicked aside shards of pottery and jammed a hand through his hair. He glanced down the hallway to Annie's bedroom.

Just where the hell *was* Ella?

He strode down the hallway, then slowed at Annie's door and forced his hands easy on the doorknob, slipping the door open as quietly as he could. Moonlight shone in through the window . . . on just Annie. Frank's gaze took in every corner, but he didn't see Ella.

He closed the door and stood for a second, not believing she really wasn't there. He opened the door directly across and found what must be Ella's bedroom, but it was empty, as well. His heart pumping, temper rising, he left the hallway and crossed the courtyard into the kitchen. Still no Ella.

His frustration ricocheted straight to Ella and fear sliced cold through his veins. Where was she and what was she doing?

His chest pricked with an instant rush of adrenaline. He didn't have a clue what Ella was up to because she had shut him out; she didn't trust him.

He saw the past repeating itself right before his eyes. He couldn't be facing this, not again. Damn it to hell, he would *not* let that happen.

Frank yanked open the front door and stepped into the night. A blanket of stars stretched to cold black ground. A serene picture if you believed in such things as tranquility.

Frank knew better. Indian land was not the boundary of some benign collective for the common good. It was a sanctuary for murderers, where enemies could hide, where killers were treated as heroes . . . and dark-eyed silence concealed hidden agendas.

A sudden chill spidered down Frank's back.

He climbed into his car and pulled away from the post.

Coriz might be right: Frank was a man without friends; but he wasn't without resources.

Frank geared down to turn left off the back road onto the paved two-lane, heading to Phoenix. At the same instant, he felt the cold cylinder of a gun at his neck.

"Turn right."

Frank jerked his gaze to the rearview mirror and found himself staring into the hard black eyes of Ben Talaqueptewa.

Frank leveled his own stare. "It's really not smart to kidnap a federal agent, Talaqueptewa."

"Tonight you are not a federal agent, Frank Reardon. Tonight, you are a white man, alone on the res."

The gun pressed hard against Frank. "Now turn right, Frank Reardon."

"Where are we going?"

"To Hoteville."

Frank glanced between the mirror and the highway, trying to keep at least intermittent eye contact with the Hopi as he slid his left hand to his waist and the handle of his gun. "What is it you want, Talaqueptewa?"

"You say my name very good!"

The son of a bitch was actually smiling back at him. "What do you want?" he repeated.

"First hand me your gun."

"I'm not armed."

The gun barrel pressed hard into Frank's neck. "Put both your hands on the wheel."

Frank complied.

"You have been looking for me, no? So now I find you." Talaqueptewa gave a little laugh as if he had just won a game of hide-and-seek.

Frank decided to play along. "Yes, you found me," he conceded. "Why don't I pull over so we can talk?"

"We can talk while you drive. It is a long way to Hoteville."

"It would be easier if I didn't have to watch the road," Frank pointed out.

"I will start," he said helpfully. "Did you tell the Navajo Coriz about the Yaponcha?"

Frank's gaze jerked to Talaqueptewa. The Hopi was still smiling, but Frank caught a measured look in his eye. "The what?" he asked.

"The sorcerer who came to visit you," he answered matter-of-factly.

"I'm afraid you have the wrong information, Talaqueptewa. No sorcerers in this part of the universe. At least not until Halloween."

"So you didn't tell Coriz. That is good."

"Just what the hell is your interest in this so-called sorcerer?"

"So-called? Oh, my friend, you have a long way to go. And not so much time."

The gloom in the Hopi's voice drew Frank's gaze. Frank saw the same deep concern there that he had seen in Coriz's eyes.

Talaqueptewa sighed. "Never mind." His voice cleared. "What I must know is, have you found the other half of the broken tablet?"

What was with this tablet? Tikui and Talaqueptewa: a crazy woman and a con man, both talking about some Hopi tablet. Frank ignored the question and asked his own. "Why do you want to know about the tablet, Talaqueptewa?"

Talaqueptewa gave a soft chuckle. "Save your strategy, Frank Reardon. You will need it later."

The implied threat skidded over Frank's skin.

"Where is the tablet?" the Hopi repeated.

"And if I have it, why would I tell you?"

"There is so much he doesn't know," the Hopi murmured as if talking to someone else.

"So, why don't you enlighten me?"

'Yes! A story for the ride! That is a good idea." The Hopi chuckled, but the gun remained firmly planted in Frank's neck.

"Let's see, did you know the whites were the last clan

to emerge? No, I'm sure you didn't. I should start at the beginning." Ben gave a sigh. "The Hopi were the first to emerge from the third world to this one. Every other clan followed, including the white people's clan. The *Bahanas,* they were called. They were so frantic to escape the third world, they didn't listen to Spider Grandmother. That's how one of the witches got into the fourth world. So the whites are to blame."

"As usual." Frustration crawled over Frank.

"They are also the ones who can set things right."

"Both the blame and the responsibility. How convenient."

"The blame, yes. And the honor," Talaqueptewa corrected.

Frank's gaze caught with Talaqueptewa's and he saw an unexpected softening in the old Hopi's face.

"You are surprised, no?"

"Not by much more tonight," Frank said dryly.

"Oh, you will be, Frank Reardon." He smiled. "Now the witch begged to stay. She promised to behave herself if she would be spared. The other clan leaders did not trust the witch, but the *Bahanas* said the witch could go with them. They did not fear her. They wanted her great knowledge."

Talaqueptewa fell silent. Frank glanced in the mirror and found the Hopi staring at him, his jet-black eyes hard with some purpose, as if to be sure Frank were listening. "Spider Grandmother put her finger to a stone and carved the figure of a man, then she broke the tablet in half. She gave half the Hopi tablet to the leader of the Fire Clan. She entrusted the other half to the leader of the white clan. In this way, she said, when a *Bahana* returns with the broken tablet we will know he is not the witch."

Talaqueptewa paused. "Smart of Spider Grandmother. But she did not count on the power of that one witch."

Frank shook off an uneasiness. "Interesting story, Talaqueptewa—"

"Listen to me!"

The Hopi's booming voice filled the Jeep. Frank had never heard such a deep, powerful voice. He gave a quick glance to the mirror, half expecting the diminutive Hopi to have tripled in size.

"Eddie Honanie died for that tablet," Talaqueptewa said softly, reverently, as if in honor of Eddie.

"Why? Why would Eddie have to die?"

"Haven't you listened to a word? He died protecting the tablet."

"Because of its value as an artifact?"

"No! Loosen your mind, Frank Reardon. This is not about stolen art!"

Frank was aware that Ben spoke the exact words of Coriz. "Okay. Why don't you tell me what this is about?"

The Hopi gave a hard sigh. "The complete tablet contains the powers of creation *and destruction.* For all the clans, including Navajo. Including the white clan, Frank Reardon."

"A kind of doomsday stone."

"Yes. It is exactly that. A doomsday stone. Spider Grandmother foretold that five signs will mark the coming of the *Bahana* with the stone," Talaqueptewa continued. "The fifth sign appeared four days ago." He leaned close. "The same day you arrived," he said right into Frank's ear.

Gooseflesh erupted on Frank's skin.

"The one who returns with the broken tablet," Talaqueptewa continued, "will have the trust of *all* Hopi. His words will tell the future and he will be believed."

"And you want to be that man, right, Talaqueptewa?"

Silence filled the Jeep. Glistening dark eyes met Frank's in the mirror, staring hard at him as if considering Frank.

"No, that man is to be you," the Hopi said quietly. The statement came almost as a plea, said so sadly, as if all hope were pinned on the wrong man.

The simple words settled on Frank with a heaviness; it was a burden he didn't understand . . .

. . . and least of all wanted.

His chest tightened around a cold hollowness. He would be the *last* man to give one minute of sympathy, or understanding, or trust.

He *was* the wrong man.

A huge crack of light split the night with such sudden blinding brightness Frank half covered his eyes with an arm. The lightning fractured. Dozens of lines jagged across the sky until the dome of night looked like a black egg about to shatter.

He lowered his arm and stared in awe at the unleashed violence spreading across the sky, and the power replenished him, stoked his own anger, cleansed him of doubts.

Damn Talaqueptewa, his sentimental stories, and his guilt-ridden expectations!

And damn every Indian who blamed every problem on the white man. That was the easy way, the coward's way.

A thunderous clap rent the air. The sound was so loud, like God's hand slamming on a drum. Rumbles resounded through the ground and shook the earth.

The highway tilted.

Was it an earthquake?

The Jeep jerked from his hands, swerved off the highway, slid sideways on the loose, sandy shoulder. He muscled it back onto the road.

He caught a glimpse of Talaqueptewa, sitting calmly in the back, as if anchored to the seat, unaffected by the wild ride, the gun still aimed at Frank's neck.

Frank spun the wheel to the left, deliberately this time, sending the Jeep careening across lanes to the far side. Talaqueptewa didn't move.

He slammed on the brakes. The sudden stop threw him forward. Frank used the motion to cover the grab for his gun. He spun around.

But the Hopi was on the far side of the backseat, his gun aimed directly at Frank, his hands steady, his face a veneer of composure.

"Put the gun down, Frank Reardon."

Adrenaline pumped through Frank, prickling up his arms and across his chest.

"Put it down. I am not the enemy."

"The hell you're not."

Lightning shredded the sky in a sudden fireworkslike explosion that turned night to instant day. Frank blinked against the glare and still had to squint in the amber afterlight that filled the Jeep.

The Hopi's eyes went immeasurably sad. Every line in his face grew deeper. "You can't be the one," he said, so very quietly. His eyelids fluttered shut and he let the gun fall to rest in his lap.

"Hand it over to me, Talaqueptewa."

Without opening his eyes, the Hopi offered the gun in his palm. Frank grabbed it. "Now get out and come around. You're driving."

Talaqueptewa opened the door, each movement excruciatingly slow, his head bent, thin arms hanging at his sides. Frank stepped out, and never taking his eyes—or his aim— off Talaqueptewa, he walked to the other side. The Hopi shuffled around the front of the Jeep, humming some Indian song—low, sad notes in the same slow beat as his steps. As he passed by Frank, Frank saw how very small he was, and so *old*. He looked ancient, as if he had aged fifty years in the last few minutes.

The Hopi's song grew louder, the notes lower still—a mournful lament as forlorn as any funeral dirge. Thunder rolled and boomed. The earth groaned, a demoniac sound like that of a great monster roaring from the subterranean depths.

Frank rounded the passenger side. A sudden wind slammed his weight against the Jeep, closing the door.

"Get in!" he yelled to Talaqueptewa over the roof.

The ground rocked right beneath Frank's feet. He fell back and flung his reach to the Jeep to catch his balance. The earth heaved, hurling him forward with brute force, slamming his head into the window.

Frank collapsed on the pavement.

Ben walked to the fallen man, crouched, and pulled Frank into his lap. "You should have listened to me, Frank Reardon," he murmured as he felt for a pulse and ran gentle fingers over Frank's head.

The wind died and *Balolokong* quieted. Ben laid a calming hand on the ground. "And you should not have thrown all your fury at this man. We need him."

The pounding in his head awoke Frank. Incessant, unrelenting pounding echoed throughout his body as if someone were using his head as a drum . . . as if he were *inside* a drum, trapped within . . . and the pounding never ceased.

He tried to sit up, one hand holding his head. Pain leapt to his touch and arced across his skull. Stars burst behind his eyes and the throbbing reached the sickly pit in his stomach. For a second Frank thought he might pass out. He pressed a hand to the ground for balance.

He took shallow, patient breaths, trying for equilibrium, trying to calm the throbbing, but it surrounded him, consumed him—the beats reverberating against the hard earth and back up his spine.

The pounding was so immense it drove straight through him to the ground. He swore he could feel the resounding thrum beneath his palm in the earth.

He *could* feel the pounding in the ground!

A pulse beat rhythmically, one after another after another. He willed his thoughts past the pain, and his ears heard the drumbeat, thumping, thumping.

He couldn't tell from where. In the pitch-black, he couldn't even determine where he was.

Cool air brushed over him, and his hand clutched scratchy ground. He must be outside, except he couldn't see the night sky.

Just where the hell had Talaqueptewa taken him?

Frank struggled to get up. The throbbing plummeted to his stomach and he paused, in a crouch, fighting waves of nausea. On a determined curse, he stood.

His head jammed against branches. He pushed with his shoulders, his arms. He was surrounded, as if encased in some stifling, prickly nest. He shoved harder and a sharp stick found his neck.

It was like shoving on a briar bush—a thick, resilient, impenetrable barrier. He tried to muscle through with his shoulder, covering his hands and bending his head, but still the branches found their mark. Frank ripped off his jacket and wrapped it around his hands.

"Dammit, Talaqueptewa!"

His voice exploded in his head, fed the pounding and the nausea.

On a surge of anger and frustration, he threw all of his weight into the side of the structure, dug his feet in and pushed. Half his body became buried in the tangle, but he didn't give up.

Panting, sweating, Frank began to realize that he wasn't supposed to ever get out.

He attacked the branches like a madman—like an animal—tearing through them, oblivious now to the pounding in his head, the nausea in his stomach, even the stabs of pain from sharp sticks.

Suddenly, there was nothing to grab, just air. He stumbled into the night and took deep, blessed breaths of the cold, fresh air.

Now the drumbeats sounded loud and clear. They came from over a ridge, about fifty yards away. An aura of yellow glowed above the ridge, as if from the light of dozens of small fires—or one huge bonfire.

Faintly aware of hundreds of stinging wounds on his hands, arms, and face, Frank started up the incline. He glanced back at the thorny jail he had just escaped. It was nothing more than a hovel of sticks in the middle of a wash.

"Damn you, Talaqueptewa," he muttered. "Wait until I get my hands on you."

Seething, Frank topped the ridge, but could not have prepared himself for the sight before him: Hundreds of Indians stood in a circle around a wide clearing. A huge bonfire—as tall as a house—stood in the center, Its flames reached several stories high, seeming to lick the sky.

Two lines of dancers snaked through the clearing, braiding in and out, gray bodies smeared with red and black. The drumbeats kept pace with every step of the dancers.

Frank now heard another sound: rattles. The distinct noise was a punctuation to every drumbeat.

But other than the drums, the rattles, and the occasional hiss and crack from the fire, not another sound lifted on the breeze from the hundreds of people. They just stood there, unmoving, impossibly silent.

An eerie sense of the supernatural settled over Frank.

For a moment, he wondered if he were asleep, caught in a bizarre dream, a nightmare of intense flames, grotesque figures, and haunting sounds in a vacuum of silence.

But he could feel the cool air, he saw the twinkling night sky above, and his feet kicked up real plumes of dust from the sandy knoll. He was not asleep.

The two lines of dancers separated, each one winding to opposite sides of the crowd, then around to the far side of the bonfire.

Frank heard a thump, louder, more powerful than the drums. The deep sound seemed to reach to the core of the earth, vibrating through the ground to his feet. The hair on his arms rose.

Another thump. Then another. One after another.

The ground shook with each thump, beat, and rattle.

One by one the dancers emerged from behind the fire. Now something hung from their mouths, something moving, something alive.

Frank stared, not believing his eyes.

Gripped in the mouth of each dancer was a snake.

The long line of dancers wound through the clearing, their lips around the snakes, their hands caressing the slithering bodies. Snake tails curled and uncurled, draped over dancers' shoulders, curved around their necks.

The sight was at once revolting and compelling—impossible to turn away from.

Unbidden, Frank's feet moved surely down the incline. For a fleeting moment, he swore he felt a gentle hand at his back, guiding him.

Drums and rattles filled the air, pulsed through the ground. Dancers and snakes circled on a turning, winding path like that of a snake's trail over the ground.

The crowd swayed with each beat, side to side, as one, caught in the hypnotic rhythm.

The dancers drew closer to the people. The snake bodies reached, stretching their tails, brushing over men, women, children.

The beat deepened, increased.

The dancers went closer still.

The snakes swung furiously.

Warnings pricked along Frank's scalp.

"Come here!"

A woman's yell rent the air. Frank's head jerked as if yanked by a string. Muddled thoughts made the sound and source seem disconnected. He blinked, tried to focus.

Suddenly, he saw white hair, whiter than sunlight.

Tikui.

And next to her was Ella, her dark eyes wide with fear.

Instantly, his head cleared, his mind focused on saving Ella. He half strode, half slid down the sandy hill, never taking his eyes off her.

But on level ground, Frank found himself overwhelmed by the crowd. He pushed between people, his aim set on where he had seen Ella.

The drumbeats heightened, now joined by heart-stopping yelps. Whether from the dancers or an onlooker, or even Ella, Frank couldn't tell.

Urgency tightened his chest. He fought his way through the throng, past people seemingly anchored to the ground. He couldn't make any headway.

A man grabbed Frank's arm, jerking him to a standstill. Frank turned and lost a breath: He was staring into the face of the painted man, the same one from Ella's post.

A ball of fire erupted in the man's hand. He tossed it

out and Frank caught it easily. In horror, he tried to drop
the fire, but it wouldn't leave his hand. He could feel the
heat, yet it didn't burn—the flames hovered just above his
palm.

The crowd gasped.

Frank glanced around and saw that he and the painted
man were the center of attention.

Logic collided with insanity.

The man's face contorted to a smile. His knowing eyes
reflected the flickering flames. He reached out a hand and
the flames returned to him.

This wasn't happening. This *couldn't* be happening!

Frank backed away. The ball of fire leapt to him. Instinctively—just to be rid of it—Frank tossed the fire up in the
air, where it danced and bobbed.

Murmurs spread through the crowd.

The man's smile widened; his gaze softened, considering
Frank with a knowing, almost kindly countenance.

The man tilted his head—no, the paint slipped to one
side! In the next instant, the mask fell away, revealing Ben
Talaqueptewa.

But this man was too tall, too young to be Ben.

He must be dreaming . . . or hallucinating. Had Talaqueptewa given him something while he was unconscious?
Maybe he was still unconscious.

Frank's mind tried to lock on reality, but he couldn't
defeat overwhelming panic.

He stumbled back.

"No!"

The scream pierced his head. For a second he thought
he might even have been the one to yell, but the crowd
gathered around him were staring off to the side, their faces
full of terror.

Frank looked over his shoulder and there was a dancer,
bent to the ground, a snake writhing in his mouth. Blood
trickled from the man's lips, snake blood, and dripped
down on Ella's fallen body.

Frank's heart slammed against his ribs. He had to reach her. Had to save her.

The thought gripped his heart in fear. And, for a second, his mind tried to connect with something, something that wasn't right, but his body charged forward.

He tore through the crowd to her side. The dancer saw him. A glint of deadly intent crossed his face. He opened his mouth and, in horrific slow motion, the snake dropped in a heap right beside Ella.

"No!" The yell ripped from Frank's chest.

The dancer stood and leapt over Ella to face Frank.

Frank shoved aside people and ran headlong into the dancer, taking them both down. With both hands, he pounded the dancer's head into the ground. He could hear yells. He felt hands grabbing him, trying to pull him away, but the rage inside multiplied to a strength beyond his own. With only a shrug, he tore loose from any grip and still held the dancer firmly.

From the corner of his eye, Frank saw the snake curl, readying to strike, its murderous gaze on Ella. He drew a fist back, struck the dancer so hard, Frank felt bones break. He had seconds now to reach Ella.

But as he rose, the sky exploded with thunder. The ground shook and heaved, throwing Frank off his feet. A lone bolt of lightning struck the earth inches away. Another hit close enough to singe his hair. And another pinned him from moving to the right.

Plumes of smoke rose from the seared earth. The crowd scattered, churning sand and dust. Desperately, Frank tried to see Ella. He pinned his gaze on where she should be. Crawled forward. Lightning struck a breath away from his chest. As if aimed at him.

He jerked his head around to see a line of the most fiercesome Indians standing on the ridge. They were tall, muscular, with long black hair whipping free over bare shoulders. One pulled back on a bow and let free an arrow. It soared high, then turned into fire midair. The fire shot to earth, straight as a lance, striking just past his shoulder. Smoke rose from the ground. Frank barely registered that he no longer saw any sign of an arrow.

Squinting his eyes to see through the miserable haze, he spotted Ella, who was braced back, her eyes wide, the snake only inches from the delicate skin at her neck.

Frank ripped off his shirt, bunched it in one hand and scrambled along the ground. Fiery arrows circled him, seeming to rain down on him.

Now only two yards behind the snake. Frank opened the shirt, held it up, and tossed it over the snake. Frantically, he gathered the shirt and twirled the snake-laden bundle, twisting the ends together. He drew the bundle high above his head, preparing to smash it into the ground, when a strong hand stayed him.

"You have proven yourself, Frank Reardon. Let the child go home."

His gaze jerked to the side. He could barely focus past the adrenaline pumping to the back of his eyes. But he saw white hair.

"Tikui."

"Yes. Now, put the child down." She pressed firmly on his arm, lowering the bundle.

Her hand slid to his fist and loosened his grip. She set the shirt down. It wobbled to one side, and the snake appeared, then slithered away, leaving a serpentine trail in the sand.

Frank crouched next to Ella and slid an arm beneath her head. "You're all right?"

But Ella didn't respond to him, even with a look. Her gaze was set on the already disappeared snake.

"Ella—"

"There is your miracle, *Kikmungwi*. Now do you believe me?"

"Believe you—" Frank started, but when he glanced up his words died. Tikui was not talking to him, but to Ben Talaqueptewa.

Frank's blood still surged with the threat of the snake; every bit of him still as focused and tight . . . and needing release. This sleazy con man provided the perfect target.

"You will wish you never met me, you son of a bitch."

The Hopi smiled. "Yes, Tikui, it is a miracle."

CHAPTER
FIFTEEN

Strong arms lifted her from the ground and carried her, holding her close. Ella drew a deep breath and filled with the scent of fresh-cut pine boughs and dust—the smells of the ground, the ceremony, the snake. Shudders fled through her body. The arms pressed her close; a whisper filled her ear. *Shh, you're all right now.* Frank's deep voice reverberated through her. A rush of warmth spread through Ella. Lips brushed her temple, her cheek—in an odd way heightening the shivers. She breathed deeply of him; her senses flooded with his scent and that of sweat and the earth. Her heart calmed and she drifted off, letting sleep conquer, knowing she was safe.

All night, Frank stared at the sleeping Ella, his heart caught on the slightest details of her face; the way her eyebrows sloped ever so gently downward, framing her eyes—closed now, but Frank imagined them open, dark, and full of expression; the full curve of her mouth, now in soft repose—but he remembered lips drawn thin in defiance, or parted in surprise . . . but not smiling. He had never seen her smile, until tonight when he carried her away, holding her close. When he brushed his mouth to her brow, her hand tightened at his neck, she breathed deeply . . . and she smiled.

As though she knew, deep in her subconscious, she was safe in his arms.

God, how good he had felt at that moment!

His fingers traced the lines of her forehead. His body tensed with the effort not to push his hands back, through her thick hair, to the sides of her slender neck, and raise her, lift her mouth to his.

Sudden guilt ripped him deep to a wound he couldn't heal.

He had no right to have these feelings for Ella!

Frank took a deep, ragged breath for the umpteenth time that night, seeking equilibrium.

He should be annoyed. Hell, he should feel betrayed that Ella would leave the store without telling him. All night he had pondered her reasons, wondering how she could have driven off, without a word to him, without arranging for Annie.

Whatever had compelled her had been stronger than her need to care for Annie, and stronger than her own instincts for self-preservation, for Ella had gone straight to the very place of her nightmares, the source of many of her demons.

He had tried to be angry. She had defied him just as Mary had always defied him, charging off to do as she pleased. A part of him had sought the anger he had always experienced with Mary.

Yet instincts told Frank that Ella's motives weren't selfish. He had *yet* to witness Ella thinking only of herself, or manipulating the situation to her own design.

His mind stopped on that thought, stilled by the insight into Ella . . . and by comparison, into Mary. Did he really believe that of Mary—that she had cared only for herself and what she wanted?

It sounded like Ella's description of Eddie, someone driven by noble causes and righteous passion, and to hell with the people around him.

Frank's mind clenched tight against the disloyalty of his thoughts.

Yet a piece of his heart fluttered, as if struggling to be free.

*   *   *

Ella awoke with a start, not knowing where she was. She lay in utter darkness, without even a sliver of light. Trying to regain her bearings, she lay still, forced calm breaths. Dust coated the inside of her nose.

She remembered the dust. The smell encased her childhood memories, suffocating her if she ever lifted the lid on that part of her mind—dust laden with oldness, dust formed from resistance, the chafing of centuries.

. . . dust from the grinding of time to a standstill.

. . . dust from the crumbling adobe walls.

. . . dust from the ground where snakes crawled.

Her body stiffened. Ella squeezed her eyes tight to obliterate the image of the snake, staring at her, considering her.

If not for Frank . . .

He had saved her life—appearing from nowhere at the very moment she had believed all was lost.

He had carried her away. She remembered being lifted as if weightless, holding on to him, breathing deep of him. Then he kissed her. Her hand went to her temple where his lips had touched.

"You're awake."

As if evoked from the vision, Frank's voice surrounded her. She felt his breath at her cheek. Ella raised a hand to touch his face and found him leaning over her, his head bent to hers. For a moment, she thought he might kiss her again, this time on the lips. The warmth within her spiraled to a place deep inside.

Then she heard the rasp of a match and soon a soft glow from a candle lit the room.

Ella looked up. Frank now stood beside the bed, a tall tower of a man, so oversized for this diminutive room. He should look awkward, out of place. Instead, the surroundings seemed to withdraw in his presence. All Ella could see was him.

"Yes, awake," she said, but her voice didn't carry past a tightness in her throat.

He crouched at eye level with her. His gaze was dark, with a look of dreadful concern, more fearful than her condition warranted. Ella nearly reached a hand out to comfort *him*.

"I'm fine," she offered.

He leaned toward her. A tingle of anticipation rushed through Ella.

Instead, his reach went beyond her to a table at the side of the cot. "There's some tea for you."

He sat back and smiled slightly, a steaming mug in his hand. "Tikui's own concoction." He grimaced. "It's not totally disgusting."

Small creases fanned from his eyes, old laugh lines that looked somehow forgotten. When the smile disappeared the wrinkles only accentuated a tiredness in Frank's eyes. He seemed so constrained, so distant from her.

Ella levered up on an elbow, but didn't reach for the cup, because now, in the soft light of the bedside lamp, she saw a myriad of cuts across his cheek and jawline. She lifted a hand to his cheek. "Where did you get all these cuts?"

"Had a fight with a bush."

His answer made no sense. "A fight with a bush?"

He bent his head and seemed to study his laced fingers. Now she noticed a streak of pinkish skin running down from his temple.

Suddenly, the horrific scene replayed in Ella's mind. She saw the warriors, the bolts of fire. "You're burned."

He raised a hand to his brow, but then ignored the wound and instead, almost self-consciously, let his hand drop to his side. "Just singed."

His matter-of-fact voice skittered over Ella. *Just singed*, as if an arrow turning to fire could be explained. Suddenly, she needed to know what he had seen.

"Singed by a lightning bolt?"

"Yes, well—"

"Or was it a fiery arrow?"

"Fiery arrow, lightning bolt, you know it doesn't matter."

Ella had never before believed in miracles or magic. But after what she had seen tonight . . . and the miracle of Frank being there in time . . .

"Except you risked your own safety to save my life," she pointed out quietly.

He looked up then, but not with a smile or even the slightest pleasure in her comment. Instead, his eyes were fierce. "Convenient that I was there."

She stared in mute startlement at his angry face.

He looked at her straight on. "Ella, we have to talk." His gaze hardened to the familiar, uncompromising Frank—not the comforter, not the hero . . . but the investigator.

Inexplicable sadness filled her. "What about?" she asked.

"Why were you here?"

"I gave Tikui a ride. She was on the highway."

"The two of you just happened to rendezvous out in the middle of nowhere?"

Ella thought of Tikui's sudden appearance at her window. She made a soundless laugh. "In fact, it happened just that way."

"Did you plan to meet Talaqueptewa here?"

"No. Well, I had hoped to find him—" The simmer of anger emanating from Frank unsettled Ella's thoughts. "But I changed my mind," she finished.

Frank shook his head. "Make sense, Ella. Are you saying you were looking for Ben? Or maybe you already knew where he was."

Ella didn't like the tone of his voice. "Yes, I was looking for him." She gave a hard sigh. "Are you going to make a federal case out of that?"

He gave the slightest start as if her words had insulted him. His brow wrinkled into the look of someone about to apologize. Abruptly he looked away and shook his head. "Just answer me straight, Ella. Did you and Ben have a plan to meet tonight?"

"No," she said, but Frank didn't look satisfied with the answer. "Like I said in the note, I didn't know if I would find him."

His brow furrowed in surprise. "What note?"

"The one I left with Grandmother." Ella registered the confusion on Frank's face. "You didn't find the note." Her tone held an apology.

"No."

"Frank, I put a note in Grandmother's pocket. I wanted her to know where I was."

"But not me."

Guilt speared through Ella. "I couldn't tell you I was going to find Ben. I knew you wouldn't let me. Or you would come along and then I might not get Ben to talk to me."

He looked at her, a flicker of sadness in his eyes that widened Ella's guilt. "Talk to him about what?" he asked.

"About the incident at the store. I thought Ben might know why it happened. Frank, I couldn't take the chance—"

Ella stopped. Frank's eyes flashed with such pain, she lost a breath. "Talaqueptewa surprised me in the Jeep tonight. He kidnapped me, Ella."

Ella sat up. She couldn't have heard him right. "Ben kidnapped you? Why?"

"Don't give me that innocent act, Ella."

The pain in his eyes reached straight to Ella's heart. "But I am—"

"You didn't deceive me tonight?"

She couldn't deny that.

"You haven't manipulated me since day one?"

The accusation rippled through Ella like a chill wind, taking her breath, speech, and leaving inner tremors in its wake.

How could he think that?

She found no warmth in Frank's cold stare.

He turned away impatiently, as if too frustrated to await an answer. He stopped in the shadows. "What was that scene outside about, Ella? Why was I brought here?'' His voice was as distant as the moon and as cold as moonglow on a marble statue.

"You said Ben brought you. Ask him."

"He's gone. Disappeared. In your truck." His tone implied something insidious.

"What are you saying?"

"You tell me, Ella."

"Are you saying that I planned this? The snake?" She shook her head. "I wouldn't . . . Ben wouldn't—"

"What? Wouldn't use you? Or me?" He faced her. "I know how things work on the res."

Ella recoiled from the bitterness in his voice. "I haven't manipulated you, Frank." Ella pushed her spine hard against the rough mud wall to counter the tremors. "You're the one who arrived with an agenda. I'm only Eddie's sister, the sister of the murder victim, remember?"

"My agenda?" He gave a sharp laugh. "My agenda did not include this night."

"My agenda didn't include this night, either. Yet here we are." She couldn't understand Frank's anger.

"That's the point, Ella."

His gaze settled on her, his eyes so dark and full of emotion. "I wish you had trusted me. Maybe all this wouldn't have happened."

Laughter bubbled from the dark hallway. "So true! So true!" Tikui's cheerful voice sparkled the room, brightening, seemingly adding light to the darkest corner.

She walked straight to Frank. "That *is* the point! You need to trust each other!"

Ella gazed in awe at the sight of the frail woman, toe to toe with Frank, her face beaming, undaunted by even his blackest mood.

Tikui reached up to Frank's face, her black shawl slipping to the crooks in her elbows. The old woman's arthritic arms could barely straighten to reach so high. She placed gnarled hands on Frank's cheeks. "Warriors have such a hard time trusting, yes?" Tikui said quietly.

Frank didn't move. But Ella noted a glistening in his eyes and her heart caught on the unexpected truth Tikui spoke.

Suddenly, Tikui whirled to Ella, her layers of clothes swirling. "And you? Are you happy to be here?"

Tikui bent and looked into Ella's eyes. Ella lost her breath at the unexpected, powerful gaze. Tikui's keen eyes focused on her, unwavering, and Ella felt a tug deep inside, as if gentle but firm fingers pried loose secrets. Ella had a moment of fear at the scrutiny, like a child facing a wise teacher . . . and no lies, or truths, were safe.

The old woman smiled kindly. "Forgiveness will come, I promise."

Forgiveness will come. The words snared on Ella's guilt. Her fears, her insecurities—her sorrow—rose swift to the surface of her eyes, shimmering inside, blurring them. She set her jaw against the onslaught and fought for control.

"Ah, child, you're safe here now," Tikui said. She ran her hand down Ella's hair and let her palm rest for a moment at Ella's cheek.

The exquisite gentleness pried loose Ella's last restraint and the shimmering tears fell.

Years of burying her emotions deep . . . only to have a wise gaze, two caring hands, and gentle words lay bare her defenses.

It wasn't fair. It wasn't right!

Ella swiped away the tears. "Yes, safe." The words choked on the emotions knotted in her throat. Ella threw back the bedcover and swung her legs to the floor, forcing Tikui to back away. "I can't stay."

"You have to," Tikui protested, still cheerful. "We have plans to make."

Tikui rose slowly but gracefully, and for an instant, Ella could see the young woman Tikui had been. It was such an odd sensation—Ella half expected the old woman to spin, shedding layers of age—that she stared as Tikui pulled two chairs close to the bed.

"You sit here, please," Tikui said to Frank and gestured to one chair. She took one for herself.

"I have to go, Tikui. Whatever plans you have might include Ella, but they don't include me."

Frank's comment didn't surprise Ella, considering his earlier accusations, his judgment of her and of Ben. She glanced up at him, expecting to see a hint of the anger, or certainly a trace of his suspicions. Instead, his expression matched that as when she had first awakened: fearful, somewhat helpless, even a bit vulnerable . . . a mirror image of what she felt inside.

Ella wanted to slip her hand within Frank's. She wanted to reassure him.

She wanted him to trust her.

"Go ahead," Tikui said.

Frank's brow furrowed. He looked quickly at Ella with such puzzlement that she in turn glanced at Tikui. The old woman was staring back at her, smiling.

"Go ahead," Tikui said again, and slanted her eyes in the direction of Frank's hand.

The old woman *couldn't* have read her mind!

Ella's mind jerked back from the possibility. "You mean go *with* him," she confirmed.

Tikui sighed hard and shook her head. "Yes, later. But not now." She glanced up at Frank. "Sit down." The old woman stared at him until he complied.

Tikui looked from one to the other, then said, "Tonight, you passed the first test. But make no mistake, that was the easiest step. Now, have you found the broken tablet?" She was looking at Frank.

"What? No. I'm not looking for a broken tablet— Listen, Tikui—" He shook his head in obvious frustration. "I have to go. Ella—"

He held her gaze for a moment, then stood. "I'm glad you're okay," he said, distance in his voice.

"You will not get far without these." Tikui dangled a ring of car keys, then slid them back into a fold in her skirt.

Frank slapped a hand against the pocket in his jacket and cursed. He had forgotten that Ben drove him here.

He held his palm out. "Hand them over, Tikui."

"Tell me, Frank Reardon, how did you explain the painted man to Coriz?"

His eyes narrowed on Tikui. "How did you know I spoke to Coriz?" He threw up a hand. "Let me guess, Ben Talaqueptewa."

"You lied to Coriz," she said. Then she turned to Ella. "And you lied to Frank."

"How did you know—"

"Aiee! You both think you can lie the truth away." Her dark eyes turned stern as she glanced first at Frank, then Ella. "How do you understand a man leaping through a locked window, Ella? And you, Frank Reardon, how do you understand arrows that grow fire and change to lightning bolts? Or a sudden earthquake, right beneath her?" She pointed to Ella. "Or a snake who watched her with eyes as expressive as any human's?"

"I don't have to explain it, Tikui."

"But you need to understand." She bent her head. "Both of you do," she murmured, gazing down.

Tikui sat so still—even her hands lay motionless in her lap—that Ella thought the old woman had perhaps fallen asleep. Frank shifted, readying to leave.

Ella leaned over for a close look at Tikui and she saw her lips moving in a silent mutter.

"Ah! I have it!" Tikui sat upright.

Both Ella and Frank started.

"I know something neither of you can deny!" Tikui said with glee, her dark eyes bright and twinkling. "I am the one who brought you together."

Ella jerked her gaze to Frank and found him staring at her in mutual confoundedness . . . and something else. She saw a flicker of caution deepen in his eyes, then disappear.

"Yes, Frank," Tikui said, with meaning. "It is possible."

Ella saw astonishment, then suspicion, traverse Frank's face. Her heart tripped over the look.

What thought of Frank's had Tikui broached?

"This is crazy," he muttered.

"By all logic, you should not be here, yes?"

"That's right, Tikui." Frank's voice was hard. "There is *nothing* logical about tonight."

"No, no. I'm not talking about here, tonight. You did not want to come to Indian land. You did not want this case. It was an ill wind blowing." Tikui intoned the last words as if they were a chant.

Frank stared down at Tikui, speechless. *How could she have known?*

She had put to words his concerns, his *dread*. He hadn't wanted to come here—to Indian land, to deal with a murder. And with every passing day here, every fear within him seemed realized—the past doomed to repeat.

Hell, no, he had not wanted this. He hadn't wanted the memories, the guilt, the whispers behind his back. None of that had been on his agenda . . . including discovering Ella. He looked at her and his heart skipped over the expression of betrayal on her face.

She believed Tikui spoke the truth. In fact, the old woman had, and nothing Frank could say would explain his intentions.

"Is it true? You didn't want to be here? You don't care who murdered Eddie?" Ella asked too quietly.

"I do care who murdered Eddie," he answered honestly.

The little woman stared up at Frank, her lips pursed, her clear eyes unblinking. "Forgiveness will come for you, too. You are not betraying her, Frank Reardon."

Tikui's soft words hit Frank in the chest, to a wounded place within. "I'm not listening to this craziness anymore. Give me my keys, Tikui." His jaw clenched around the words.

"You must both work together," Tikui said, then turned her attention to Ella. "You, too. As I said, I brought you together."

"Eddie's murder brought me here, Tikui, not you," Frank said. Then his eyes flashed. "And you were the witness, Tikui, weren't you? What else do you know about that murder?"

"What I know you won't believe."

"Try me," Frank challenged.

Instead of answering him, Tikui rolled back the sleeve on her garment to above her shoulder. There, on her upper arm was the drawing of a waterbird, the same as the one Frank had seen in the picture of Eddie.

Tikui raised her gaze to Frank and smiled, then she turned to Ella. Gray eyes full of gentle sadness looked deep within Ella. Tikui's hand found Ella's and squeezed—the firm grip of a friend about to impart heart-wrenching news. Inexplicable panic swept Ella. She wanted to stop Tikui's words.

But the old woman was already speaking. "Eddie died for you," she said. Her gaze held Ella's as if Tikui meant to shore Ella's heart with only the strength in her eyes.

Tikui faced Frank. "And also for you. He died protecting your destiny."

CHAPTER
SIXTEEN

She dreamt she was on horseback, galloping across the desert. She could feel each hard beat of the horse's hooves pounding up through her. She flew, jumping cedar bushes, vaulting arroyos. Each leap was too far, too risky, and sent her heart to her throat. But the horse jumped, cleared, and raced ahead, out of her control. The obstacles came more frequently, were larger, more dangerous. The landscape mutated to horrific proportions. Dry washes grew to flooded, raging rivers; sand hills grew to monstrous mountains with craggy peaks.

A scream lodged in her throat. She yanked on the reins, desperate not to die. Still, the horse charged forward. She couldn't make him stop . . . she couldn't make him stop. Her mind froze, locked on the inevitable.

She could hear only the rush of the wind, the effortless breathing of the horse, an exquisite, soulful quiet. The quiet filled her with joyous peace. She laughed out loud and the echoes of her joy rushed through her—even the horse, who ran faster, faster. She let the reins slip from her hands, relinquishing all control.

As if by a miracle, the barriers disappeared beneath her feet. Suddenly, she was flying alone, the horse gone, only her and the sky and the earth. Nothing could stop her. Tears of joy filled her eyes. The freedom made her invincible. She had never felt so powerful, so alive.

A hard bump jolted straight up her spine. Ella winced.

The dream faded. She squeezed tight her eyes, clinging to the images, trying in vain to keep them alive.

The dream dissolved, but the powerful emotions remained: a glorious feeling of euphoria; a heart-stopping joy as if she had taken a terrible risk and prevailed.

For the first time in her life, Ella had felt what it was like to be fearless, daring.

She glanced at Frank, wanting to share, only to see the same stony face he had worn since Hopi. She didn't understand his determination to stay angry, even after her explanations. His features had hardened to a mask of suspicion and distrust—like the one he wore when they had first met, when he had come to the post . . .

. . . when they were still strangers.

. . . before he had held her in his arms, brushed his lips against her forehead.

. . . before he had risked his life for her.

Sadness in the wake of that glorious dream pinched Ella's heart. She wanted to again have the Frank she had only just discovered.

She wanted to step past their impasse.

The power of the dream surged through her.

She slanted a glance to Frank, then shifted in her seat to face him. "I had the most amazing dream."

Frank didn't want to listen. He didn't want to look. He didn't want to confuse his anger with awareness. But Ella's voice dragged across Frank, pulling his gaze to her as surely as if her hand were at his cheek.

Evidence of sleep still lingered on her: a tendril of hair clung to her temple; reddish creases from the window frame imprinted her forehead. She had a slightly unkempt, sleepy softness that stirred something deep in Frank.

"I was on a horse . . ." She paused. "Have you ever had the feeling of stepping off a precipice? I mean, that moment of total fear?"

She couldn't have known that her question immediately conjured Frank's recurring nightmare. "No," he whispered.

"The horse was fast. Jumping impossible distances. Charging ahead. I couldn't stop him. I couldn't control him."

Unreasonable anxiety crept through Frank. His nightmares might have nothing to do with a horse . . . just a yawning abyss at the edge of his sanity . . . but he understood, intimately, the fear of losing control.

"So, I let go," Ella said. "I risked getting hurt."

Frank's heart jumped.

"But as soon as I let go, the fear went away. It was as if an incredible burden had been lifted and I floated over the obstacles, weightless." Ella's voice quieted to a whisper.

Frank glanced over. She had a look of awe on her face.

"I don't remember ever feeling that way." Her eyes shimmered in the sunlight.

Frank's heart lodged in his throat. He wanted to tell her everything would be all right, but he couldn't get past the emotions strangling his thoughts.

Fear doesn't go away.

Love goes away.

The maelstrom of thoughts tangled with anger, loss, and a deep need he couldn't name.

It was the same feeling he had when he thought of Mary, desperately needing her to be here because she could make him whole again.

He had believed Mary's love completed him. That when she was yanked from his life, it tore loose a part of him, inflicting a mortal wound, and he was slowly bleeding to death. If only Mary were here, he could take deep breaths without pain, he could live again.

Except that was a lie. Mary's love had only masked the hole, not healed it. He was fatally flawed, missing something significant, lacking a vital piece of humanity.

"—just a dream."

Ella's voice pulled him from his thoughts.

"I know that." She took a deep breath. "I can't be that way. I can't not worry, not plan. But Eddie could." She gave a short, stifled laugh. "He never seemed to have a plan. Just charged ahead, challenging anything, everything. He was so ready to fight, as if he were born with a mission—"

God, Ella could be talking about Mary, who rushed ahead with only passion to guide her; a zealot blindly trusting in some universal code of fairness and justice.

Frank jerked his head to Ella. She was looking at him, her dark eyes glistening. "He was difficult, my brother. Seemed like he was always causing trouble. He was so determined, so opinionated, so unafraid. I couldn't talk to him. I didn't *want* to talk to him. He made me *angry*. He was my brother, but I was always mad at him."

Her brows creased as if puzzling an answer from the inside out, a truth she couldn't fathom because it was too painful to admit: being mad at the one you should love.

Anxiety tightened Frank's chest, just as it had every time he had tried to reason with Mary. His words were always hitting a brick wall of idealism.

The wound on Frank's heart stung as if seared by something caustic, an emotion too black to name. He could never be mad at Mary. Frank clenched his jaw, desperate to hold firm against a sudden surge within him that scratched at the back of his eyes.

"In the dream I . . ." She paused, then rushed ahead. "I was fearless. I felt what that was like. To take a step past what I understood, just on faith. It gave me a sense of what drove Eddie."

She looked at him. The shimmering in her eyes threatened to overflow. "I çan't get out of my mind what Tikui said—that Eddie died for a reason, to protect me."

Frank couldn't speak. He almost dared not breathe for fear of losing the shred of control he had over the enormous knot of emotions in his chest.

"You hate talking about Eddie," she said quietly.

"No." His voice was choked. He swallowed hard. "But it doesn't do any good to look back."

His whole body tensed with the strain of holding his own memories at bay.

"How is it that the champions of the world end up alone?"

She was talking about Eddie, Frank knew that. She was thinking of her brother, not herself. Never herself. As if somehow she had failed Eddie by not being there for him.

But when had he been there for her? Now, it was Ella who was alone, struggling with her store, with her niece. In Frank's eyes, she was the one with the courage.

"All Eddie had to do was slow down, Ella, and he wouldn't have been alone. His life was his choice and it's not your fault."

Frank's own words resounded through him, an echo of something important, something he should understand, just beyond what he could grasp—

"Frank, I want to see where Eddie died."

"What?" Frank cut a glance to Ella. "You can't be serious." But he saw she was. "Why?"

"Because it took a dream for me to feel even in the least connected with my brother."

Frank could think of a million reasons she shouldn't go there. She didn't need to see the scene of a murder. She didn't need that memory. His own heart beat fast and furious.

"I don't think it's a good idea, Ella." His voice came tight.

"I have every right," she said quietly. "Please."

He couldn't ignore the plea in her voice. Reluctantly, Frank nodded. He couldn't explain his resistance. He shouldn't care about the site of Eddie's murder. It had nothing to do with him, despite what some crazy woman might say.

Ella studied the silent man beside her. Frank hadn't spoken since he agreed to take her to the canyon and Ella wondered what had made him so distant. He stared ahead, his face stern, his jaw set, every fiber of him tense—from the pulsing vein at his forehead, to his hands gripping the steering wheel, to the bunched muscles at his thighs. For all Frank's fierceness, Ella considered, more than once, reaching across and rubbing the muscles of his neck, or brushing the hair aside on his forehead—a carefree gesture to make him smile.

She wished, most of all, that she knew his thoughts, because she needed to understand him, all the myriad facets of him. She thought back to his first appearance at her store: the poster man for the FBI. Tall and imposing behind dark glasses, without a hint of emotion or concern for anyone's feelings.

But that layer of Frank was a thin veneer. It had split at Grandmother's, when he carried *Sani* in his arms, and when he gathered remains from the *alch'i'i*. It cracked wide open in her store after the break-in, when he pulled her into his arms. He had held her, just as he had at Hopi . . . soft lips caressing her temple, his breath in her hair, his large hands pressing her to him. Then he had pulled away, staggered back, as if somehow betrayed by his own feelings.

Ella thought of what Tikui had said to him. *You are not betraying her.*

Instant pain had filled Frank's eyes—his response as immediate and deep as if Tikui had struck an open wound. What truth had she probed? *Who was Tikui talking about?*

What person evoked such acute anguish in Frank?

Ella's heart had recognized Frank's profound, involuntary reaction. She knew the vulnerable place inside from where it sprang: the defenseless domain of love. The same spontaneous, helpless urge *owned* Ella whenever she thought of Jenny.

The aura of the rising sun outlined the eastern horizon, casting the ground in beautiful yellows and pinks. But only Ella seemed to notice. Her gaze settled on the implacable man beside her and she wondered about the love within him that caused him so much pain.

The path wound over dunes and down into arroyos and crawled over landscape only fit for lizards.

With every mile gained, Ella saw Frank set his jaw tighter. Whatever thoughts captured him seemed to also press his foot to the pedal, attacking each rut, as if by sheer will he could dominate any obstacle. Ella wanted to understand what tormented him. More than that, she wanted to offer Frank a chance to *talk,* just as he had once offered the same to her.

For the last five miles, the Jeep bounced and lurched unmercifully over ground that had never seen a path. Ella gripped the seat with one hand and braced her other hand on the dashboard, her body tense, her mind riveted on one thought: *Why here?*

The arroyo they drove through broadened and flattened to a wash, lined with tamarisk and Russian olive trees. Mesas that had been only distant purple tabletops now loomed close, their jagged walls reaching into the desert, warding off encroachers. Chills fled over Ella's arms at the sight of the awesome wildness.

The mesas stepped closer to the wash, forming towering walls of red sandstone. Frank and Ella had reached the canyon.

He navigated the Jeep over rocks and sagebrush, around errant junipers, and fallen trees, back and back into the chasm. Ella's gaze rose to the lofty cliffs scraping the sky that allowed only a strip of turquoise-blue to show. Desert varnish, the dark pigment in canyon walls, ran in streaks from the top of the cliffs almost to the floor. Shadowed crevices hinted at caves and Ella caught glimpses of ruins crouched within the caves high on the walls—the telling stacks of adobe bricks nearly camouflaged in the terra-cotta sandstone.

No one could look at the crumbling homes, seemingly inaccessible from any approach, without recognizing the defensive location of the ancient dwellings. The haunting sense of utter isolation crept over Ella.

Frank pulled the Jeep to a blessed stop, but then made no move to get out. He turned in his seat and faced Ella.

"Are you sure you want to do this?"

No she wasn't, not anymore, not faced with a very real menace she felt in this place.

Eddie died protecting your destiny.

Tikui's words curled through Ella. She had never, not a day in her life, been able to depend on Eddie. Yet she was to believe he had died for her?

A lump formed in Ella's throat.

She had had only herself to rely on. The rest of the world may have been able to call Eddie their champion, but not her.

The lump grew, tightening her chest.

"Yes, I'm sure," she managed past the knot of emotion.

Frank led her around a copse of tamarisk to the base of the cliff. "Up there was where Tikui was hidden."

Ella scanned the cliff wall and spotted the cave directly above. "That was her home?"

She looked back at the ground, then to Frank. She wanted to know exactly where Eddie had been found, but Frank was already walking away, toward the cliff, as if he meant to climb to Tikui's cave.

"Do you want to come with?" he called over his shoulder.

Ella stared after him, puzzled by his behavior. He seemed distracted, almost in a hurry. "No. I don't," she answered.

He stopped, his leg already bent to the talus slope. Ella turned back to the canyon floor, the area just beneath the cave. She took a few steps closer, unsure where to walk, not wanting to disturb anything. She heard the crunch of Frank's boot heels on rocks just behind her.

"It happened over there." His voice was strained.

Ella glanced at Frank to see where he meant, but he stood to the side, his gaze off to the distance, his face as stone-hard as the cliffs, the silhouette of a lawman one step away from losing control.

She had never seen such a fierce expression. Ella reached a hand to him.

"Animals," he muttered, his tone full of loathing.

Her breath caught on his hatred. Her thoughts fled back to the only other time she had heard such animosity in Frank—the night he talked to her and Jenny about AIRO. "Frank?"

Frank heard Ella call his name, but he couldn't answer past the lock of anger and hatred in his throat. All it had taken was seeing the place where Eddie had knelt before getting a bullet in his neck, and Frank had been instantly transported to another place, another time. It hardly mattered that Eddie had been executed and Mary had caught an accidental bullet—they were both murdered by the same aberrations of humanity.

"Frank, talk to me."

He jerked his gaze to Ella. She staggered back a step and Frank realized the hatred encased his features. He cursed the emotions claiming him.

I should be thinking of Ella, of her pain for her brother.

He closed his eyes and took a deep breath, struggling for control.

"I want to know what you're thinking." Her voice, gentle, coaxing, drifted up to him. Frank opened his eyes and saw Ella right in front of him.

He lied. "Just thinking about Eddie."

"No. You're not. You're thinking of someone else. Who?" The light in her eyes shone like a laser straight to his soul.

He raised his gaze to the cliffs beyond. "Ella, leave it alone. It's none of your business."

She flinched, but didn't move. "You're right. No more my business than it was yours when you asked about my childhood, or when we talked about Jenny and AIRO."

The mention of the murderers sent an iron rod through Frank. "Ella, don't," he managed.

He heard a gasp and glanced to Ella. Her hand covered her mouth, her eyes were wide. Slowly, she lowered her hand. "When you said 'animals,' you were talking about AIRO, weren't you?"

Frank looked back at the cliff wall. Embedded sparks of

sand glistened in the sun. The pristine beauty chafed against the ugliness in his thoughts. "They *are* animals, Ella."

"Why do you hate them so much?"

Frank faced her. Ella drew a breath at the fierceness etching his face. His eyes shone cold black, devoid of any warmth.

"I thought I explained that at the post. To you, to Jenny. Which part didn't you understand? The stealing for guns? The kidnappings? The murders?"

His lips drew back on the last, as if he could commit that very act, right now. Ella saw he *would* kill if he were faced with his enemy.

What would drive *anyone* to this amount of hatred? *He* was like an animal—a predator, stalking an enemy, driven by some basic instinct to survive . . . to protect.

Suddenly, she knew what could drive Frank over the edge: AIRO had struck too close to him. Worse than that, she knew. Ella's heart tripped and caught again, stumbling over a realization: AIRO had struck at *someone* close to Frank. That explained his ferocity, the vicious words he chose to describe them, the savage glare in his eyes.

"Who—" The question stuck in her throat. Ella swallowed, walked to Frank and laid a hand on his arm. "Who are you avenging, Frank?"

Muscles at his jaw clenched with some extreme effort for control. Ella gripped his arm tighter, to bring his attention back from whatever edge he faced.

He glanced down at her, his black eyes full of emotion. "My wife," he said simply. "They killed my wife."

He turned from her, walked several steps away, then just stopped and stood there, staring down the canyon.

"No," she whispered. The unshed tears she had seen in Frank's eyes sprang into her own. She could barely breathe for the wave of sadness flooding her.

She walked to Frank, put her hand to his chest. "I'm sorry. I'm so sorry."

He didn't look at her, but kept his gaze ahead on the deepening canyon.

"How, Frank?"

"At Red Earth." He winced, as if reliving the moment. "She wouldn't listen to me," he whispered into the air.

Ella's heart stuck on the helplessness in his voice. She thought of when she had left the post, sneaking away, deceiving him. Understanding of his relentless anger dawned on Ella—and with the understanding came the realization that her actions had caused him more than frustration, more than anger.

"I'm sorry," she said again, as much for what he suffered now as for what she had caused.

Frank threw a hand up at the air, the gesture of a man desperate to stop the memories. "No, I'm the sorry one." He looked at her. *Stared* at her. His eyes were so focused on her, Ella felt she had never been really looked at before. An arc of pain drew his brows tight. Then he did the most amazing thing.

He pulled her to him and wrapped his arms around her as if he were holding on for dear life.

Ella could feel his heart thumping furiously. She pressed her hand against his chest, letting his fury, his anger, his desolation seep within her palm, where she would crush it—if only she could.

He clung as if *needing* her in his arms. His fierce mask had dissolved, his defenses had crumbled.

Ella's heart swelled.

Minutes passed before his hold loosened. He straightened, but kept an arm around her shoulder. His hand absently rubbed up and down on her denim jacket. "I wish we ... I can't ..."

Frank couldn't finish the sentence. Hell, he didn't know his thoughts. A part of him had wanted to never let go of her. Even now, faced dead on with his guilt and sorrow for Mary, he had found himself reaching for Ella. All he knew was that he thanked God for Ella.

The thought stilled his heart and mind, but he dismissed it in the same instant. He *had* no heart. Only a hole, where it should be.

He took a few steps toward the cliff, but Ella dragged back.

"I was going to show you, Ella. The place you came to see."

She shook her head. Her black hair shone, but not as brightly as her deep eyes when she looked up at him. "I don't need to see it now, Frank. I don't want to," she added.

Her eyes were clear, certain. Frank's heart expanded to this woman with such quiet strength.

He nodded. "I'll meet you back at the Jeep, then. I want to look around."

She started to protest.

"I'm an investigator, remember?" He forced a smile. "It's okay, Ella. *I'm* okay."

He watched her walk away, then turned back to where Eddie was murdered, and walked the periphery of the scene. He saw indentations in the sand, and the splatter of blood. Frank slammed his emotions behind a steel door, and focused on the larger picture.

He walked to the facing cliff, where Coriz said there was evidence the bullet had been dug out. Frank found the hole in the sandstone, and the clean gouges of a knife. He looked back at the site, imagined Eddie on the ground, the murderer behind, and realized the murderer would have had to crouch for the bullet to lodge here in the wall.

His chest tightened with the realization this murderer had calculated every detail, including how to retrieve the incriminating bullet after it cleared Eddie's head.

"The cold-blooded son of a bitch," Frank muttered to himself.

He went back to the site and studied the imprints. He could see where Eddie's knees and the toes of his shoes marked the sand. Just behind were another set of shoe prints, different from Eddie's, but familiar.

Frank knelt and leaned close. He traced the tread of one shoe with his finger, and remembered.

"Son of a bitch."

CHAPTER
SEVENTEEN

Ella watched the landscape sail by in a blur of browns, reds, and pinks. As soon as Frank had hit the highway, he pressed his foot to the gas, sending the Jeep roaring down the road in the direction of her store, as if in a race against time, or desperate to escape.

Maybe that was precisely his goal. She knew he hadn't wanted to come here in the first place. Now, she understood why: He carried a wound within him—a wound he blamed on Indians. She thought about Frank's rudeness when they first met, his impatience, his easy frustration. At the same time, larger images of Frank filled her mind: his strong arms cradling Grandmother; those same arms wrapped around her tight; the sincerity in his eyes when he *promised* he would keep Jenny safe.

She thought of Tikui's words: that Tikui had brought Frank and Ella together.

She couldn't believe Tikui had that kind of power, but if she did, Ella was grateful . . . with all her heart.

Something in Frank had also connected to this place, to her—Ella knew it. She only wondered whether Frank would ever, could ever, admit it. Could he get past the hatred he had carried with him for so long? Or would it drive him right out of this place, back to Denver?

It struck her that any day, without a word, he would simply leave, never to appear at her store again. She glanced at Frank, saw the determination in his face, the purpose in his focus, and Ella realized that moment of departure could even be today.

A sudden ache spread through Ella down to her bones.

Frank drove the road to Ella's post as fast as the ruts allowed, his mind set on one goal: to talk to Annie.

He had noticed Ella's silence beside him, but had not wanted to analyze it, to consider where her thoughts had taken her, especially if she were pondering his loss of control back in the canyon. Instead, he had kept his mind on what he had found at the site, and his hopes pinned on one possibility: that Annie had not told them everything about what happened at her place.

He pulled up to the post, only to find Annie standing at the doorway to the store, her arms crossed over her ample chest. The worried expression on her face made Frank uneasy. He jumped from the Jeep, dust still swirling, and strode to her.

"Annie, are you all right?"

"I need to go home," she said, not looking at Frank. She stared at Ella approaching.

"*Sáni*, what's wrong?" Ella asked.

"I *need* to go home!"

Frank exchanged a worried glance with Ella.

"Grandmother, you can't. I thought you understood—" Ella started.

"I need to be there when Mr. Chambers comes back. He said he would be back. Now I won't be there."

Frank's nerves sparked. "Who is Mr. Chambers?"

"Ella knows. He trades at the store."

Frank stared at Ella. She shrugged, obviously puzzled.

"Trades with her how, Annie? Is he Indian?"

Frank's sharp tone racheted Ella's concern.

"Oh, no. Not Indian."

"Grandmother," Ella said gently. "I don't know a Chambers."

"He said he knows you. That you buy from him. He was nice, *sitsói.*"

"He was nice." The irritation in Frank's voice made Ella look. Hard, focused lines creased his face and sent a chill over her arms.

"Annie, what did he look like?" Frank asked.

"Not tall. Long brown hair."

"What was he wearing?"

The old woman furrowed her brow, then her face brightened. "I remember a denim jacket."

Frank shook his head in obvious frustration.

"You shouldn't worry, Frank Reardon. He came to help me keep my home." Then, Grandmother's face shadowed and she looked out across the desert. "Now I won't be there. I should have left a note."

Frank faced Ella. "Think, Ella. Do you know a Chambers?"

"No . . . I don't—" She could barely think past the intensity in his stare. "Frank, what is it?"

"Maybe you just forgot," Grandmother said, now sounding a little perturbed herself. "He has been busy with AIRO."

At the mention of AIRO, Ella felt the energy in Frank sizzle hotter than the air. He stared at Grandmother. "Annie, this is very important. Did he actually mention AIRO?"

"Of course. He said he is very important with AIRO. Eddie would know him."

"*How* would Eddie know him?" Frank demanded.

"Because of AIRO." She raised her chin. "They were going to help me."

Ella took a deep breath. "Grandmother, AIRO can't help you. Eddie couldn't have helped. He would have wanted to," Ella added. "But he couldn't."

"Of course AIRO can help." Grandmother was defiant now. "Mr. Chambers just had to find something first, then he would be back."

Frank took her arm. "Find what, Annie?"

Both Ella and Grandmother started at his urgency.

"I don't know," Grandmother said. "He just asked if

Eddie had left something with me. I told him that Eddie left me many things.''

''Annie, did he look outside for this thing?''

''No. I don't think so. He was in a hurry.''

''Hurry to go where, Annie?''

''I don't know. He just said he and Jenny had to leave.''

Ella's heart caught. ''Jenny was there and you didn't make her stay?''

The old woman looked from one to the other, her eyes confused. ''I don't know where . . .'' Her voice trailed off. Then Annie's gaze settled on Ella. ''I could not make Jenny stay. She makes her own choices, *sitsóí*.''

Frank glanced to Ella. The need in her eyes lanced straight through him—a desperate need to keep Jenny safe, sound, happy. That same need pumped through him.

''When was this, Annie?''

''The night before last.''

''The morning before we found you—'' Frank cut the sentence off, but he couldn't avoid the images of Annie, crumpled on the ground.

Grandmother bent her head. ''I should not have said anything. He told me not to say anything.''

''And you would listen to him, Annie?''

''He came to help me. I shouldn't listen?''

Ella shook her head. ''You let your only great-granddaughter leave,'' she said so quietly that Frank barely heard. ''And you don't know who she left with or where they went.''

''She left with Mr. Chambers and they were going to AIRO.''

Frank jerked his gaze to Annie. ''Where, Annie? Did he say where AIRO is?''

''Oh, no. That's a secret.'' She nodded proudly.

Frank clenched his fists at his sides.

''I told him he should rest. He shouldn't do so much with that bad leg.''

''A bad leg? What kind of bad leg, Grandmother?'' Ella asked. The interest in her tone drew Frank's attention.

"He got it in a battle," Annie declared. "I understood his bitterness."

"Chandler!" Ella declared. "Was it Chandler, Grandmother?"

"Yes. I think so."

Everything stilled in Frank. He knew the name—from Ella and from Fuller.

"Was it his right leg?" Ella asked. "And he walks with a limp?"

"Yes," Annie said. "Such a bad thing. Poor man."

"Tell me about this Chandler, Ella."

"He's a trader I buy from. He travels the west, buying, selling." Her brows creased. "I never guessed he would be involved with AIRO. He's too weird."

Frank's chest tightened. "Weird? How?"

"Just everything—" Ella paused. "The way he dresses: leather pants, fringed coat, saddlebags with all his inventory. It's like he thinks he's some old-time mountain man. He's gone for months, then shows up and hovers around the gallery all afternoon."

"He is lonely," Annie offered.

"Yes, I've thought that, too," Ella agreed.

Frank blew out a harsh breath. "And what does he talk about when he's hanging around?"

"He doesn't, much. He just seems to like the company."

"What *do* you know about him?"

Ella's quick look told Frank she didn't like his tone. "I don't interrogate my customers or suppliers, Frank."

"Ella, you're the one who said he was weird."

"He is. But then so are most of the traders. They're loners, literally living on the periphery of civilization."

"Do you know his first name?"

"I don't think he ever told me. I just know him as Chandler." She shook her head. "We never talked much, except about the pieces he would show me. He loves the old stuff—pawn, estate pieces. It's like he's caught up in the past."

Annie snorted. "You deal with him for years and know

so little. I can tell you he is a brave man. He fought for what he believed in, but doesn't complain about his wound.''

"Did he say how he was wounded, Annie?"

"I told you. In a battle."

"What was this *battle,* Annie?"

"With the white man's government."

She seemed to draw up straight right before Frank's eyes. Her eyes locked with his and Annie softened, smiled at him. "Please take no offense, Frank Reardon."

"No offense taken, Annie." He barely managed a smile. He was thinking this man had the perfect cover for AIRO reconnaissance. How the hell would he track him down?

Frank started for the Jeep. "I'll see what I can find out about him at the bureau."

"Oh, he won't be in your files. He says he knows all your tricks."

"All *my* tricks?"

"You are FBI."

Frank stopped in his tracks. "What do you mean, Annie?

She looked away, her lips tight.

"Annie, did Chandler mention the FBI?"

She stared ahead, unblinking. Frank thought that was the end of it, but then she said quietly, "You helped me."

Frank saw her wavering. "Yes, I helped you. And I want to help you again. I also want to help Jenny."

Annie only stared back, as if his comments were obvious and not worth a response.

Suddenly, Frank had an idea. "I might even be able to help Chandler," he added. He exchanged a quick glance with Ella. "Does Chandler need something from the FBI?"

"I don't know," Annie said thoughtfully, then her face brightened. "Maybe you could make things right about South Dakota?"

Frank's heart literally stopped. He gulped for air. "What did you say?"

"He said no one would listen. But maybe you will?"

In three strides he was in front of her. "Annie, did he say where in South Dakota?"

"Everybody knows of Red Earth." She cast her gaze to the side. "A bad time," Annie murmured.

Annie couldn't know how bad. Shadows of that time stole over Frank, like black clouds passing over his soul, chilling every drop of his blood.

Red Earth, South Dakota. A breeding ground of militants, violence, bloodshed.

What else had this hell on earth spawned? *Who was this guy?*

"Ella, tell me everything you can remember about Chandler. When was it you first met him?"

"Why? Do you—"

"Just think, Ella!"

Frank saw her stare at him from the corner of his eye.

"He showed up about two years ago," she began. "He had only a few things and I really didn't need any inventory, but they were nice old pieces. He had that bad limp and he was trying to make a living."

"Two years ago," Frank said to himself. A year after Red Earth. "Did he say where he was from?"

"He looked to me like a down-on-his-luck Easterner. I felt sorry for him. Bought a few pieces to help him out."

Splinters of adrenaline pierced Frank's chest. "Easterner? What part of the East?"

"I don't know. It was just the way he talked. Fast, aggressive. He said he was starting a new life." She sighed hard. "We get them out here. Misfits looking for a home, the simple life. They think the West is still a frontier."

"But he didn't ever say where he was from?"

"No," she answered thoughtfully.

"Anything else?"

"Last spring he came in without the bandanna he always wore across his forehead. I didn't recognize him at first because he had also cut his hair some and shaved his beard." She was quiet a moment. "I remember noticing a scar on his face."

An image flashed into Frank's mind—the face of Ritter smiling even as Frank bent over Mary, his hand pressed to her belly to staunch the blood. But there was too much, and too many other wounds, all bleeding, leaking her very life. And there was Ritter, in the crowd, smiling, triumphant: He wasn't looking at Mary or Frank, but at the AIRO member he had just shot, his grin macabre for all the blood streaking from a gash over his eye.

The briar of adrenaline tightened around Frank's chest. It couldn't be, he told himself. Chandler couldn't be Ritter.

"What kind of scar?" He didn't recognize his own voice. It sounded squeezed from someplace distant.

"Right above his right eye."

Every bloody memory of Red Earth flashed through Frank's brain—and every frame had Ritter's face superimposed.

He couldn't be here, not now.

Frank's mind jumped to the FBI in Phoenix: dead of night, agents hovering, desperate for a message from their undercover man in AIRO. What if Ritter was the inside man?

Frank's gut twisted. Hard. His hand shot to his side.

"Frank! Are you all right?" Ella's hand went to his arm.

"Nothing. It's nothing."

But he lied. Something was definitely wrong.

How had Ritter gotten back in the bureau after the debacle at Red Earth? He thought Ritter had left. He had even tried to find him to talk about what had happened—but Ritter never returned his calls.

Frank knew, then, that his partner had turned against him, the one man, besides Frank, who really knew what Red Earth had been about.

What the hell was he doing here?

He had to find out, with or without the cooperation of Harris.

"Frank, what's wrong?"

A hand pressed to his chest. His heart screamed.

Frank looked at Ella and saw the sheer terror in her eyes.

"Nothing," he said again. "I might have an idea who this is. I have to check something out."

"You know who Jenny is with?"

"Maybe."

For a moment, Ella was quiet, though Frank knew she was staring at him. "You know and you're afraid."

"I won't let anything happen to her, Ella."

The words pounded through Frank in the rapid-fire beat of the fleeting white lines. *I won't let anything happen to her*.

Ella stared after Frank as he pulled away from the post, the Jeep's tires spitting sand and gravel. He drove with the same intensity and purpose as when they left the canyon, only now with even more fury . . . and she knew the fury that fueled him: hatred for AIRO.

She had seen that hatred come alive in the canyon. Now she saw the hatred claim every bit of him.

She thought of what he had told Tikui—that he cared who murdered Eddie.

But that was a lie.

Frank had only *one* agenda: revenge for his wife's murder.

Everything else was a lie.

CHAPTER EIGHTEEN

Her arm was asleep and her nose itched from where the fly had landed, but Jenny didn't dare move. She had already lain this way for two hours and she would for another two, however long it took to gain her freedom.

A sob filled her throat and instantly pricked the back of her eyes. She pressed her face to the already damp pillow, stifling even the barest breath of a sound. Crying only seemed to anger him more.

Anything she did seemed to anger him.

The sob rose, a knot of ache fighting past the muscles in her neck. Jenny bit down on the pillow. The salty wetness stung the new wound on her lip and forced more tears through her lashes.

Jenny clenched her eyes tight, pictured her own room, her own bed. She imagined herself there. The heaviness across her waist was only the weighty quilt, the one Great-grandmother had made especially for her.

Jenny's mind flashed instantly to yesterday morning's early hours when she and Chandler had visited the old woman in her hogan. She could feel the small woman's powerful hug. She saw the joy on Great-grandmother's face, the unconditional love in her eyes. *Sáni* had been so happy to see Jenny.

But Jenny had brought with her the devil.

What must Sáni think now of her only great-grandchild?

Jenny clutched the pillow tight to her and squeezed her

eyes shut. She wanted to black out the rest of that day, erase it, make it go away . . . make it not happen.

Yet again, she saw Great-grandmother trundle off to the corral. She saw Chandler watching, waiting, until *Sáni* was out of sight, then he disappeared over the ridge.

There's nothing there, she had called out. He didn't stop.

She should have called out to *Sáni*. She should have run after Chandler. Instead, she had stood there, frozen, denying the evil spark she had seen in his eyes while her heart jumped in her chest, a small hand beating on her from the inside.

Chandler reappeared over the ridge, his hands empty. He struggled over the top, looking determined but vulnerable, his limp more pronounced from the exertion.

He had hurried her to the car, pushing her along, his hand on her elbow. He drove down the road and abruptly stopped, muttering that he had not told Great-grandmother what he would do about her hogan.

When he stepped out, Jenny saw the bottom of his jeans: red earth, brown sand . . . and jagged specks of white.

White clung to his jeans, a spattering that reached inches up Chandler's leg, as if razed from the earth on a cloud . . .

. . . a precious cloud of bone and ashes.

What have you done?

The words echoed through her head now.

She didn't remember climbing from the car or running down the road back to *Sáni*'s. Had she run or had she walked? Her mind stuck on the question, as if it mattered, as if she could turn back the clock, dictate her actions, change the outcome, replace the next image.

Her heart cracked again, as it had a thousand times that morning. She had told herself there were things she didn't understand. She had convinced herself he knew more and whatever he did was for AIRO, just as her father had.

Except now she knew it had all been a lie!

She gripped the pillow tight to her face, clenching against the rush of shame she felt every time she faced what Chandler had done, the man she had brought to *Sáni*'s.

Everything *Sáni* owned littered the ground in her home. She watched him drag the mattress off the cot, his limp making the burden awkward, enraging him. He spotted her and his eyes flared with hatred.

He reached into his pocket. When he withdrew his hand, Jenny saw flecks of white.

As the powder drifted from his clenched fist onto *Sáni's* bed, Chandler's face contorted into an evil grin.

Jenny's heart pounded against her chest.· A scream lodged in her throat.

A faint whimper ·pierced her mind, rang in her ears. A leg pressed against hers and the present slammed into her consciousness.

For a terrified minute, Jenny held her breath, trying to hear past the thundering pulse in her ears. Had she awakened Chandler? If she turned her head would she see his eyes open?

Soon, she heard the deep breathing behind her. With agonizing slowness, she let air escape past her lips.

She was safe.

The thought drove through her with the force of a spike impaling her to the spot.

Safe was not here. Not here.

Why hadn't she taken the car when she had the chance? If she had, maybe she could have stopped Chandler. Or she could have yelled for *Sáni,* put her in the car and driven away.·

Then she wouldn't be ·here.

She would be free. She would be back with Great-grandmother. She could explain, apologize, beg forgiveness . . . help *Sáni* put everything back.

Except everything couldn't be put back. Remnants of those things that mattered the most now ringed the bottom of Chandler's jeans—which lay in a heap on the floor right beneath her. If Jenny dangled her hand over the side, she could touch the denim. She ached to do just that: gather some of the white dust, smooth it between her fingertips, rub it deep into her skin, under her skin, if she could.

She shifted, ever so slightly, edging her arm an inch at a time to the side of the bed.

A hand squeezed her waist.

"I like you right here."

His low drawl breathed down her back. Every muscle in Jenny instantly tightened.

That drawl used to send tingles to her belly, raise goose bumps of anticipation on her flesh. She remembered wishing to hear that slow roll of words right next to her ear, like she did now.

God, how could she have been so stupid?

The hand spread across her stomach and pulled her from her side onto her back. Sharp, spiky hairs brushed her neck. Her nerves jumped, repelled at the touch.

"Don't be so skittish. You know you want this."

Jenny's stomach roiled so violently, she felt the churning in her throat, filling her throat, pushing over her tongue. She was going to get sick.

She pushed back the cover, her elbow connecting with something hard, and fled to the bathroom.

"Bitch!"

Chandler's curse rose over the sound of her retching into the toilet. But if he heard her throwing up . . . shivers fled down Jenny's bent back. She reached for the faucet and turned the water on high.

Gradually the spasms subsided. She sank against the porcelain, sweat on her brow, her stomach still turning. She had to get out of here.

The shadow of a man crossed the threshold and stretched along the bathroom floor. "What the hell— You're puking?" Angry red blotches spread up Chandler's neck to his cheeks.

Jenny scooted back into the shower door. "Must have been something I ate."

His lips curled into a sneer. "I don't think so, chickadee. You look scared to me." He walked in.

Jenny flattened her back against the glass. "No, I'm sick. I really am."

God, please let him have an ounce of decency.

He crouched next to her, so close she could see every black inch of his eyes, so close she should see the irises in his eyes—but there were none: He had the flat black eyes of a viper.

"You know," he whispered, his sour breath heavy with cigarettes and booze, "in this dim light, huddled on the ground, you bear a striking resemblance to your father."

My father. The comparison, so sudden, caught Jenny off guard. Did she resemble her father?

Jenny's heart squeezed so hard her eyes watered. She tilted her head up, determined not to cry. She bet Eddie never cried. He would have been brave.

Maybe that was Chandler's point? Maybe he had made the comment to remind Jenny of her responsibilities?

"I should have known better," Chandler said.

The judgment in his voice struck its mark: She couldn't let him down. She couldn't let her father down. If only Chandler would reassure her that everything would be all right in the end, then she would do what he said, she told herself.

She wanted to apologize, wanted even more to understand, but when Jenny looked up, the words died in her mouth.

Chandler stared back, his face pinched as if repulsed by a sudden rancid odor. "Yeah, you're just like him. Worthless." Contempt, anger, absolute hatred filled his voice and was mirrored in his eyes.

Chandler hated her father.

Jenny's mind stumbled. Her heart, her breath, jammed in her throat. The floor beneath her dissolved to nothing but a black hole and she was falling with nothing to stop her, nothing to cling to, nothing left to believe in.

Vaguely, she heard a yell, but she couldn't focus, couldn't respond . . . and if Chandler hit her, she didn't care. She had been such a fool.

She heard more shouting, two different voices—Chandler and someone else.

". . . not ready!"

". . . hell's going on?"

Jenny didn't listen, she didn't care. All she could see was her father; his face filled her mind, but he wasn't the smiling Eddie she knew.

". . . insignificant little shit."

". . . understand. Be patient." It was Chandler. His pleading, almost whining tone was superimposed on Jenny's thoughts of her father. An image emerged: Chandler, the bully, but scared; Eddie, her father, always sure of himself, independent . . .

Why did Chandler hate her father? What had he meant, *huddled on the ground?*

Jenny's heart stilled. She crawled close to the bathroom door.

". . . not calling the shots, do you understand?"

"I know that. But this is worth waiting for," Chandler said.

"You keep saying that, but you don't show us anything, Chandler."

"I haven't let you down yet. I told you about Eddie Honanie, remember? I'm the one who found out about his plan to set you up. And I took care of that problem, didn't I?"

"So you said."

Jenny's heart froze on the truth.

An image crystallized . . .

A canyon, dead of night. Her father and Chandler—one proud, one a bully . . . one on the ground, the other, Chandler, standing, whining.

"And I'm the only one out there, trying to clean up all the loose ends," Chandler continued.

"By playing around with some child? You're sick, Chandler, and we don't want you around."

"She's the link, don't you see? She knows something."

"What makes you so sure?"

"She's as much as told me Eddie hated AIRO."

Jenny's heart slammed against her chest. She wanted to jump up and yell.

"That little shit. Where is she?"

"In the bathroom."

"So she can hear us? You idiot."

Jenny heard footsteps coming toward the bathroom door. She scrambled to the toilet, leaned over it and closed her eyes.

"She's sick," Chandler called out. "Puking her guts out."

Jenny felt the creak of the floor as someone walked right up to her.

"She looks passed out, Chandler."

The voice came from right above her. Jenny's heart thundered in her chest.

"What have you done to her?"

"Nothing. Something she ate, she said."

A big hand pressed against her back. Jenny forced out a moan and put a hand to her stomach.

The hand went to her forehead, lifting her hair, and pressing against her skin. A shudder ran through Jenny.

"She's clammy, Chandler. Get me the blanket off the bed."

A moment later, soft warmth settled over Jenny's shoulders. She wanted to say "thank you." But she didn't dare. Could she trust this man any more than Chandler, who right now stood only a few feet away anyway?

"I want her out of here, Chandler."

"Let's go talk in the hall," Chandler said.

The floor creaked. Jenny peeked an eye open and, through her lashes, saw black cowboy boots disappear out the door.

Their voices diminished. Jenny scooted back to the door.

"There's no telling what trouble she and her dad had cooked up," Chandler said. "But I have a plan."

The door slammed, shutting off the voices.

Cautiously, Jenny leaned around the bathroom wall. No one was there. For the first time in four days, she was alone.

She jerked her head to the window . . . and freedom.

Jenny dropped the blanket, grabbed her jeans from the floor, and pulled them on. She got her shoes and shirt and ran to the window. With a simple flick, she unlocked the latches, then pushed up on the frame. It moved.

She could get out of here.

Her heart raced, jumping her pulse, jerking her thoughts like a skipped stone.

I have a plan.

Chandler's words skittered through her head. What plan? For who?

He had lied to her. Lied to AIRO. Lied to *Sani*. Whose side was he on? Who would he hurt next?

He had trashed *Sani*'s place, probably destroyed *alch'i'i*. AIRO wouldn't do that. Something told her AIRO had no idea what Chandler was up to. People were listening to this guy, believing him, and he was evil.

You have to be your own person, Jenny.

Aunt Ella's voice cut through all the confusion in Jenny's head with the clarity of a shining light. She saw her aunt, standing alone in the store, her gaze sure, honest, uncompromised . . . strong.

Jenny's hands stilled on the frame. Her heart quieted. A calmness slipped over her.

She could stay, find out Chandler's plans. Or she could run. The choice was hers.

Jenny pushed the window down and locked the latches. Giving herself no time to reconsider, she walked to the door and leaned her ear to the wall. All she could hear were the muffled voices.

She slid over to the door and cupped her hands around her ear.

". . . don't like you."

"Sanchez . . . a chance . . ."

Jenny couldn't hear enough. She laid her hand on the knob and, ever so slowly, turned it, cracking the door a fraction of an inch.

"Leonard wants you out now."

"He's making a mistake, Sanchez. You all are. You need me."

"Like we need cockroaches, Chandler. Pack your things."

"You can't. Not now. Not when I've put everything on the line—"

"Just what have you risked? Your shady reputation as an itinerant trader? You've got *nothing* on the line, Chandler. That's what has bothered me from the beginning with you."

"What's bothered you, Sanchez, is that I'm white. That's why you don't trust me. You're ready to throw me out over some *Indian* girl. Without a thought to what I've done for you. Real open-minded, aren't you?"

"Open-minded doesn't keep us alive, Chandler. Being safe does."

"Then answer me this, how are you going to take care of the threat from the Feds without me?"

"The Feds?" The man laughed. "The Feds are not a threat. We got as much chance of seeing an agent at the door as an elephant in the desert. And the Feds would be about as subtle.

"You've already got Feds crawling all over the place."

"What are you talking about, Chandler?"

"I'm talking about information I have that you obviously don't."

"Enlighten me."

"Maybe I should be talking to Leonard."

Jenny heard a scuffle, and when Chandler spoke, his voice sounded about an octave higher. "Okay, okay. You ever heard of an agent named Reardon?"

Jenny's breath caught.

"He's all over your shit."

"The one in charge at Red Earth?"

"That's right, Sanchez. He caused all the trouble there. Got fired and now he's on a grudge. He won't rest until all of AIRO is dead and buried."

"Where is he?"

"Around."

"Do better than that, Chandler."

"I will! What do you think I'm telling you this for?"

"You got one day, Chandler, that's it."

"You think I don't know? I'm working on it."

"In the meantime, I want her out of here. Get the information and get her home."

"I'll take care of her."

"And Chandler, you better make our wait worth it."

"Oh, it will be worth it. I guarantee. You'll be so surprised."

"I don't *want* a surprise from you, Chandler."

"Right."

Chandler's voice was close.

Jenny ran as fast and quiet as she could to the bathroom and turned on the water. She dunked her hands in the icy water and splashed her face, trying to look as if she had just cleaned up.

The outer door slammed. She heard something crash to the floor. Loud footsteps stomped to the bathroom.

"Good, you're dressed. Let's go."

"To where?" she managed.

But Chandler was already across the room, grabbing his shirt. He pulled it on and faced her, smiling. Jenny's heart jumped to her throat.

God, what was she doing?

"We got one day, chickadee. Then he gets the surprise of his life. And he won't even see it coming." He walked over to her. "They never do," he murmured, trailing a finger down her cheek. Evil flickered across the dead black of his eyes—the evil of a man who held death in his hands.

He could kill and never think a thing about it.

He *had* killed.

The truth squeezed her heart so hard Jenny thought she might faint: Chandler had killed her father.

Her vision blurred. She reached a frantic hand to the sink for balance.

"Don't even think of getting sick again, bitch."

A hand grabbed her arm and yanked her from the bathroom.

Utter hatred leapt through her veins, as if shot through her from the tips of his fingers. In one crazy tilt of reality, her balance righted, his hatred rushed through her and gave her purpose.

Somehow, someway, she would make him pay. He would not get away with murder.

Frank pressed the Jeep to its limit. His foot to the floor, his gaze was focused straight ahead on the highway, but in his mind's eye a myriad of images flashed by faster than the landscape flying by in a blur—and every one included the man he knew as Ritter, a man who had at one time been Frank's partner.

He had seen Ritter only a few times since Red Earth, but they hadn't talked. They'd been kept apart almost from that very day, separated at duty, then sequestered in interrogation. It was by-the-book procedure to assure unprejudiced information from every witness. Frank had understood. Until, somewhere along the line, he had stopped feeling like a witness and more like a suspect.

He hadn't cared then. He hadn't even thought about it. Truth was, for about the first six months after Mary died, he had done his best to keep his mind incapable of thinking *anything*.

He could *smell* the drunkenness even now. His world was colored a tired, fluid amber that washed around him, through him, as he sat numb, motionless, resigned to any punishment for any crime—that would have been all right with Frank.

Nothing mattered. Nothing made sense.

How could he have let Mary die? What the hell had she been doing there? How had she gotten past him to AIRO?

The questions swirled; dark images floated just beneath the surface of whiskey in every glass he poured into his body one after the other, as if he could drink away those last hours, drown out the voices in his head.

But they were always there in the next glass and the one after that. Until one day, he simply stopped reaching for the glass. Instead, he had reached for the phone and called Ritter. The man had been at Red Earth. He was his partner. He could explain things. Frank needed them explained.

Two years later, Frank could remember the phone call as if it were yesterday: Ritter's surprise, then his evasive, hurried answers as if Frank weren't his old partner, as if they hadn't been through hell and back together . . . as if Frank were the last person in the whole world Ritter wanted to talk to.

When the final judgment came in, Frank was sober, and Ritter was gone. Frank never got his questions answered . . . instead he faced more questions in the eyes of every agent when he returned to work. Frank had heard the whispers that he was to blame for Red Earth, for the deaths of the agents, the civilians . . . and the near death of his partner.

Ritter had gotten his own punishment: The man was crippled at Red Earth and couldn't possibly work in the field anymore—or so had gone the talk.

So how had Ritter ended up back with the bureau? Even more of a puzzlement: How had he managed to be assigned to undercover on AIRO?

Frank knew he wouldn't get any answers from the office. But he had a back door to the bureau: All he needed was a computer.

He pulled into the Navajo Tribal Headquarters and parked. As soon as he opened the Jeep door, Frank heard heavy drumbeats and chants drifting from the great sandstone arch. He stood there, hand on the door frame, the deep beats of the drum pounding through him to his feet. His thoughts fled to the ceremony at Hopi. Were the Navajo now marshaling their own powers?

The voices of the chanters rose, the drums beat louder. The air pulsated with urgency.

Frank headed for the front doors and entered an empty lobby—no duty cops, nobody even in the receptionist booth. He pushed open the glass door leading to the squad rooms and walked past unoccupied desks, their phones ringing unanswered.

This was not normal . . . unless there was a full-scale emergency.

He threw a glance at an available computer, cursed and headed for the hallway door. As soon as he pushed open the thick glass door, he heard voices coming from a room at the end. The talk was agitated, electric.

Frank's instincts fired. He strode to the room, turned in and found himself in the midst of a war room: cops gathered around a map of the res tacked to the wall; other cops bent over enlarged maps of the res on the conference table, tracing routes. And every face in the room wore the look of crisis.

He spotted Coriz and maneuvered through groups of Indian cops.

"What the hell is going on?"

Coriz looked up. There was an instant before he recognized Frank and for that moment, Frank saw a man in acute pain: his face drawn tight, his eyes red and tired.

"Coriz, what happened?"

The Navajo's eyes cleared on Frank and turned instantly hard. "I can't talk to you."

"What do you mean you can't talk to me? What's going on?"

Coriz stared back. "AIRO has closed down the interstate highways." His gaze narrowed as if measuring Frank.

"When?"

"As of about an hour ago." Coriz still stared, scrutinizing Frank.

Frank could strike a match from the jet-black flint of the Navajo's eyes. "Coriz, what the hell is your problem with me?"

"You're the one with the problem, Agent Reardon."

"What?"

"You're persona non grata."

"What the hell are you talking about?"

"Come with me, Agent Reardon."

Coriz put his hand on Frank's elbow and started to the door. Frank's instincts fired. "Just what the hell is going on, Coriz?"

Coriz didn't answer until he had Frank down the hall in the squad room. "You'll have to answer that, Agent Reardon. Right now, just have a seat while I make a call."

"The hell I'll have a seat, Coriz. What is going on?"

"You're being detained, Agent Reardon, by order of the FBI."

CHAPTER NINETEEN

Ella wandered the rambling building, unable to fix herself to any one of the hundred tasks needing attention, unable to muster the slightest interest, unable to find any strength within. She soon found herself outside her home, her store, standing in Apache's domain, staring at the painted dunes.

As if beckoned by her footsteps, the prairie dog popped his head from his hole and scrambled out to her, chirping hello. He sniffed the hem of her skirt, then rose up on his hind legs, his nose to the air, his whiskers twitching. Ella couldn't help but smile at the little creature; his expectations were simple and obvious.

"Good morning, my little sentinel." Ella reached in her skirt pocket and withdrew a handful of sunflower seeds. She sprinkled them on the ground, but Apache showed no interest, just stared up at her, his small body perfectly balanced.

"So you just came to say hello?" Ella knelt to him. She ran a finger over his head and down his narrow back, releasing small puffs of dust from his fur.

Gray hairs tinged his tiny cheeks. They were the first sign of his age she had seen. She thought of Jenny's concern about how long Apache would live. Ella remembered her own response.

Maybe one day he'll just go underground and never come out.

No, Jenny had said. *Apache is a warrior. He will die defending his family.*

The words filled Ella's mind, overwhelming her with immense sadness—irrational, out of proportion to the significance of this little fellow.

Her gaze blurred. Her hand faltered on Apache.

No! she thought fiercely, fighting the flood of grief. Yet the great sense of loss welled from her heart, lodging a sob in her throat.

Soft fur slipped through her palm and Ella glanced at her loyal friend. "But you're not gone yet, are you?"

She gazed intently at him, wishing he could answer, that he would promise to stay . . .

. . . but she knew it wasn't Apache's promise she wanted.

Ella drew a ragged breath and raised her eyes to the horizon, to the bald dunes rolling off into the distance, and it occurred to her that Apache's view never altered, his world never changed. He peeked from his hole each morning, knowing what he would see.

How comforting, she thought. *How safe.*

She had yearned for that same certainty, it seemed, for her entire life. She had thrown all her energies into *building* that world for herself—a place of abiding peace, stable . . . unbroken. A reasonable goal, she had thought. Now she questioned whether the world abided reasonable people.

Ella heard the creak of the screen door.

"Shouldn't you be cleaning the store?"

Ella glanced over her shoulder to Grandmother. The little woman stood in the doorway, an apron tied around her substantial waist.

"Yes," Ella answered absently and returned her gaze to the sand dunes.

"Already three Navajo are gathered outside, Ella."

"They will wait."

"They should wait while you feed that rodent?"

"Apache," Ella corrected.

Ella heard the *shoosh* of *Sáni*'s moccasined feet across the ground. Apache dove into his hole.

"You *named* the prairie dog?"

That was the same question Frank had asked. "Why does everyone find that so improbable?" Ella muttered.

"I was just—"

Grandmother's quiet, halting voice drew Ella's glance. The old woman looked down, her gaze thoughtful, as if thinking back. Then she focused on Ella. "I was just thinking," she said. "That was something your mother would have done."

Ella stared, speechless. She *never* could have expected that answer.

"She related to animals," Grandmother continued. "More than people, I guess." *Sáni* sighed. "So you have some of your mother in you." She smiled at Ella.

Ella barely registered the kind smile; instead, her heart registered the comment as a judgment. "I don't care more about animals than people."

Grandmother's eyes widened in surprise. "Of course you don't. Anyone can see that."

That response threw Ella even more off balance. Since when had Grandmother given two thoughts to what Ella cared about?

"But your mother—" Grandmother shook her head. "She had her mind on other things, I think."

"What other things?" Ella shifted slightly to look directly at Grandmother.

"I don't know," Grandmother said, her voice truly bewildered. "To me, she *had* enough to occupy herself—a home, a husband, children. To her, not enough, I guess." She let out a hiss between her teeth.

The sound lingered in the air. Grandmother's face was drawn in distaste.

Ella stared. She had never heard Grandmother speak so openly, and with such disdain, of her own daughter. The question Ella needed answered rose to her lips. "Why did she leave, *Sáni*?"

"No fortitude," *Sáni* said, without hesitation. She gazed on Ella with eyes suddenly solemn and wise. "Not like you, child." Then she smiled.

"No fortitude," Ella repeated, but the words barely escaped past the knot in her throat.

She saw the kindness in *Sáni*'s eyes, but all she could think was, *You're wrong. I'm not strong.*

She couldn't bear one more test, not one more expectation, not one more disappointment. She had no more room in her heart for cruel reality.

Ella stared at the ground, shaking her head.

"Will you give up like your mother gave up? I suppose you will just walk away, too?"

Another hiss escaped Grandmother's lips just before she turned and walked back into the store, the last sound in the air another creak of the screen door.

No, I won't walk away. When have I ever walked away?

A flash of anger sparked in Ella. Her heart lurched—a flutter of life against heavy sorrow.

Ella pulled herself from the ground and walked into her home, through the kitchen, courtyard, and straight to the gallery. She dragged the broom from the office, resigned to restoring some semblance of order. She swept from the far end of the gallery toward the counters, gathering up broken pottery, rolling rugs to hang later, righting sculptures. She tried to stay dispassionate, focused on cleaning, but every broken shard, every ragged bit of wreckage, tore at a wound inside Ella, reminding her of all in her life that needed repair.

I only wanted a home. I only wanted a safe place!

Her head went light with dizziness and Ella braced a hand against the wall. She had always seen her way to a solution, been able to forge ahead, her sights set on a goal. But she couldn't see the end this time.

Why had this happened?

A bubble of anxiety burst past the barrier in her chest, carrying with it a wave of fear: This time she couldn't make things right.

The loud squawk of a bird bristled the hairs on Ella's arms. The next instant, the magpie swooped from the rafters and landed on her shoulder.

"Damn bird! Shoo!"

Ella jerked her shoulder forward and back, but the bird wouldn't move.

"What are you doing with that Hopi bird?"

Grandmother's demand echoed from the doorway.

"*Hopi* bird? Grandmother, it's a magpie."

"He shouldn't be here."

"Believe me, I've tried to get rid of him. I think he sneaks in around sunset. He must have a nest up in the beams."

The bird pushed through Ella's hair and nestled, much to her chagrin, at her neck.

"Get out of there!" she yelled, bending one arm, then the next behind her, trying to reach the bird.

He evaded her, getting more and more tangled in her hair.

"Grandmother, can you help me out?"

"No, no, leave him be."

"Leave him be? You just said—" Ella drew a frustrated breath. "Will you at least open the door?" she pleaded.

Sáni wouldn't budge.

Ella made her way to the door, still struggling to reach the magpie. She opened the door, stepped outside, and waved her arms through the air. The magpie cackled and chortled, as if laughing at her efforts.

Worn out, Ella finally dropped her arms. To her amazement, the bird immediately settled quietly. She thought of the pellet rifle and took a step back inside. The magpie flew straight from her shoulders up to the rafters, yanking a few strands of hair with him.

"Ow!" Ella spotted the gun behind the counter and grabbed it.

"No! You can't shoot him!"

"You just told me to get rid of him."

"Child, don't shoot that magpie."

Ella glanced at her grandmother. The old woman's face was skewed in wonder. *Sáni* looked at her. "He is a Hopi bird, Ella. He is the bird of the east, of the dawn, and of water and the underworld. He shouldn't be here, that is true. That is what is amazing."

"He's just a bird, Grandmother. And he poops on my rugs."

Grandmother shot her a stern look. "The magpie causes divisions of people, Ella. But he has rested here. That is good. Maybe he has already seen too much division." With that, she turned and disappeared back down the hallway.

Ella stared after her grandmother, disbelieving what she had just heard. *Sáni* was worried about division among people? Was this the same woman who just two days ago had argued against any peace with the Hopi?

Ella followed her grandmother down the hallway and to the bedroom. "Are you all right?" she asked.

Sáni stood at the window, gazing at the western sky.

The little woman seemed even smaller in this room, surrounded by the heavy, dark wooden furniture. Ella had imagined her grandmother here, but could the old woman ever really make this her home?

Ella stepped quietly inside the room and over to the chair. She lifted the backpack she had brought from Grandmother's hogan.

"Not mine," Grandmother murmured, with barely a glance.

Ella glanced over to *Sáni*. The old woman was looking at the bag.

"I packed some of your things inside, Grandmother."

"Not mine," *Sáni* repeated.

Ella let the bag rest. "Why don't you come to bed?" Ella lifted the covers for Grandmother to climb in. Her hand went to *Sáni*'s forehead, tucking back hair in the same way as Ella would for Jenny.

"I am so very tired," *Sáni* said, closing her eyes. ". . . find some peace," she murmured.

This little woman, always full of vigor and fight, now

lay so quiet—at odds with her nature, contrary to the spirit integral to *Sáni*.

The time Ella had wished for—for *Sáni* to stop fighting, to be practical and rational—now seemed a time out of place, out of step . . . out of balance.

Ella felt out of balance.

She backed away from the bed, her steps awkward, her legs unsure.

She bent down and straightened *Sáni*'s shoes. She folded Grandmother's shawl and laid it neatly on the bureau. Her gaze rested on the backpack slung over the chair. She could unpack Grandmother's things, put them away.

She unzipped the bag and pulled out *Sáni*'s clothes. Her hand paused on the brush, then she set it next to the shawl. She opened the bottom drawer of the bureau and reached for the backpack. It made a hard *clunk* against the wood.

Ella looked inside the bag again, only to find it empty. She turned the bag around, searching for another pouch, but there were no zippers, no other access.

Yet *something* weighed down the bottom.

She turned the bag over and suddenly noticed a five-inch line of stitches, as if someone had resewn the bottom to the pack. Her fingers manipulated the canvas, feeling around the edges of something hard and square, like a book . . . or a block of stone.

What is in there?

Her gaze went to *Sáni*.

Not mine. Grandmother's words echoed in Ella's head. Chills raised the flesh along Ella's arms.

She closed the drawer and left the room, backpack in hand. In the gallery, she grabbed a pair of scissors from behind the counter and snipped the new threads at the bottom. She reached within. Her knuckles scraped painfully against something rough.

Gripping the object, Ella tore it loose from the hidden cache in the backpack.

A triangle of greenish-gray stone slid onto the counter—

with two perfectly even sides and one long, ragged edge as if the stone had been broken in two.

She didn't recognize the material. It was too thick to be turquoise, too hard to be serpentine. All shades of green swirled in layers like marble. Yet it was too light to be marble.

She ran her fingers across the top. They slid, unhindered, over the smooth, satiny stone—no pockmarks, no pits or blemishes. A material so impossibly perfect couldn't exist in nature.

And it was *warm*.

Her fingers trembled inexplicably.

Ella turned the stone over and her breath caught.

There, carved in the center, was half the figure of a man. The other half of the man was gone—part of the missing piece broken from the stone.

She traced the etching. It was primitive, reminiscent of the prehistoric Anasazi carvings on canyon rocks. Except this was not a canyon rock.

Her gaze went to the break. The exposed, unpolished stone should be dull and chalky, yet it gleamed in vibrant hues of green.

She had never seen anything so beautiful, so carefully carved . . . so precisely broken.

The jagged imperfection ran exactly diagonal, a clean break across the image of the man . . .

. . . as if deliberately broken.

Who made this?

Ella knew the answer. She knew it in the timeless beauty and simplicity of the piece she held, its extraordinary color, the magic of its warmth.

Was this the stone everyone searched for? The stone Tikui wanted?

She stared at the stone in her hands. Could she truly be holding the Hopi tablet? Did it really exist?

What was Grandmother doing with it?

Uneasiness crept through Ella. Her gaze went to the hallway.

Not mine, Grandmother had said, looking at the backpack. Then whose?

Ella tore through the bag, both hands searching for something, anything that would identify the owner. All the time one name pounded through her head and the uneasiness swept through Ella, carrying an eerie foreboding.

She yanked on the bottom flap, ripping through the stitches, tearing back the canvas. There, jammed in the back, wrinkled from the weight of the stone, Ella saw a paper. She pulled it out, unfolded it, and read through a receipt for a storage locker, made out to Eddie Honanie.

This was Eddie's bag.

The full impact of that realization drove through Ella with the violent turbulence of a thunderbolt. She dropped the receipt—as if the paper carried an electric charge. Her insides quaked.

She had denied every one of Frank's arguments, even knowing how irrational she sounded. But she couldn't deny the truth facing her.

Eddie had stolen the art. With it, he had stolen this stone and, like a thunderstorm on mountains flooding arroyos miles away, that theft—that one decision—had changed the landscape of their lives.

She stared at the hard stone in her hands. The foreboding chilled her blood. Instant shivers stole through her with the certainty and clarity of the truth.

Her body shook with pent-up anger, a rage she had never before experienced.

What made this worth a life? What made this worth Eddie's life?

And who had determined his life was due in payment for this stone?

She knew the legend. A myth of ancient peoples crawling from a hole in the ground. A story of hope, of reconciliation . . . and the tablet represented honor and destiny.

This was Eddie's destiny? To die for a piece of rock? For a legend?

Ella's body shook, repulsed by the hoax.

She grabbed the stone, meaning to shove it into the backpack. But at first touch, her fingers tingled with such alarming suddenness, Ella nearly dropped the tablet. She gripped the stone tighter, determination steeling her against the thousands of needlelike stabs pricking her fingers, her palms, and running up her arms in the speed of a breath. Agony ripped through her chest, crushing a moan from her lips.

Ella shoved the stone into the satchel, desperate for relief. She pulled out her hands, each as weighty as an ingot of silver. When she rubbed them together, she couldn't feel them, just a thick, piercing numbness and a leaden ache throbbing to her shoulders. For several moments she stared at the stone, disbelieving the sensations even as she furiously kneaded the pain in her arms.

No stone could cause this . . . yet it had—attacking her, almost like something alive, fighting for its life.

She pushed away from the counter, her hand grabbing the receipt, and walked out of the gallery. Ella paused in the hallway, uncertain of where she meant to go.

Her body sank against the wall. She clenched her fist around the paper.

What could Eddie have been thinking? What had he planned to do with it?

For all Eddie's impulsiveness, Ella had never known him to do anything illegal. He hadn't been a criminal or a thief. He was an activist, with lofty ideals, always driven by the next cause.

Ella's thoughts jerked to AIRO. What was it Frank had said about them? They preyed on people with noble ideas.

Had AIRO preyed on Eddie?

Her heart seized around the thought. Had they put him up to stealing the art?

But they couldn't do anything with the art—they wouldn't do anything with the art. It was Indian art, precious, special. A part of the heritage AIRO itself defended.

It didn't make any sense. Ella shook her head, rocking it back and forth against the hard stucco wall. Whatever Eddie's plan, it hadn't worked.

Her fingers flexed around the clenched receipt. She now held a vital piece of evidence for Frank. Maybe the art was still there . . . all but one piece.

She yanked her gaze to the doorway of the gallery and, beyond that, to the stone.

That tablet was somehow at the crux of everything. Ella knew it to her core. If the art had been for AIRO, why had Eddie withheld that one artifact?

It was Eddie's destiny.

Ella's blood raged on every word, churning her insides with helpless frustration. She felt as if she were a pawn in someone's grand scheme. It seemed everyone around her had an agenda, except herself. Maybe it was time that changed.

The Hopi wanted the tablet, of that Ella had no doubt. She could take the stone to Tikui and be done with it. But what about AIRO? Did they know about the tablet? Had they put Eddie up to the theft just to gain possession of the artifact? Only to be betrayed when he kept it?

Ella paced up and down the narrow hallway, her thoughts swirling, her nerves charging. Her body, every fiber within, screamed for action, as if facing imminent danger.

Had *they* killed Eddie and were now using Jenny to get the stone? And here the stone sat on her gallery counter.

Ella stopped. AIRO had Jenny, but Ella had the stone. She just had to find a way to get to AIRO.

She thought of Frank—the most obvious choice, but would he cooperate? Would he deliver to AIRO what they wanted, when they were the very ones who had taken what was precious to him?

Frank had told her he wouldn't let anything happen to Jenny. He had held Ella's face in his hands, looked her in the eyes, and *promised*. And in his gaze, she had seen a man *needing* to keep that promise.

God help her, she believed him.

Ella strode down the hallway, her mind set. She grabbed the backpack. Then, with a glance at the ripped bottom, reconsidered, and tossed it into a corner. She found her leather satchel and laid it on the counter. She grabbed the closest thing available—two polishing gloves—and covered her hands. She reached for the stone, then stopped.

Her hands paused in midair over the stone, her whole body screaming against picking up the stone. For several moments she stared, frozen in terror of a stone, her mind racing over alternatives. But she didn't have a choice; she had to have the stone with her when she went to Frank.

On a breath, she poked a finger to the stone, inching it toward the satchel. Nothing happened: no tingles, no numbness, no stabbing pain. She pressed firmly on the stone and slid it within the satchel. All she felt was a warmth flowing through her, settling over her, like a comforting blanket.

Why hadn't this happened before when she first held the stone? Why had it been so easy this time?

Ella stepped back from the counter, all the time staring at the now-plump satchel.

She swore she heard, from far away, a deep sigh.

It had to be her.

Ella pulled up to the FBI building in the midst of dust and commotion. She wasn't surprised to see men in Arizona police uniforms, others in Navajo Tribal navy, and still more in Hopi law enforcement uniforms. They swarmed on the sidewalk and open space, each in their own distinct groups—just as they had been at every road block she had encountered . . . and then been waved through when recognized as Indian. Only when she had gotten close to Phoenix had she begun to worry about ever reaching her destination. Instead of Indian blockades, she ran into checkpoints run by the feds. They had not appreciated the eagle feather dangling from the rear view mirror on Mitchell's truck. Once more that day, Ella wished that Ben had seen fit to return her own truck.

Ella parked in the lot and worked her way to the front door, past a group of men in suits. FBI agents, she guessed.

"And the helicopters?" one asked.

"Waiting on the governor."

"He should give us tanks, while he's at it. Blast those sons of bitches."

Someone laughed. "Back one hundred years, where they belong."

"Not gonna happen," another said. He gave an obvious glance to a group of tribal cops.

"Excuse me," Ella ground out as she walked right through the middle of the group. The agent turned, Ella tried to sidestep, but the backpack caught on his arm.

"Jesus!" He leapt back as if hit by a lightning bolt.

The other agents converged on Ella. "Where do you think you're going?"

Ella's heart pounded. "I need to see Agent Reardon."

"Damn, lady, what's in the bag?"

"Nothing."

But someone was already pulling the strap off one shoulder.

"It's nothing!" she repeated.

"Stand back." It was the agent who had wished for tanks.

Ella stared helplessly as they opened the satchel. One reached a hand inside. "Hell!" he yelled and yanked his hand out. "What's in there?"

"Just a stone. I traded for it. It's a new marble," Ella said quickly. "Is Agent Reardon here?"

"And why would you want Reardon?" A deep voice came from behind Ella. She faced a small man, but somehow knew immediately he was in charge. He had the same commanding look as Frank, though even more fierce. His piercing blue eyes held not even a trace of compassion.

"I need to talk to him."

He looked her up and down and gave a cold smile. Chills shuddered down Ella's spine.

"And you know him from where?"

"I own a trading post."

"An Indian post?" His lips flattened to a thin line. "Why don't you talk to me." His eyes gleamed.

Ella's shudders rippled into tremors. "No, it has to be Reardon. I have some information for him. Please, where is he?"

A black sedan pulled up in a cloud of dust and stopped. Four doors swung open, four men in suits stepped out. One in back was Frank.

"Frank, I need to—"

"A friend of yours, Reardon?" the agent interrupted. "Someone you need to talk to?"

Ella recoiled from his menacing tone.

"Don't know her," Frank said.

"Really? She says she has some information. What would that be?"

"Haven't the faintest."

Frank turned his gaze to hers. His eyes were flat, expressionless. "You know these Indians. Always working an angle," he said, his voice hard.

He walked past her. Ella nearly reached out to stop him. Two agents suddenly appeared on either side of him, flanking him, as if escorting him to the door.

Frank shot her a quick glance—his eyes begging her not to say another word, *commanding* her. And though she would have disobeyed out of confusion and concern, she saw something else: fear for her.

Ella withdrew her hand, let it drop to her side. Frank kept walking, surrounded by agents who walked so close they jostled him, left him no room to even step to the side . . . or away.

She suddenly understood; they were there to be sure he *didn't* step away.

Her heart pounded so hard, she could hear it. Something was wrong, very wrong for Frank.

Ella followed, pushing past through the crowd to keep

Frank in sight. When he reached the doors, Frank glanced over his shoulder, his eyes searching the crowd. Ella stepped around a bystander and Frank's gaze settled on her, his eyes warm. He mouthed a word.

Go.

CHAPTER
TWENTY

Ella backed away, her gaze on Frank as he disappeared into the building. Why had he pretended not to know her?

She felt a hand at her elbow. She jerked free, stumbling back. Two hands caught her and righted her.

"Whoa, take it easy."

Ella swung around.

"It's me, Ella. Chandler."

Every nerve in Ella's body fired—jolts of surprise compounded by a rush of adrenaline. *Chandler. The man Grandmother said was with Jenny.*

Ella started to ask for Jenny, but something in Chandler's gaze stopped her. He stared back at her, his eyes dead-black. Ella thought of Frank, the terrible urgency on his face when he had first learned of Chandler.

"You can't say hello to your old friend?"

"No . . . it's not that . . ." Ella pivoted, searching faces in the crowd. Was Jenny here? She pulled her gaze back. She wanted to shake him, demand he tell her where Jenny was.

"You don't look happy to see me."

"I'm sorry," Ella said. "It's just such a . . . surprise." She offered a small smile.

Chandler stared back. Ella saw a hardness in his eyes. Her insides tumbled, a cascade of dread.

She couldn't do this! She couldn't pretend at normalcy!

"You really look distraught, Ella. By the way, heard about Eddie."

He put a hand on Ella's shoulder and squeezed a little too hard. Ella flinched, looked at him.

His focus was intense on her. "Too bad. He was such a . . . passionate guy." He gave a quick, sad smile.

Ella wanted to take a step back, but Chandler still held her shoulder. "What brings you here, Chandler?"

He kept staring for a moment longer than necessary, then he glanced to the building. "Funny, I was wondering the same thing, Ella. You have friends in the FBI?"

Ella paused. "Not really," she answered.

He slanted his eyes to her. "You always were cautious, Ella," he said. "That's good. Especially these days."

His grip tightened on her. "Ella, I know about the investigation. You must feel all alone against . . ." He glared at the black-windowed building. "Those bastards." He faced her and grabbed her other shoulder. "I'm sorry I didn't get here sooner."

"It's okay—"

He leaned in close. "I saw Eddie not long before he died. He told me his plans. He was so . . . brave." He breathed the last word in her ear.

Ella took a deep breath, not believing what she was hearing.

"What plan, Chandler? I don't know—"

A man in a suit approached them. "You two. You need to move along."

Chandler took Ella's elbow. "No problem," he said over his shoulder. "Let me get you some lunch, Ella."

"No. I mean, I just haven't had much of an appetite lately."

Still holding her arm, Chandler walked. "I'm here for you, Ella. And I can help. We can help each other. For Eddie's sake." He looked so sincere—a look she had seen on his face many times before in her store.

Could he have wrecked Grandmother's home? Was he the one who had destroyed the alch'i'i?

She had always considered him harmless. An eccentric, yes; also a loner. A lone man on the road . . . in a way, a lot like Eddie.

But what if Chandler were dangerous?

Ella's thoughts fled to Jenny. Chandler was the last person Ella knew of who had been with her niece.

Ella's heart collided with her tumbling stomach. She couldn't let Chandler drive off without her, without *knowing*.

She let him guide her to his car, a huge utility vehicle. It might have been tan at one time, maybe even a light yellow, but now it was the color of dirt and mud—layers of different earth tones from all over the West.

Chandler pulled open the side door with a nasty creak and waited until Ella climbed in before slamming it.

Her heart jumped.

As he pulled away from the curb, Chandler looked at Ella and smiled. "I'm so glad I found you, Ella."

Ella shifted the backpack off her shoulder to her lap and gripped the straps with both hands.

Chandler's hand patted her thigh. "Don't you worry. Everything is going to work out just fine, now."

He turned the corner and Ella's gaze went to the impenetrable FBI building, to the blackened windows, and she imagined Frank gazing down, watching. She hoped with all her heart that he saw her.

A low moan came from the leather satchel on the seat next to her.

Frank slammed into Harris's office, knocking back the glass door into the wall with a resounding echo. "What the hell is going on?" Agents on either side of him grabbed his arms, dragged him to the middle of the room.

Harris brushed past and walked to his desk. He nodded to the agents, and they released Frank and left the office.

"Have a seat, Agent Reardon." Harris gestured to a chair. "First, who's the girl?"

Frank ignored the chair. "I told you. I don't know her."

"She just picked you out of the crowd of agents and called your name."

Frank tried to look puzzled. Whatever shit was about to hit the fan, he didn't want to get Ella involved. "Why the hell am I here?"

"Why do you think?"

What Frank thought was that his Honanie investigation must be getting hot on the trail of something or *someone*. Someone the FBI didn't want him getting close to . . . like the undercover agent in AIRO.

Frank had a good idea of the identity of that undercover agent . . . Ritter; and his skin itched with frustration that he might be pulled from the murder investigation before finding out for sure.

Harris might have his agenda. Frank had his own and he wasn't about to let on for a second. "Cut the crap, Harris. Why am I being detained?"

"Let's talk."

"Fine. Talk."

"Sit, Agent Reardon." Harris pointed again to the chair, and this time did not lower his arm. Frank had the sense Harris could stand there like a statue through the night if necessary.

As far as Frank was concerned, Harris could just do that.

"You already *have* a reputation as an uncooperative asshole, Reardon." There was a warning in Harris's tone that Frank didn't like.

Frank walked straight to the deputy's desk. "And you have a funny way of asking for cooperation: having me detained at Navajo Headquarters, then sending agents to drag me here. Why?"

Harris glanced at Frank, then paced to the window and back again. Suddenly, Frank got the distinct impression that *he* wasn't the one in trouble. Harris was. And whatever the man had on his mind, he was hard-pressed to talk about it—especially with Frank.

Harris let out a deep breath, as if blowing some sort of

distaste out of his mouth. "Where are you at in the Honanie investigation?"

Frank felt inner satisfaction. "Don't have the murderer, if that's what you mean. Are you offering to help?" Frank smiled.

Harris's face remained stony. "But you have an idea about the murderer, don't you?"

"Why the sudden interest?"

"You know why, Reardon. And I don't have any more time for this cat-and-mouse game. What connection have you found to AIRO?"

There it was.

"There's been plenty of mention of AIRO everywhere I look. Criminal records, interviews, background checks on suspects, you name it," Frank answered honestly. "Not a surprise, though, considering the situation here. What do you hear from your inside man?"

Harris sliced a quick questioning glance.

"From the night I was here?" Frank reminded him. "You were waiting for word."

"Right." Harris nodded. "As I recall, I also ordered you to keep me apprised of anything you found out about AIRO."

"I can't know any more than you already do from the inside."

"That's for me to judge, Reardon."

Frank studied the agent facing him. Worry lines cut deep on Harris's forehead and his eyes had the red lines of a road map to purgatory. Frank saw all the signs of a man under severe pressure.

He realized that Harris was worse than in trouble: He was hanging by a thread.

In that instant, Frank had the sense of staring at himself, as he had been three years ago at the nadir of the situation in Red Earth.

A sick pit opened in Frank's stomach.

Ritter was the inside man—Frank knew it as surely as

he recognized the desperation on Harris's face—and now something had gone terribly wrong.

"You want cooperation from me, Harris? Why don't we start with you telling me why?"

"You arrogant son of a bitch. You don't give a flying damn about the next guy."

"And who is the next guy, Harris? You? I've been where you're standing. I can even see myself there and I was one sick son of a bitch, thinking I knew everything."

Harris's eyes flared.

"And let's not forget Eddie Honanie. But then, you already *have* forgotten Eddie, haven't you? He was just a blip in the big picture."

"You don't want to say another word, Reardon." Harris's lethally quiet tone raked over Frank.

Frank braced his knuckles on the desk and leaned toward Harris. "Or maybe I should give a damn about your man in AIRO? What happened, Harris? Did he screw things up? You know what? If he did, he's not to blame. You are. That's the way it works, Harris. *You* take the blame for *not* knowing everything." Frank stood back from the desk. "Now who's the arrogant asshole?"

The look that passed over Harris's face was pure torture. "He's dead." Harris turned away from the desk and faced the window.

For a second, Frank stood speechless. *Ritter was dead?* Frank shook his head. "What?"

"The agent. He's dead," Harris said over his shoulder.

The pit in Frank's stomach grew to a yawning hole, dragging him within a maelstrom of emotions. "How?" he managed.

"Shot. At least that's what the message said."

"What message?"

"Fax." Harris's face contorted to a wry smile. "It came in early this morning."

If Ritter was dead, where was Jenny? Did anybody know?

Frank's mind raced, thinking of the people he could

question: Joe Miller, Tillen Chavez, Ben. Even if he could find any one of them, would they talk, would they know where he could find Jenny?

Frustration pounded through his veins, pulsed at his temples like the beat of a clock, ticking away the seconds.

"You had a situation like this at Red Earth, didn't you, Reardon?"

Frank jerked his focus to the agent.

"When the inside man was discovered?" Harris was studying Frank from across the expansive desk.

"Yes."

"And you sent in another agent?"

"We had reason to believe the first one was still alive." *And he was, but not for long.* Everything had fallen apart. He should never have approved Ritter going in. The man had insisted he could keep control—of the situation, of the negotiations . . . of his own temper.

Sending in Ritter had been the beginning of the end.

"And was he? Alive?"

"Yes." Suddenly, Frank saw where this was going. "You're not sending someone in, are you? You already know the agent is dead."

"Well, that's the question, isn't it? The message included a description of our man and it came to this fax number. Pretty good case the agent talked, under duress." Harris took a deep breath. "Then again, maybe it's a bluff. There's only one way to find out."

Harris turned from the window. "You've been in this situation, Reardon. You know everything you did wrong."

Frank's stomach turned. "And you're asking the wrong man for help."

Harris's eyes narrowed on Frank. "You're even worse than they say. I should have sent you back to Denver the second I heard you were here."

"But you didn't. And you won't now, will you? You dragged me in here because you *don't* know what to do."

Harris smiled wickedly. "Not exactly."

"Then why?"

Harris rounded the desk and stopped only a few feet from Frank. Frank saw his answer in the agent's eyes.

"You're the man I'm sending in," Harris said.

Frank's gut twisted. "You're making a mistake," he forced out between clenched teeth.

"Why is that, Reardon? Isn't that agent important enough to you?"

Frank heard the derision in Harris's tone, but his thoughts were on Jenny. "You have no idea, Harris. But no one can negotiate with those fanatics."

Harris stared for a moment, every bit of his low attitude for Frank written all over his face. "Well, you don't have a choice, Reardon." He walked back around his desk and pulled a file out. "This is your contact in Gallup. With any luck, he'll set you up with the leader of AIRO. I think you know him from Red Earth: Leonard Bluehouse."

The name tripped all the nightmarish memories: the deafening echo of endless gunfire; people screaming; the loud, deathly explosion.

"Yeah, I know the name. And he knows me. This won't work. You'll have to get somebody else."

"That he knows you is the point, Reardon. He also knows what happened at Red Earth."

"He *caused* what happened at Red Earth."

"Some people say the same about you, Reardon."

Frank stared at Harris, an invective on the tip of his tongue—except Harris was right. "All the more reason not to send me."

Harris stared back. "You're right. In fact, if it were up to me, you wouldn't go. But I don't have a choice. They asked for you."

"Who?"

"AIRO."

The ground shifted beneath Frank. He wasn't standing in the office anymore. He was on a grassy ridge looking down at a compound. Men with guns guarded the walls. Men with guns snaked through the grass for vantage points.

One moment of quiet to change his mind. But he didn't. He nodded to Ritter and the agent drove the empty road down the hill to the compound. With that decision, Frank had destroyed his own life.

Now AIRO had assembled the two key players from Red Earth.

"It didn't occur to you that they have a motive? Someone wants to finish what was started at Red Earth? That those bastards are hell-bent on *forcing* an outcome?"

"I think that's obvious, Reardon."

Frank slammed his hand on the desk. "You want to do it all again? You didn't get enough kicks out of Red Earth?"

"That's for *you* to answer, Reardon. This doesn't have to be Red Earth."

"You know as well as me, Harris, that it doesn't matter if that agent is still alive. Now, he's as good as dead."

Frank's statement hung in the air. For a moment, neither man said a word, only stared at each other—two men who knew better than to hope, who lived with the odds every day . . . two men who accepted death in silence.

"But you'll send me, anyway."

"Yes." Harris stared, his clear-blue gaze right on Frank.

"And you've known this from the moment I walked in here. Son of a bitch."

Harris nodded, his unwavering gaze on Frank. The agent didn't couch the request in any pretense of optimism.

Frank grabbed the file from Harris's hand. "Who knows? Maybe we all learned from Red Earth. Maybe this time will be different. Maybe this time, Ritter and I can walk away without casualties."

"What?"

"Ritter. Your man inside?"

For the first time that afternoon, Harris looked truly befuddled. "What are you talking about, Reardon?"

Despite Harris's question, the obvious puzzlement on his face, Frank tried again. "Code name Chandler?".

"There's no Chandler, Reardon. And no Ritter." Harris now looked concerned. "I thought you knew. Ritter's been out since Red Earth."

"Yes, but . . ." Frank shook his head, struggled to comprehend, make sense of his jumbled thoughts. "Ritter's the inside man, right?" Frank insisted.

"No. It's Sam Hernandez." Harris approached Frank. "Why would you think Ritter was inside?"

His thoughts raced over what Ella and Grandmother had said about Chandler—a bitter man, stuck in the past, with stories of glory from Red Earth; a man with a bad right leg and a scar over his right eye; a man who *knew the tricks of the FBI*.

It *had* to be Ritter. Frank knew it. This was all some sort of game.

"Does Sam Hernandez walk with a limp?"

"No. Answer me, Reardon. Why would you think Ritter was inside?"

Frank studied Harris, saw more than concern in the agent's eyes—something closer to doubt about Frank's faculties. A part of Frank wondered about the same thing, but every one of his instincts said he was right. "A man fitting Ritter's description has been on the res—"

Harris interrupted. "Why would Ritter be on the res, Reardon? He left the bureau right after the debacle at Red Earth. Are you saying he retired to spend quality time with the very people he hated?" Harris shook his head.

"The man fitting Ritter's description has been on the res from about the time of Red Earth," Frank finished. "He's got a limp, a scar over his eye, and he talks about the battle at Red Earth—"

"That could be a hundred—"

Frank walked to a few feet from Harris. "He has connections to AIRO *and* to the FBI."

"You're hallucinating, Reardon. You know, maybe you're right. You can't do this."

Frank leveled his gaze on the agent. "It's Ritter. You can bank on that. And if he's not working for you, Harris, then why is he here?"

CHAPTER
TWENTY-ONE

Chandler took a back road out of Phoenix, heading north through desert hill country. To where, he wouldn't say.

"I'm glad you came with me, Ella." He glanced over to her, smiling. "You know, we've never really had a chance to talk. This will be great." Just as swiftly, his lips drew into a tight, fierce line.

The contrast sent a chill through Ella.

"Yes, great," Ella said.

The small talk chafed against her. She wanted to know where they were going, whether he was taking her to Jenny.

"Yeah, it's a good thing I found you, Ella." He smiled again.

Ella couldn't remember ever seeing him smile. The expression was out of place, so unfamiliar to his face that the muscles looked contorted and tight and gave the impression of a smile bordering on anger—a smile that filled her with fear.

Ella told herself Chandler couldn't possibly mean to hurt her. He had walked right up to her, then stood and talked with her in a crowd of police from every agency. Soon, hers would be the only truck sitting in the lot. Someone would have to notice—except it wasn't her truck. What she counted on were Chandler's words: that he wanted to help.

"Yes, it's great, Chandler," she managed. "It's been hard since Eddie's murder." She glanced at Chandler. "You said you saw him?"

"That's right. Ran into him in a bar in Gallup. Man, was he glad to see me!" He let out a loud laugh.

"Really? Why?"

Chandler slid a look at Ella. "Eddie was in some trouble. I think he hoped I could help him."

"What kind of trouble?"

"You know, I don't mean to speak bad of the dead, Ella, but you have a right to know. Eddie was in over his head with some bad people. The kind of people you don't mess with."

"What people, Chandler? Did he say?"

"Yeah, but you won't believe it. *I* didn't believe it." He gave her a long look as if for emphasis. "Eddie was tied up with the FBI, Ella."

Ella stared at him, stunned. She had expected him to say AIRO. She had been prepared for that. But the FBI? "Eddie would never work with the FBI. Not in a million years."

"That's what I thought, too. It gets worse. The FBI had Eddie working a frame on AIRO."

"You have to be wrong, Chandler."

"I'm not. Look, I know you don't believe me, yet. Just hear me out. It all started out with Eddie trying to help AIRO. They needed money. You know how Eddie was, always trying to help the next guy."

Ella nodded slightly.

"Well, he had an idea. There was this crooked dealer in Indian art out of New Mexico. Eddie found out he had a load of stuff stored in a storage unit there."

"He stole the art."

Chandler looked surprised at her pronouncement.

"I already know about the art, Chandler."

"Yeah, our boy decided to liberate that Indian art from the dealer." Chandler smiled. "Pretty gutsy. But he didn't get far. That's when the trouble started. He got caught by the FBI."

"No—" Ella shook her head in confusion. "They're investigating that stolen art."

"That's what they want you to think, Ella. But they're not investigating any stolen art. It's all about AIRO. They used Eddie to get to AIRO."

"That doesn't make any sense—" Ella shook her head. "Eddie wouldn't help the FBI."

"He would if he didn't have a choice."

Ella's gaze slid from Chandler to the passing landscape. "Eddie always had choices, always had open doors, Chandler."

"Yeah, he called his own shots." Chandler chuckled.

Ella looked at him.

"But not this time," he added. "Not this time." His lips drew up in a satisfied grin.

Ella clenched her fists against the rush of anger trembling through her. "You look happy about that, Chandler."

"Me?" He shot her a surprised look. "No, no, I was just appreciating the passion of that boy, Ella. Even against all odds. You've got to respect that."

His face sobered. "Ella, he didn't have a chance. The FBI had him all sewn up. It was all a part of their grand scheme. And they have their master schemer in charge. Agent Reardon."

"Frank." His name slipped from her lips on a breath.

Chandler looked at her, one eyebrow raised. "That's right. Agent Frank Reardon."

"No . . . you're wrong." Ella stumbled over her thoughts. "He's investigating the art and Eddie's murder."

"Think about it, Ella. Why aren't the Navajo cops investigating the murder? Eddie was an Indian killed on Indian land. Why are the FBI involved?"

"Because of the art. They have Eddie's fingerprints on the storage place in Denver, Chandler." Ella started to see the hole in Chandler's logic. "Frank came here following the trail. Now he's trying to solve Eddie's murder."

"You're right that he came here following a trail—to AIRO. That's all he's had on his mind for three years."

Ella's mind fled to the canyon, to the moment Frank had

told her of his wife's murder. She could see his face in her mind, as if he were here beside her, the anguish on his face, the pain tearing him apart from the inside, blinding him with hatred. Her heart quickened for the man, so consumed with sorrow.

"Tell me this, Ella." Chandler broke the silence. "If Reardon gives a damn about Eddie's death, just what has he been doing to *find* the murderer? Who has he been questioning?"

"The investigation *led* him to AIRO, Chandler. He found a connection. He was trying to solve the murder."

"Ella, he already *knows* who murdered Eddie."

She shook her head. "No. It isn't true. It can't be true."

She didn't want to hear another word. *Chandler had to be wrong.* He had to be making all this up . . .

"Look, Ella, I know this is all hard to take in and coming at you mighty fast. But you have to believe me. The FBI had a plan. Actually a brilliant plan." The twisted smile spread across Chandler's face. "They ordered Eddie to plant the stolen art on AIRO."

"But Eddie would never—"

"You're right," Chandler said, his voice tense. "He wouldn't." The angry lines on his face bordered on hatred. The minutes ticked by and Chandler didn't say a word, just stared ahead—a man riveted on anger.

His silence, the frozen intensity of his face, scared Ella. She took a sharp breath. "He wouldn't help the FBI?" she prompted.

Chandler blinked. A veil seemed to lift from his eyes. With what looked to be extreme effort, he regained composure and his features relaxed, if only slightly.

"No, he wouldn't help." He glanced at her. "You really should be proud of Eddie. He told me he wouldn't cooperate. I guess he meant it."

"Wouldn't cooperate with the FBI," she confirmed.

Chandler nodded. "And that got him killed. The bastards."

Ella's heart jumped. "What are you saying? Who got him killed?"

"The FBI, Ella. Haven't you been listening?

She stared at him in horror. "You're wrong . . . you're making this up . . ."

He looked over at her, his eyes fierce. "Believe it, Ella. Believe it for the sake of Eddie. Believe it for your *own* sake."

Ella's heart jumped at the implied warning.

"I've got almost everything in place," he said, staring ahead. "I've been working hard. Very hard." He sounded almost as if he were talking to himself.

Chandler fell silent, his black eyes sharp shards of jet focused straight ahead on the highway as if he could bore through any barrier. He glared out the window. His whole face was taut with hate.

Ella recognized that intense stare. She had seen the same fixed purpose in Frank's eyes whenever AIRO was mentioned—an anger Frank could barely contain.

Anger like she saw in Chandler. Anger like she had seen on the faces of Hopi and Navajo . . . on Jenny's face . . . on Grandmother's face.

They were all lightning storms, converging from different directions, flying across the land, angry people on a collision course.

Ella saw herself dead center, at the moment of impact.

Suddenly, Chandler looked at Ella. "There's just one more thing. That's where you come in."

Ella's breath caught. "I don't come in, Chandler. I don't know—"

"But you do know, don't you? You *have* to know!" His look dared her to hold anything back.

Ella fought for calm. "Chandler, Eddie and I barely talked. He wouldn't tell me any important plan."

"*I* know the plan, Ella. But you have something I need."

Ella thought of the receipt she had found for the storage locker. *That must be it*. He wanted the art.

But she needed the receipt. If Chandler didn't take her to Jenny, this receipt was all she had to trade with AIRO for her niece.

Ella's thoughts swirled in a tempest. "I don't know . . ." Ella started.

Anger flushed Chandler's face.

"I'm trying to think," she amended quickly. "I've been so worried . . ."

"I'm the answer to your worries, Ella."

Her skin crawled beneath his evil tone. Fear sliced straight to her heart. The man was a liar. The man was dangerous—and all Ella could think of now was Jenny.

Her hands gripped the leather backpack. Heat emanated through the canvas to her skin, through her pores, through her blood, inexplicably quieting the storm of terror racing through her.

Her mind stilled so she could think. "You told me you wanted to help, Chandler. I believe you," she said, the words biting her tongue. "Maybe we can help each other. Maybe if you can first help me find Jenny," she offered, holding her breath.

Chandler barked out a laugh. "Help you find Jenny?" His tone was taunting.

Ella's heart plummeted.

"No problem," he said.

He pulled to a stop. Ella jerked her focus up to see they were parked in front of a storage unit. *Oh, God. What was going on?*

He got out of the vehicle, then bent his head to look at her across the front seat. "You want to find Jenny? Get out of the car."

Ella's trembling hand went to the door handle. It took all her weight to push the door open. She stepped to the ground, bracing herself on the window.

Chandler stood at the storage unit, grinning.

Fierce dread stole the breath from her lungs, the strength from her muscles. She stared at Chandler, unable to speak.

What have you done?

He pulled a key from his pocket, opened the padlock, and grabbed the handle at the bottom of the door. With a loud clatter, the door rolled up. Chandler motioned for Ella to join him.

She thought her legs would collapse beneath her. Ella walked without feeling the ground to the open door and peered into the darkness. Paintings, cradle boards, masks, and boxes and boxes filled the unit. She squeezed past a heap of Navajo rugs.

There was Jenny, her ankles bound, her wrists bound, a strip of tape across her mouth.

Ella's heart slammed against her chest. She reached a hand to Jenny's head, terrified she would find her dead. At Ella's touch, Jenny groaned.

"Jenny, shh, I'm here." The words choked in her throat.

Ella slid an arm beneath her, rolled her gently forward. Jenny blinked, saw Ella, and her eyes filled.

"It's okay, now," Ella whispered. "It's okay, now."

Jenny had her eyes on her, so full and dark and expressive. Saying everything her mouth couldn't.

Anger swept through Ella, but she smiled to Jenny. "I know, I'm here." She fumbled at the tape covering Jenny's lips, her vision blurred, her fingers barely able to function.

Ella peeled back the tape.

"Aunt Ella!" Jenny breathed. Tears slipped from her eyes.

Her wrists still tied, Jenny leaned forward into Ella's arms. Ella pulled her close. "Shh, shh," she murmured. She ran a hand up and down Jenny's back. "Are you okay? Are you hurt?"

"She's fine," Chandler snapped.

Ella's hand fisted at Jenny's back. Anger turned to rage. She whirled on Chandler. "She's fine? What kind of animal are you?"

His eyes went flat black. "Animal?"

Ella's heart caught at her throat, but her fury was stronger than her fear. "You've treated *her* like an animal, Chandler. Get that tape off her!"

Chandler slid a knife from his pocket and smiled when

Ella flinched. "Glad to," he said. The blade ripped through the tape at Jenny's wrists and ankles.

Ella threw her arms around Jenny, held her so close she could feel Jenny's heart pounding. Ella set her jaw against the sob pushing through her.

"Nice," Chandler said. "Now for your part of the deal. Where's the tablet?"

Surprise jerked Ella's gaze to Chandler. *How did he know about the tablet?*

"The tablet, Ella," Chandler demanded, his eyes hard. "The one your brother *died* for." His voice held a threat.

Ella nodded toward the front seat. "It's in the backpack."

"You had it *with* you. Good." He smiled, as if proud of her. "This is very good," he said, as he went to the passenger side of the car.

Chandler unzipped the bag and looked inside. "Good," he said again and tossed it onto the front seat. "Now for phase two."

Ella panicked. "Chandler, you have what you want. You have the art, you have the tablet. Why don't you let us go?"

"Right." He chuckled. "No, you're still of use to me. Start loading up the car."

Ella looked at all the boxes, the heavy rugs. Her arm shifted around Jenny's waist, supporting her. "Jenny can't, Chandler. She's too weak—"

"Get the hell over here!"

Anger flooded Ella, pushing aside reason, caution. She faced Chandler down. "You want my help, you leave Jenny alone. Or do it all yourself."

Chandler stared at her a moment. He glanced at his watch, then back at her. Ella didn't budge.

"You have two hours."

Ella settled Jenny in the front seat. Just as she started to straighten, Jenny grabbed her arm.

"I'm so sorry, Aunt Ella."

Ella could barely look at Jenny's face, at the dark rings beneath her eyes, the red line around her mouth from the tape. Anger at what he'd done pumped through her. "This is *not* your fault, Jenny."

For an hour, Ella hauled things to the utility vehicle, filling it to the ceiling. Halfway through, Jenny had insisted on helping. The whole time, Ella's mind raced over possibilities, ways to escape or talk their way out. The storage facility was on the edge of Window Rock, and there was no place to run and hide. She kept hoping other renters would drive up, but they were still alone when Chandler slammed the hatch down on the back end.

"Get in," he ordered.

Ella took hold of Jenny's hand. "Chandler, let us go. We've done what you wanted. You don't need us."

He turned and, in one swift move, hit her across the face. Ella staggered back. Jenny caught her.

"Eddie thought he could tell me what to do," he said with menace. "Get the hell in the car. Now is when the fun begins."

The black sedan rolled past an endless succession of protestors. They lined both sides of the highway for miles, sometimes three deep. Frank stared through the tinted windows at the countless Indians—young, old, men, women, even children. It looked to him like the whole Navajo tribe was assembled along Interstate 25.

"This is not just AIRO," he said.

"No shit, Sherlock," said the agent driving.

Frank glared at the agent from his seat in the back.

His ears picked up the noise of helicopters. He pressed his face to the window and saw two Army choppers hovering. One swept closer to the ground. Its blades churned the air, lifted the sand and hurled it around. Frank heard screams.

"There are children out there!" he yelled, over the chopper's roar.

Frank met the agent's gaze in the rearview mirror. The man's lips curved to a thin smile. "This is where you get out, Reardon."

The car stopped and Frank looked out the window at the angry protestors shaking their fists, yelling at the government men in this car.

"Thanks," Frank said, opened the door, and stepped out alone onto the blacktop.

As soon as he closed the door, the sedan backed away, turned, and hauled off in the opposite direction.

For just a moment, the crowd stilled in surprise, then picked up momentum again, shouting right at Frank. Frank drew in a sharp breath and looked down the road. One hundred feet ahead, a crowd of Indians stood gathered on the highway, forming a human barricade.

Frank walked down the middle of the road, ignoring the jeers from the sides. Within twenty feet, he saw what he faced: at least fifty men who had to be hard-core members of AIRO.

He would know their look anywhere: every one of them with long hair, some with black headbands, black armbands, black sunglasses. He didn't see guns, but had no doubt they were armed. They stood defiant and quiet, some with arms crossed against their chests, staring at the white man approaching.

Images of Red Earth flashed in his mind.

The hilltop.

Guns firing.

People screaming.

Blood everywhere. Mary's blood.

They were no better than terrorists, with no conscience, no morals, no humanity.

He hated every one of them.

He let the hate flow through his body, pump his heart, pulse through his veins. It filled the hole in his gut, healed the wound he had carried for three years. Never in his life had he felt so alive.

He walked straight to them, stopping only a few feet away. "I'm looking for Sanchez."

"Who the hell are you?" A young, lanky Indian sized him up.

Christ, he was only a kid. "Agent Reardon, FBI."

"You got a lot of balls, Agent Reardon," said another, older Indian.

Frank bet he was Sioux. In fact, he would wager there wasn't a Navajo in the group.

From the corner of his eye, he saw some of the men move to the side and a tall, lean man stepped out and faced Frank.

"So, you're Reardon."

Frank's skin bristled at the tone. He leveled his gaze on the Indian, but didn't say a word.

"This is the agent from Red Earth!" he announced.

A grumble of expletives rose from the men.

"Your *disrepute* precedes you, Agent Reardon."

"I don't think we've met," Frank said through his teeth.

"I'm Sanchez."

"Then I think *you* have orders to take me to Leonard."

Frank could see the glare through Sanchez's dark glasses. Then, without a word, he turned and disappeared into the group. Frank followed, his muscles tensed against the deliberate pushing and bumping from the crowd.

He emerged from the crowd and saw Sanchez standing beside an open-air Jeep. Sanchez raised an arm and suddenly two men grabbed each of Frank's arms.

"What the—"

Then he felt the brisk frisk of hands down his sides, down his legs, and up the inseams.

"He's clean," one yelled.

Sanchez nodded and Frank was shoved forward. He had barely climbed in the Jeep as Sanchez took off, across the desert. Frank held on with one hand on the roll bar.

Sanchez pulled a cellular from his pocket, flipped it open, and punched a number.

"Got him," he said, then closed the phone and pocketed it.

They drove north, not on any road. The Jeep careened up dunes and down washes—flying over wild ground only coyotes would cross. Nearly forty minutes later, Sanchez brought the Jeep to a skidding halt at a juncture of five sandy back roads in what had to be the middle of nowhere.

"Get out," Sanchez said.

Frank stepped from the Jeep, and Sanchez took off, spewing sand and rocks.

Five minutes later, a cloud of dust down a different road announced the approach of a vehicle. A black Jeep stopped within two feet of Frank. The window opened and Frank saw Leonard Bluehouse behind the wheel.

"Get in, Agent Reardon."

Frank climbed in and Bluehouse steered off the road, back into the desert, and down into an arroyo. The wash widened, deepened, and descended between banks. Soon, they were in a small secluded canyon, where Bluehouse stopped and got out of the Jeep, without a word to Frank.

Frank followed the leader of AIRO to a cluster of fallen boulders.

Bluehouse faced him. "So, Agent Reardon, we finally meet."

"I didn't know this was a moment you waited for, Bluehouse."

The Indian slid off his sunglasses. "Oh, yes, Reardon. I have waited for this day."

Frank stared at the man who had led the insurrection at Red Earth. He was a big man, with black hair past his shoulders. He didn't seem to have aged a day. Neither had Mary, Frank thought with a vengeance.

"You're under arrest, Leonard Bluehouse, for the illegal uprising called Red Earth."

Bluehouse let out a big laugh. "So you have waited to see me again, too."

"You're in a lot of trouble, Bluehouse. You want to talk about that?"

"I don't think I'm the one in trouble, Reardon," Bluehouse answered. Sharp black eyes stared back at Frank.

Foreboding skittered over Frank. "I don't have a problem with trouble," Frank countered. "But you've got a lot of it out there on the highway, Bluehouse. Haven't you got enough men? You have to use children?"

The Indian's eyes hardened. "They choose to be there, Reardon. They *choose* to make a statement of sovereignty."

"You better hope no one *chooses* to make a show of power."

Bluehouse's lips curved to a thin smile. "We're not the FBI, Reardon. You're the ones who have to make a show of power."

Frank's gut twisted. "We don't jeopardize the lives of civilians, Bluehouse," he said, his voice so tight with fury, he barely recognized it.

Bluehouse frowned at Frank. "That's exactly what you do. That's exactly what you did at Red Earth."

"We didn't kill—" Frank stopped at a sudden, jabbing pain in his chest. He shoved down the agony. "You're the murderers, Bluehouse."

The Indian breathed out a long sigh. "You think of your wife, Frank Reardon. She is one reason I asked to meet with you."

Frank stared at the man. "Go to hell, Bluehouse. I'm not talking about her with you."

Bluehouse studied Frank, his gaze calm, thoughtful— while a violent rage stormed through Frank, pushing him to the edge of his control.

"We'll leave that for now," Bluehouse said, turned his back on Frank and walked a few paces. "I was surprised to learn you were again working AIRO," he said over his shoulder.

Frank didn't say anything.

Bluehouse faced him. "I was *glad*."

Frank stared, speechless.

"That surprises you."

"Not much," Frank said finally. "You're looking to repeat Red Earth?"

The Indian's face turned as hard as the boulder Frank rested against. "No, I do not want to repeat Red Earth. Do you?"

"I'm not the one using children to blockade highways, Bluehouse."

"This isn't about the highways, Reardon!" Bluehouse's voice boomed through the canyon.

He advanced on Frank. "If you don't want another Red Earth, why are you using the same tactics?"

Frank didn't have a clue what Bluehouse was talking about. He kept his mouth shut.

"You planted undercover with us again, no? Now he's dead."

"Tell me something I don't know, Bluehouse. Or is this a confession right before surrendering to me?"

"We didn't kill him." Bluehouse stood right in front of Frank, his face drawn in fierce lines. His unwavering gaze held Frank's. Frank even thought he saw a flicker of pain in the Indian's eyes.

God. He was the best damn liar.

"Sure, Bluehouse. Just like you didn't kill the one at Red Earth."

"We didn't." Bluehouse breathed the words. His jet-black eyes stared into Frank's. "You *know* in your heart something was wrong with the way Red Earth went down."

Frank breathed past the instant memories assaulting him. His hands fisted at his sides.

"I watched you at Red Earth, Reardon. And I've watched you since. You are a man devastated by what happened there—"

Unbidden, Frank's hand rose faster than a breath and connected with Bluehouse, sending the Indian to the ground.

Bluehouse rubbed his jaw. "My point exactly," he said, and pushed himself up to one elbow.

"Get on your feet, you son of a bitch."

Bluehouse didn't move. He just stared at Frank with those same considering eyes.

"You were double-crossed at Red Earth, Reardon. Just like you're being double-crossed now."

"Why the hell would you tell me that?"

"Because I *don't* want another Red Earth."

"Right. Get on your feet, Bluehouse. You can tell your story to someone who gives a damn."

The big Indian rose. "Answer me this, Reardon. If it's a story, how did I know you were working on AIRO?"

Frank's mind stumbled for just a second. Then, "You obviously tortured that out of Hernandez," he said, though he knew that was impossible. Hernandez didn't know Frank. And Frank *hadn't* been working on AIRO.

"I told you. We didn't kill Hernandez. No, I found out about you from the second undercover. Funny thing. He voluntarily dropped your name."

Adrenaline flashed across Frank's chest, down his arms. "You're lying."

"Am I lying about this? That man's name is Chandler." *Ritter.*

Frank turned away and walked a few paces, struggling to right his thoughts.

How did Ritter even know Frank was here?

Frank's mind fled over the last few days, back to Annie's, to the man she called Chandler, but who was really Ritter. He'd been with Jenny. Jenny could have mentioned Frank to Ritter.

Why the hell would Ritter mention Frank to AIRO . . .

. . . except to get Frank out of the way.

The pieces tumbled into place in Frank's head, forming a sick, evil picture. The shoe prints at Annie's. The same prints where Eddie was murdered. And everywhere Frank looked, he saw Ritter.

A cellular phone rang, piercing the canyon silence. Bluehouse answered, turning away from Frank. Just as swiftly, he turned back, his face in a rage.

"When?" he said into the phone. After a pause: "I'll go!" he yelled into the phone. He looked at Frank. "I have just the man they can talk to."

CHAPTER
TWENTY-TWO

Chandler arranged the Navajo mask just so atop the pile of Navajo rugs. "Perfect, don't you think?"

Ella nodded weakly from the doorway of the old adobe house and continued on outside for another load. Jenny peeked around the open hatch as Ella approached.

"There are only a few more things, Aunt Ella."

Ella could hear the fear in Jenny's voice.

"I know, honey."

Jenny grabbed her arm and Ella looked into her niece's young, terrified face. "Aunt Ella, he'll kill us. I know it."

"No. He won't." A rush of steely resolve flowed through Ella. She leveled her gaze on Jenny, imparting her own strength to the girl. "I won't let him."

Jenny's haunted eyes, the terror she had already endured, drove straight through Ella. Still the child faced more. Ella drew her into her arms. "That bastard is not hurting you any more," she whispered into Jenny's ear. She glanced quickly back to the house, then added, "I have a plan."

The flicker of hope in Jenny's eyes nearly undid Ella. She tore herself away from Jenny and grabbed a box from the back of the Suburban into her arms. As she passed by the front seat, she glanced in the window for the hundredth time to her leather satchel—and the tablet. What she hadn't told Jenny was that her plan amounted to no more than a bluff: She was betting Chandler didn't know the legend of the Hopi tablet.

She walked into the house and set the box down by others. Chandler immediately moved it to an angle with another box, pulled a weaving from the stack, and draped it over the two boxes. Then he stood back and seemed to reconsider the placement. "How much more?" he demanded over his shoulder.

"A few more boxes," Ella answered, "some rugs, and another mask."

"I am going to *bury* them in stolen art," he muttered. He glanced at her, his face an ugly contortion of anger and delight. Ella could hardly bear looking at him.

Then he approached her, his steps awkward, his limp even more pronounced, as if maintaining the level of fierce anger demanded all his strength. Ella tried to look anywhere but to the foot he dragged across the floor.

"They did this to me," he said to her.

Ella stared off to the side.

"Look at me! No one can live like this!"

Her heart pounding, she slid a glance to him, then away, sure that if she really stared, he would only be angrier.

"They *won't* walk away from this."

Abruptly, he stuck a rough finger beneath her chin and forced her head up. He looked half-crazy, his lips drawn tight over his teeth. His eyes were wild, dilated.

And Ella couldn't miss the message in his gaze. Chandler didn't intend for her and Jenny to walk away from this, either. Framing AIRO with stolen Indian art would cause a scandal . . . planting two murdered Indian women at their headquarters would damn them.

Ella knew her and Jenny's time had run out.

She willed her heart to calm, the tremors within to still. On a deep, silent breath, she played the only card she had.

"It's too bad you don't have the other half of the tablet."

He jerked his head to her, his eyes were unfocused. "What are you talking about?"

"The Hopi tablet. The legend. I thought you knew."

"I could care less about some goddamn Indian legend."

"I know. Me, too." Her heart pinched at the bit of truth in what she said. She had an instant of sorrow, of regretting the words. She shook off the sensation. "But the Hopi believe. I thought that was why you wanted the tablet. The other half is what provides proof." She tried to give a casual shrug just before taking a step toward the door.

He grabbed her arm. "What proof?"

Ella felt a stir of satisfaction. "Proof that you're the one."

"The one what?"

"The man of honor." She forced herself to look at him, to say the words with conviction, without getting sick right there on the spot.

She saw the words sink into his brain, the cloud of craziness in his eyes lift. His black eyes stared at her. "How do you know about this?"

"I'm half Hopi. I know the stories."

"So what about this 'man of honor'?"

"He brings back the tablets from the emergence. It's the proof he's meant to lead." She paused and added the final enticement. "The legend says he will be a white man."

Chandler's lips curved into a smile.

"I was just at Hopi yesterday where they had a ceremony, preparing for his arrival. They're sure the time has come."

His eyes narrowed in suspicion. "Why are you telling me this?"

"I have my reasons." She looked to the side, pretending not to want to say.

"And what are they?" His fingers bit into her arm.

She drew her gaze up to his. "I want the Hopi embarrassed. I want them shamed, like they shamed me. I want them hurt for all the years I lived as an outcast." Ella spoke the words, expecting the anger she had buried her whole life to surface, but it didn't. Instead, a wave of remorse flooded her, welled in her eyes.

Chandler stared at her, obviously taken with her emotional reaction. "So, where is the other half?"

"I'll take you there," she answered.

Chandler's hand tightened on her arm. "You'll tell me now."

"No."

He glared at her. "I can kill you where you stand, you know."

"Then you won't get the other half."

He glanced out the door. "There's also Jenny."

Ella's heart pounded furiously. "You lay a hand on her, Chandler, and you might as well kill me, too. I'll never tell you where the tablet is. And *you* will miss your chance at destiny." She forced the words between clenched teeth.

Instant anger rose in his face. Ella drew a breath, sure that her bluff had failed. She wanted to run for Jenny. Maybe they could still escape, somehow outrun Chandler.

He dropped his hand from her arm. "Get the last of the stuff in here. Now! We're leaving."

For a second, Ella couldn't believe his words. Then she pivoted and ran out the door. "He bought it," she whispered frantically to Jenny. "He bought it."

She grabbed an armful of the rugs. "Help me get everything in before he changes his mind."

They hauled the rest of the stolen art into the house. Chandler gave it a last glance, closed the door, and went to the car. "You better not be lying," he said to Ella and slid a look to Jenny.

Ella didn't miss the threat. She squeezed Jenny's hand.

The late afternoon sun cast elongated, twisted shadows from the junipers and drained all the desert colors to a dull brown. Frank glanced to Bluehouse beside him, negotiating the Jeep over the wild terrain with apparent ease. It struck Frank as symbolic: this Indian, long, black hair whipping in the wind, commanding a Jeep, driving into the sunset. He even had a moment of regret, then winced at the undeserved sentiment.

He couldn't deny, though, that Bluehouse's revelations had turned his thinking inside out and made him question everything he thought he knew about Ritter . . . and Red Earth.

For three years, he had avoided thinking of those days because the slightest memory brought back the full force of his pain, his guilt. Bluehouse was right: Frank had questions about Red Earth, questions he had tried to ask Ritter long ago, questions he had finally buried deep inside, given up to never knowing. It didn't matter, he had told himself, because no amount of understanding would bring back Mary.

Now the uncertainty ate away at him, gnawing at the wound inside . . . and he didn't have the power to overcome the assault. The only one who could was Ritter. Except Frank had no idea where the son of a bitch was.

The sun slipped below the western mesas and the horizon erupted in brilliant orange and deep pink, spreading across the low-hanging clouds like fire eating the sky. Helpless frustration crawled over Frank. What the hell was he doing with Bluehouse?

Bluehouse drove the Jeep through a stand of cottonwoods, and down into a bosque of wetlands, nourished by mountain runoff. He stayed close to the cover of reeds, finally pulling out of the wash, and up an incline, where he suddenly stopped.

Ahead, Frank saw what looked to be an abandoned adobe home, sheltered in cottonwoods. He got out of the Jeep and followed Bluehouse to the front. When the Indian opened the door, nothing could have prepared Frank for the sight: Staring him in the face was a hoard of Indian art, some of which he immediately recognized as stolen from Fuller.

"Shit!" Bluehouse strode inside and stood over the display.

"I'd say so, Bluehouse."

The Indian faced Frank, his face fierce. "Did you know about this?"

Bluehouse's anger electrified the room. For a second, Frank bought the act. For only a second.

"I knew you were behind the stolen art, Bluehouse. This will finish AIRO."

"Listen to me, you son of a bitch, you think I would bring you here if I *knew* about this? This is the work of Chandler, Reardon. Believe it, or don't believe it, I don't give a shit."

He headed for the door.

Reardon stepped in front of him. "Where the hell do you think you're going?"

"Where do you think? Wish I could stay and watch you have your fun slandering AIRO, but you understand. Now move."

Frank laid a hand to the Indian's chest. "You're not leaving, Bluehouse. I'll kill you first."

The big man stared at Frank. "You would, wouldn't you? You have let that hate consume you, Frank Reardon. What will be left inside you when you discover you hated the wrong people?"

"That won't happen."

"There will be nothing left of you," Bluehouse continued. "Is that what your wife would have wanted?"

Rage overwhelmed Frank. He hit the Indian, swiveled, caught Bluehouse's leg, and brought him to the ground. Frank bent over him, his fist raised, ready to smash it into Bluehouse's face.

"Our bullets didn't kill your wife." Bluehouse stared up at Frank without a hint of fear in his eyes. "Ritter knows that."

Pain exploded in Frank's chest, taking his breath.

It isn't true. It can't be true.

His mind stumbled, confused. He couldn't think straight. His head filled with the image of Mary in his arms, the life flowing from her. He saw Ritter, saw the Indian Ritter had killed lying at Ritter's feet. Ritter had said he shot the man who killed Mary.

"No," he murmured, his mind still full of the memories. "It was the Indian, not Ritter."

"What gun did Ritter hold?" Bluehouse's voice prodded Frank's memory.

Suddenly, Frank saw clearly. He focused on Bluehouse, the Indian's lie exposed. "He didn't hold a gun, Bluehouse."

"That's because he dropped it, Reardon. I saw from across the road. He shot that man in the back and the bullet went through him . . . and through your wife."

Bluehouse's eyes glistened with the memory. Frank eased back, not wanting to believe what he saw in the Indian's eyes, unable to get his mind around the truth staring him in the face.

The Indian raised up on an elbow. "You see now, don't you?"

"Why are you telling me this, Bluehouse?" Frank didn't recognize his voice. It sounded far away, pleading.

"Because it's the truth, Reardon," Bluehouse answered.

Bluehouse pulled himself out from under Frank and stood, leaving Frank on the floor.

Frank didn't think he could stand, he didn't think he could move. The anger had ebbed, disappeared like water on the desert, and left him cracked and lifeless. For a panicked moment, his heart frantically sought the anger, his lifeblood. Instead the vision of Ella's face filled his mind, her long black hair flowing behind her. He realized she was on a horse, flying through the air. It was the dream she had described to him—the dream she told him had given her freedom, by letting go.

"By the way, Reardon, next time we meet, I won't let you hit me." Bluehouse laughed and started for the door.

Frank was already on his feet. "You're still not going anywhere, Bluehouse. I need your Jeep. And your gun," he amended.

Bluehouse laughed again. "I'm not staying here to greet the FBI and the media."

"You have to. I'm going for Ritter."

Bluehouse's eyes narrowed. "So you have shifted your hatred to Ritter, now?"

"I'm keeping a promise I made to someone. He's the last one seen with Eddie's daughter."

Bluehouse's face hardened. "A young girl?"

Frank's heart drummed in his chest. "Was she all right?"

"She was sick."

Frank pushed past Bluehouse and headed for the Jeep. He heard the Indian's steps behind him. Bluehouse climbed into the passenger side. "Drop me at the highway, Reardon. I'll get a ride out of here." He glanced at Frank. "Do you know where to find them?"

Frank had been asking himself the same thing. Where would Chandler take Ella and Jenny?

Where would a killer go?

"I have only one place to look."

Ella had watched the same colorful sunset with the same helpless frustration. She would have traded a lifetime of beautiful sunsets to have it over with, now, and bring on the blackest of nights. In another hour, they'd be in the canyon. She prayed there was no moon tonight.

She also prayed the bluff would hold up. In just a few minutes, she would tell Chandler to turn onto the dirt road leading to the canyon. He'd already grown impatient and more suspicious as the drive wore on. As soon as she pointed out the turn, he would *know* where she was taking him. Would he still buy her story?

Ella saw her landmark and took a breath. "Turn up here."

Chandler threw her a glance. "Just where are we going?"

"You'll see soon enough."

"You better not be playing with me, Ella."

Her skin crawled to hear her name come out of his mouth.

By the time they got to the canyon, the cloak of night finally shrouded the sky.

Chandler turned off the car and shifted in his seat to face

Ella. "If you're lying, or thinking of pulling anything, this is where you'll die." The corner of his mouth curled to a menacing grin.

"What reason did you have to come here . . . before?"

His eyes narrowed. He knew what she meant. "It was Eddie's idea," he answered finally.

It was the answer she had hoped for. She didn't think Chandler would have taken the time to drive Eddie all the way out here for no reason. Her brother had probably hoped for the same thing she did—a chance to escape. That this had been the end for Eddie, Ella tried not to think about.

"What's the point?" Chandler demanded.

"Don't you see? He probably knew of the other tablet, too."

Chandler's gaze flitted to the side and back to her. She could see he was trying to follow her logic.

"Just where is the tablet, then?"

"In Tikui's cave," Ella said, without hesitation.

Chandler's eyes darkened. "The crazy woman?"

"She is the Hopi sorceress." Ella thought Tikui might even like that description. "So, she's the guardian of the tablet. She told me the power is great when the two halves are brought together. In the hands of the wrong man . . ." Ella stopped, hoping she hadn't gone too far with the story.

Chandler looked up at the cliff. "I searched that cave. There was nothing there but dirty scraps of whatever she collected. No tablet."

"It must be hidden. I know it's there."

He raised a brow at her. "Let's *all* go see." He climbed from the car.

Ella and Jenny got out and walked around the Suburban. Ella faltered when she saw the gun in Chandler's hand. "Remember what I said, Ella."

She nodded and gripped Jenny's hand.

He motioned for them to lead the way.

"Wait a minute," he demanded.

Ella watched him go around the car and reach through the window to the glove compartment. He pulled out something. The next instant, he flicked on a flashlight.

Her heart sank. She hadn't thought he would have a flashlight.

He hesitated a moment by the car, then grabbed her bag by the straps. Maybe he thought he would put the stones together as soon as he found the other.

Except there wasn't another stone.

Ella's gaze darted down the canyon and up the other cliff, trying to find a place they could run to. But Chandler followed too close, with the light right on their backs. They wouldn't have a chance.

They reached the talus slope to the cave and started to climb. Ella's thoughts fled over alternatives. Maybe she could catch him off guard and push him over the side.

They struggled up the loose sand and rocks, Ella sometimes pulling Jenny along. Soon, there was no more slope, but a wall of sandstone angling nearly straight up. Chandler swung the light over the cliff.

"There's a path here somewhere," he muttered.

The light caught a narrow ledge.

"There!" The excitement in his voice ratcheted the fear within Ella. She had to think of a way out.

Too soon, they were at the cave, and Chandler was kicking the dirt, searching for soft ground to dig in.

"It's hard!" he yelled, his anger echoing through the cave.

He strode to Ella. "You lied."

"I didn't—" She looked from him to the edge. He was too far to push.

A sudden crack on the side of her head sent her sprawling to the ground.

"Aunt Ella!"

For a second, Ella saw nothing but stars in the blackness. "I'm okay," she managed. She pulled herself up, her head instantly dizzy and threatening to make her sick. But she had to show Jenny she was all right.

She felt Jenny's arm around her, her hand at Ella's head.

"Help me up," she whispered to Jenny.

Once on her feet, she found herself facing an enraged Chandler. "I warned you." He advanced on her. "*This* is as good a place as any."

"Wait, Chandler! I have an idea!" Her thoughts raced ahead. "The other stone. Use the other stone."

He stared at her for a moment, then looked at the bag. "You mean the power," he said.

Ella couldn't believe he still bought the legend. "Yes, the power. Maybe it has powers alone."

She watched him consider, his attention on the bag. As he walked to it, Ella angled behind him. He bent to grab a strap and Ella ran at him, knocking him to the ground. The gun flew from his hand across the cave. "Jenny, run!"

"You little bitch!"

He swung the backpack over his shoulder, hitting the side of Ella's head, but she didn't feel it any more than a sudden wind. Ella tried to grab for his arms, but he yanked free. She didn't know how long she could keep him busy. From the corner of her eye, she caught sight of Jenny still standing there, her eyes wide.

"Jenny, run! Now! Get out!" Her yell startled Jenny. Ella craned her neck to see Jenny make her way out of the cave.

Chandler grunted, reached behind, grabbed a handful of Ella's hair, and yanked hard. Pain screamed across her scalp. She bit down on Chandler's shoulder, locked her jaw around a hunk of his back. He let out a wild yell and the next second flipped her on her back—the pain she caused him seeming to give him brute strength. He straddled her, his knees pinning her arms.

Ella stared up at the face of a man ready to kill.

"You first," he panted. "Then your niece."

He grabbed the satchel, raised it over her head, and swung.

Ella closed her eyes, thought of Jenny, prayed she would get away. A swift breeze blew through her hair.

"What the—"

Ella's eyes flew open. Chandler was staring at the backpack. He swung again. Ella flinched. A gust of air swept her face.

Ella stared at the bag. He couldn't have missed her twice. Her thoughts fled back to the post, when she had touched the stone the second time and it didn't bring her harm. She couldn't make sense of it, but something told Ella to get the bag from Chandler and open it, free the stone.

Chandler scrambled off her, dropping the backpack, and dove for the gun. Ella ripped back the zipper and grabbed the stone. The minute her hands touched the tablet, it started to glow. Iridescent green filled the cave, rippled over the walls, like waves of green water.

Chandler's eyes flew wide. He pulled the trigger and the bullet pinged past Ella's head. The stone grew hot in her hands. Without a cognizant thought, Ella threw it at Chandler. The stone hit him in the chest and knocked him backward. He grabbed the tablet and let out an inhuman screech.

The ground beneath them began to rumble. Ella scooted back to the wall, only to feel the solid rock behind her shake. She saw Chandler try to stand, but his lame leg buckled.

Rocks fell from the ceiling, pelting both of them. Ella covered her head with an arm and crawled to the cave entrance.

"You can't leave me here!"

Ella glanced back at Chandler. His hands still gripped the stone. His face was ravaged with agony. Her choices sliced through to her heart.

She grabbed his arm and pulled, dragging him behind her. With each passing moment, the violence in the earth increased, buckling the very bedrock of the cave floor. They reached the ledge, and Ella had to brace Chandler with her own body.

She moved as fast as she could. The whole world seemed to be breaking apart all around them. Ella's foot caught an edge and she slipped. She scrambled to get her balance, but Chandler's weight leaned back on her. Ella fell backward. She grabbed for the wall, grabbed for the slightest ridge of rock. Her hands found the ledge. She was dangling eighty feet above the canyon floor.

"Chandler! Help!"

He glanced down at her, his gaze full of terror. He shook his head, pressed his back against the cliff wall, and, step by step, inched away from Ella.

Frank roared down the wash and ground gears to gain the incline, praying he was right and Ritter was here. Praying Jenny was still all right. He remembered his promise to Ella, to keep Jenny safe. She was right. He *was* just a man and he had made that promise without thought, with only his arrogance, his hatred of AIRO, making him think he had the power to take on anyone, *make* the world the way he wanted it.

God, I'm a fool.

He rounded the corner to the canyon and the Jeep bucked, nearly rolling. Frank thought he'd hit a fallen tree. Then the earth heaved, sending the Jeep airborne.

Another goddamn earthquake?

He ground the gears and gunned the Jeep, fighting uneven terrain that rocked underneath. The Jeep stalled, its headlights aimed at the cliff wall. Frank saw a flash of denim, a sweep of black hair. His heart stopped at the sight of Ella hanging from the side of the cliff.

He ran toward her, his gaze never leaving her, and nearly collided with a Suburban. Heart pounding, desperate to reach Ella, he dropped to a crouch, pulled Bluehouse's gun from his belt, and looked in the window. He instantly recognized the small black head, peeking over the seat.

"Jenny?" he said, just above a whisper, and stuck the gun at his waist.

She turned, her eyes terrified.

"It's Frank, Jenny."

She scrambled to the door, unlocked it, and fell into his arms. "Aunt Ella—" she choked out.

"I know. I saw. Where's Ritter?"

"Who?"

"Chandler. Where's Chandler, Jenny?"

She pointed to shadows to the left of Ella.

"Get back in the car, Jenny, and lock it."

Frank ran toward the cliff, the gun in his hand. The canyon sounded as if it were under attack: Trees popped and screeched with strain, rocks flew by his head, and a booming roar echoed through the ground under his feet. He charged the talus slope, only to lose balance and have to scramble up on all fours.

A crack of thunder rose the hair on Frank's arms. Wind moaned through the canyon. Frank swore he heard a loud whoop from the distance, but he kept all his attention on Ella.

"Ella! Hold on!"

"Frank?"

"I'm here. I'll get you."

He saw her turn her head carefully, trying not to move too much, or lose her grip. She saw him and smiled.

"You found us." Streaks of blood ran from her temple, scratches grazed her cheek.

"I found you. Now don't go anywhere," he ordered, his voice tight.

He climbed higher, stretching for any jutting rocks, balancing his feet on the smallest ledges. He was within five feet of her when he heard a menacing splinter, as if the ground were going to rip wide open. He threw all his strength into reaching the upper ledge.

"Ella!"

He lunged for her, grabbing her around the waist with his free hand. He pulled her to him. The ledge crumbled beneath his fingers. The whole face of the cliff started to disintegrate into an avalanche.

"Hold on to me!"

They slid in a landslide of rocks, sand, and earth. Frank fought for footing, grabbing anything, finally stopping them on the root of a juniper.

He brushed sand and debris away from Ella's face. "Are you all right? Ella?"

"I . . . think so."

Rocks cascaded over them.

"Ella, we can't stay here. Can you move?"

He angled an arm under hers and pulled her up.

"Chandler," she said, suddenly.

"I don't know where he is."

"Frank, he has the stone." She looked up at him, her eyes pleading. "We have to get the stone."

He stared at Ella, confounded by her concern for a stone. "Let's get down first."

The ground moaned and grumbled. Foreboding threaded down Frank's spine. Another slide of earth and rocks took the ground beneath their feet. Afraid for Ella, afraid to *lose* her, Frank wrapped himself around her and held tight until the barrage stopped. When he opened his eyes, he found them on the canyon floor.

Ella coughed and pressed a hand to her head. Before Frank could stop her, she pushed herself to stand. "The stone . . ."

She sounded so weak, Frank thought she might collapse. "Forget the stone, Ella!"

Thunder boomed and lightning rolled across the sky.

"There!" she yelled.

He followed her gaze and saw Ritter, crumpled on the ground not twenty feet away.

On a surge of anger, Frank clambered to his feet. He staggered toward Ritter, his partner, a man he hadn't seen in three years . . . a man he now knew had double-crossed him.

An unworldly radiance spread underneath Ritter. Frank shook his head, trying to right his eyes. The glow remained.

A scream of whoops descended from the top of the facing cliff. Frank ignored the sound, every bit of him focused on Ritter.

"Ritter!" His voice grumbled from deep inside.

He didn't move.

Frank jabbed a boot toe to Ritter's side and rolled him over. Fluorescent green bathed the night, momentarily blinding Frank. He blinked, refocused, and saw the light came from whatever Ritter grasped in his hands.

Frank grabbed his collar, dragged him from the ground. Ritter moaned and opened his eyes.

"You," he breathed.

"Me," Frank answered.

Frank stared into Ritter's face and didn't recognize the man. He saw dead eyes, a face drawn in such evil ugliness, he could barely stand to look.

"Why?" The question rose on his lips without his thinking.

"You have to ask? They killed your wife."

"No they didn't, did they?"

Ritter's eyes widened and Frank saw the truth, the truth he really hadn't believed until this very moment. Rage flooded him, claimed him, and he clenched his fists around Ritter's collar, pulled his face within inches of Frank's. "You son of a bitch. All these years. You let me think—"

He drove a fist into Ritter's side.

The man doubled on a groan.

"It was all worth it," Ritter choked out. "Whatever I did, whatever you suffered." He angled his gaze up to Frank. "Don't you see? That's what it takes to get those murderers."

Frank flinched from the acerbic words, words he might have spoken himself not so long ago—the only words he had been left with after Mary's death.

He stared at the pathetic example of a human he clenched in his hands and the years of anguish, of bitterness, of hatred, flooded through him without barrier to a torrent he couldn't stop. Didn't want to stop.

He drove another fist into Ritter. Pulled his hand back to throw one at his face,

"Frank, stop!"

He heard the voice, but his mind tumbled around the image. He thought it was Mary, but it couldn't be. It was Ella. He stared at Ritter, his anger seething just below the surface, but the image of Ella filled his head. He couldn't shake her loose.

"Frank."

Her voice poured through him. He felt her hand on his arm. Her quiet strength pulsed on his blood. He staggered back from Ritter, letting the man drop to the ground.

A rain of fiery bolts struck the ground all around. The whoops rose to an earsplitting level. Frank looked to the top of the canyon and gasped.

A hundred warriors lined the cliff. Their yells rang through the canyon, resounding off the cliffs, and reverberated through Frank to his core, producing a fullness, a completeness . . . in the same way as Annie's song had swelled him from within.

Unbidden, Frank's hand went to the tablet and he took it from Ritter.

The land settled, the moans ceased, the wind died, and stars blanketed the night. For a moment, the warriors stood silent, their arms bent, bows aimed skyward.

Frank bent his arm beneath Ella's legs, swung her to his chest, and walked away from Ritter.

The air screamed. Frank pivoted, clutching Ella, and saw hundreds of fiery arrows pierce the sky, then curve to the ground—to where Ritter lay.

Frank pulled Ella close and walked. He breathed in the sweet grass of her scent. "If not for you—" he started, but couldn't finish.

Ella looked up at him, her black eyes shining in the starlight. She leaned toward him. He could see the passion in her eyes, the belief in him, and Frank thought his heart would explode.

He lowered his mouth to hers, drew her close, and *knew* he had found the reason for being alive.

CHAPTER
TWENTY-THREE

He could have carried her in his arms forever. For the strength he felt, he could have walked out of the canyon, carrying Ella all the way back to her store—preferably with his mouth pressed to hers the whole way.

The image provoked a deep chuckle. Ella looked up at him. "Are you all right?"

"Never better," he answered and realized it was true. The burden of guilt he had harbored, even protected, for so many years, had disappeared. His angry world of black and white had taken on the blush of hope, of promise ... of love.

He squeezed Ella closer to his chest, to his heart, wanting to hold her this way and never let go.

It was a miracle, he thought, and smiled again at the realization he truly *had* witnessed miracles.

"You sure you're all right?"

Frank stopped and looked into Ella's dark eyes, the quiet depths of her, and he answered her question the only way he could.

He bent his head, pressed his lips to hers, and his heart swelled impossibly more. He had doomed himself to never loving again, told himself he no longer *deserved* to love.

Now, the unexpected, unbelievable sensation of feeling love, of wanting Ella, wanting to protect and be there for her, soared through Frank, flowed to every limb, producing an ache he hoped never to relieve.

The passion in Frank's kiss spiraled through Ella, a cyclone of warmth, of *want*. Her fingers spread across his neck to pull him closer. A shudder fled through Frank beneath her hands. He deepened the kiss. Desire drew Ella tight, pulled the blood from every source to a pool someplace deep inside. She went weak with the need for more.

Her practical mind tried to fight the response.

This can't last. Nothing good here lasts.

Ella refused to listen, to be defeated by doubts. Today, she had learned she could face the greatest odds.

Now she knew that no matter whether the odds against Frank deciding to stay here were enormous, no matter whether tomorrow he were to leave—this moment, this heaven with him, was worth any risk.

He pulled his lips from hers and looked into her eyes. Ella caught a breath at the passion she saw there.

"Does that answer your question?" he asked. His voice rumbled through her chest.

"I forgot what I asked," she said in all honesty, lost in these newfound emotions.

He smiled and walked to the Suburban, where he rapped a knuckle against the window. The door immediately opened, as if Jenny had sat watching, her fingers ready on the handle. She looked at Frank, then to Ella in his arms, and grinned.

"How romantic," she cooed.

Ella felt a flush of heat spread up her face. In a rush of embarrassment, she tried to slide free of Frank, but his large hands held firm. He opened the door wide with his knee.

"Come on, Jenny. We're going home."

Ella stared at him, wondering at his choice of words.

At the Jeep, he settled Ella in the front seat, and placed the stone in her lap. It seemed dormant now, its glow faded, but the warmth remained.

Jenny scrambled into the back. "I was worried about you, Aunt Ella. The rocks crashing, the lightning. The earthquake . . ." She stopped. "Ohmigosh, do you think Ben was right about the miracle?"

"Yes," Frank said, ahead of Ella.

His answer startled Ella. She looked at the man beside her, a man she never would have thought could believe in miracles. But then, she hadn't thought she could, either.

"What happened to Chandler?"

Ella looked out the front window. A rain of fiery arrows saturated one particular spot in the canyon.

"He let the anger consume him," Frank said quietly, staring ahead.

He backed the Jeep away and out of the canyon. He drove in silence, staring ahead, one hand on the wheel. He seemed to be deep in thought. "I'll take you back to the store," he said, suddenly, as if that settled something in his mind.

Anxiety pinched Ella. She wanted to ask his plans, change his mind if he meant to leave. She squelched the urge. She didn't have the right to ask. She didn't have the right to expect anything from Frank. She assumed her customary stance: Let be what will be.

Except this time, she didn't experience the familiar security in that approach. Instead, the anxiety spread. Her heart pounded with urgency, demanding she *do* something, *say* something.

She fought the desire the whole drive until, by the time they reached the store, she was so tight with determination she fairly sprang from the Jeep, the stone in her hands.

She heard Frank get out. "Ella, can I make a few calls?" he yelled.

"Of course," she said, over her shoulder.

She strode through the kitchen, across the courtyard, and straight for Grandmother's room. Her door stood open, but *Sáni* wasn't there. Panic grabbed her heart. Ella raced down the hallway to the gallery and slid to a stop.

Grandmother was behind the counter, waiting on a tourist couple, her face intent with that particular expression of a salesman. *Sáni* glanced up at Ella and her eyes widened in alarm. The couple turned toward Ella and froze.

"*Sitsoi*! What happened?"

Ella placed a hand self-consciously to her face and felt the grit of dirt and dried blood. She hadn't even thought of how she must look. "I'm fine," she said, backing out of the gallery and down the hallway.

Ella slipped into the bathroom and closed the door. She walked to the sink and, as she set the tablet on the counter, she caught her reflection in the mirror.

No wonder Grandmother was alarmed.

Blood caked at a gash in her forehead and matted the hair at her temple. More cuts, more blood, and a layer of dirt made her look as if she had barely survived some terrible assault.

Footsteps approached the door. "*Sitsoi*, are you all right?"

"I'm fine," Ella repeated, quieter this time. She stared at the face in the mirror and was suddenly hit by the magnitude of all she had endured, of all Jenny had endured.

She *had* barely survived.

If not for the miracle of Frank . . .

A warmth sprang from deep within her and filled her eyes.

More footsteps and muffled voices echoed in the hallway. Ella heard Frank's low voice and then Grandmother's voice. The door opened and she knew, without looking, with only the instant response of her body as evidence, that Frank had entered.

His hand weighed on her shoulder. Ella's heart leaped to his touch. He bent his head to catch her reflected gaze in the mirror and smiled at her.

"Annie said you scared the customers."

Warmth spread through her, just to be looking on his face, just to be seeing that too-infrequent smile crease the wrinkles at his eyes.

"Let's see what we can do about cleaning you up."

Strong hands slid beneath Ella's arms and lifted her. For a suspended moment—just before he settled her onto the tile counter—Ella thought he meant to draw her into his arms, as he had in the canyon. Her pulse skipped, raced . . . then plummeted when he stepped back.

She could hear Frank open the medicine cabinet and rummage through the contents, but Ella stared ahead trying to quiet herself, to regain composure.

How foolish she was being! And how vulnerable! Why couldn't she control these crazy feelings?

Frank's hand brushed her cheek. Ella drew a sharp breath at the unexpected tingling rush that rose to his merest touch.

"It's just water." He held a washrag out for her to see.

Ella couldn't reply. She couldn't trust her voice to be normal. She couldn't trust her thoughts not to betray her.

"I promise to be gentle," he murmured close enough that she felt his breath on her face.

She inhaled for strength and was filled with his scent. All her sensibilities strained to withstand the tide threatening to overwhelm her.

"You were so brave out there, Ella," he said.

The wet cloth pressed at her temple oh-so-gently and Ella felt her tenuous hold slip through her fingers.

"I'm just glad—" He stopped.

Ella heard the tightness in his voice and glanced up. He was staring at her, the rag seemingly forgotten in his hand. His eyes were filled with a soulful, intense look—as if whatever he meant to say were lodged there.

Ella thought she understood: He was glad she was fine. He was glad Jenny was fine. Mostly, she thought, he was glad all of this was over. She wouldn't let herself hope that he also meant he was glad to be here. No, she wouldn't hope that, because then she would only be more devastated when he left. She had no right to hope he would stay. None.

She looked away from him. "I'm glad, too, Frank," she answered and reached for the rag. "I can finish this," she added.

He didn't step back. Instead, he ran a hand over her hair,

smoothing it. "Okay," he said, finally. Still he didn't move to leave.

Ella felt his finger beneath her chin and he lifted until her gaze met his. He stared back, unblinking, inches away, then closer still as he lowered his mouth to hers. His palm curled to her neck, drawing her pulse to the surface.

He angled his head, deepened the kiss. Ella reached to him, put her hand at his nape, threaded her fingers through his hair. She felt his other arm brace her back and he pressed her so close Ella's heart seemed to beat against his, thumping hard in unison.

He drew a breath and rested his forehead on hers. "I've got some calls to make," he whispered and brushed a kiss to her cheek, then walked out the door.

The room shrank in his wake, closing in on Ella, suffocating her, as if he had taken all the air with him. She slid from the counter with a hand pressed to her chest, to a need forming there she *would not* acknowledge.

She stepped to the sink, braced her hands on the edge of the counter, and stared into eyes she didn't know, a gaze that wouldn't conceal her deepest fears . . . or wishes.

Ella twisted the faucet and cupped her hands beneath the water. Splash after splash of water rinsed away blood and dirt. When she finished, Ella grabbed a towel and dried off, then dared to look again into the mirror, where she stared and stared until she was confident she had successfully regained control.

Ella pulled herself up straight and ran a smoothing hand over her shirt and jeans. She slipped into the gallery, trying not to disturb Grandmother, who now worked with another group of customers. She didn't see Frank.

Then she heard his chuckle and looked past *Sáni* to her office. Frank stood with his back to her, one hip against her desk, long fingers around the receiver. She walked toward him, determined to ignore the quick flutter of her heart.

Once inside her office, Ella faced the surprise of everything set back in place: The file cabinets stood straight, and her papers were stacked on an upright desk. She turned around in a daze. Through the doorway, she now noticed that the whole gallery had been restored.

How in the world had Grandmother managed?

Then she spotted a cage, fashioned of scraggly juniper branches. Inside sat the magpie—plumper, Ella thought. She gave Grandmother a sharp look, though *Sáni* didn't notice, she was too preoccupied with making the sale. Ella walked to the cage and rotated it slowly. There wasn't a door, just a big gap between two of the branches, so the bird could leave anytime. He obviously had no intention of doing so.

Ella glanced back to her office. Frank hung up the call, but then dialed numbers for another one. He swivelled on a foot and faced her, as if he had sensed her gaze. Ella paced to her desk, straightened papers that didn't need straightening, angled the stack of bills just-so.

Frank couldn't help noticing Ella's nervousness. He had watched her wander from the office to the gallery and back again.

He smiled. She wouldn't ask him what he was doing: That was far too intrusive for Ella. He knew she wouldn't ask him his intentions, either—assuming she was curious. No, she would let the world spin on its axis while she continued on her way, living her life. The saying "steady as she goes" must have been created with Ella in mind.

The voice on the other end of the phone finally returned.

"That's right, Coriz. I'll pick Tikui up, if you can assemble the rest. We'll meet at noon."

He hung up and glanced over his shoulder. Ella had left the office and was talking with two Navajo men as she looked over their jewelry. Her brow creased in concentration, and then she would smile with genuine interest. He leaned against the desk, his legs crossed at the ankles, and watched her at work, envying her ability to put people at ease. If he got his way, he would see to it she never had to worry again.

It struck him suddenly that she might not approve of his plan, might not even *want* him around. The thought sent a shudder across his chest and brought him up straight.

Frank walked from the office, intending to wrap his arm around Ella's waist, test her reaction, but then she stepped from his path, as if sensing his approach.

Cold doubt lowered his arm, propelled him forward. He paused on the other side of the case, simply to catch her attention before he left.

Ella glanced up from the jewelry. Her heart tripped over the smile creasing his eyes.

"I have something to do," he said. "I'll be back in two hours and then I need to drive into Window Rock."

Ella said the only fact that registered in her mind. "You're leaving."

"I need to take care of the stone, Ella."

His expression had sobered. He looked at her with a gaze already set on his own purpose.

"Where is the stone, Ella?"

"In the bathroom. On the counter," Ella answered absently.

He strode from the gallery. Ella's gaze settled on the juniper cage, where the magpie sat preening.

In that instant, she decided she *couldn't* let things be.

Patience be damned. Control go to hell.

When had they served her well? When had they ever brought her what she really wanted, and not just what she would settle for?

She rounded the counter and caught *Sáni*'s quick smile. Then the old woman actually winked at her! A flush of excitement raced through Ella and her heart pumped faster as every step took her closer to the bathroom.

She got to the door and could hear water running. Ella took a breath and knocked. He didn't answer.

She hesitated a moment, then closed her fingers around the knob, turned it, and walked in.

The first thing she noticed was the pile of clothes on the

floor. Her gaze went to the shower. Her pulse jerked to her throat.

"Frank?"

"Yes?"

The deep timbre of his voice reached beyond the curtain and glided over Ella, catching on every pore of her, brushing against every fine hair on her arms. She had never known such hyper-sensitivity to just the sound of someone's voice.

"It's Ella," she answered, her voice tight.

"I decided to rinse off some of the mountain," he said. "I hope that's okay."

Ella couldn't speak. She stared at the shower, suddenly clearly aware of the precipice she faced, the risk she dared.

Seconds passed. Her heart thumped harder. Her mouth went dry. What was it she meant to say or do?

I don't want to lose him now.

The thought filled her mind.

Her hands raised to her shirt. Her fingers undid the buttons and she slipped from the sleeves. She unsnapped her jeans, let them fall to the floor, then shed her undergarments. Steam from the shower settled on her bare skin. She glanced at the pile of her clothes mingled with Frank's, took a deep breath, and slid back the curtain.

Cool air wafted across Frank. He started to turn his head, when hands skimmed under his arms and across his ribs.

He drew a sharp breath, clasped Ella's hands in his own. Her fingers spread and pressed him back against her. Her body curved to his. Taut breasts grazed his back.

"I don't want to lose you," she whispered. Her breath skated over him.

He turned within her arms and stared into Ella's eyes, filled with passion and uncertainty.

He cupped her face in his hands. "You can't lose me," he murmured, lowering his head.

His mouth covered hers. He wrapped an arm across her back and felt Ella stretch up to him. An immeasurable ache lanced straight through Frank, drawing him tight, breathless. A pulse grew within, deep and pounding.

Ella backed up against the shower wall, pulling him with her. Hot water pounded against his back, sprayed over his shoulders, slid down his chest. His nipples drew taut. He brought Ella's hand to his chest. Her fingers splayed at his breast, grazed the nubbin, now tight. The ache jolted straight to Frank's groin and forced a groan from between his teeth.

He swept his hands behind Ella, lifted her, and braced a foot on the rim of the tub. Her arms reached to his shoulders, her fingers ran up his neck and through his hair. She pulled herself higher, positioning herself. And, as she lowered herself onto him, she gazed at him, her eyes brimming with passion.

He slid within and gasped. Every muscle tensed against instant release. His heart slamming at his chest, Frank held his breath, willing himself to slow down.

But Ella's body defeated him.

She tightened around him, pulsing, moving. His body clenched, shuddered, and all thoughts dissolved. Frank drove harder. Ella moaned into his shoulder, captured his neck in her lips. She murmured words his mind couldn't grasp but his heart heard.

He heard her need him, want him.

He heard an elation, a freedom.

He thought of the dream she had shared: the dream of leaping off, taking a chance.

He heard her heart and the message squeezed his own heart until he thought he might cry . . . because he heard her love.

And Frank held on tighter, taking the leap along with Ella.

EPILOGUE

Ella watched Frank's Jeep approach the post and she was out front before he had barely opened his door.

"Frank." Ella started talking, still five feet away.

Then she saw that Tikui was in the Jeep.

"What—" she stammered.

"Ella, get in. I want you to see this." A grin spread across his face.

Ella couldn't help smiling back. "See what?"

"Please," he said. "I want you to be there."

Ella glanced back at the store and decided Grandmother would probably not even miss her. She walked around the front of the Jeep and climbed in. "Where are we going?"

"We're going to Window Rock," Tikui announced from the back seat.

"To do what?" Ella looked at Frank.

"For one, to take care of the stone." He reached across the seat and gripped her hand.

He stayed that way the whole drive, even taking her hand with his when he changed gears. Ella could hear Tikui's giggles drifting from the backseat. For herself, she wanted this to be the way she traveled from now on, her hand in Frank's.

On the outskirts of town, State Road 264 widened to the divided Highway 264. Ella noticed Indians lining both sides of the road. Frank slowed to a crawl, then stopped. Ahead,

Ella could see a huge crowd of Indians, Navajo and Hopi, blocking traffic. To the side, surrounding them, were police from every agency, including federal government cars.

At the center of the crowd, Ella saw the black armbands, the dark sunglasses of AIRO. She faced Frank. "What are you doing?"

He smiled. "You look worried. Don't, Ella. I didn't come here for trouble. At least not with them." He gestured ahead.

"He is a smart man," Tikui said from the back.

"Yes, but—"

Frank's brow rose at her agreement with Tikui.

"He is the man of honor," Tikui continued.

"Yes, but—"

"He has decided the destiny of the stone," Tikui said, louder this time, as if determined to make her point.

"I thought the destiny of the stone was for it to be returned to the Hopi," Ella said.

"The destiny of the stone was to bring unity," Tikui said quietly. "Frank Reardon has pointed that out to me."

"What *are* you going to do, Frank?"

"Well if nothing else," he quipped, "I'm probably going to lose my job."

He opened the door.

Ella grabbed his arm. "Wait. Frank. I—" Ella laid a hand against his cheek. "I want you to know I believe in you."

His smile vanished. Ella's breath stuck in her chest.

Then he leaned to her, placed a hand on each side of her face, and drew her to him. She saw passion well in his eyes, just before he lowered his head and took her lips to his.

"So romantic," Tikui cooed.

Ella chuckled. Frank caught the sound within his mouth and she forgot any world existed but them.

Ever so slowly, he pulled back, the flush of passion still

in his gaze. "I'll be back," he said, and stepped from the Jeep.

Ella's gaze caught on the lanky stride of the man who chose to deliver peace. "Thank you," she murmured.

"You're welcome," said Tikui.

Dear Reader,

The idea for *Broken in Two* began with the birth of two white buffalo calves, streaked through my imagination with the occurrence of two comets, grew with an eruption of earthquakes in New Mexico, and finally found an anchor with the discovery of a newspaper article. The newspaper article included an interview with a Hopi medicine man who claimed the cluster of unusual occurrences signalled the deliverance of a Hopi prophecy. Who wouldn't be intrigued?

Each tribe of the Southwest has its own creation myth—fantastic tales of emergence from other worlds. The Hopi myth is particularly detailed, including legends of migration of the different clans across hostile lands until they gathered at their rightful home: Hopiland. The stories read like fables: boys turning into antelopes, sons of village chiefs facing terrible monsters of the underworld. But they also include tantalizing tidbits of history and ancient sites—enough to tempt modern researchers to study the tales for insight.

And so the Hopi prophecy sparked my own insight. Life for any creature in the Southwest is precarious at best, a constant struggle to keep balance. Yet, the balance among the desert dwellers has been sorely tested over several decades, with factions cutting across the cultures as deeply as arroyos eroding the landscape. The Hopi story inspired a tale of destiny and reconciliation. I hope you have enjoyed *Broken in Two*, where I imagine a world of miracles and wonder—a world where hope prevails and legends come true.

I love to hear from my readers. You can reach me at the base of the foothills of the Sandia Mountains, or, better known to the postal service as P.O. Box 23203, Albuquerque, NM 87192. You can also reach me by email at: lbaker10@aol.com

Sincerely,
Laura